C. G. Leeder is an up-and-coming author who has always loved reading, creating, and indulging in fantasy stories. She enjoys recreational activities along with spending time with her family and children. She believes herself to be a down-to-earth person who appreciates the individual flavor of every being, which gives inspiration to her characters.

Dedicated to Les Clarke, my loving partner,
and my mom, Cheryl, who always believed in me.

C. G. Leeder

THE OLYMPUS TRIALS

The Story of the Untold Tale

AUSTIN MACAULEY PUBLISHERS™

LONDON • CAMBRIDGE • NEW YORK • SHARJAH

Ordering Information:
Quantity sales: special discounts are available on quantity purchases by corporations, associations, and others. For details, contact the publisher at the address below.

Publisher's Cataloging-in-Publication data
Leeder, C. G.
The Olympus Trials: The Story of the Untold Tale

ISBN 9781641828123 (Paperback)
ISBN 9781641828130 (Hardback)
ISBN 9781645366171 (ePub e-book)

Library of Congress Control Number: 2019914967

The main category of the book — FICTION / Fantasy / Action & Adventure

www.austinmacauley.com/us

First Published (2019)
Austin Macauley Publishers LLC
40 Wall Street, 28th Floor
New York, NY 10005
USA

mail-usa@austinmacauley.com
+1 (646) 5125767

Big Les and Julie Clarke – thank you for helping me
grow into a better person.

Preface

Nirvana.

Within a land we do not call our own, lies a place where all languages are spoken and all the stories told. This is the place where you might find yourself peering up to, questioning life's purpose or blissfully wondering what lies above. It twinkles as it tells the story you wish to know, in a language you no longer remember, in a story untold. It is the place that knew you before you knew yourself, this place we know of as Nirvana. The place where the first indigenous were born; this place is your birthright: it is your zodiac home. Within this land lie twelve zodiacs, ones you may have read about, ones you may not know. Now all their secrets are going to be relinquished to you from the day they were born. Travelling through the harshest lands of the Scorpio's Solitudiem Desert, through the Libra's harmonious village known as Arbor Domus, hidden within the tallest trees of Pacem's Forest, you are about to witness the dawn of time.

The Twelve Constellations

Capricorn Constellation
Region colors: Black and Indigo
Region stone: Garnet

Aquarius Constellation
Region colors: Gray and Ultramarine Blue
Region stone: Amethyst

Pisces Constellation
Region colors: Sea green and Aqua
Region stone: Aquamarine

Aries Constellation
Region colors: Red and Scarlet
Region stone: Diamond

Taurus Constellation
Region colors: Green and White
Region stone: Emerald

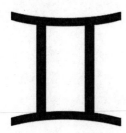

Gemini Constellation
Region colors: Green, Yellow, and Orange
Region stone: Pearl

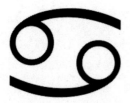

Cancer Constellation
Region colors: Sea Green and Silver
Region stone: Ruby

Leo Constellation
Region colors: Gold, Orange, and Yellow
Region stone: Peridot

Virgo Constellation
Region colors: Green, White, and Yellow
Region stone: Sapphire

Libra Constellation
Region colors: Blue, Jade, and Green
Region stone: Opal

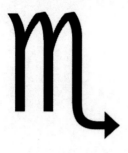

Scorpio Constellation
Region colors: Red and Violet
Region stone: Citrine

Sagittarius Constellation
Region colors: Light Blue and White
Region stone: Blue Topaz

Introduction

Time is an illusion within this realm, but it was during a fragmented moment in Nirvana history, the land became stuck within turmoil. Nirvana was confronted by a dark hand, Apophis, the snake, a trusted and respected friend who held great power, he was the only one who could read the creator's language known as Unum, who did not embody a physical form: he was everything and one with all. The zodiacs relied heavily on Apophis to see unknown forces and predict futures one could not foresee. No one knows why Apophis had turned on them but the zodiacs' grief of betrayal became his gain, creating a dark spell, intertwined within a lullaby which enchanted them, placed them under his control, and captured the weak who had lost faith. Those who became enchanted would leave their homes and family to live within the darkness of the uncharted forest, the thick woodland beyond each Constellation where no zodiac would now dare venture. Once lost, they withheld extreme power, an extension of Apophis himself, but became shells of their former selves. Apophis is now believed to live deep in the uncharted forest amongst those zodiacs who follow his every command and sing the same lullaby to others who step into the forest that they succumbed to. These zodiacs are now known by the name 'Infernum.'

During this time, chaos and ruin began to riddle the land as the Constellations did not know how to fight such evil and were unable to work together due to different ideologies. As tension and hatred grew between them, the lullaby became stronger as more zodiacs lost faith and the enchantments increased in numbers. Apophis was one of the oldest and first born to this world, created by Unum's hand, gifted with an exceeding power and intuition aided by his third eye. Zodiacs were terrified as they knew the power he withheld. So, they tried anything to protect themselves and those they loved from building large walls around their Constellations, stopped leaving their homes, boarding up doors and windows, never to be seen alone. The Patriarch and Matriarch, Virgo pair chosen by the now twelve paired elders, one male and one female, allocated to their own region, led Nirvana back into a strong working unity. First banding the Constellations together to fight back and designing the Olympus Trials – theory and physical base studies – put together from each region to have a broad understanding of how each Constellation works to become the reputable zodiacs who learnt to work together, which eventually made them somewhat defiant against the once impenetrable spell as their faith started to re-build.

As they grew stronger, the enchanted lullaby was only heard by those who had not entered the uncharted forest, now thought to target the innocent who still suffer with self-doubt and disbelief. The sturdy walls built around the Constellations were kept to separate the zodiacs from the now dangerous and infested uncharted forest. They wanted to diminish every aspect that factored into a possession, like the visual of the enchantment which caused initial scarcity and fear within the shadows of the dark woodland. So, building the high walls created safety and false security within. Eventually, time lingered by and the strong system, "The Olympus Trials," was established for future generations. But before a zodiac sits the trials, they first become secluded within their Constellations when they are born, brought up and groomed by their family and peers to endure the most mentally and physically challenging tasks that is deemed acceptable by their paired elders until they come of age 21, learning all about their traditions and way of life within their Constellations in the hope that when they make the journey through the uncharted forest to the Doh to participate within the Olympus Trials, they will be strong enough to resist a possession. But unfortunately, every year zodiacs are still taken from each Constellation when they embark upon the journey. But it's the cost they must make; few weak lost for the strong who keep the land united.

The Children's Tale

There once was a snake called Apophis, one of the very first born to this world, able to understand our creator's messages and calls. In the beginning, Apophis was known as the wisest creature of them all. Zodiacs waited many a time to converse with him, foretelling certain futures, of what to avoid and what to build to prevent harm from ever bestowing upon them. But on a particular day, for no good reason at all, he disappeared with not a whisper, not a story told. Zodiacs banded together looking high and low, travelling to places they should not venture, hoping they had not been left alone. It was on this unfortunate day, Apophis was witnessed slithering into the now identified uncharted forest.

Zodiacs calling his name, but he did not answer, not one word at all.

Our creator, whose name was Unum, gave us everything you see before you. Not a face to the creator, as he catered to you. He did not have a body as he embodied what we reflect too. Coming to us at unexpected times and at the perfect times too. How he never made sense when he spoke our name, giving us advice in the most peculiar ways. Apophis, you traitorous snake, he also spoke Unum's linguistic taste. And on that dark day, Unum's voice would cease to be heard even by the most sensitive ears. Did Apophis kill Unum in a way we do not know; he was the wisest of the wise, how were we supposed to know. Taken by greed, he now wants to consume us all, eaten by gluttony we hear him call. Be wary, do not let him in; do not strike a tear. As sadness is the key, it is the one that allows you to hear the enchanted song, the one that makes the call into the darkest place, the one that has no soul. We call them Infernum, the embodiment of hell.

Now another lullaby was made to keep us at bay, one you may hear within each sturdy wall, the one children sing as they play:

Deep within the forest, Infernum would creep
If you would hear one, beware the end of sleep
If blackness consumes you, beware your family too
That's why we stay away from Infernum view.

Now you've heard the woeful tale that places fear upon this land. Let me take you to the girl who will continue this story, one who lays within the Taurus land. She is not like any other nor does she entail that of what is known to be a bull. Constantly faced with adversity, some which you may know too well. Now let us begin the story of the untold tale.

Chapter 1

The Girl

Conformity, the mask that drowns individuality and desire.

Hidden amongst bushes and trees, I can see the moonlight glimmer upon an open field, but I am constricted within a tight warm blanket. I peer up at a woman who holds me, feeling deep security and comfort. Her face is unfamiliar but I feel an unconditional attachment to her. I press my head into her chest, hearing her heart beat, the pulsating rhythm lays a blanket of comfort. Now, it begins to pick up pace; I feel anxious as her skin becomes clammy and her eyes dilate. Her breathing becomes irregular and heavy. I feel hot, claustrophobic. I try to speak but only a curdling cry escapes through my mouth. She cradles me close, hushing to give me comfort, "shhh amica mea shhh." Suddenly deep rustic voices are heard nearby, "Did you hear that? She's over there!" Galloping hooves now trample hard and fast towards us, stopping right above us. Silence lingering with the deliberate sound of the horse's snorts, rapidly reiterating through its nose. The woman places her sweaty hand gently over my mouth. I feel her tremble. I hear the horse's hooves break twigs and branches between its feet as they move slowly around our poorly concealed position hidden by the darkness. An anticipated silence dissipates for a moment. Until a high-pitched scream and a giant horse stands above us and comes down hard, nearly crushing us. The woman holds me tight and I squeeze my eyes shut.

She whispers in my ear, "*Tu es via, veritas et vita. Nemo venit ad Patrem, nisi per te.*" I don't understand the language she speaks, but I can see deep within her sorrows, this is goodbye. I start tearing up. She looks at me with her big blue eyes, attempting to smile as a single tear travels down her face and her last words are spoken, "*Te amo.*" She lets go of me as she is pulled upon the horse and I fall to the ground with a strong thud. My small body trembles as I struggle to breathe. I start to scream, a bewildering cry after my lungs grasp the air once more. I become shell-shocked, taking a few deep, quivering breaths. Trembling, the struggle of commotion quietens to complete silence, then the woman's body hits the ground beside me, startling me and staring at me with empty eyes. Tears fall down my face, her mouth begins to slowly expire, and I wriggle from the tight blanket, extending my tiny hand as a strange illuminating blue aura expands from my fingertips. Then blackness consumes me.

I wake up with a heart-wrenching feeling of guilt as though the woman's death, who I do not know, is somehow my fault. How can I feel guilt towards a woman who is only a figment of my imagination? I look at the picture frame of my father, Adonis, thinking how many times he's told me this reoccurring nightmare never happened. He too continues to tell me it's a reflection of my deep feelings that yearn for my mother beyond the grave whose old picture sits beside mine and my father's as she too holds me when I was a baby. I always wondered if the woman in the dream was her, but they look nothing alike. I linger at the pictures of a time when my father appeared to be truly happy. Then I place my hand on my sheets realizing they're soaked through, breathing heavily, I shut my eyes bringing myself back to reality.

My heart skips a beat as two big bangs slam on my door. "Taura, get up! You got registration today!" I rub my face and sit up. It's the year of my 21st birthday, and I have to register for 'The Olympus Trials,' studies every 21-year-old must endure, living away from home within the Doh's walls, residing with every other zodiac I never encountered. I pick up my introductory scroll that lays unraveled on the floor, reading it for the second time since yesterday when my classmates and I received it, leaving our last lesson.

Skimming through, I begin reading through bits and pieces:

"The trials can take a few years or decades depending if you show little or great promise, then you are classed, assigned a career you're best suited to, which is carefully chosen by the elders."

But I fear I won't even make it to the trials, as we have to pass through the uncharted forest, the place where the Infernum infest the shadows of the woodland. I continue reading on.

"Region: The Taurus Constellation, a village on a large, flat, green land known as Herba. You are the descendants of the bull. Strong-headed, independently determined, generous, and patient at times, although Tauruses are stubborn and ignorant of others' emotions when expressing their truth.

In the Taurus Constellation, the males have large horns and the females have small stumpy horns, both with a bull tail, being incredibly muscular and lean; only the females are much smaller in stature. Their power is that of incredible strength, making them natural great warriors. Their ability enables them to pick up any weapon and wield it with great accuracy, agility, and strength. Although this talent comes at a price with an upbringing of toughness and rigid routines. If a Taurus wants to make it to adulthood, they must be fastidious in their approach, otherwise they'll perish as the elders are incredibly regimented, constantly testing their physical capabilities. They're generally seen as great officers/second-in-command within the Nirvana Army as they are great at following orders, rarely failing to deliver.

Every zodiac takes years to master their abilities and power before reaching their full potential, especially young zodiacs. Lacking the maturity and wisdom to control their abilities properly. So, depending on the classification it will depend how much time is spent on learning to control and master the abilities, as it might not be necessary for the field of work. This structure maintains protection, order, balance, and purpose which must be kept for the zodiacs faith within the Nirvana unity, reducing the risk of another Infernum infestation."

I drop the scroll on the ground again, feeling a gag growing within my throat. I pick up my *Zodiacs Appearance, Ability and Power* book, that sits on my bedside table and flick through the other 11 zodiacs, who I may meet at registration for the first time today, if I can make it through the uncharted forest. I open the first page, reading over a particular part that always caught my eye before reading on:

All zodiacs have some form of human appearance with aspects of their descendants. Although a human is only myth and the only human connection known is that of Adam and Eve, but even that is only legend. It is still unknown as to how we came to evolve in this way.

I continue on:

Aries:

Descendants from large mountain goats. They are incredibly loud, courageous, and adventurous although you do get the impression that they love to argue, as they genuinely have to be right all the time. They have large circular horns, athletic stature, and back legs of a goat, standing upright. They have the ability to run through anything once they pick up enough speed, so stand out of their way, as they'll break through anything. This ability is derived from mountain goats as they protect their territory and land by literally ramming with their heads. They are generally seen within Demolition throughout the Nirvana, as they are great for clearing large areas for construction. They're genuinely good with small weapons as they are incredibly agile, and are quite nifty with a bow and arrow.

Gemini:

Descendants from yin and yang, they used to have two heads but now their good and evil are split in one body. They are incredibly charismatic, intelligent, and witty, but they lack consistency as they are always in two minds about everything which can make them quite anxious. Their appearance is split down the middle: one side has black hair with malevolent looking features and the other has

19

white hair with innocent, delicate features. They can split both sides into two separate zodiacs, yin and yang, as two beings, being able to move as fast as lightning, though this transition can end in destruction if not taught properly. They are genuinely used for big tasks within the Doh, such as geography, architecture, writing history and much more. Having two people in one can produce a large amount of work in a short period of time.

Cancer:

Loving, protective, and faithful zodiacs, but they are overemotional and pessimistic if failure occurs. They're descendants from a crab. They have black eyes and small sharp spears that protrude from the top of their forearm that expand into long sharp weapons. They have the ability to produce a shield of protection that inhibits anything from penetrating through. They are great soldiers to use for the frontline in many numbers for battle.

Leo:

A loyal, optimistic leader who always speaks the truth. But their famous ego has the tendency to undo them. They can be quite dominating and impatient too. Descendants from a lion, they are lean but athletic looking. The males always bigger than the females, they have lion tails and ears with golden eyes and thick golden hair. Small fangs protrude from their mouth and sharp nails that stick out from their hands. When in battle or threatened, they have the ability to transform into a bigger animalistic version of themselves with a more muscular frame. Their claws grow longer, sharper, and their small fangs become more prominent. Once this transformation occurs, they become resilient to pain, making them great animalistic fighters; they're generally great commanders within the Nirvana Army as they are great delegating leaders.

Virgo:

Intelligent perfectionists that pay great attention to detail; however, they are overcritical and judgmental as everything must be perfect. Virgos are tall and slender as they are the descendants of angels with large angel wings and piercing eyes. Their wings grow larger with age. They have the ability to fly and power to control elements of the wind to help guide them in the direction they wish to go. They are genuinely great in political roles within Nirvana.

Libra:

A romantic diplomat who uses great tact when getting things done. Libras are the descendants of scales eluded by superficial beauty and can be prone to changing their minds as they struggle with making decisions. Libras are radiant and beautiful with an elf-like appearance; if unbalanced, their eye color changes, one blue and the other green, if balanced both eyes stay blue. They have the ability to control the minds of others, but if not taught properly, they'll only carry an influence over others. They are genuinely used in quarrels over Constellation matters, as they are great diplomats.

Scorpio:

They are brave, ambitious, faithful friends, who can read people very well. Do not cross them as they are incredibly resentful, jealous, and possessive creatures; they do not handle deceit well. Descendants of Scorpions, they have a long black tail that attaches from the base of the neck all the way down to their tailbone, which grows out from the body. Thorns protrude from their elbows, knees, ankles, shoulders, and head. They have strong features with black hair. Scorpios have the ability to store two separate poisons in their tail: one that can put you to sleep and one that can kill you. They are incredibly bad at controlling both poisons when they are young, so stay clear if you are another zodiac as they're immune to their own poisons. They're genuinely seen as guards within the lands of Nirvana, as they put those to sleep who disturb the peace, and their poison is used in death sentences on those who sin. Unless either of those are Scorpio, then other approaches must be taken.

Sagittarius:

A vivacious, intelligent, and generous zodiac who has a great sense between right and wrong. They are tactless when it comes to the brutal truth and at times take things for granted. Overconfident as they perceive themselves to be perfect. Descendants of horses. Appearance of a horse body and attached from the base a human torso, sitting upright from the neck. They are magnificent creatures with large lean muscles and strong attractive features. They have the power to talk to the forest and have a great ability in archery, rarely missing a target. They are genuinely seen as hunters and gatherers of food and resources.

Capricorn:

Practical, cautious, and most ambitious of the zodiac. Born with great wisdom, never going against the odds. Stubborn, never changing their minds, can be perceived shy as they only enjoy the company of close friends. Descendants of a goat and a fish; although a strange mix, they have an incredible aura of beauty about them. Having a light orange and golden-tinged skin, some with an elongated fish tail and others with a small goat's tail, they have horns that track from the front of their forehead, curling only slightly around to the back with slightly pointed ears poking through their thick hair. Eyes that are large and oval-shaped with a small flat nose. They have telekinetic power, the ability to manipulate objects with the mind, although without constant practice, this skill can diminish quickly. Generally seen as great teachers and mentors within Nirvana.

Aquarius:

The humanitarian of the zodiac. Famous at the ability to make a lot of friends, intelligent and independent. Although they can be inconsistent as they never follow a particular pattern, detached at times and stubborn as they do everything to the extreme. Descendants of man with water. A large zodiac, similar size to that of a giant but not as big with thick bluish hair. They have the power to talk to animals and other creatures depending on how skilled their tongues are. Being such radiant humanitarians, they make great doctors who care for the injured, sick zodiacs and animals throughout the land.

Pisces:

A kind, selfless, and compassionate zodiac. They are incredibly intuitive, which they rely on to make a lot of decisions. Although famous for escapism when things become hard, they are over sensitive and pessimistic when things don't go their way, and idealistic situations can seem mediocre to them. Pisces are slender and delicate looking zodiac. Descendant from a fish which is portrayed strongly within their appearance with a thick, leathery bright blue skin with tinges of orange sporadically intervened into their illuminating physique. They have big oval eyes with small fins that grow from the outer corner. Two large fins that grow from the bottom of the knee, sprawling out at the top of the ankle and two fins grow from the wrists expanding out at the end of the elbow. These fins enable them to swim swiftly through the water at high speeds. Thick leather like rope hair, with webbed feet and hands. They have the power to control water and must always have access to it, as it's a part of their life source; they make great sorcerers/alchemists.

Closing the book, I get out of bed, putting on my tattered constellation clothes; they are plain brown and don't fit me correctly, with holes from being second-hand over the past few generations, but I feel comfortable in them, which makes me feel safe and familiar. We are not wealthy but we have a roof over our heads and enough food to keep us nourished. I stand up, walking over to my small old mirror that's lost its youth; it was supposedly my mother's. Rubbing my hands through my hair, I look at my plain green eyes, small features, and long mousey brown hair sprawled out over my shoulders. I don't believe I'm a stunning Taurus, more average, but I was never meant to be special. I walk out to the small but homey living room. Breathing in the scent of the smoky old fireplace, touching my hand against the cold brick wall, ducking under pots, pans, and herbs from the garden that hang from our low ceiling. My father is standing in his usual big bear coat, thick brown leather pants, and black leather shoes tied with an old rope above each ankle. He has a thick brown beard with Taurus tribal tattoos on his neck, dark brown eyes, noble nose, and thick long brown hair that's half tied up at the back, not to mention his huge horns that nearly take out the cottage door every time he steps through; he has a thick bull tail that insists on whacking me in the face whenever we're in close proximity. He also has the number one imprinted on the back of his neck, known as our 'purpose number'; you obtain this on your registration day. It determines your traits and purpose for this lifetime along with your characteristics of zodiac ancestors, from where you are born, and also enables you to teleport to and from the Doh. His number is a representation of leadership, hard work, determination, self-motivation, ambition, independency, and innovation. This gives you your individuality within your community. There are nine known purpose numbers which helps us relate to one another and aids the Elders in allocating our classification.

My father is an old-school, tough Taurus, overcoming many difficult times in his life, like the Infernum dark era. Becoming one of the biggest heroes throughout the land as he fought hard and strong against them when many wouldn't and couldn't. Helping to keep the last residing zodiacs' faith strong. His biggest hardship was my birth. But he has always been incredibly noble, supportive, and loving father. He is not only my dad but also my best friend. In his hand, he holds the same repulsive medicine I've had to take since I can remember. It's a potion to keep my immune system strong. When I was born, I was incredibly weak and fragile, which is considered futile within Herba, meant to be carried to the uncharted territory and left to die.

When a baby is born, the Elders determine if it is strong enough to represent the Taurus Constellation. Like I said, being a natural great warrior comes at a price; you are carefully selected. Adonis told me when I was born: he knew I wouldn't be accepted by the Elders. I was his first and only offspring, as my parents had trouble conceiving, ending in many heart-breaking miscarriages. So, the thought of leaving me to die without a chance to live was unbearable, telling the Elders when they came to inspect me that I was a stillborn and they had already buried me. They kept me a well-hidden secret for a while until someone saw me and reported it, knowing Adonis and Penelope had no children. Before they could hide me, soldiers came and took me and my mother away, ripping Adonis of all his rankings, which left him with nothing but this old abandoned cottage at the end of the Constellation, and now he hunts within the dangers of the uncharted forest to put food on our table. But Adonis, being one of the most respected Tauruses, was able to pull some strings to keep me and my mother alive. They told him they'd make an exception for his heroic acts in those dark times. But one of us had to be made an example of so this occurrence could never happen again. Otherwise the

Taurus Constellation would become weak and the way of the Taurus would perish. They tried to convince him to take mine, warning him that I'd never be accepted by the other Taurus children. My whole life would be a struggle and once I'd come of age, I'd certainly be taken by the Infernum as a lifetime of bullying will weaken my heart making me susceptible. My father was torn, but my mother chose for him. She told the Elders to do as they wished in order to save my life. They murdered her in front of all of Herba. Adonis had to watch as the community had to see a great warrior broken, knowing simple NC folk like themselves could not risk or endure the same heartache. Using fear to counteract repeated history. Adonis never told me the details of her public massacre, obviously wanting to protect me but not wanting to lie either. I try to remember my mother, Penelope, but there isn't a single memory that comes to mind. It's as though she never existed within my reality.

Adonis hands me the cup. "Here you go, same as usual." I gulp it down as fast as I can; it's revolting. It's like itchy grass mixed with dust, doused down with water and the backside hair of a bull. But no matter how bad I despise this potion, it keeps me alive, because without it for long, I'll most likely die from illness due to my undeveloped immune system. That's why Adonis never lets me do much; he blames the condition for my lack of capability for everything. Although he still believes I'm incredibly special somehow, I don't have the natural ability of strength and I can't lift much in contradiction. I still have my small horns on my head and a bull tail. I'm lean like everyone else, but I lack the muscle. I'm sublimely bullied and judged by the community due to the life I've been allowed to exhibit. A big part of me understands and takes on the guilt of their pain from ones lost, but there's a part of me that wishes to disappear. So, I spend most of my time indulged in my books, reading about all the zodiac powers, history, and astrology. I don't feel like I belong anywhere but in the pages of times past.

Adonis sits down and his expression becomes serious. "Now Taura, remember what we have spoken about; you must not let fear seep into your heart when you enter the uncharted forest. I want you to think about your achievements; you're very intelligent, smarter than any other Taurus in Herba. You must have courage and remember to have an inner strength."

My countenance is unfulfilled. I agree with Adonis but I shouldn't even be doing the trials. He continues, "Taura, the Elders are well aware of your condition, but unfortunately, they must treat you like everyone else. It was part of the agreement when you were a baby. I don't want you to go either. But I cannot fight this, Taura, and I can't lose you too."

I peer at the ground as his words stab me. I can't stand the thought of him going through any more heartache. I reply with a strong undertone, "It's okay, Dad, you won't. I promise I'll stay strong. You'll see me straight after registration today." Adonis takes a big sigh of relief, trying to take in my words convincingly, and shutting his eyes, he opens them and says, "I know."

We embrace one another for a long moment. I step back, smiling with confidence and say, "I'll see you tonight and tell you all about it." He smiles with a strong affirming nod. We walk over to the small front door. Pulling the broken door open and jarring all the way, Adonis hands me my backpack that sits on the small stool next to the front door. The light now shines through from the morning haze, hearing the searing cries of crickets. We stare at the broken door. "Should fix that today," he says expressionlessly.

I nod. "Good idea."

He grabs my shoulder and squeezes it, gently pushing me through the door; he kisses me on the forehead and shuts the door behind me.

I linger at the door for a moment, glancing over our conventional clay and white cottage with small crooked windows on each side and a giant old tree that grows in the back corner, casting a giant shadow over our home which keeps the house cool when hot days occur. I turn around, breathing in the smell of fauna and crisp fresh air of the morning residue, grabbing the straps of my backpack, pulling it higher on to my shoulders and begin walking towards the Halls of Ivy.

I follow one of the many narrow gravel dirt paths that have been intercepted into Herba. It's a nice warm day as the sun warms my back, listening to the bird's chirp as they swoop down amongst the grass, grabbing bugs for breakfast. I eventually come to the small village where most Tauruses live and within the center are large brown clay cottages that aren't much nicer in appearance than our small home. Some sell and provide all different kinds of services and goods, although they would never trade with the likes of me or my father. There's also a small old arena not far from here and I can hear the sound of swords colliding and the grunting moans and panting of early training. Although the culture is selective and rigid, the Taurus community live off the land, never taking more than they need, although they're ironically materialistic when it comes to particular ways of life, especially with the security of a home and the finer things that supply comfort. Cows and bulls from our Constellation are mooing loudly as the village begins to wake; they're ginormous in size, the females weighing up to two thousand pounds and the male bulls weighing up to five thousand pounds. They're highly respected and honored within the community as they are a representation of our ancestral bull, and they keep the ever-growing grass neatly cut. The NC Taurus villagers that live within the Constellation are outside already emptying their toilets, cleaning towels and mats by smacking them against outside walls. And their penetrating eyes follow me as I walk by. I know their pain as I see it on Adonis's face every day, the guilt. I know their resentment lays with the children who were deemed unworthy of life and I'm a reminder of that pain they try so hard to forget.

I continue on my route for the Halls of Ivy, but I find myself appreciating the smell of fresh food from the market, finer than anything we've ever consumed. Briefly closing my eyes, I imagine myself indulging in such exotic nourishments. Then unexpectedly, I find myself falling as I hit something hard, my face colliding with an unpleasant slimy texture.

As I pull myself on to my feet, wiping the substance from my face, I hear a deep penetrating moan, "Mmmooooo!" A large female cow stares at me as her jaw chews from side to side, attempting to warn me. I sigh with annoyance, cleaning myself up as good as I can. Then I feel sharp pains coming from the palms of my hands. Wiping away the slimy residue, I notice they're scraped and bleeding with bits of who-knows-what stuck in the wounds, reminding me of how delicate I am. I also notice I'm missing a shoe. Looking around, I see it under the cow's large hoof and I know there is no saving it now. I take off my remaining shoe and decide to go bare foot today.

I leave the village in the distance and walk through a large grassy field to cut time short, finding another footpath that leads towards the Halls of Ivy. I stop unexpectedly to a school of duckas, crossing the path from one side of the meadow to the other. Duckas are a small bird with an abnormally large spiky shell attached to their back necessary to stop larger birds from picking them off. They waddle past me and I smile in awe of their cuteness, until their mother hisses in warning. She watches me carefully as her babies disappear into the tall grass and she stares at me defyingly. I put my hands up in submission and she follows after her babies through the tall grass.

I now come to the school which is built on top of a high hill. I keep one hand on a strap of my backpack and I extend the other, sprawling my hand out and touching the tips of the grass. Breathing deeply, I try to alleviate the anxiety I'm confronted with. The Halls of Ivy is a large wooden structure with a high ceiling and small windows. It has the Taurus emblem engraved in our Constellation colors: green and white at the front, with two large doors at the entrance and beneath the emblem it has written our Constellation's poem:

April 20 – May 20

Taurus, a bull we see,
Oh so generous is he.
Dependable and patient,
Loyalty nor absent.
One as Independent,
Persistent intendant.
Tunnel like vision,
Move for revolution.
With good there is bad,

Possessive gone mad.
Stubbornness breeds,
Like self-indulgent needs.
Beware color red,
Fixed arrow makes his bed.

Chapter 2

The Uncharted Forest

Our dreams sometimes take us through the darkest of places.

As the school draws closer, I think about our teacher, Constance Terran, the female Taurus Elder from the Doh. I picked her a bunch of poppies, another one of our Constellation's emblems, to say thank you, as she has been a great mentor and close friend of my father, supporting him after my mother's death. I remember her being around a lot but the visits became few and far in between once I started school. She has always remained a close companion, looking out for me when she can. The Elders have a lot to do with their Constellation community, making sure all is well and secure within the working unity. Except for Iden Terran, the male Taurus Elder and Constance's partner. He was the one who ordered either my mother's or my execution to make a strong visual impact on the community so history wouldn't repeat itself. I heard his purpose number is eight – authority, efficiency, organization, vision, ambition, toughness, and materialism. Calculations, outcome, and the bigger picture kind of Taurus. I've never met him; he stays within the Doh and Constance stays within the community, implementing what is ordered. She's a purpose number seven – mystical, intuitive, sensitive, dreamer, playful, introspective, and perfectionist. I guess that's why she's so involved, feeling obligated due to Iden's lack of virtue.

Approaching the Hall, I take my backpack off and pull it around, taking out the bunch of poppies I freshly picked yesterday afternoon. Seeing a familiar figure near the Hall as I come closer, I realize it's Isa Edlyn, the girl with a chip on her shoulder. She has dirty, blonde, frizzy long hair tied into a plait. Hard features and more muscular than the average Taurus female with angry threatening tattoos covering the majority of her body. She's someone I try to avoid at all costs. Beating up some of the toughest Taurus males in combat, she's one angry hotheaded bull.

I keep my head down. Isa leans beside the two big entrance doors. As I attempt to push the door open, she places one hand on my shoulder. "You think you can just walk past me without saying hello?" Without changing my stance, my eyes stare at her thick strong hand and large forearm engulfing my whole shoulder. She could crush me in an instant. But I hate it when she patronizes me.

"No, I just want to head inside is all."

Isa tightens the grip on my shoulder. "Don't play coy with me, runt."

I become irritated and retaliate, "Look, I don't want to do this today, Isa."

She smiles and releases her grip on my shoulder.

"Okay," she says with intent, making me become anxious and annoyed. I step inside and all of a sudden, the front of my collar pulls tight around my neck and I'm propelled backwards hearing my clothes tear. The poppies fly high into the air as I land straight into the mud. Isa's expression becomes stern. "That'll teach you for being rude and stupid." I don't say anything, trying to save the poppies that now disintegrate into the mud. Isa comes storming over, standing over me dominatingly; she holds her foot up for a moment and slowly squishes the poppies deep into the mud. I look up at her with ferocious tears welling up into my eyes. She smiles then spits on the ground beside me. My anger subsides as tears begin travelling down my face in defeat. Then I hear a deep familiar voice, "Isa!" Strong steps approach me from behind and I feel two large hands lift me up. "Get inside."

Isa holds my gaze for a moment. "Why? A Taurus as pathetic as her won't even make it pass the uncharted forest any way." Pained by her words, I know she only speaks the thoughts of everyone else in the village. After all, I'm the exception no one else was allowed to be; it's probably my fate to be taken by the Infernum. Isa looks me up and down and storms into the Hall with a gruff. I wipe the tears from my face, turning around to see Demetrius Ambrosia.

He looks like a younger version of my father. Huge and muscular with long sandy hair and dark brown roots. The Taurus symbol is tattooed on either side of his shaved head with the middle of his hair draping down into a ponytail. Strong features with kind grey eyes and noble nose. He wears armored plates with our Constellation colors, green and white.

Demetrius is an SNC, our overseer – every new-blooded zodiac Constellation has one. They're particularly important when you first start the Olympus Trials as they'll be your guide in the first few months. So, while in the Constellation, he is Constance's right-hand man. Demetrius is another Taurus of few words. His purpose number is also one like my father: teaching us how to harness our power of strength within our fighting technique and combat skill. I've never participated within those classes as Adonis has forbidden it, due to my condition. If it wasn't for Demetrius, Isa probably would have killed me on several occasions, although it's also considered insolent to let someone else fight your battles.

"Are you okay?" he asks and I nod. Looking ashamed, I wipe the tears as he bends down to pick up the single poppy that hadn't been crushed and hands it to me.

"Thanks," I manage to muster.

"Don't mention it," he says without judgment.

I try to rub the dirt from my clothes, and unexpectedly Demetrius carefully grabs my arm, reaching over with the other hand and grabs my face within his large hand, directing it towards him. I go stiff and rigid as he wipes away a tear I'd missed with his rough thumb, scraping against my soft, paper-thin skin.

"Tears are a delicacy…keep them hidden," he says softly but with a serious undertone. Gently letting go, I stare at him in shock with a bright red face. Then in a startled awkward panic, I pick up my backpack, gather myself together as my heart rattles frantically. I look at Demetrius and not knowing what to say, I hurriedly head inside.

I pull the large creaky door open, now struggling against the weight, I quickly shut it behind me. Leaning against its warm panels, heated from the morning sun, I sigh with relief as though I'd survived a strange sense of excitement. Is that what they call attraction? I shake such a thought away as I know he only meant to advise me to keep such pain masked, as Infernum prey on the weak-hearted and it's only through strength that I'll survive. Besides, Demetrius would never court me, he's only following orders sentenced by Constance.

Calming myself down, I walk down the long old wooden hallway, smelling the musky heaviness of a room so dense with history. Tiny bits of light shoot through the cracked timber. Portraits hang of all the old Tauruses who have made history within Herba. Even Adonis's picture hangs, one saying 'The most heroic of our time,' but someone has scratched the heroic word out and replaced it with traitorous. I always noticed the obvious distress of those around him when I've walked with my father through our village, sporadic terror spreads like fear of a plague. I've never asked why, I just presumed it had something to do with me. Fear of me tarnishing those around me or maybe the average NC Taurus is scared of someone as historic as my father, but that wouldn't explain the traitorous statement. I just accept things for the way they've always been. In my eyes, my father will always be my hero. I rub the dust away from his engraved name with the end of my sleeve. 'If only I had come out right.'

Unexpectedly, I become aware of the commotion coming down the end of the hall. Realizing I'm already late, I hurry down to the small green door to our usual and only classroom where all eight Tauruses wait, who also turn 21 this year. I see Isa with her two disciples, Dalton and Henrietta Hamlyn, the twins. They're not built like Isa, but they're both athletic with large ears sitting low on their head, poking out from below their horns, missing adult teeth with unproportioned features, greasy light brown hair with identical tattoos on both their faces and arms. Their hygiene is also distinct as it's non-existent – flies even stay clear. Although they're undesirable and physically repulsive, they're one of the most innovative Tauruses, always building new contraptions to help out the community, even though they constantly bicker amongst themselves. They stare at me as Isa stands with a strong penetrating exterior, arms crossed, leaning against the wall, giving me an arrogant look of superiority. Then I turn to see Europa Castellanos.

"Taur!" relieved to see my best friend. I admire her beauty as I believe she is one of the prettiest Tauruses I know. She has small blue eyes with wavy, long blonde hair and a small strong physique reflecting her elegance when she fights, more agile than brawn but still immensely strong. She doesn't have many tattoos like the majority; they're mostly on her hands and feet with the Taurus emblem on the back of her neck.

I smile as she beams. "Am I glad to see you," I say. She looks at me up and down inquisitively. "Don't ask," I state.

Glancing over at Isa, who now stares out the small window as the twins bicker, Europa grabs my hand, lifting it up to get a better look. "Your shoes too?"

I manage to smile awkwardly, "Oh no, that was my own doing. Clumsy effort."

Europa smiles.

Looking down, she notices the wilting poppy I still hold within my hand. "And what's with the dying poppy?"

I bring the poppy up to eye level. From all the trauma, it just looks sad now. I can't give this to Constance, it would be insulting.

"Oh, I picked it before. But looks like it won't survive the trip." I place the dying poppy in my bag and she looks at me solemnly.

"Wanted to take something to remind you of home?"

I nod, not wanting to elaborate. Then she gives me a big hug and I go stiff and rigid, never being used to affection from others. But Europa is one of the most affectionate Tauruses I know, as Taureans are generally only affectionate to their children and only physical to their romantic partners when they procreate, or from what I've read. Although they are passionate about their individual purpose, they also see affection as a sign of weakness. But I believe that has become apparent through their hard times, built up interior walls that have been passed down to generations. But it hasn't seemed to affect Europa and I admire her for that. She is confident in displaying who she is.

Constance walks in, she has such wisdom and a calming aura within her presence, but her strong youthful physique looks like she hasn't aged a day past 21. She has full lips, big blue eyes, tattoos covering her whole right arm up to her neck, long brown hair that's tied into a neat high plait and a necklace that has a peculiar tooth tied at the end. She stands at the front of the class, wearing a tight green and white dress with long black tights. She tucks the necklace under her garments and begins.

"Alright, everyone, as you know this is the most important day of your life, registering for the Olympus Trials. And gaining your purpose numbers which will define you as individuals and allow you to obtain teleportation. As you are all aware, you must first survive the uncharted forest. This is your first test to see if you are strong at heart, if not, you will be taken by the Infernum. There is no easy way to say it. You must stay strong or the forest will try and play tricks on you, and I don't mean children's mind games. Pulling on your heart, it'll psychologically target the most vulnerable and the deepest parts of your subconscious. You won't hear the lullaby right away, it will try and enchant you first. So don't indulge in its nonsense, because once you hear that lullaby, there is no coming back. You will become possessed, forever a part of the Infernum. If you make it through once, you'll probably never have to embark through it again, depending on your classification and title. For instance, an Elder of my position or Demetrius, who is your overseer, but that title is an incredibly hard position to obtain or come by. Now, let's get this over with, there is no point holding back now. Every new-blooded zodiac in Nirvana will be embarking on the same venture this morning… Stay strong and good luck."

The energy becomes uneasy and tense within the room. Not a single voice is heard after that as reality sets in. Europa grabs my hand with an intensity and gives me a strong affirmative look and we both nod diligently. Then Constance announces, "It is time," and signals everyone to follow.

She turns, walking over to the small door at the back of the classroom. Opening it, I instantly hear the soaring cries of crickets, louder today than normal. We band together and follow behind Constance, walking down the withered old wooden stairs as the hall sits high from the ground, followed by a drop at the back. The bright hot sun now beams down on us and the flies begin to attract. I notice Demetrius walking down the steep grassy hill, now catching up to walk besides Constance.

We follow through the tall green grass to the big gates that will introduce us to the uncharted forest footpath, eventually leading to the Doh. No one talks, only hearing the sound of footsteps and grass moving in the wind. I linger at the high wooden barriers surrounding our village, thinking how my whole world is made up within the safety of these walls and the idea that we are now willingly venturing into the uncharted forest feels like a total illusion as fear has been embodied through stories told. Everyone knows someone will be picked off today by the Infernum. It happens every year and I know everyone believes it will be me as it should have been when I was born. But I know that idea supplies comfort, so I don't mind being a comfort to lean on, considering the pain I have caused many families. Europa stares defyingly ahead, gripping my hand tight. And I think of the nightmares I had as a child about the uncharted forest and the Infernum. Now the day has come where I'm supposedly ready to face this nightmare. I realize my head is starting to get to me. So, I take a big breath, trying to control my nerves. I try to clear my mind, feeling the grass beneath my feet and listening to the birds singing and the trees rubbing against one other as though they talk amongst themselves. Their leaves rustle and the wind howls distantly.

We now approach the large wooden gates where six other Taurus soldiers wait our arrival, armed from head to toe. They fence us: two in the front, two in the back, and two in the middle, either side. Everyone from the village is here waiting; they too stand still in their demeanor. They have come to show respect and stand together strong as a mental support knowing the now eight Tauruses will soon lessen. I try to look around for my father, but I cannot see him and I'm soon distracted by Europa, who squeezes my hand, looking at me with a 'here we go' expression. Constance walks up to the two guards that watch from two high platforms on either side of the tower and says, "Let the new generation commence!"

Everyone stays quiet until a murmuring of foot stamping begins to take the lead, becoming louder and louder as their stamping feet take on a rhythmic tune. The vibration through the ground is almost comforting as Constance throws her hands in the air, the giant doors begin to open. I squeeze Europa's hand, squinting as a cold gust of wind comes bouldering through. Birds fly high and the doors sway, creaking loudly and slamming open. Dirt and dust blow hard into our faces.

Constance places her forearm over her eyes, turning to face us as she says with a loud and confident voice, "Everyone who witnesses now is honoring the transition you'll be making from boys to men and girls to women. Although it will be your choice to make that transition as no one else can be strong for you. Now, do not leave the group. You all know what lurks deep within the uncharted forest. We have done all that we can as a community to help you grow into the hopefully strong men and women. Now the rest is up to you. Good luck, Taureans."

She gives us a strong, confident nod, making eye contact with every one of us. Slowly turning around, she signals for us to follow. Demetrius stays close to Constance as he signals the other guards in an aggressive manner to move and they hit their chested armor once with stern affirmative grunt. We begin to walk and I see the long tree branches hanging down on either side of the deep, dark forest path and I feel as if time comes to a standstill. The Herba community begins stamping their feet again to give us strength. But now I cannot hear them as fear unwillingly begins to take control of my heart. The children's nursery rhyme enters my head, continuously playing over and over again as though they whisper it specifically into my ear and all the other noises drown out.

Deep within the forest, Infernum would creep. If you would hear one, beware the end of sleep.

If blackness consumes you, beware your family too. That's why we stay away from Infernum view.

The thick sturdy wall passes us gradually. The wind immediately changes, feeling more chilling in its presence, and an eerie, vulnerable sensation of terror consumes me. Even the sun disappears above the thick, tall trees, and we now stand on the other side of the wall, completely susceptible to the uncharted forest.

The gates slowly begin to creak shut until they slam loudly together, cutting off the small glimmer of light that held the warmth of the morning sun. The stamping feet become a far distant memory and a cloud of dust covers us all; as the dust settles, everyone goes eerily quiet as the forest is dead silent. Instinctively, there should be some sign of an animal or creature. A footprint, scamper, chattering but not even a bird sings a morning song, making it apparent how the sound of nature is reassuring to an unsettling mind. The dirt path isn't very clear as the forest has almost overgrown it. The forest is incredibly green with ginormous trees that travel for miles. If you weren't aware of the danger that lurks within, ignorance could possibly save your life. Demetrius breaks the stillness, signaling to the surrounding soldiers. He lifts his long thick sword from its sheath and the others replicate the action. Blades echo as they slide out, hearing the clear sharpness in their vibration to the very last tremor. Our attention is then sought by Constance, who presses her index finger to her soft lips, signaling us to follow. She turns and begins walking along the small trail with Demetrius close by her side. Demetrius and the soldiers begin hacking back the overgrown fauna as we walk. Feeling the cold branches and leaves scrap against my exposed skin as water formed from the condensation leaves its residue, bringing a chill to the surface of my skin. Europa squeezes my hand so tight I begin to lose circulation. But I know it brings her ease, so I don't bring it to her attention. Sweat begins to perspire relentlessly, bringing an even colder chill to my already cold body. And as I hesitantly but curiously stare deep into the forest, listening to the blades slice and branches fall, I lose track of time. As I find the sequences of movements and path becoming uncannily familiar, over and over again, suddenly I find myself colliding into Latham Hampton, one of the other Taurus students. Strong male who I always recognize from his giant ferocious Taurus's emblem tattoo engraved on his back. He always complains about being too hot, so he rarely wears a shirt and I wonder if he regrets that decision today. I wait for him to continue but he's stopped unmovable in his tracks. He unexpectedly stumbles back into me and I fall straight on my arse. Europa pulls me up, now letting go of my hand, which tingles as blood rushes back into it, and I rub my hands together as the uncomfortable prickling sensation kicks in.

Latham's head hangs as his long hair drapes over his face and his big horns tip forward as his tail drapes lifelessly on the ground, dead still. Europa slowly reaches out to touch his shoulder, seeing if he is okay, but she is tersely stopped by Constance. Strongly grasping her hand in resistance, she shakes her head in a stern but sorrow manner. She places Europa's hand by her side. Constance then pushes Europa and others, who stand beside back where she stands. Everyone moves accordingly, making a small spacious circle around Latham. All is still for a moment, as our anticipated eyes lay upon him, feeling he fights turmoil within him. Then he abruptly screeches in the most horrifying and penetrating scream, echoing through the eerie, silent forest. And you instantly feel his pain tremor deep within your core. He grasps his hands over his ears, falling to his knees. We all jump back even further with readiness as the soldiers push us back, drawing their swords as he continues to scream chaotically and horrifically. I place my hands over my ears, squinting my eyes, feeling the extensity of my eardrums about to reach their limit. I glance back from where we came but our Constellation is no longer in sight. I look back at Latham as the screaming subsides and he now cradles himself on the ground. His stare is not one of his own. Is this the Infernum? I anxiously look around, waiting for something to appear. I catch Europa in my eye who holds a clenched fist on her heart and the other over her mouth as she watches in wretchedness. I open my mouth to speak, but I feel a large hand press against my face, firmly and softly at the same time. Peering up, I see Demetrius' stone-cold face looking down at Latham. He presses me into his chest but leaves my nasal way free to breathe. I see his large dagger at a ready by my side. Latham now sits in an upright position on his knees, head hanging as he strongly presses his knuckles deep into the earth. Suddenly, he relaxes. Standing up without struggle or resistance, I feel his aura change as Latham disappears. Everyone takes another step back as Constance indicates everybody to move fast. He makes no initiation to lunge at anyone, only turning slowly around the circle in an elegant and creepy manner. Demetrius grasps me even tighter and I feel his breathing change to a steady pace as though he braces himself to fight. Latham stops by Demetrius, becoming instantly apprehensive. I wait for them to collide, but nothing appears to happen as Latham makes distinct eye contact with me. And I notice his eyes are now a bright shade of purple. Demetrius roughly and quickly turns me away, pointing the sword at Latham's throat. As I manage to see from my peripheral vision, Latham says expressionlessly in a non-threatening voice and one that is not his own, "This is an unstoppable force… Soon, all will be restored," after every word spoken a vibration of repeated words echo as though many voices speak at once.

Demetrius says nothing, then Latham turns towards the fauna and walks leisurely past Demetrius as he follows him with the end of his sharp dagger. Latham keeps secure eye contact with me the whole time as though he is trying to look for something. He stops for a moment, glancing up to Demetrius, giving him a questionable look. Glancing back at me, he turns his head and coldly disappears into the uncharted forest.

Demetrius continues to embrace me within a strong hold and I begin to struggle against it. He relaxes and releases me. Turning me around, he holds my gaze for a moment, looking over me with analyzing eyes, nodding affirmatively as though to confirm I'm in good health. Placing the dagger back within a small sheath, he takes a big breath of relief and pushes me close within the center of the group and walks over to Constance to have subtle words which no one else can hear. I turn around and everyone is staring at me with the expressions of bewilderment, probably thinking that I cheated death again as I too have the same thought, because Latham was obviously the stronger one out of the two of us.

Europa stands beside me and grabs my hand again in reassurance. Clenching her fist, she pounds it twice firmly against my chest and nods. Then the attention is pulled towards Constance, who swiftly goes around the group counting our heads with an anxious look upon her face. She looks at Demetrius and then he peers around at the group several times and shakes his head in dismay. Constance places one hand to her face in sorrow and I feel the chill of the forest become more prominent than ever before. Europa squeezes my hand to get my attention. She displays six fingers, switching from eight to six, pointing to the group. I look around; we started with eight Taurus students and now there are only six. But we only witnessed Latham become consumed by the Infernum. Then I realize another Taurus is missing, Beverley Fleur. Beverley genuinely kept to herself, I guess that's why no one noticed she was gone. I may stick out like a sore thumb, but Beverley just blended into the background, never making a fuss, always did well and she was great with a glaive too.

Everyone begins looking around frantically and before chaos breaks loose, Demetrius bangs his fist against his armored plates, grabbing everyone's attention. He points two fingers forward and insists we keep moving. He grunts to the surrounding soldiers, making a hand gesture circling around us, and clinches his fist into the palm of his other hand. The soldiers push the rest of us together, now completely constricted of personal space. Europa and I are together at the back of the group with two large soldiers stepping closely behind us as their armor clinks loudly with each step. I feel claustrophobic as I'm used to my own space. I begin taking big breaths, focusing on a focal point in front of me which happens to be Kendall Warren's full head of black dreadlocks, half tied up at the back. He's an unusually tall Taurus, so he makes a great focal point. As I try to keep basic thoughts, ones that won't make me drift towards negative emotions, not too over powering, just simple, my skin becomes colder as the initial sweat brings a chill to the surface of my skin and dampens my clothes. Then I hear a distant movement coming from deep within the forest, a slithering sound. My heart nearly stops and as my eyes widen, I try to stay focused on Kendall. Then I hear a 'hiss' as though it was slithering right beside us. I glance to Europa and the others, but either they're ignoring it too or the Infernum is trying to enchant me. Although I have no recognition of a snake in my recollection, I used to get Adonis to kill them on hot summer days, prone to sit in front of the cottage as they'd bask in the morning sun. The hiss intensifies and grows in strength, perpetrating deep into my ear. Catastrophic fear begins to seep in and spread within me. My heart pounds hard beneath my chest. I do not look its way. I refuse to let my father down. I will not let the Infernum take me!

Then it speaks in a high-pitched hissing tone, *"Tu es via, veritas et vita. Nemo venit ad Patrem, nisi per te."* I feel as though everything falls silent within my mind and around me as those same words repeat in my head from the woman in my dream. Then the lullaby sung by children, who cannot be seen in a daunting whisper, repeating themselves over and over again:

Deep within the forest, Infernum would creep.
If you would hear one, beware the end of sleep.
If blackness consumes you, beware your family too. That's why we stay away
from Infernum view.

I turn to face the creature with defiance, but I'm suddenly overcome by a hot burning ray of light piercing through the outline of a tall, robust tree. I place my forearm over my eyes, squinting as they adjust from the dark forest. There is no snake to be seen, only endless forest. I turn to the front and see an open field in the distance as the trees begin to separate and disintegrate far from one another as we approach. The sun now pierces through and I can see the Doh.

As we approach, picking up speed, we hear and feel big bells echo through the forest floor, everyone pushing one another to peer down the path as the soldiers fastidiously cut down the remaining fauna that's in our way. Birds fly high at the beginning and the edge of the uncharted forest, hearing our loud feet approach without subtlety. The sun becomes increasingly bright as we step out from the damp, cold uncharted forest and into a large meadow where I can see the Doh in clear view now, a tall white tower with large white stone walls, circling around the edifice structure.

The field is saturated with grass and a large white footpath lays before us, leading our sector towards the tower. It's the most enigmatic structure I've ever seen. The path we stand on has our Taurus emblem now illuminating above us, with our constellation colors – green and white – rotating as we stand idle. I've seen a little magic but not much as our sector is one of brawn not magic. We all stand still at the edge of the forest as every other zodiac begins to appear evenly around the large circular meadow, related close to the direction of their sector. Their zodiac emblem lights up above them too, rotating with their Constellation colors as each one emerges. First, Aries: red and scarlet; then Gemini: green, yellow, and orange; Cancer: sea green and silver; Leo: gold, orange, and yellow; Virgo: green, white, and yellow; Libra: blue, jade, and green; Scorpio: red and violet; Sagittarius: light blue and white; Capricorn: black and indigo; Aquarius: ultramarine blue and grey; Pisces: sea green and aqua.

Constance's voice suddenly grabs our attention, and I notice Kendall's withdrawn expression, knowing him and Latham were best friends.

"Alright, everyone, I can't allow you to stay this close to the border, you saw what happened to…" she pauses for a moment, swallowing and looking away momentarily.

She continues, "Beverley and Latham. I warned you, it is a common occurrence. But we will not remember them in sadness; we shall remember them for the strong Tauruses they were as they are no longer the Taureans you once knew. When we get back to the Constellation, we will celebrate their never-forgotten existence."

Everyone grunts loudly in agreement and bangs their fists on their chests in honor. We begin walking along the path and I see the other zodiacs also head towards the Doh surrounded by guards from their Constellation and an overseer SNC in front. And I notice not all the Constellations have an elder teacher, like Constance, which makes me have even more profound respect for her.

The paths are long and narrow as we approach the Doh with our Constellation emblem following us from above. I can see each zodiac Constellation path leads towards a separate entrance. The Gemini's are to our right, looking very similar from afar. Their white and black hair split down the middle, abstract, as though you are looking at an optical illusion when they walk together, much like their diverse personalities from what I've studied. To our left are Aries, who stand tall with their strong goat legs, chest pushed out, looking as courageous as what I've read, covered in tattoos much like ourselves but their horns curl around unlike ours. We approach an open gate and a shadow is casted over us from a large statue that sits above the entrance. Nirvana's emblem – 'The Wisdom Tree' – one sits above every entrance with a thick base and enormous branches expanding outwards that fall elegantly down far from its trunk. It stands tall and sturdy, painted in a brassy gold color. We walk under it and golden leaves begin to fall all around us. Looking up, I notice the tree now moves in the wind as though it becomes alive in our presence. We place our hands out and the leaves delicately land on the palms of our hands, disintegrating as they touch our skin and blow away in the wind.

Constance gathers us around in a circle and says, "This is an impersonation of the real Wisdom Tree. Every leaf is meant to be a representation of a single essence lost and reborn. As you know when we pass away in this life, our essence is drawn from our bodies as we are laid under the Wisdom Tree to die. We are given back to Unum, as he is everything and one with all. Although Apophis was our direct interpreter of Unum, it doesn't mean he still doesn't exist within our world. Because if we lost our connection to Unum and he did perish, we would cease to exist as he uses our essences to restore what is lost and without that natural cycle, Nirvana would fall. Now, pay your respects."

Constance, in admiration, blows away the golden leaves she's accumulated in her hand to the sky. We stand under the tree in awe and I watch a singular leaf fall on to the tip of my finger, thinking how something so delicate can be so powerful. No one has ever seen the Wisdom Tree as it is forbidden and sacred. It is only in your last passing minutes will you be able to undergo the most beautiful experience of our time – death.

Chapter 3
The Doh

Prodigious is only great if those roots grow deep.

Big bells begin to vibrate again, trembling through the ground, tingling the tips of my toes. Then a deep, dominate voice echoes, "Welcome!" Turning around I see the pristine white tower that could possibly be touching the brim of the universe, whilst strange winged creatures circle around the higher parts of the immeasurable tower. On a singular, unbelievably large balcony looking tiny in comparison to the building, the patriarch Theophilus Malis Virgo stands. Even though he seems small from this view, it's apparent his wings are beautiful but unusually large for a Virgo, as wings of that size would usually indicate an ancient age. But in comparison to his physique, you would not believe it to be so. He now steps forward.

"Good morning, my new-blooded zodiacs!"

Enlarged holographic images begin to appear around the tower, so all who are not in view can see him speak.

"Let me start out by giving you my condolences. I know the journey through the uncharted forest is not for the faint-hearted, you lost those who were close to you. But we must remember them for who they were and not what they are now. Look to the future as we shall reclaim our lands as long as we stay strong, working together as one. Their lives will not go in vain. Apophis will not be our undoing. Because we will take down his Infernum army! Now cheer, so he can hear you! Let him know his tactics to take our friends and loved ones will not crush us! We are strong together!"

Everyone cheers loudly and I notice each individual Constellation are expressing themselves in individual ways, depending on their culture. Different grunts, snorts, magic, and elegant movements are articulated on the ground to give forth their honor and gratitude. A large circular carapace horn sits next to Theophilus. And at almost three times his size, it is blown in congregation with the cheering of the Constellations. It has a deep stifling horn, pressing through the ground and walls. I squint as it shimmers bright in the morning sun and as it diminishes, I see a stumpy hairy creature step down from where it's appeared to be played. Everyone falls silent as Theophilus holds a gentle hand in the air,

"Thank you, New Bloods. Now being the year of your 21st birthdays and the beginning of your Olympus Trial studies to better understand our world and those who live around and within it. You'll be registering today as you know, retrieving your purpose numbers, dignifying you as individuals. As you've probably been informed when you leave today, you will not be going back through the uncharted forest as your purpose numbers allow you to teleport back and forth from the Doh. But when you come back here tomorrow, you will spend the next chapter of your lives endeavored within the Olympus Trials. So we can better understand you as individuals, enabling us to set you up for the remaining chapter of your lives within the specific classifications you are best suited too, allocated to particular career paths as you are well aware of. But this process takes a long time, we need to watch you grow, monitor your behavior and individual patterns, so we know precisely how you work. Your Constellation overseers will guide you through the beginning of this process until you get the hang of your whereabouts and devices. But now I'll let you get registered. Good luck. And let strength lay beside you."

Theophilus stands for a moment then his wings begin to expand, blocking out the morning sun. He leaps off the balcony and flies off circling around the tower, casting a shadow over all who stand below. Flying away, we watch him slowly disappear into the distance.

I look down and see the disintegrating leaves gather around us, slowly blowing away in the wind. Europa stands beside me and says softly, "I knew you could do it," I look at her, "I'm glad one of us did," and smile.

Constance signals us and says, "Alright, everyone, you will follow me to the Taurus statue ahead, where you'll be given your purpose numbers and then you can enter the Doh. After that we are going to head to the dining room where you'll sit and eat with the other zodiacs then be placed within your Constellation Dormitories."

We follow Constance and we approach another larger, white, pristine wall. There is no entrance, only the Taurus statue of the bull sitting large and profoundly exotic in all its glory. As we come towards the bull, it slowly starts to break free from its solid, rigid composure, moving in distilled fragments, transforming into a live statue of our ancestral bull. My mouth widens with amazement, green and white spray off as it bursts into life, amazingly animated. Out of the corner of my eye I catch the Gemini's statue of yin and yang, their ancestral twins. Green, yellow, and orange fly from both of them as they peel apart and transform into life. And to the left, Aries' statue, the ram, bucking and kicking as their red and scarlet colors flail off him.

Constance stands before us and smiles, allocating Europa to be the first to step forward and present herself. She grabs her hand and says to all of us, "Now don't be coy. He's just going to simulate you with your purpose numbers. Then you'll be able to enter the Doh. Now go ahead, Europa," Constance guides Europa over, letting go of her hand. Europa pauses for a moment with hesitation, staring at the giant beast whose horns could easily remove a valley or destroy a large group of strong soldiers in one thrust. Constance presses her forward and Europa slowly walks over to the giant bull who now sits calmly by the primeval wall. Demetrius now stands beside me and Europa cautiously approaches. I intently watch her as she nods sternly to the bull and bows in honor. He looks at her for a moment as if analyzing her. He blows through his nostrils and leans down as an emerald necklace slips off the top of his horn and gently falls over her head. Then a green aura illuminates from her, displaying the number five.

And in an influential and earthly voice, he speaks, "Europa Castellanos, you bear the purpose number five. Magnetic, fun-loving, adventurous, curious, flexible, restless, and a free spirit. You have the ability to adapt to any new situation, unafraid of the unknown, captivating and persuasive with words. Although you are easily distracted, have a tendency to have a lack focus, terrible with routine, and you can be too self-indulgent. Those are the things you must be most wary." He turns his head and gestures to the wall. She looks at the wall in confusion but continues. She stands in front of it for a moment then places her hand against it and it falls through as though it were imaginary all this time. She snaps her head back in shock and he says, "Sometimes things aren't always what they appear." She smiles and steps through the wall.

Isa pushes past me and attempts to push me over, signifying her superiority against me. But I manage to keep my balance. Then Dalton and Henrietta follow closely behind, finishing the job, and I find my face reconnecting to the familiar hard surface. Dust fills my lungs as I follow through with hard, painful coughing. Lifting my head, I catch Demetrius looking down at me and I know he can't defend me in this scenario as it would be seen as favoritism, and I should be able to defend myself at this age. Kneeling on my knees, I wipe my already scrapped hands on my shabby clothes. Standing, I attempt to remove the dirt from my face. Demetrius glances at me with intent, maneuvering inconspicuously beside Constance who stands meters in front, surprised by the eager Isa who walks up before her. She allows Isa to go forth confidently taking the first step, she unexpectedly trips over, landing face first into the hard, dirty pavement, and I see Demetrius' foot slowly return back to his normal stance. Dalton and Henrietta both blurt out into laughter and I find my mouth slowly curling into a large smile, trying to cover it with my hand. Isa's hair has come undone, her frizzy hair expands into a giant hairball. Her head snaps back at Dalton and Henrietta, and they quickly drop their amusement, coughing and elbowing one another to quieten each other down. Isa hurriedly stands, pulling her hair back into a rough knot. She looks at Demetrius with an expressionless countenance then glances back at me, wincing, and continues forward with masked pride.

The bull looks down upon her and says, "Be careful of the concoction you choose to drink as thy will only cause cancer within one's self." Isa says nothing and stands as though he did not speak, most likely blinded by rage and unable to see or hear anything else but the furious noise in her mind. The creature bends down and once again an emerald necklace slides off the end of his horn, landing softly on to her shoulders. Breathing deeply into his lungs, he relaxes and a green aura illuminates from her too, displaying the number four. Then he speaks, "Isa Edlyn, you bear the purpose number four. You are strong, honest, determined, practical, hardworking, down-to-earth, and organized. You have the ability to accomplish large projects due to your organizational skills and perseverance, due to your honesty and integrity, others know they can trust you. And you are comfortable expanding small projects into large ones, though you have a tendency to be bossy and a bit of a know-it-all. You can be ridged at times and are quick to place judgment on others. You can be overly cautious, which can lead to missed opportunities. This is where you must be most wary."

Isa nods determinedly and walks through the wall into the Doh as though she had done it several times before. Dalton and Henrietta now wait impatiently before Constance, and she nods for one of them to proceed forward as the creature now chews its jaw from side to side in a bull-like manner· patiently waiting as they both quarrel about who will go first. Then he speaks as he chews, "Both Hamlyns, come forward."

They look at one another with excitement and walk in sync. He looks down upon them and says, "Both, one of the same." Continuing to chew, he leans down and takes a deep breath in; they chuckle, finding it ticklish. Two emerald necklaces appear on either horn and gently slide over their heads in a synchronized motion with the illuminating green aura displaying the number three. He says, "Dalton and Henrietta Hamlyn, you bear the purpose number three. You are creative, generous, charismatic, playful, joyful, optimistic, and witty. You are amazingly creative and innovative, communication comes easy to you, others are drawn to your charming, magnetic personalities, and your energy and happiness uplifts those around you, though you have a tendency to hold grudges when hurt by those you trust, tough time with managing finances, you also have a tendency to procrastinate, have a lack of focus when something does not interest you, and you constantly need praise and affirmation from your peers to keep your spirits high. This is where you must be most wary." Dalton and Henrietta look at one another and nod with big smiles, convinced by the bull's reading; they turn to the wall and leap through.

Demetrius and Constance both turn to look at me simultaneously. Then I look at Kendall who stands patiently beside me, not appearing to be in any rush. I glance either side, at both Gemini and Aries Constellations, who are nearly finished with their purpose number simulations. Then Constance remarks, "Come on, Taura. Aren't you excited to find your purpose number?"

She places her hand out and I walk forward. Demetrius gives me an affirming nod and I walk slowly towards the ginormous bull. Standing in front of him, he glances at me as he did the others, leaning down I feel the ground tremor beneath my feet, feeling the absorbent power within his presence. He breathes in deep and unexpectedly snorts mucus all over me and around me. He stares at me with sudden fear and astonishment within his eyes. I freeze. He says with caution as his muscles tense then slowly relax as he comes to a realization, "You only see things as they appear to be, not what they truly are. How did you end up here?"

I'm completely stiff with not only fear and confusion but a sudden eerie sagacity. Constance walks up from behind me and looks at Taurus carefully. They stare at one another for a moment before he goes back to his original composure and says, "This is the child?" I look up at Constance who now nods slowly and her expression has an obvious secrecy intended behind it. He holds eye contact with her then glances away, as though he is ashamed in some way, acknowledging my already sick, insecure feeling of not belonging. He looks at me with an expressionless composure, drops a necklace that lands clumsily in front of me with the number ten imprinted on it. No illuminating green aura appears above my head. Constance whispers in my ear, "It's okay, my Taura. You can walk through the wall now, into the Doh." She pretends to act composed but is clearly rushed by the now infuriated Taurus as she gently guides me with a soft hand on my back and the other hand placed on my shoulder. Walking me through the wall, she says with humility, "Don't think too much on this. You're perfect just as you are." Those words do not supply comfort; how could I not think on it. Adonis and Penelope should have left me in the woods where I belonged.

As I walk through the illusionary white sturdy wall, I feel a warm sensation slowly crawl over my body from front to back as though walking through water. I shut my eyes until I feel my feet land on secure ground. The warm sensation rolls off my body and fresh air touches my naked skin, feeling properly washed for the first time. Burning into me, I feel the necklace melt into my chest. I look down and see it absorb into my skin, glowing bright green until it slowly fades, now burning the back of my neck. The wall gentle peels off the remaining remnants of my body, rippling as it detaches, returning to its illusionary representation of a wall.

I analyze myself. Then look up to see the inside of the Doh for the very first time, my mouth drops slightly open. Europa, Isa, Dalton, and Henrietta all stand ahead of me as I walk slowly towards them, unnoticed. The room is large and circular, brightly decorated with golden outlines around historic art and every zodiac appears from their Constellation section, appearing through the wall as I did, with their region emblem displayed above, glowing brightly as they enter. I turn around to see ours too, slowly fading as I step further into the Doh, snippets of significant events told to us as children appear and disappear amongst the tall walls. As I look up into the infinite tower, there seems to be thousands of floors separated between a large twirling staircase made of hard stone. It appears to go on forever, a spinning hole of the unknown, making you dizzier the longer you stare.

"Taur!" Europa's now standing beside me. Looking at her chest, I notice her necklace, too, is gone. She continues, "Isn't this amazing!" she says, noticing me staring at her bare chest. "Oh yeah, it happened to me too. Burnt for a bit. But it transfers to the back of your neck. See," she turns around, moving her thick blonde hair, displaying the number five, distinctly seen through any original tattoo. I rub the back of my neck, realizing the purpose for the burning sensation. "What was your purpose number?" she asks. I look ashamed, even though I don't know the purpose behind a number ten. But from the bull's expression, it did not seem good. And I hear Isa murmur beside us, "Bet she didn't even get one."

Dalton and Henrietta both chuckle. Europa spits them a livid glare. "Ten," I say with slight malice.

She gives me an inquisitive look and says, "Ten? What purpose number is that? I thought there were only nine and the master numbers?"

I shrug, "So did I, he didn't give me an explanation," not wanting to elaborate on the disappointing event.

Europa realizing this, changes the topic, "So have you checked out the other zodiacs? I can't believe we're so close to one another. It feels so surreal."

I smile slightly and nod, "It's incredible, this whole place."

We both look around, taking in the moment and say no more. Kendall Warren now approaches the group as the last Taurus, visually seeing the purpose number nine now burning into his chest, but his facial expression barely changes from the discomfort. He appears to embrace the pain, representing a true determined Taurus. All the zodiacs now gather in alignment within the circular room, standing next to one another, reflected within Nirvana's layout, from a bird's eye view.

The Geminis now stand closely to our right, their black and white, yin and yang distinctions look nothing alike up close. Every individual has their own unique appearance, with youthful slender builds. They all glance around frantically, unable to miss a thing, making humorous witty comments as they point and chuckle to one another. Beside them is Cancer: their black piercing eyes with pristine porcelain skin, a malevolent, innocent contrast as their skeleton armament pierces through their forearms. Their exteriors are guarded and protective of their small colony. Next to them is Leo: their lean athletic builds are a better representation of my own, golden eyes glimmering in the light, sharp nails sprawled at a ready, lion's ears slightly protruding back in attentiveness as their tails flicker with an ego and dynamic presence, as though they wait in thrilling anticipation. Next to them is Virgo: tall and slender, bright green eyes pierce

45

through you with large wings pinned behind their backs. Dressing neatly, they stand inflexible in clear judgment of everyone, taking in every detail and analyzing every feature, their intelligence does not go unnoticed. Next to them is Libra: radiant and beautiful zodiacs with pointed ears and mystical looking unconventional clothes from the forest. They stand without judgment and little curiosity, only skimming through everyone. A few have one green eye and the other blue, representing an unbalanced emotion or turmoil, probably reflecting their nervousness within this unknown situation. Next to them is Scorpio: hard-looking zodiac with thorns extending from all jointed parts of their body, fierce long black stinging tails standing high above their heads, strong features, and jet-black hair. Their whole aura is represented with bravery and focus. They watch silently, barely moving, making them incredibly hard to read. Next to them is Sagittarius: standing tall and noble as their horse hooves clop from side to side. They have a strong, no-nonsense presence about them. The men look rugged and the women fierce, as they look at some zodiacs with impressiveness and some with disappointment, clearly noted by their facial expressions. Next to them is Capricorn with a shy presence: they stand huddled closely together, watching everyone in a cautious, inquisitive manner. Some distinctly with a long fish tail, trailing along the ground and a couple with a small goat tail. Their mysterious beauty does not go unnoticed. Next to them is Aquarius: the largest of the zodiac, having an Amazonian look about them. Although they may be large with an incredibly strong and powerful physical presence, they have a calming, safe, and protective aura in contrast. They look at everyone in a friendly and welcoming manner. Next to them is Pisces: the fragments of their sporadic orange color shimmers brightly as the light hits their waterproof skin on the right angle. They have a soft and gentle presence about them, watching everyone in an affectionate manner as though excited to get to know us. And I notice, unlike their pictures, their fins are tucked away when outside the water. Next to them and us are Aries: they stand courageous and lively, beaming in a positive and arrogant dynamic manner as though they wait impatiently to get started. Their restless energy stands in center of attention.

We all stay close within the safety and familiarities of our Constellations, now waiting for one of our overseers to guide us away from this surreal confrontation. But as stillness lingers throughout the murmurs of conversation and judgment, silence quickly diminishes every voice heard as blue sparkles begin to fall from the Doh's high-proximity ceiling, falling delicately and disappearing as they hit the old stone floor. Everyone slowly looks up; it appears to be manifesting from out of nowhere, decorated by the twirling staircase that twists around the circular perimeter of the Doh's infinite tower. And as we follow the falling diamonds down to our eye level, we begin to hear words spoken by a profound, deep, and memorable voice; his words appear within the raining blue diamonds, lighting up with every word spoken.

He says: "Welcome to the Olympus Trials. Theory and physical base studies you're now registered within, to enhance your power, ability, and skill to become the strongest version of yourselves. This system was devised to bring unity back between the twelve Constellations due to an unseen evil force you know of as the Infernum that had shattered the land in the past and divided the twelve Constellations. The Olympus Trials has been made to give you a clear understanding of where each and every one of your residing zodiacs came from, giving an appreciation to every zodiac's inhabitants and way of life, coming together as one working unity as opposed to the perception placed upon you at birth.

"You are classed by the 12 paired Elders, two from each Constellation: one male and one female, who will be introduced to you today. The main two who oversee all major decisions are the Patriarch and Matriarch, chosen by the elders. They speak for all the Elders and have the greatest power and knowledge. They designed the Olympus Trials.

"There are three classifications you'll be classed within once you complete the trials and this depends on what promise you show within the whole of your studies. This is established over time, after much rigorous testing. The first classification you know of is the 'Nebula Classification,' also known as NC. Second is 'Planetary Nebula Classification,' also known as PNC, and the third is the 'Supernova Classification,' also known as SNC. NC is for those who are set in their ways, unable to change, staying within their Constellation and never leaving. During the trials, they'll generally display continuous and predictable traits from their upbringing, unable to innovate and adapt to the unfamiliar environments or task given at hand. PNC is for the zodiacs who work and live within the Doh. This classification is determined by those who show quick initiative, solutions, and broad intelligence within stressful environments which is needed within the Doh's working environment. SNC is for the ones who give service to the Nirvana Army, created to defend against the prehistoric enemy, the 'Infernum,' as not every zodiac has the ability and mentality to take on such an evil and powerful force; this is a hard class to determine, as you must show great courage, intelligence, and profound skill.

"During the trials, if deemed worthy, they'll be submitted into the army to learn the skills to enhance their unique talents, making them the strongest zodiacs within Nirvana."

Then the voice ceases to be heard and the falling blue diamonds disappear almost simultaneously and unexpectedly behind the Scorpios, who stand rigidly. Then comes a loud creaking noise of doors slowly opening. All the zodiacs turn and watch as a light slowly illuminates delicately over two large ancient doors that

I had not noticed before now as though they magically appeared. All the zodiacs' emblems are crafted in great detail on the surface of the radiating doors with the wisdom tree centered in the middle with leaves falling. The door begins to crack as though it's breaking. A deep breathing noise follows as it heaves open, straight down the middle of the animated tree. Its leaves still fall as the doors move to reveal a room which has a real tree with small multi-colored orbs moving within it. It looks much like the ones above the entrances just before entering the Doh, except this one is ginormous. A long horizontal table lays before it on a podium with twelve paired seats, leaves disappearing as they land on the surface. Twelve other tables lay vertically below the podium, each individual table displaying the Constellation colors of all twelve regions, obviously delegating where we must sit. The multi-colored orbs move around the large room, flowing in and out of the tree. The Leos make the first initiative, one saying, "Well, come on, what are you all waiting for!" The Aries, confronting any given opportunity to express their notorious courage, immediately raise to the occasion along with Sagittarius, the most intrigued about investigating the unknown. It makes sense that all the fire signs are quick to light the flame of enthusiasm.

We merge into the room slowly, taking in the magnificent display. I stay close to Europa as we enter, but she is completely consumed by the elaborate room, unaware of my movements. The temperature increases to a warm and comfortable texture, making me relax. The little colored orbs dance around the room, scooting in and out of the tree as though excited about our arrival, reminding me of fairies but only the colors are visible as they glow. Once we had entered and before sitting down at our tables, they come flying over. Every color colonizes towards different zodiacs. The Capricorns gather orbs of white, Aquarius collect orbs of grey, Pisces blue-green, Aries yellow-green, Gemini orange, Cancer rose, Leo red, Virgo brown, Libra blue, Scorpio violet, and Sagittarius gold. Yellow bulbs hover above us. Before we get the chance to look closer, they all fly straight back amongst the large branches of the huge tree. Then the Elders appear from behind the tree, now approaching their seats that lay behind the long table on top of the podium.

We all rush to sit down; every Constellation has the exact number of seats for each new-blooded colony. Six seats wait for Europa, Kendall, Isa, Dalton, Henrietta, and me. A long skinny satin cloth is laid centered in the middle, draping over either end with our Taurus emblems knitted beautifully into the material with the colors green and white, and a replica hanging over the back of our wooden chairs just like every other Constellation with their individual color scheme and emblems, making it obvious where we are to be seated. Beautifully lit candles are also on display with large golden cups and plates with stunning cutlery.

"With this kind of display, I expect the food to be just as good!" Europa whispers to me with eagerness as we pull our chairs in. Then the table begins to tremble. I hold on to my seat and I look at Europa who beams with enthralled excitement, and an illuminating, sparkling, green hologram emerges through the table. It's our Taurus bull, and I notice everyone else's symbols of their lineal ancestors appear through their tables too. I suddenly jump out of my seat as the hologram cries, "Moooooooooooooooo!" and shoots into the high ceiling, followed by Gemini's twins, Cancer's crab, Leo's lion, Virgo's winged virgin, Libra's scales, Scorpio's scorpion, Sagittarius' emblem reflecting themselves, Capricorn's fish goat, Aquarius's pot with spilled water, Pisces' two fish, and Aries' horned goat. Green sparkles fall upon us and I take my right hand and let them fall on my open palm, blowing them into the air watching them disappear. Then brightly colored explosions begin to blast above us and my heart begins to race as a rush of excitement and pleasure overwhelms me. I notice the Elders clapping with joy as though this was some kind of entertainment, so I relax and marvel at the falling, beautiful colors.

"Those explosions are much like Father's farts," says Dalton to Henrietta who chuckles at his comment. "I bet he could give them a run for their money," says Henrietta. Both laughing hysterically at their unamusing humor.

Isa rolls her eyes, "Don't you two ever have anything worthwhile to contribute to a conversation." Both look at Isa who sits sternly, unimpressed by the display that continues to fall delicately upon us.

"Those farts are pretty worthwhile if you ask me!" says Dalton and they both continue laughing uncontrollably. Isa sinks deeper into her seat, arms crossed, rolling her eyes, unimpressed by their sarcasm.

Europa whispers to me, "They should never reproduce."

I lean towards her, "Well, they wouldn't exactly have many suitors."

Europa snuffs, "Yeah, but they're stupid enough to settle for one another and then we'd really have problematic offspring." We both chuckle and now the show is over.

The Patriarch and Matriarch, Theophilus Malis and Adora Malis, continue to stand proudly in center as all the other Elders take a seat. They are both draped in long elegant robes with the Virgo constellation colors: green, white, and yellow. Both are tall and slender with piercing green eyes. The beautiful Adora takes a seat and Theophilus continues to clap in a slow, interval, stern rhythm. Stopping, he calmly lays his hands down in front of him and clasps his hands together elegantly and says:

"Well, it's nice to meet you all up close, my new-blooded zodiacs. I hope that enthralling display made you feel more at ease within the Doh's premises. I see you've already met your totems; they have been very eager to meet you." He raises his hands high and the colored orbs begin to act lively, flying in and out and in-between the tree branches in their unique mannerisms. Then Theophilus brings his hands back to his original stature and continues, "You have probably never heard of your totems as they are unique to the Olympus Trials, born into this space once you obtain your purpose numbers. But you'll be educated on them at a later time during your classes. First, we must eat and rejuvenate ourselves as it has been a catastrophic morning for you all. Then dormitory placement will commence and you can start to get settled before going home for the last night. But before we begin anything, I will introduce you to your residing Elders."

He clears his throat and announces, "Capricorn Elders: Aldous and Amelia Darcy!"

Everyone praises them as they stand. Aldous has a goat tail and Amelia a fish tail. Aldous has long dark brown hair tied back with two thick bits draping down either side of his ears. He looks concealed but wise and noble. Amelia has long, salty-looking, indigo-colored hair as though it's dried that way from salt water. She looks guarded and strong-willed. They both wear comfortable clothing in their Constellation colors, black and indigo. Amelia begins speaking in a strong and delegating voice, "We are the ambitious of the zodiac: practical, wise, disciplined, persistent, and cautious."

Amelia steps back and Theophilus adds, "If you want guidance or advice, they are the best mentors and teachers as their philosophical connection to life comes exceedingly natural in regards to the balance of the universe." Everyone applauds. They both bow in acknowledgment and Theophilus gestures towards the Aquarians, "Aquarius Elders: Cassidy and Brigantia Dion!" They stand eagerly but nearly take out the table in the process due to their large size. Pulling it back, they reframe themselves and smile welcomingly, making you feel drawn to them. Cassidy has long blue dreadlocked hair with different fauna immersed within it; he has a large smile and jolly appearance. Brigantia has two long blue plaits draping down the front of her; she too has fauna immersed within her hair, and she looks loving and caring. They both wear clothing that appears to be made by all sorts of fauna, colored with grey and ultramarine blue as their Constellation colors. Brigantia raises her large arm and says in a welcoming kind voice, "We are the humanitarian of the zodiac: friendly, intelligent, creative, independent, and loyal."

Theophilus adds, "If you or the creature you know have a life-threatening injury, they are the ones to see as they are the greatest healers in Nirvana and advanced in any language." Everyone claps and they both wave and carefully sit back down in their larger seats, sarcastically gesturing to everyone.

Theophilus smiles then moves on to the Pisces, "Pisces Elders: Galen and Calypso Murdoch!" They both stand delicately; their illuminating eyes look over everyone in the room, observing carefully. Galen has bright orange eyes, soft features with his rope-like hair tied into a large bun at the top of his head; he looks kind. Calypso is fragile but gentle looking; she is small in frame with tiny facial features, but her eyes are on the darker side and her rope hair lays freely down her back; she looks feeble. But I get the impression not to underestimate her. Neither wears clothes as their leathery, scale skin already covers their naked bodies, instead they have painted themselves in their Constellation colors, sea green and aqua. Galen now speaks in a soft but confident voice, "We are the intuitive of the zodiac: imaginative, kind, compassionate, sensitive, and selfless."

Theophilus continues, "There's not a spell nor potion they cannot conjure and not a curse they cannot cure. They are the greatest sorcerers and alchemists of our time." We applaud and they compassionately and calmly nod in gratitude and sit down. He moves on to the Aries, "Aries Elders: Ardon and Anthea Cadman!" They both stand animated, demonstrating a strong, proud demeanor, chests pushed out and hands sternly on their hips, exuding complete confidence. Ardon is a strong and muscular Aries with hard features, short beard, strong eyes; tattoos cover the majority of his body with a large Aries emblem imprinted on his chest. He holds his head ardently high. Anthea is also a tough and striking female Aries. Her hair strongly tied back into a short ponytail. She too is incredibly athletic; she stands tall, appearing to compete over the attention Ardon claims from the crowd. They both wear minimal brown leather clothing, only wearing face paint to show their Constellation colors, red and scarlet. Ardon takes the stand and speaks boldly, "We are the courageous of the zodiac: confident, lively, ardent, bold, and daring."

Theophilus adds, "They have the strength to destroy mountains and clear any area with their large strong-headed horns, having the courage and determination to step up to any challenge that exceeds most." Everyone applauds, especially the Aries Constellation as they egg each other on.

Theophilus raises his hand and everyone instantly falls silent. Then signals Taurus, "Taurus Elders: Iden and Constance Terran!" We all thud our chests hard and in sync as the air from our lungs makes short grunting noise. This is the first time I have seen Iden. He is hard and tough looking; his facial expressions speaks only of hard work ethic, and efficiency, clearly showing great dominating demeanor over Constance, who stands slightly behind him. He has muscular features with a thick, long, clean-cut beard and dark brown eyes, standing with his arms crossed. They both wear conservative clothing with our Constellation colors, green and white. Iden speaks with a strong and resolute tone, "We are the determined of the zodiac: independent, generous, down-to-earth, patient, and persistent."

Theophilus continues, "The most diverse weaponry skilled zodiacs. If you want to learn how to fight, they are the only zodiacs who have the patience and skill to teach and produce great warriors." Everyone claps and we hit our chests twice efficiently in sync and sit down, like the good soldiers we were trained to be, although I'm aware I look out of place.

Iden and Constance both nod their heads and sit down. Theophilus then gestures towards Gemini, "Gemini Elders: Eldryd and Amora Findal!" They both stand quickly with intent, dynamic in their presence. They look enthusiastically around the room. Eldryd's black side looks solemn and watchful, hard in its appearance with a pierced eyebrow, and his white is playful and calming with two piercings in his ear. Amora is incredibly pretty with a delicate appearance, her eyes are big with long eyelashes. Both their black sides portray wickedness in contrast to their white, kind sides, both sides connected as one. They wear expensive attires with their Constellation colors: green, yellow, and orange. Eldryd smiles with enthusiasm, rubbing his hands together vigorously and says, "We are the charismatic of the zodiac: compelling, witty, intelligent, versatile, and enthusiastic."

Theophilus adds, "They are able to create the most beautiful pieces of architecture, like the Doh you see before you. Their attention to detail and diverse intelligence can manage many tasks at once, having the initiation and speed to complete these masterpieces." The Gemini Constellation enthusiastically cheer for their Elders and everyone claps in acknowledgment. They both wave uncontrollably fast.

Then Theophilus points to Cancer, "Cancer Elders: Dimitri and Selena Griswold!" They both stand with a cool and detached demeanor, unable to give much away with their piercing black eyes although I feel they deliberately want to portray that for their own self-protection. Dimitri stands with his arm protectively around Selena's back, demonstrating a caring and loving partner. He is mysterious looking with stern features and a large scar protrudes on an angle from one side of his face to the other. Selena stands confident with Dimitri by her side: faithful and strong in appearance with girly looking features and a shaved head with decorative pattern shaved into it. They both wear tight fitting clothes with their Constellation colors, sea green and silver. Selena speaks with a humble and light voice, "We are the passionate of the zodiac: loving, protective, faithful, caring, and unassuming."

Theophilus includes, "The most nimble, agile, and unassuming zodiacs, initiating a murder before being aware of their passing and produce a force field so vast it could cover the Doh's grounds." After that comment, they both bow and everyone follow up with an applause.

Theophilus clears his throat then signals the Leo partners, "Leo Elders: Leander and Albertina Maximillion!" The Leo Constellation energetically give a positive and loud ovation as the couple stand with pride and intent although they appear to be magnetic in their demeanor. Leander is strong, athletic, and handsome with long rugged golden hair half tied into a bun and bright golden eyes, covered in tattoos even on his face. Leander is feminine and sensual; she moves in a promiscuous way and has beautiful long golden hair tied into a long draping ponytail with beads entangled. They both wear armored uniform in their Constellation colors: gold, orange, and yellow. Leander speaks with a proud and licentious voice, "We are the leaders of the zodiac: optimistic, magnetic, captivating, self-assured, and fiery."

Theophilus continues, "The fiercest animalistic hunters of our time, to see their transformation into their lion ancestors and to watch them hunt or kill is something you should hope to see in your lifetime."

Everyone applauds and they confidently sit back down in their seats as Theophilus gestures to Libra, "Libra Elders: Adlai and Isadora Dempster!" The Libras clap in a very pleasing manner as their Elders stand conservatively; their energy is harmonious and calm. Adlai is striking as his skin is porcelain white with not a mark to be seen with clear, crystal blue eyes and long, light brown hair which doesn't have a strand out of place. His presence is reassuring and alluring. Isadora is incredibly beautiful with the same porcelain skin and with the same crystal blue eyes. She has bright, strawberry blonde hair that glows in the light. Her presence draws you in a sensual, calming, and comforting way. They both dress in immaculate attires with their Constellation colors: blue and jade green. Adlai speaks convincingly with a self-connected undertone, "We are the diplomatic of the zodiac: charming, romantic, honest, respectful, and harmonious."

Theophilus continues, "Their skill in mind control goes beyond any Constellation; they are able to control everyone in this room, all at once if they wished. You'd be surprised to know their beautiful appearance is part of their mind control and this even grows with age, it's hypnotizing."

The applause continues and they sit down looking detached but pleased. Theophilus then looks to Scorpio, "Scorpio elders: Archibald and Ambrosina Erhard!" They stand strong and focused as does their Constellation. They are expressionless, giving nothing away. The only zodiac I find unreadable. But I'm aware I wouldn't want to anger them. Their resentful sting is something I never want to experience. Archibald is rigid and intimidating; his features are coarse and his hair is cropped short and his stinger hangs high above his head in a threatening manner. Ambrosina is fierce and deadly looking; her threatening appearance is attractive in an enigmatic way. Half her head is shaved with a Scorpio emblem shaved into the side with bright orange eyes which I have never seen before. They both stand freakishly still as though a part of the furniture. Their tails are painted red and violet representing their Constellation colors. Ambrosina speaks with a coarse and brave tone, "We are the mysterious of the zodiac: fierce, focused, brave, faithful, and instinctive."

Theophilus continues, "These zodiacs implement the death penalty, their skin is impenetrable and their two poisons are the most lethal of any Scorpio. Do not upset or cross these elders – they do not show mercy."

The claps are unsure and few and far between, as no one knows if the Scorpio Elders would be happy with acknowledgment or not.

Then Theophilus moves on to Sagittarius, "Sagittarius Elders, Emanuel and Abigail Galloway!" The two Sagittarius already standing as their horse bodies cannot be seated. They stand sturdy and robust, having an earthy philosophical aura about them and a deep sense of connection to the wild. Emanuel is ruggedly good-looking with a down-to-earth appearance. His hair is rough like his hands worn from living in a harsh forest. He is covered in tribal tattoos and has dark, deep beautiful eyes. Abigail has a femininity, sensual, and earthy aura, complementary to her dark skin with bright blue eyes. Her hair speaks nothing but the wild and her character appears blunt. They both have their Constellation colors, light blue and white, painted on their arms and chest. Archibald speaks with a wild and robust voice, "We are the adventurous of the zodiac: straightforward, intelligent, philosophical, generous, and inquisitive."

Theophilus adds, "The greatest trackers of all time, being able to find zodiacs weeks and even months after disappearance and their ability to converse with the forest exceeds any Sagittarius." The Sagittarius ruthlessly applaud their Elders much like our approach, but they stomp the floor and everyone applauds as they nod in gratitude.

Theophilus claps slowly then raises his hand for silence, "And last but not least, Virgo. We are the perfectionist of the zodiac: analytical, reliable, humble, altruistic, and strong-minded. I myself, Theophilus, and my wife, Adora Malis. We are the Patriarch and Matriarch of the Nirvana as I'm sure you're aware, controlling the lives of everyone who lives within this land. And we welcome you to the beginning of the Olympus Trials!" Everyone cheers as the energy in the room becomes joyous and more fireworks explode, displaying all the Constellations' emblems exploding in all represented colors. Theophilus sits down and we turn to find our table saturated with food, covering every inch of space. Large grass juicy patties piled up to the brim. Grass sweet cakes, grass fried chips, hay curries and hay salads – all the types of grass and hay recipes I have only ever dreamt about as I used to watch the NC farmer Tauruses make them in the market stalls, but they wouldn't dare to sell me a portion. It was their way of expressing their revenge against my existence that insulted their dead children's graves.

Henrietta and Dalton both say in perfect sync, "My favorite part of the day!"

Isa already starts towering up her plate and Kendall appears to be doing some sort of prayer. Europa turns to me, "It's the meal of a lifetime!" I nod with excitement as saliva begins to accumulate in my mouth. Never have I seen such an abundance and delicious amount of food, reminiscing on the days when father and I had lived of such scarcity within the dark winter years. I can still taste the rubbery rabbit jerky he used to make and store, so we could maintain our much-needed portion of protein as much as I hated it. I pretended it wasn't too bad for my father's sake. But I could still see the disappointment in his eyes, being unable to provide for his daughter.

Once our bellies were full and everything on the table is good and gone, Theophilus stands again and says, "I hope you enjoyed the meals; we need you to stay healthy and strong during these times so you can continue to grow stronger and demonstrate your full potential. Now your overseer will guide you to your dormitory to get settled. Then you'll be shown how to teleport back to your Constellations and we will see you bright and early in the morning to officially start the Olympus Trials. Oh, and I'll leave you with a bit of advice: spend this time with your families wisely as it'll be the last time you'll see them for a while. And congratulations on making it through the uncharted forest and always remember to let strength lay beside you."

The twelve overseers march out from behind the tree and I immediately spot Demetrius who walks down standing before our table.

He says assertively, "Alright, follow me and I'll show you to your rooms." The large doors from where we came begin to creek open and we all stand from our seats, heading out in a big group. Everyone noticeably begins to relax as some Constellations start to mingle, especially the friendly Aquarians, famous for their ability to make a lot of friends. I attentively watch Demetrius making sure not to lose sight of him. Our group slightly spreads out, Europa now intrigued by a Cancerian. Her ability to speak to new individuals astounds me.

We stand at the bottom of one of the large twisting stairwells, the steps slightly worn in the middle from the constant impact of feet. Some of the zodiacs are eager to get going, especially the Gemini, who are constantly on the move, easily bored. The stairs are pristine, made from ancient stone and are well polished. Different statues of creatures are integrated into the climbing wall. The Sagittarius stand at the front, ready and impatient to take on the unknown. They begin clopping up the stairs, led by their overseer as the rest of us follow. I place my hand on the stone railing as the stairs are large and not built for my small frame. Every step feels so big and tiresome. Soon, other zodiacs begin to pass me and my backpack becomes noticeably heavier than before. After we pass a couple of doors and weirdly arranged entrances, I come by a terrifying statue and written below is 'The Wendigo' from the Libra region. It stands on a large platform. A frightening creature with abnormally long muscular arms expanding from its shoulders with two minor arms curling around from underneath its armpits. Both sets have incredibly sharp long claws. It has large hind legs with long, rigid horns, growing from its malevolent skull with big sharp teeth, hollow eyes, and pointy ears. From what I've read, it lives within the shadows of their Pacem Forest, below their beautiful village. They gain longevity by eating those who get lost within Pacem. Others have stopped to stare at the creature as you can only read about these monsters. Unexpectedly, I swear its eyes move, but it's hard to tell as they are hidden within the dark passages of its skull. I peer closer and I see granite fall from its body as it begins to move, I freeze. It stretches onto its hind legs and relinquishes a horrific, screeching cry, penetrating the ears and echoing up and down the Doh's narrow internal spine. I fall backwards on to another, who catches me. A Gemini who passes by begins to laugh at himself as he too got quite the fright and the Wendigo goes back to a still original composure. Everyone stops for a moment as a Pisces overseer remarks in a soft voice, "Everything has a life of its own within this place…along with watchful eyes," he adds with a cautious undertone, and everyone continues up the stairwell.

The individual who still clutches me remarks, "Well, I guess you've learnt, it's rude to stare." I quickly turn around to find a rugged Leo staring at me with bright golden eyes, holding an amusing smile.

His head is clean-shaven around the left side with the Leo emblem shaved within it and the rest is thick, rugged, shoulder length hair flowing everywhere. He has intense eyes, sunken in to create an alluring shadow around them with a defined jaw. Tattoos cover his whole right arm with Leo representations, and the name Cedric Sol is written on his forearm. I become annoyed by his insensitive comment, so I pull on the straps of my old backpack and continue up the stairs.

He follows closely behind, "I've heard Tauruses can't take much of a joke, take things too personally. But surely we can come to some sort of a silver lining? I mean I did just save your life."

I become instantly angered by his confident arrogance, saying nothing in return.

"Ah your stubbornness exceeds you. What's your name?"

I flick him a livid stare. "None of your business," I remark and he smiles, almost enthralled by the presenting challenge, "That's not nice to say to your savior."

I roll my eyes, keeping them fixed on the stairs and ignoring him. Then Europa comes pounding down, "Taura! There you are! I was wondering where you got to."

She looks at the Leo inquisitively standing beside me, curiously she asks, "Who's your friend?" as it's unusual for me to be seen conversing with anyone I don't know.

"He's not my—" and the Leo rudely interrupts, "Leon Sol is my name, your friend," he pauses for a moment and looks at me with triumph, "Taura…was just introducing herself." I roll my eyes and Europa looks at me with an estranged expression. But we are abruptly interrupted by Demetrius.

"Taura! Europa! What are you doing? Dormitory placement has already begun," he says sternly.

Then his eyes shift towards Leon and his expression immediately changes, eyebrows crease together, clearly angered by his presence. I notice the doors laying above from where he stands, realizing now we are the last three stragglers and the big wooden doors sit wide open, waiting for our arrival.

Demetrius looks intensively at Leon, "Why aren't you with your colony, Leo?"

Leon ever so slightly smirks and replies, "Taura fell willingly into my lap. I couldn't help but introduce myself."

I feel the blood rush to my face, knowing I'm now obviously turning red with awkwardness. Demetrius, unable to hide the emotion behind his face, becomes exceedingly mad and abruptly says, "Well, don't."

Leon, now expressionless, replies, "I guess that's up to her." Being a fire sign, he naturally wants to challenge the situation due to a contradiction of rules now individually delegated towards him as we are encouraged to mingle with one another. Demetrius, fighting with the internal battle of rage that Leon ignites within him, presses down each step with deliberation and promise of Leon's demise, "Know your place, feline."

Leon doesn't say another word but neither backs down from Demetrius' threatening scowl. Suddenly, a Virgo overseer appears from within the doors, "Demetrius, what's taking so long?" Demetrius holds Leon's stare for a moment longer. The Virgo repeating, "Demetrius!?"

Demetrius, still not taking his eyes off Leon, says firmly, "I'm coming," turning towards the wall he gestures for us to go up the stairs, carefully watching Leon as he follows closely behind.

We walk into a chamber of rooms with high ceiling, built out of bricks with six rooms to the left and six rooms to the right, all allocated with our Constellations' emblem and birth stone residing above each door, delegating where we now live for however long the Olympus Trials take us to complete independently. Down the end of the hall is a magnificent, rotating golden statue, dedicated to all our ten residing planets within our solar system, each planet representing each constellation on behalf of our individual gods. Each planet seen within the night's dark sky, rotating around our precious Nirvana world. I admiringly watch the planets and name them with their residing gods as they move majestically around the golden figurine: Uranus, god of the sky, represents Aquarius; Neptune, god of the sea, represents Pisces; Mars, god of war, represents Aries; Venus, goddess of love, sex, beauty, and fertility, represents Taurus and Libra; Mercury, god of trade and profit, represents Gemini and Virgo; Moon, god of emotion, represents Cancer; Sun, god of light and energy (self), represents Leo; Pluto, god of the underworld, represents Scorpio; Jupiter, god of heroic actions, represents Sagittarius; and Saturn, god of cause and effect (karma), represents Capricorn. But I count eleven planets, not the residing ten that live amongst the stars. One I have not seen before. It's not like the others – ordinary in its composure and quite small in stature. I watch it diligently as we walk towards the contraption, trying to figure it out as all the revered planets move around in their primitive nature, held up by nothing but their own weight. Everyone is huddled around the moving figurine, admiring its authentic beauty. While the overseers stand idle on the perimeter, presumably awaiting our arrival. Demetrius and the Virgo both annoyed by different reasons, begin walking towards the group, firmly signaling us to follow. As we pass each door, I read each Constellation poem written above:

Capricorn

Birth Stone: Garnet
*A goat fish we see
oh so ambitious is he,
patience embedded,
caution dreaded.
Practical thoughts
wise as thy never sought.*

*Change of mind
don't react kind.
Stubborn creature
shy nature.*

*Don't be blind
by this frontier state of mind.*

Aquarius

Birth Stone: Amethyst
*A large man we see
such a humanitarian is he
friendly as a giant
all or nothing defiant.
Interest range wide
but an independent tide.
Loyal friend,
nothing he can't mend.*

*Be careful one so big
unpredictability runs thick.
Detachment is a trait
inconsistent always runs late.
Aloof he may seem
deep thoughts dream.*

*Power to talk
with animals that walk.*

Pisces

Birth Stone: Aquamarine

A fish we see
oh so selfless is he.
Sensitive in nature
compassionate savior.
Intuition so strong
never guided wrong.
Imagination runs wild
thoughts never mild.

Hard times are near
escapism is clear.
Idealism never found
as pessimism bound.
If interest hazy
fish become lazy.
Emotions run wild
water controlled, they smile.

Aries

Birth Stone: Diamond

A ram we see
oh so versatile is he.
Lively with passion
positive worn fashion.
Courage he bares
circle like horns impairs.

Impulse burns
stubbornness churns.
Arrogance, strong
thinks no wrong.
Stand for confrontation
With this combination.

Fierce like fire
Adventure inspire.

Taurus

Birth Stone: Emerald
A bull we see
oh so generous is he
Dependable and patient
loyalty nor absent.
One as Independent
persistent profound intendant.
Tunnel-like vision
move for revolution.

With good there is bad
possessive gone mad
stubbornness breeds
like self-indulgent needs.

Beware color red
fixed arrow makes his bed

Gemini

Birth Stone: Pearl
Two heads we see
intelligent is he
such wit and humor
enthusiasm glamour
soft-spoken words
the adversity crossword.

With air comes miss direction
adds self-destruction
in constant two minds
anxiety binds superficial lacks detail
fall through cracks and fail.

With one head
two shall break the bread.

Cancer

Birth Stone: Ruby

A crab we see
oh so creative is he
loving and faithful
shield of protection grateful.

Passion runs wild
drives the inner child.
Praise thy with love,
comforting glove;
emotion beware
as suspicion lives there.
Drop of pessimism,
raging alcoholism.

Illusionary shielded exterior,
raw flooded interior.

Leo

Birth Stone: Peridot

A lion we see,
a leader is he.
kind and caring,
optimistic wearing.
Loyalty strong,
beware thy wrong.

With arrogance
a king advance.
A head so strong, patience lacks. Ego dominates,
as possession gravitates.

Beware this king,
or watch his teeth sink in.

Virgo

Birth Stone: Sapphire

Angel wings we see,
oh so watchful is he.
Intelligent and practical

perfection unstable.
Eyes see from a far,
analyze and alter.
Reliable we trust,
perfection is a must.
Fastidious from within,
the building blocks begin.
Harsh spoken words,
judgmental eyes stirred.
Overcritical kind,
endures fussy mind.

Conservative exterior
fly from above, inferior.

Libra

Birth Stone: Opal
Scales we see,
oh so charming is he.
Tactful in approach,
diplomatic coach.
Romantic lover,
balance thy mother.
Always fair,
two sides take care.

Sociopath detach,
drawn by superficial catch.
Decision nor made,
unreliable behave.

Eyes beware,
the unbalance can declare.

Scorpio

Birth Stone: Citrine
A scorpion we see,
Oh so brave is he.
Focused ambition,
strong intuition.

Faithful friends,
beware the back end.

One strike,
resentful bite.
Secrets build
and jealousy in field.

Manipulation mastermind
be careful pretense 'once mine.'

Sagittarius

Birth Stone: Blue Topaz
A horse we see,
oh so straight forward is he.
Generous heart,
intellectual head nor so far apart.
These think as one,
philosophical thoughts run.

Tactless bare no bounds
as self-perfection runs around.
Consistent difficult,
impatience comes result.

Stern creature,
Iconic archer feature.

As we come toward the slow, passive movement of the golden planets, I begin to shorten my stride, noticing the ceiling raises again, burrowing down a deep pungent tunnel as the planets move between the large space. They make a powerful murmuring sound as each one passes us by, showing off their radiant size. Leon leisurely walks back to his small group of Leos, keeping me subtly within his gaze, Demetrius now watching him with hawk eyes, and I wonder why he does not particularly like Leon and how would he know him outside of today?

We now stand by our dormitory door with our Taurus emblem and stone glowing as we stand by idly. There's a doorknocker shaped as a Taurus head and it's slightly worn by the recurring pounding motion, noticeable damage through everyday knocking. Demetrius stands in front of our small group and stares at the knocker as though he was waiting for something.

Then suddenly its eyes open, followed by an irritated yawn, "What is it?" it spits in a high creaky voice.

Demetrius stands rigid and repeats the poem from above the door. The doorknocker looks up, rolls its eyes, and grunts, "I guess you guys really did get lazy, huh? Can't even remember your own poem without it plastered in front of your eyes…tsk tsk tsk."

Demetrius says without remorse, "Another doorknocker would be an easier option." The handle looks up through his thick sunken eyebrows and grunts with a sneer. He begins to levitate from the door, followed by a repeated pounding knock that's delivered with his sturdy golden head, followed by a click and an old creaking sway as the door begins to open.

A large room ornamented with thick tree roots creates our six green and white sheeted beds with white pillows inserted and comfy looking mattresses. The roots expand from our beds and attach to the walls, crawling up the ceiling into a great tree that grows upside down, flourishing dense old branches with dark green leaves and red poppies that grow from the end. Some have even fallen in the center of the room, still glowing with life. And the same yellow orbs we saw from the dining room move around within the branches. Our names are exclusively carved and painted white into an old dark wooden plank upon each bed. Europa's and mine lay next to one another which brings warmth and comfort to me, knowing I'll have some familiarity in this chapter of my life.

Demetrius stands at the door and says as we investigate our individual quarters, "Leave all your belongings on your bed and come with me." I take off my backpack which relieves my tired, sore shoulders, and I glance at Isa whose bed sits on the other side of mine; she snorts with disapproval. The twins Henrietta and Dalton have bunk beds, fighting over who gets the top, smooching each other's faces as they both try to climb. "You have the top at home!" says Dalton.

Henrietta pushes her hand down against his head to get leverage, "And that's why I should have it here. I am three minutes older, so it only makes sense," he grabs her leg.

"How does three minutes older make any sense?!"

Henrietta jabs her foot into his face and he falls to the ground with a big thud, winning the commotion. She pokes her tongue out and Dalton glares at her cracking a tantrum and throws his belongings on the bottom bunk. Isa rolls her eyes in disgust as though there had not been better suitors for friends. Even though we were once good friends when we were young and I still wonder what happened to this day, why does she hate me so much? Kendall quietly sits on the end of his bed with his possessions lying next to him; he hasn't spoken a word since the disappearance of Latham.

After settling in within our dorms, we're told to gather around the outskirts of the rotating golden planets. All twelve overseers stand close around its perimeter.

The Capricorn overseer signals her Capricorns to follow her as she steps in between the large moving planets and they slow as she steps on. The rest of the Capricorns follow as instructed but look a bit wary. They stand uncertain in the middle of the platform; their residing planet Saturn moves quite high above their heads and begins to press down as though it were going to crush them. The Capricorn soldier states: "It's okay, everyone. This is how you teleport home. Now visualize your inhabitants, close your eyes and chant our creator's name, Unum, together. Unum, Unum, Unum, Unum." They all begin chanting together as Saturn casts a bright light over them. So bright, everyone else glances away momentarily and once it diminishes, they're gone. Aquarius are next, their residing planet Uranus casting them home, followed by Pisces residing planet Neptune, Aries residing planet Mars and then Taurus. Standing on the platform, I watch our planet Venus slowly move down toward us; the number ten on the back of my neck begins to burn and spread as it crawls over the rest of my skin, tingling the top of my head. I shut my eyes, visualizing my cottage, Adonis and the grasslands followed by chanting Unum's name. The large grounding pressure of Venus becomes more prominent as I feel it crawling toward us but a warm sensation takes over as the same white light flashes beneath my eyelids and I feel myself expand from the heat.

Chapter 4

The Unbeknown

Identity is the story we have foretold.

As the day falls, I watch the orange-tinged sky fall behind my small, worn-out cottage home. Tall trees shadowing the background and it brings me warm, familiar comfort as I walk back from an unusual day. I think how worried Adonis must be and how thrilled he'll be to see me whole and intact. Demetrius told us we have to be back at the Halls of Ivy by dawn tomorrow morning after the teleportation brought us back to the classroom. I glance back to the village to see illuminating lights celebrating Beverly and Latham, forever lost to the Infernum within the uncharted forest. Fireworks are drawn and music is played as the community drowns its sorrows in the comforts of exterior pleasures that will never bring back their loved ones. That's why I knew I couldn't go when Europa had begged me to go and to bring my father. "No one will care at a time like this," she had said. But I'd just be a constant reminder, stabbing an already open wound and they don't need that; right now they need to drown their sorrows and forget that I exist. Because everyone knows it should have been me... I know it should have been me.

But selfishly, I'm glad it wasn't me because it'll bring my father such happiness. He's rarely allowed himself that pleasure, poisoned by the guilt of my passing mother. I hear wood being chopped, noticing several dead rabbits skinned and hanging from a line beside our family home. He's obviously kept himself busy today. I walk around the back grazing my hand lightly on the old pinewood, carefully trying not to get splinters. Skipping around the old shovels and rusty axe, I see my father, who has not yet noticed me and for the first time I notice how worn out he looks. A deep line creases between his eyebrows, dark bags drop heavy under his eyes as he wipes sweat, dripping down his forehead with his forearm.

"Dad," I murmur. Adonis stops, his back turned, slamming the axe into the big plank of wood.

He wipes his face and pulls back his hair with both hands. "Taura, is that you?" unconvinced and maybe thinking it's the enchanting voice who preys on vulnerable hearts.

"Yes, Dad, it's me," I say, strong and reassuring this time. He turns and sighs with relief.

He sprawls his arms out with a big smile and says, "Taura!" He runs over, picks me up, and embraces me tight. I can smell the old pinewood and dark oil that stains his clothes. Placing me down, he kneels to my level and engulfs both large hands over my shoulders.

I sigh glancing down. I slowly look up at him. "I can't believe I made it, Dad, I really can't, especially because Beverly Fleur and Latham Hampton were both taken. It was sad, really sad, Dad, especially for Kendall, he didn't mutter a word all day after that."

He creases his eyebrows together, making the line between his eyes grow deeper, showing his unidentified old age. "I do feel for their parents, but we all know the risk. I'm just grateful you're okay."

I nod in agreement but refuse to tell him how we were invited to the celebration of their lives; we both know it wouldn't be the time or place. I tell him about the Doh and all that happened today and he nods his head, his expression never changing, only watching me as though he may still be dreaming. After I finish, he waits for a moment and says, "Yes, the Doh is an extraordinary place. I doubt any one has seen all its untouched walls. We know so little about it."

I nod and touch the back of my neck where the purpose number ten is imprinted and ask, "Dad, today the Taurus gave me the purpose number ten. But I didn't realize such a number existed? He was even dissatisfied by my presence. It's because of what I am, isn't it? What I represent? How my livelihood lets the Constellation down."

Adonis stands there for a moment, thinking carefully. My whole life he's had these moments, thinking of the best way to explain things, because I am so different. He looks intently into my eyes and says, "Sometimes, we have to look beyond what we see in front of us. Be patient, my dear. I'm sure all will be explained to you in good time." He kisses me preciously on the forehead, holding on to me just a little longer than normal. "Now, I've made you supper, go inside. I'll be there in a moment. I just have to finish chopping this fire wood before the cold night comes," feeling there's a subliminal message behind his remark. I still find myself damped by this unknown number.

And I become contorted as to why my father never fully explains anything to me. "Dad, do you regret it?" I ask in an insecure tone.

Adonis turns around carefully. He waits a moment once again thinking upon his words. He sighs and says, "Taura, you are the apple of my eye. I don't regret a damn thing. I'd do it all again if I had to, just to have you. Keep such thoughts away, because they will destroy you. Such thoughts are conjured up by our own insecurities. And so many die from such poison drunk too often. No matter what happens, always know I love you... No matter what you hear..." he lets the words linger in the air for a time and adds, "So come on, let's get you inside. The sun has nearly ended the day and the cold will make you sick. Your supper is sitting on the stove, keeping warm."

I look up at him with sincerity. "So you did think I'd make it?"

His eyes squint as a warm smile spreads across his face, showing his hidden wrinkles. "I never doubted you."

I open the creaky front door, getting a whiff of my favorite supper, rabbit and pea corn soup. Taurus don't normally eat meat but rabbits are a common pest and they keep our bellies full. So, I am grateful for their infestation. I've gotten use to eating meat as the NC farmers won't trade with us because of my existence and they're the ones who own all the farmland. So Dad makes do with the little he has – lucky he's a good hunter. I shut the door, securing the wooden handle as it has a tendency to swing open, especially during windy cold nights. I take my jacket off and place it on the old wooden hanger. I sigh and walk over to my freshly served soup, sitting on the stove. Taking a deep breath in, I smell the deliciousness, love, and care Dad has put into my favorite supper. As I mix it around the bowl, scooping it up with my dinted, thick old wooden spoon, all the chunky bits fall, plopping into the dense juicy liquid, I think about how much I love being home, wishing I didn't have to participate in the Olympus Trials. If only I could stay here with my dad and help him, considering he will have no one once I'll be gone for who knows how long.

"You only see things as they appear to be, not what they truly are. How did you end up here?"

I reminisce about what the large Taurus statue had said to me and I become slightly irritated as it was not my choice. I think about the snake-like voice that spoke to me within the uncharted forest. The enchantment calling to me within my subconscious as they said would happen. I have never told anyone about those words spoken to me by that woman within my dream, not even my father, who is the only one aware of the nightmare that haunts me to this day. And I wonder why Apophis did not take me. *"Tu es via, veritas et vita. Nemo venit ad Patrem, nisi per te,"* probably the same reason why no one else wanted me. But what do those words mean?

I sit down and begin to sip on my meal, feeling the fire warm against my back. Then unexpectedly, I hear a noise coming from my bedroom as though something got knocked over. I jerk my head up not making a sound, listening carefully but I hear nothing. I become anxious and tense as a balmy sweat begins to drip down my neck. Slowly I turn around, apprehensively peering through my half-opened door where only darkness lurks. Steadily I stand, trying to step on floorboards softly, attempting not to make a sound. Peeking through the dark crack in my door, I can only see the moonlight shine upon my mismatched bed cover. Slowly I push my door open and it squeaks louder and louder, slowing down to a complete stop.

"Who's there?" I demand nervously with masked confidence. A large hairy figure steps into the moonlight and I slowly grab the container that conceals my fireflies, shaking them to life. My room gradually lights up, and I see a large creature covered in hair from head to toe; it has a long beard, a round stumpy body with long limbs and large hands. I have a strange feeling I have seen him before. His eyes are bloodshot with a worn-out look on his face.

"Who are you? And what are you doing in my bedroom?" I demand, feeling my adrenaline making me shake profusely. I squeeze the door handle so I don't look so fraudulent. The oddly looking creature fidgets, extremely agitated.

"I have come here to warn you, Taura Andreas," he says with urgency. His voice is croaky and insecure, contradicting his large appearance. I lean back, grabbing a steel rod from the fireplace that sits next to my door, not taking my eyes off the creature and carefully shut the door behind me, looking to see if Adonis has walked in. I hold the steel rod in my hand.

"How do you know my name? Who are you? And where did you come from?"

It jitters, suspiciously glancing out my bedroom window. He shuts his eyes and shakes his head. "No, No, no. None of that matters right now. You must heed my warning…you have an unbeknown secret power you do not know of as yet. When you become aware of its growing presence, you must know its evil and never use it and tell no one. Suppress it if you must, just do what you have to so that no one may ever know of its existence. Do you understand me?"

I become shocked and confused. "What do you mean? Is it a side effect from my medicine?" I ask.

He shakes his head. "No it's not. You must never unleash its power as it'll cause tragic repercussions, many zodiacs will die, and the ones you love. Do you understand me, Taura? Your life depends on it, you're in great danger."

I become frightened.

"Tell me why? I don't even know of such power you speak of?" I plead.

He becomes enraged with frustration. "Just promise me you will not use it! Tell no one!" he demands.

I say nothing.

"Promise me!" he insists.

"Why? What will happen if I do!?" I query.

He looks away and says, "You will die, Taura, murdered, annihilated, torn apart! By those who seek its worth. Such power causes those with blinded eyes to become greedy with control as they want it for themselves."

The room becomes still and I feel my hair stand on end. He looks me dead in the eye and says, "Many will die… And you will be to blame. Now promise me!"

Suddenly I hear Adonis walk into the cottage, banging his dirty shoes on the ground and securing the rickety door. The creature looks at me in eagerness. I look back and whisper, "Okay, I promise, but you must leave now."

He sighs with relief, nods, then opens the windows. As he sits on the windowsill, he looks back, staring at me intensely and murmurs, "You cannot tell anyone about this, especially your father," and jumps out the window; I hear his footsteps disappear into the far distance as the window doors bang against the windowsill.

Adonis walks in my room. "Taura, what are you doing? It's freezing outside," he storms past me and up to the window. I hurriedly follow closely behind him, making sure the creature is out of sight. I grab his large arm but he rips it away and gives me an annoyed expression. I jump on my bed and peer out the window, the creature is gone. I sigh with relief, sitting back on to my squeaky bed.

"For goodness sake, Taura, what's gotten into you? Are you trying to catch pneumonia?" He shuts the window and rubs his shoulders, chilled by the cold. He picks up the old thick blanket folded at the end of my bed that my mother Penelope had knitted when she was with child and wraps it around me. "You must stay warm, it's going to be a cold night."

Adonis walks out of the room and I remain on my bed, peering out the window for a short time but there was nothing to be seen but the now fading reminisce of footsteps. What was that creature on about, unbeknown power?

"You have an unbeknown secret power you do not know of as yet...you must know its evil and never use it and tell know one...many will die... And you will be to blame...you cannot tell anyone about this, especially your father..."

My thoughts pause for a moment; why didn't I tell my father? And why did I have this churning feeling. Maybe it is a side effect from my potion, *illusion*, lingers in my head. I take a deep breath, not being able to make sense of it all. How did it know my name? I sigh as I remain on my bed wondering if that was all just a dream. And why did I feel as though I recognized him.

I watch Adonis bring in loads of freshly cut firewood. He never says much, only signifies a lot by his actions, words are only used when needed. I reminisce about a time when I was young; it was late and I had had a terrible day at the Halls of Ivy. Isa had been especially cruel to me that day, after she had caught me staring at a large bruise on her eye that appeared to be infected. I know she trains hard but it appeared whoever had beaten her up was just as angry as that eye. I sat in this exact spot, sobbing. Adonis came in without saying a word and took my hand. I had asked him where we were going but he just said, "You'll see."

We walked to the farthest part of the Constellation on the highest mound. He picked me up, wrapped me in this exact blanket, and laid me down on my back as he laid next to me, submerging my small hand within his and stared up into the stars. He didn't mention the events of the day, only pointing out each zodiac alignment in the sky, land marking where each Constellation resides beneath their star sign glowing from above. He would point with his index finger and say, "Each zodiac star was the first of our kind and now they watch over us."

"They must not watch over me," I'd replied. He lay there without a word, instead pinching my tiny hand with his index finger and thumb, lifting it up to the sky and going over the Taurus alignment.

"How could they not," he'd remarked. I sighed, feeling my father did not understand, thinking the gods don't watch over those who were never deemed worthy.

"Why am I not like everyone else?" I asked with a sad tone.

Adonis once again didn't react. "You don't want to be like everyone else, my dear."

This comment made me mad. I rolled over, glaring at my father, angrily snapping back, "Well, that's stupid, why wouldn't I want to be a natural great warrior? I'm weak, small, and unable to defend myself. Like today, I looked pathetic. Everyone hates me."

I instantly felt regret about yelling at the one person who truly loves and cares for me. But once again Adonis did not react, in fact he kept the same composure. I sighed, rolling on to my back, staring at the stars, adding, "I'm sorry, Dad."

Adonis glanced at me from the side, calmly rolled over and said, "One day you'll know how special you really are, but until that day, enjoy this time for what it is."

I had said nothing more after that as I did not understand. But for some reason I always felt it had true relevance. Remembering what my father had said not too long ago. *"Sometimes we have to look beyond what we see in front of us. Be patient, my dear. I'm sure all will be explained to you in good time."*

Does my father know about this unbeknown evil power?

I pull the blanket over my shoulders, thinking I should go spend some time with him before the trials tomorrow. I slide off my unstable bed that creaks as I stand. Walking into the warm living room, I sit down and continue eating my now cold supper. I look at Adonis who stands still in front of the fire, his back towards me, lingering at its luminosity.

"Dad?"

I wait for a moment. He remains still only slightly moving his head to the side. His shadow casts upon the distant wall next to me, over-exaggerating his already large muscular frame.

"Yes, my darling? What is it?"

I watch him curiously as he does not face me. Something seems off about him tonight. I see him rubbing something in his jacket pocket, remembering how he carries an old picture of my mother around with him.

"Tell me a story about my mother, Penelope." I feel Adonis is tense, he stops rubbing the picture, taking his hands from his pockets and holding them out in front of him. I have never asked about my mother, only accepted what he has told me which wasn't much. I can tell it hurts him to speak about her, but I feel this is the right time to find more about who I truly am due to all these uncertainties.

Adonis sighs, glancing at me, "If you eat the rest of your supper." He waits and I begin eating my cold and now unfulfilling meal. "What would you like to know?" he asks with dictation. I continue eating my soup pondering on the question as I know he won't allow me to stay on this topic for long.

"How did you fall in love?"

He waits a moment, never answering any question without a full thought. He rolls his shoulders back, relaxes, and says, "Penelope was beautiful. I first saw her in the Halls of Ivy on the first day of school. I was a quiet kipper, never said much." *Not much has changed*, I think to myself. He continues, "I was only determined and focused by the task at hand. Somehow, she seemed taken by me. I don't know why, there were many qualified suitors. I never showed an interest back. I was too focused on passing the trials, doing well in Orbis Bellum fights, and qualifying as an SNC. For many decades, I continued to serve Nirvana, until my last order when I was sent out to deal with another encounter with the Infernum, it was…" he paused and my mouth slightly drops open in anticipation. My father has never spoken about my mother or even touched base on the Infernum and his interactions with them, only stressed that I was never to venture outside the Constellation walls. He sighs again, continuing to gaze into the fire, he added, "it was, torturous, Taura. I am still haunted by that particular incident today and now I must face it every day…reminded. But after that day, I realized there was more to life. Penelope never married, and she hadn't accepted another male to court her ever. Even though she had proposals all the time. For some reason, she waited for me. Knew I'd eventually come around. So, I relinquished my love to Penelope and soon after you were born and she gave her life to you…" he says no more and I circle the soup around with my spoon, taking in the story. What event had tortured him so? My father, the great Adonis Andreas, humble, never bragging about his achievements. I don't dare ask, as I know he would only end the conversation, sending me to bed.

This was the most information I've ever gotten from him, so instead I ask, "What was she like? My mother, Penelope."

My father lifts his right hand, wiping what I presume to be a tear, the first tear I'd ever see him shed or maybe he is weary from the past couple of days. "She was kind, your mother, patient, always giving. Even when she could see someone was using her. She continued to give until the end…she was perfect…she is you." He takes a big breath and sighs. I ask no more questions; instead, I decide to sit in the blissful silence with my father. I know I'd touched a wound he'd been keeping closed for many years and I did not wish to open it further. I don't want to see the only man I have ever loved in pain. After all, he is my hero.

I finish my supper and Adonis picks up my bowl and spoon, placing them in the basin and says, "Alright, time for bed, you have a big day tomorrow." I pull the blanket over my shoulders, yawning I walk to my bedroom and place the blanket on top of my bed. I glance outside the window, pondering on the creature who was in my bedroom not long ago. I make sure the window is secure and I hop under the covers, choosing to forget about what the creature had said as I would know if I had some unbeknown evil power. Adonis walks in, pulling the wooden chair from my desk and sits beside me. "My dear daughter, I know you have struggled with your differences but zodiacs just don't like different, it scares them. So, don't underestimate yourself, there is more to you than you yourself could ever imagine. I love you." He kisses me on the forehead, drawn out, tense and raw. His eyes sear shut. Turning quickly away as though already regretting the words, he leaves the room without another sound. Slowly shutting the door behind him, leaving a slight crack to let the light seep in as he has done so since I was a baby. I am never fond of the darkness, it reminds me of the uncharted forest that sits just beyond our backyard. He lingers at the door for a moment, bows his head and I listen comfortingly to his slow and heavy footsteps. I have never seen my father act the way he has tonight, something must be haunting his thoughts. Maybe I shouldn't have asked about my mother. He appears to be reliving the event all over again and what memory of the last day he served the SNC army scares him so, my father, Adonis Andreas. I pull my hands from under the covers, analyzing them. *"You have an unbeknown secret power,"* the words come unwillingly flooding back into my thoughts. I roll to my side, staring at my hands, eyes heavy, unaware of my exhaustion. The heaviness quickly consumes me.

I awake suddenly screaming, my door slams open.

"Taura!"

My father is standing at my bedroom door with an axe, held at a ready. Sweat drips down my forehead, my sheets soaked through. It is that dream again, it's becoming more distinct every time, as though I am reliving a memory. That woman's face so vivid I have to take a second look at the picture of my mother Penelope on my bedside table to make sure it is not her.

"Tu es via, veritas et vita. Nemo venit ad Patrem, nisi per te." I take a big deep breath, closing my eyes. Adonis drops the axe on the ground, hurriedly walks over and kneels beside my bed and holds me within his arms. "It was that dream again, wasn't it?"

I nod without saying a word and he rubs my head, pressing my hair against my sweaty neck. He grabs my tiny head within the clutches of his large callused, war-torn hands, so rough it scrapes against my soft skin, unconditioned for such toughness. He looks at me for a moment then pulls out a small green vial from his pocket and gestures me to open my mouth, pouring it down my throat. I nearly regurgitate but I know the medicine is important, although I've never seen it in that fancy vial before. As I contain the urge to vomit, I fixate on a particular wooden panel to keep my nausea at bay.

Adonis stands appearing to be his usual self this morning. He places his hands on his hips. "I purchased a hundred of these green vials yesterday," holding up the now empty vial, "I spent all night making a large batch of your medicine so you can keep your dosage up while you're away doing your studies for the Olympus Trials." He takes a moment before he speaks again, he looks at me intensely, "And Taura, as much as I believe immensely in your capabilities in who you are, you must still be aware of you limitations due to your illness, just always remember that. It's very important, your life is very precious and delicate."

I don't say anything, only nod as the nausea slowly subsides. He walks up to the bed waiting for an answer. I sheepishly look up as his aura has appeared to harden from last night, almost having to make up for being too soft. "Yes, Dad, I understand,"

He nods sternly. "Good, and one other thing, this too is incredibly important... you must never, and I mean never, inform any one of this medicine within the Doh as it could be used against you. Do you understand?"

I nod assertively.

"Good, because I'm very serious about that detail. Now I've made your breakfast. Hurry, otherwise it'll get cold." He walks out of the room and I notice my bag is already packed and ready. Presumably it is crammed with those vials of medicine as I have already taken my necessities to the Doh yesterday.

After I've dressed in the same old clothes I wear every day and reminisce on the events of the night before, I walk out of my bedroom with the very heavy backpack. Adonis places a bowl of hot porridge on the table, with bits of residue from the hot pan floating amongst it. The same old wooden spoon is placed beside it and I now empathize with the term 'ignorance is bliss,' after being exposed to yesterday's delicacies, understanding the impacting turmoil my father carries upon him, the constant inability to provide for one's child that comes so easily to those around him.

I sit down feeling the weight of the day ahead and begin eating the lukewarm porridge, feeling the cold stone beneath my feet. I wonder how Adonis makes the vials not clink together. Opening the bag, I notice he's stuffed small strands of straw between them – clever. Adonis doesn't say all that much as though keeping his inner thoughts to himself. After I've finished, I place my dish in the sink and look at Adonis who stares sternly out the window beside me.

"Dad, will I be able to see you during the trials?" There is a long stillness for a moment, as though he'd wish I hadn't spoken.

He replies without turning away from the window, "Unfortunately not, as the Elders feel it may interfere with the way you perform. But I'll see you during mid-semester. I can give you more vials of medicine then." Adonis walks over to the front door, awkwardly opening it as it jars against the ground. The sunshine crawls in and the heat of the morning sun warms my cold face. "Okay, my dear, it is time to go," he says, looking at me with unconditional love. My eyes begin to well up and as I walk slowly toward the door, standing at the front entrance, I embrace him, not wanting to go. Unable to get my small arms to fit around his waist, I squeeze as tight as I can and breathe in the scent of him. He stiffens then relaxes, rubbing my back as I unwillingly release my grip. A single tear drips down my face and he crouches down, wiping it away with his large rough thumb. He kisses me on the forehead.

"You'll be just fine and you'll see me sooner than you know," he says with sincerity, guiding me out the door. Adonis smiles and slowly I hear the long creak of the door as it clunks shut behind me. I linger at it for a while then I take a deep breath, feeling the fresh air of the morning fill my lungs. I feel the gravel beneath my feet with the memories of last night filling my head. Had it just been a figment of my imagination to believe I am something that I'm not? I guess worrying about it won't bring me any answers, only time will tell and I'll take it from there. I begin walking up to the Halls of Ivy. I turn around one last time to my small old cottage to see Adonis staring through the small front window. I slowly reach my hand up to wave, but before I do, he's gone and all I can see is darkness within the house. Creasing my eyebrows together, I try not to think too much on it and continue walking.

I reach the Halls of Ivy and see Demetrius standing at the front assertively waiting. His eyes raise as I approach.

"Are you ready?"

I nod, still feeling the weight of the last twenty-four hours.

"Good, everyone is inside," as I go to pass him, he adds, "and Taura..." he pauses for a moment, his face exclaims regret after the words left his mouth, "...never mind, I'll meet you inside."

My eyebrows crease together in curiosity, but I think nothing of it. As I walk in the classroom, the air is cloudy and full of dust, disturbed by numerous feet. I notice a large map of Nirvana drawn with chalk on the wooden panels of the floor. Whoever had drawn the emblem hadn't been a very good illustrator as it's barely circular. Isa, Dalton, Henrietta stand together in their usual small group. Kendall stands by a window, patiently waiting and still looking distant from the days prior. Sunshine distinguishes the heavy dust in the air and Europa is analyzing the terribly drawn chalk drawing. Demetrius' footsteps stamp loudly from behind me, echoing through the preceding hall.

"Alright, everyone, gather 'round!"

Europa now notices me and runs over to stand by my side in excitement. She gives me a hello expression then draws her attention towards Demetrius who now stands in the middle of the badly drawn Nirvana map, right where the Doh should be located.

"Okay, everyone, I'm going to need you to stand within the Taurus Constellation."

The sector where our Taurus emblem is drawn is incredibly small. I don't know how all six of us will fit. Firstly, Isa steps on then Henrietta and Dalton both scramble to stand beside her. It always appears their constant need for Isa's approval and direct attention is never about her but the thrill of being better than the other; it makes Isa feel important and so their relationship always feeds each other's dynamics. After Kendall steps on, I follow Europa, trying to stand as far away from Isa as possible.

Then Demetrius speaks, "Good, now place your middle and index finger on the back of your necks where your purpose numbers reside and repeat after me." I place my two fingers on the back of my neck and I outline the number ten against my fingers, '*Who are you?*' my subconscious questions. It begins to pulsate slowly with heat as though it recognizes my touch.

Demetrius then says, "Chant with me and visualize the dormitory from yesterday and whatever you do, don't open your eyes until I say so," he says sternly, shutting his eyes and begins, "Unum, Unum, Unum, Unum, Unum."

Demetrius now appears to be in a trance. Kendall starts to chant next and then we are all chanting together with our eyes shut.

"Unum, Unum, Unum, Unum, Unum."

I suddenly cannot tell my up from my down, and I feel as though I'm floating. My purpose number now burns with radiated heat, not enough to hurt me but enough to know its pronounced distinct presence. Then a warm sensation slowly crawls over my body and in an unexplained way, I feel I am here but I am not, until I am gone.

Chapter 5

The Theory Behind Number Ten

When pursuit ignites, adventure takes flight.

My feet are now planted firmly upon a creaky floor and my hands shake profusely; my eyes are still securely shut and I wonder if I'll ever get use to this teleportation disorientation.

"Alright, you can open your eyes now," Demetrius' deep dominating voice commands. But I still don't open my eyes until I feel an object skim past my nose at an unearthly rate. Reflexes immediately make my eyes spring open as my heart begins to pound through my chest. My whole body goes stiff in a flight or fight mode until I see what lays before me.

"A library," I whisper under my breath; my body relaxes and I become entranced in awe. But the library of books appear to be alive as one tall old book floats in front of me; it has large eyes but no mouth. It looks down referring to its title, *Language of the Purpose Numbers*, it has written. Its eyes nearly squeeze shut as though it were smiling at me, then it wisps away amongst all the other books that wiz around up high above the tall ceilings as zodiacs walk around on the floor. The magnificent room is filled with floors upon floors, staircases upon staircases of books, and zodiacs sit and study or chase their desired book around the room as it freely teases them. I watch a particular Gemini as he hides behind a case of books, trying to catch a large book that hides at the other end. He begins to split to try and outsmart the book. As he rips himself apart directly down the middle, I wince at the method as body parts crack, pop, rip, and tear. Mucus drops on to the ground once they are separate, looking much like residue from a placenta. Even in pictures, this process looks painful. A young Gemini can really struggle to control both his yin and yang once split, but this Gemini appears to have great control over both; this comes with considerable practice. Now his yang goes down one aisle and yin goes down the other, attempting to block the book off. The book glances to each side, then pushes its back against the wall, sliding up with a taunting expression. The yin and yang agilely tiptoe and spring from around each corner and simultaneously the book flies up. The book looks down and bounces with amusement. The Gemini, now entangled between its yin and yang, slowly morphs back into one entity with a frustrated expression; it curses the book that levitates above.

I look over at Demetrius who seems frustrated. "This wasn't supposed to be the destination, how did this happen?" he remarks.

The others had already subtly started looking around, slowly breaking away from the group.

Demetrius says, "Hey! Don't go wandering off. I have to go check when you're needed in the dining room. Don't get lost. Stay together until I return." We all nod as he assertively stomps out of the room. Pulling open the two large, thick, heavy doors with beautiful golden handles, which have been decorated out of an open book's pages. They creak open and his back muscles contract and ripple, demonstrating his sheer strength and beauty. He leaves the doors widely exposed and they begin to close behind him, coming together with a deep, low, creaking impact and everyone glances over for a moment and then goes back to what they were doing.

Europa now stands next to me. "Is he ever in a good mood?"

I shrug as she follows up with, "Seriously, have you ever seen that guy crack a smile. Probably doesn't find jokes funny either."

I laugh. "To be honest, they'd probably go straight over his head," I say.

She laughs and nods in agreement. "How amazing is this place! Who ever thought books could come alive? Just your kind of pastime."

She winks at me but before I reply, I notice the book that had wisped past me not so long ago, idly floating not too far in front of me. I grab Europa.

"C'mon, I want to get that book," I remark.

She unexpectedly and clumsily follows after me.

"Wait, we're not supposed to leave the group!" she yells out after me.

I don't take my eyes off the book as it now darts away, yelling back, "Since when have you cared about not supposed too?"

I hear her suddenly pick up the pace and she becomes deliberate with each step. I think to myself, *That's what I thought.* As we are on the chase, we knock into other zodiacs who become annoyed with our recklessness and lack of respect. One Sagittarius yells, "Watch it, you heavy footed cows!" Europa, who now runs beside me, turns back and pokes her tongue out. The book glancing back, not realizing how close we are to catching it, darts down a narrow corridor. We both stand side by side, trying to block any spaces with our arms sprawled out. It dances about appearing to become apprehensive on where to go next and just as we come into arm's length, it bounces up and over our heads.

"Damn it!" I remark. Then out of nowhere, a strange creature pounces on it from above, flattening the book to the ground. It's very small, with long gangly legs for hands as feet; long, skinny, hairless body, with long rangy arms, tiny wings, small head with a long thin beak. The book bounces around as the small creature keeps a tight grip until the book gives in and completely stops. Europa and I look at one another in a 'what the heck' expression and begin to approach.

The creature carefully opens the book and slides its delicate fingers over each page, appearing to clean it carefully with its narrow beak. Bugs and moths fly out of its pages and it quickly gobbles them up, enjoying the taste for a brief moment until it goes back to its urgent work. We stand above, watching.

Europa whispers to me, "That's one ugly...imp?" without taking her eyes away. The creature, undisturbed by our presence, turns its back to us as if to be insulted, making a high-pitch grunting noise.

Unexpectedly, a confident but fast-paced spoken voice is heard from around the corner, "He's a Liber Amundans, which means 'Book Purifier,' but we just call him Emun. He cleans all the books in this library. He lives of the bugs and moths from the books he cleans. Full-time job, but he takes it very seriously. Oh, and I'll warn you now, he doesn't like being called imp. He believes it as a vast misconception and massive insult."

I look up to see an elderly Gemini lady, who wears large glasses that are broken at the bridge, fixed up with large amount of unnecessary tape as though she got too excited in the process. The glasses do not fit her but they emphasize her malevolent and innocent eyes that reside side by side. The white side of her hair is now grey and the black is now a dark blackish grey. Her hair is incredibly long and almost touches the ground, and she lets it fall where it lays as though she does not care for her appearance. Her lips are thin and she looks tired but knowledgeable. She quickly notices me watching her as a Gemini does not miss a thing, and I quickly take my attention away from her untidy appearance.

Europa asks, "Who are you?"

The old Gemini lady smiles enthusiastically as though her patience were running thin. "Well, I'm the one who runs this place! I'm Bibliotheca, but everyone calls me Bib. I'm the Librarian. I noticed you both recklessly running after this particular book, so I was going to tell you off. Or at least get the book for you before you made some sort of large mess. But I can see Emun has already helped you out. If you saw when you first walked in, the sign says no running. But I've learnt the new bloods need a little guidance at first." She looks around the large library as though appreciating it for all it is.

"I've read every book in this place and I'm now over half way through reading it all again for the five hundred and twenty-six thousandth time. Need something to keep this old mind sharp, you know what I'm saying?"

She winks tapping the side of her head and adds, "I love a good challenging question! So, if you need any help, I'm your lady."

She smiles with warmth and the wrinkles crease hard upon her face. I've never seen a zodiac as old as her; she must have been here since the dawn of time.

Europa puts her hand out to shake. "Well, I do apologize. I'm Europa and this is my best friend Taura. She was adamant about getting that book."

Bib puts her old wrinkled and knuckled hand out and shakes Europa's at an unearthly rate, making Europa's body bounce up and down.

"Well, I wouldn't expect any less from a Taurus, always up for the challenge. But next time let's do it more quietly, okay?" she says in a quick but efficient manner.

Europa smiles, slightly ashamed, and I notice Emun has finished cleaning the last page, closing the book ever so gently. But before the book has a chance to fly off again, Bib splits her yin and yang so fast down the middle as though it's a natural process during her everyday activities, normally so challenging to any Gemini. The yin black stays beside us, closely watching us with its malevolent expression as yang white enthusiastically grabs the book and merges back with it now as one entity again. She presses her unfitting glasses back on to the high bridge of her nose as they were the only thing disturbed during that whole process. And she reads the title: *Language of the Purpose Numbers.*

She looks at me from above the brim of the book, her eyes largely emphasized, and adds, "That's interesting, you would have learnt about the purpose numbers in the Halls of Ivy…" she pauses for a moment, skeptical, "You must realize this book has a much wider range of information. Very good, it will probably answer the purpose you seek then."

She hands the book to me and smiles, wrinkles ever so deep up close. A part of me wants to ask her age, but I don't dare. "Thank you," I say quietly, barely raising my voice.

She releases the book from her grip, places her hands behind her back, standing up as tall as she can and says, "My pleasure, now remember, if you have any questions, please don't hesitate to ask."

Then she turns to walk away and I notice a large scar down her back as though electricity had struck her. I don't dare ask, but Europa blurts it out. Obviously unable to contain herself, "Miss Bib…what happened to your back?"

My eyes widen and I look at Europa shocked. Bib glances back expressionless and says, "That is for another time…when your minds aren't so enclosed within the space your entrusted thoughts," and she walks away.

I abruptly look at Europa. "You shouldn't have asked such a personal question."

Europa shrugs, "She didn't seem to be bothered. Besides, you wanted to know just as much as I did."

I don't argue as she's right. I look down at the book whose eyes I can no longer see, now only displaying an ordinary book. "C'mon, I want to read this before Demetrius gets back."

Europa replies, "Okay, but if I knew a book could make you run so fast, I would have thrown one into training long ago."

I suddenly realize I was running faster than Europa, which has never happened before. I'd always believed I was so weak and futile. The words from the night before, spoken by that strange creature enter my mind, *"You have an unbeknown secret power."*

We find a table amongst hundreds dedicated to studying. Does this place ever end, I wonder.

As Europa sits next to me, she asks, "Why is this book so important anyway?"

I realize I hadn't told her any of the events that happened from the night before, but I'm not sure if it was even real. But why was that creature so familiar. I go quiet for some time, staring at the book, then I look at her intensely.

"What's wrong?" she questions.

I begin to explain to her what happened when I got home, not looking at her once as I tell her about the incident, ending with, "So when I saw this book, I thought it might have some answers. The purpose number ten might give me some insight to why I am the way I am. Just seemed too ironic that it was the first book to float in front of my face as though it knew I was calling it. I just had a feeling."

I slowly look up at her and her face is unreadable but confused all at the same time.

"The creature didn't tell you what the power was?" she questions, not even doubting my story.

I shake my head, "No, I have no idea."

She looks at the book coming to some sort of conclusion, "Surely Adonis would know, did you ask him?"

I shake my head, "No, the creature said I could not speak of this to any one, especially my father."

Her eyebrows raised. "And you believed him?"

My expression becomes stern, saying it out loud did sound odd. I add, "I don't know, Adonis was acting weird that night. I couldn't bring myself to ask him. I can't explain it."

Europa nods slowly, now sharing the same confusion as me.

"Okay then. Well, let's take a look at this book, surely they'll be some answers," she remarks brightly. I always feel comforted by her optimistic vibe.

Opening the book, I realize how old and decayed it is. The heavy front-page lands hard on the table, but it's immaculately clean from Emun. As I start flipping through the pages, I notice it's all blank, I become anxious. Europa and I look at one another in mistaken expressions. I continue to flick through them back and forth. I leave the book open on the first page sighing.

"Not even a table of contents? Prologue? Nothing?" I remark defeated. And instantly after those words slip from my mouth, words begin to appear on the page. As if typing itself out for the very first time.

Table of Contents

Master Numbers

The Theory Behind Purpose Number 10, Chapter 13

My eyes widen, planting my index finger on 'The Theory Behind Purpose Number 10.'

Europa smiles.

"Quickly flick to page 180," she retorts.

I begin scrolling through, 110, 150, 165, 179…191. I flick back and forth, looking closer I realize the pages have been torn out from 180 to 190. I remorsefully touch where the pages had clearly been ripped out in a hurry, leaving large jiggered pieces behind. Whoever did this, clearly wanted no one to ever know about this strange number and no one wanted to talk about it either, dismissing the idea that I even had it planted distinctively on the back of my neck. Europa had said nothing this whole time, probably finding no comforting words. We both sit back and sigh. Then without warning, a voice startles us, "There you are! I told you to stay in a group!" It was Demetrius. "Come on, we're already late." He turns and walks away with everyone else who stands close by. Europa stands to follow but I do not want to leave the book behind. I notice there is a spare compartment in my bag at the front, just enough room to fit the book, whilst no one is looking, I shove it into my bag and follow closely behind Europa.

The big doors open to the dining room. Everyone is already seated and waiting, pausing momentarily as blatant and impatient stares project our way. Demetrius bows in an apologetic manner, referring to Theophilus, who stands at the head of the usual large table amongst the other Elders who sit either side, "Apologies,

Patriarch and Matriarch, we were unfortunately teleported to the library. I am unable to explain why but I understand that is no excuse."

Theophilus says nothing with an expressionless look. For a moment, I am sure he glances my way. He gestures for us to take a seat. More food is abundantly waiting for us. Everyone looks ravished. We're hesitant to begin as the room is stone-cold quiet. Theophilus, still standing, looks around, almost torturing us for being disrespectfully late. Then he nods, taking a seat and all start to dig into breakfast. The room begins to become lively with conversation and other Constellations begin to converse. Our table hasn't really been one to socialize when there is food around as we are too preoccupied with our obsession over our stomachs.

Europa now turns to me and whispers to me with a mouth full of food. "I wonder who would go out of their way to specifically tear those pages out," she questions.

I shrug, thinking the same thoughts, "I'm not sure, but now I'm starting to regret not asking my father... Although I'm not sure he would even tell me...if it's as evil as that creature says it is. Knowing Adonis, he'd probably try to save me from the heartache. And address the situation, himself, without my knowing."

Unexpectedly, amongst the quiet murmurs of chewing, an explosion of food is plastered against the back of Kendall's skull; he stops and raises his head. We all turn to see where the food came from and I'm instantly captivated by the colors red and scarlet from the Aries constellation as they laugh amongst one another, punching one particular Aries with playfulness. He has bright red hair himself that's shortly cropped with young features and a chiseled jawline. He's a typical Aries, ardently strong. Even though none of them look their actual age, being the child of the zodiac also explains their mischievousness.

Isa becomes enraged and stands abruptly, almost toppling her seat over. "Well, aren't you going to do something about that Kendall! I mean he just disrespected us. You must put him in his place!"

Kendall, who still hasn't spoken since the uncharted forest, shrugs in an uncaring manner and doesn't even attempt to wipe off whatever remnants are left on the back of his head and continues eating.

"Stop being so pathetic, Kendall, we have all lost loved ones. Grow a backbone for crying out loud," she protests as though coming from experience. But I didn't know she had lost anyone; both her parents are still alive and she only hangs out with Henrietta and Dalton. I wonder whom she speaks of.

Suddenly, Kendall is holding Isa by the throat, slowly crushing her airways, intently looking deep into her eyes.

"Just because you've turned your sadness into resentment, doesn't mean we all have to do the same. You have no backbone as you thrive through hurting others. That's not strength, that's sheer weakness. Now leave me be!" he says with anger as tears well up into his eyes. He releases her, sits back down, and places his elbow on the bench covering his face and pretends to eat. But I've noticed none of the food he's been eating has been touched, only played with as he slowly chews the tiniest of pieces. Isa sits back down, not saying another word, guilty in her expression and embarrassed, which I know isn't a good sign as she'll sit there and stew upon it. We all fall completely silent and continue eating as though nothing happened.

I look up at the Elders, who don't appear to have noticed anything, too preoccupied within their own conversation. Then Theophilus turns deliberately in my direction, making eye contact. I look away quickly, feeling incredibly inferior to such a hierarchy. I glance over at Isa, who now looks livid with anger and refuses to eat any more. Europa whispers to me, "If she refuses to eat, I know we're in for a whole lot more trouble." I say nothing in response, not wanting to get on Isa's angry bandwagon today; she's going to explode any minute. Then I look up to see the Aries celebrating in victory, butting heads and mucking about.

After our bellies are full, Theophilus stands again.

"I hope you enjoyed that delicious meal. Remember, I must remind you to take advantage of every meal to stay fit and strong during your trials as it isn't just about theory, you'll be tested physically too. In fact, today you'll get to experience such a class called Orbis Bellum, the fighting arena. Where over time you'll get to fight one another to enhance your abilities, power, and skill in combat. But that'll be later on once you've learnt the basics of one another's strengths and weaknesses. Since today is your orientation, you'll be meeting your Capricorn mentor and they'll take you through a short class to brief you of your studies. They teach a little differently from what you're used to, unless you're from the same Capricorn region but they are the best mentors. So make sure to embrace it. This is all beneficial to understand one another, your land, and especially an understanding of who you truly are. This all makes a strong unity, because without purpose and awareness of each other, we are doomed to the Infernum and that snake you know of as…Apophis. Now your SNC overseer will be taking you through this all today. So, I wish you all the best. And let strength lay beside you." He brings his hands together and bows, showing off his magnificent wings that sit tightly behind his back, and I'm surprised they don't throw him off balance as he bends over.

Everyone stands as we are led out of the dining room. My thoughts linger towards the twirling stairs that curl around the Doh, praying the classes and Obris Bellum aren't too far up. As we stand waiting for further instruction, I notice the same fiery redhead Aries approach us amongst the crowded new bloods. He has a large scar I had not noticed before across his left cheek, it must have been a deep wound. A large fire tattoo climbs up from the base of his neck, flickering up across the borderline of his face and he carries a bow around his body, but without any arrows. It must be some sort of statement. It's obviously too tight as it places an immense amount of pressure on his chest, skin bursting out either side of the thin bowline.

I shove Europa to look as he confidently comes and nudges Isa arrogantly. She loses her footing and stumbles to the side. And I know today is not the day to be upsetting her.

"So, what makes you think you don't have to abide by the rules?" he says, slowly making individual eye contact with all of us. "Think you're better than the rest of us?" he contorts.

I can see they're wanting a fight, typical Aries, never afraid of confrontation, always up for a good fight. I know this is not personal. They're probably just bored wanting to cause a bit of mischief. I notice Europa tensing up and same goes for Henrietta and Dalton, but Kendall just watches idly, uncaring for the situation. The red-headed Aries smirks then tenses, readying himself as does the other eight Aries around him, all wanting this outlet just as much as him.

Then with added arrogance he says as though taunting us, "By the way, the name's Manley Luther," and winks, probably knowing us Tauruses have thin skin when it comes to those who challenge us, especially on a personal level. Or maybe their arrogance is just irritating in general when they're on a rampage of self-satisfaction. Then before there is a strike, Isa comes out of nowhere with an upper-cut to the chin. Unable to hold it together, she probably doesn't want to hear the sound of his voice any longer. And as if in slow motion, Manley flies up, his head leading and his body follows, rotating up and smashing down into the ground.

The fight begins to break out. Dalton and Henrietta charge in behind Isa and I notice Europa already dashing forward to help. Feeling obligated, I feel my first footstep push forward almost out of my control, due to obligation to my Constellation. But Adonis's voice seeps into my head as one foot steps in front of the other. *"You must still be aware of your limitations due to your illness, just always remember that. It's very important, your life is very precious and delicate."*

But I've made a commitment now, so I make my steps confident, staring at a long strawberry blonde-haired Aries. Riddled with tattoos and bulging muscles, he scrapes his hooves on the ground, looking at me as though I'm easy meat. He must be able to smell my fear from a mile away. He awaits impatiently for my embrace and now my confidence completely diminishes. But my feet don't stop, for the embarrassment of running away would be unimaginable. Then by the grace of Unum, I am forcibly stopped by an immensely strong force that wraps itself around my waist as I am pulled aside out of the firing range and into the surrounding crowd.

"We got to stop running into each other like this," a familiar voice says. I turn around and I am confirmed by the bright golden eyes, Leon Sol.

"What are you doing?" I demand, trying to act confident.

"Ah…saving your life? Much like last time. You really have a knack for throwing your life around aimlessly," my lips purse together and he adds, "Oh come on, you and I, and the rest of the crowd know you couldn't have taken on that monstrous Aries. Have you looked in a mirror lately?"

I cross my arms angrily glaring at him.

"Cute," he says with a wicked smile. Deep down I agree with him, although I'd never admit it due to his egotistical appreciation of himself. I feel steam coming out of my nostrils and with blinded rage, I try to re-join the others, even if it means broadcasting my suicide. But he picks me up and restrains me as though I am placed into a straitjacket, and holds on to me with little effort.

"Put me down! Put. Me. Down…or you will suffer the consequences!" I demand as he chuckles with pity. This damn Leo makes me so mad. I go limp as I tire myself out. I notice through the crowd the fight is over. It appears to have been broken up by a calm and beautiful Libra who stands directly center of the commotion. Leon places me down and I watch Demetrius guide our group away, smacking the back of Isa's head in disapproval.

The SNC Aries overseer moves his Aries group aside, hearing him yell, "Why are you young Aries so defiantly difficult to manage in your younger years! Get a grip! Is this the way you want to represent our Constellation as a simple goat, just looking to butt heads with others!" I notice both the Aries and Taurus look dazed in their expressions as though they've been bewitched. Both sides still look pretty banged up from the turmoil between them.

The Libra, who still stands center, wears Libra's Constellation color blue, long-sleeved gown, holding her hands gently together with two white stripes strapped over each shoulder and draping either side to the floor were the gown ends. She has a very dark complexion with platinum blonde hair and white eyes contradicting to their usual blue residing eyes. She looks around the room as we all admire her exotic beauty and suddenly the sensation in the room begins to become warm and relaxing, making me feel happy. "My name is Harmonia Ishta and I am one of the few Libra Diplomats who reside within the Doh, dealing with quarrels within Constellations and outside, like the one you just witnessed. I encourage you to not condone this type of behavior as only one warning is warranted. And this is that warning. If I have to settle another matter such as this one again, everyone involved will suffer the consequences. This is for the safety of you and everyone living within the Doh as this is a communion place and we can't have such behavior breaking our unity that has taken so long to overcome." Although she is very logical and straight to the point in her tone, she speaks it in a very pleasing manner, soft and alluring to the ear.

Her white eyes grow incredibly bright then diminish to their usual and gorgeous blue eyes.

The strong happy emotion fades but I now feel calmer within myself. Harmonia now raises her right hand to the sky. A loud powerful flapping sound is heard as a strong gust of wind is penetrated against us, pressing our hair and clothes down. A large black bird which I have never seen or read about before comes floating down and I put my hand up to cover my face, protecting it from the strong wind it pushes out. One of its large clawed feet grabs her hand and she is expelled into the air as they fly high into the fading vision of the Doh's infinite twisting walls, until they are out of sight. Everyone stands in complete awe and shock of what just happened, feeling themselves as though there had been some kind of phenomenon.

I murmur out loud, "Why were her eyes that glowing white?"

Leon leans towards me and whispers, "Surely you've read about their ability to control our minds?"

My eyebrows crease together. "Of course I have," I say bluntly.

Leon smiles, "Well, Libra Diplomats are PNC authorized. They're not as strong as an SNC Libra, but they do have great influence over our emotional state. When their eyes glow that penetrating white, you know that's when they are using it. That's why you feel so calm and happy right now."

I nod and question, "How do you know so much?"

Everyone now starts to move along, guided by our overseers and we move with the crowd as he says, "Let's just say I have a little bit of experience with this place." He winks at me again and I roll my eyes.

Suddenly, I notice Demetrius spotting me from within the crowd, standing with the Leo he has made clear he dislikes. He stampedes through the crowd and they either get out the way or they're thrown to the side. The way he moves depicts the image of a raging bull. As he stands in front of us, panting heavily with anger, he says, "What are you doing with her?"

Leon puts his hands up in the air patronizingly and says, "It's okay, I was just stopping her from committing arbitrary suicide."

Demetrius looks at me then looks at Leon, "Well, next time…" he pauses, appearing to be lost within words of anger, "don't."

Demetrius grabs me tightly around the arm to pull me away and I see Leon's expression become impatient as he kicks his head to the side in irritation and says though the words fall unintentionally from his brain to his mouth, "Well, I didn't see you around."

The zodiacs in earshot gasp as no one ever talks back to an SNC overseer, taught to have respect for those who have dedicated their lives in mastering their skill in order to protect us. Especially overseers, they need to be strong to take care of numerous amount of unpredictable new bloods who can't control their power or ability as yet. Demetrius stops dead in his tracks, uses my arm to sternly direct me behind him, and walks purposely toward Leon with a livid countenance. He looks him dead in the eye. "I know exactly what you're up to, child. I warn you. Stay away from her."

Leon's eyes slightly crease but do not flitter from Demetrius' over-dominating presence towering over him. Although Demetrius may appear much bigger in frame, I have not seen the comparison from a Leo's animalistic transformation and by not doing so, makes a point in itself.

Demetrius drags me back to the group. He lets go of my arm and I didn't realize how hard he was holding me until he releases me, blood rushes back with slight skin burns from his hard grip. He kneels down to my height and looks me dead in the eye.

"Promise me you'll stay away from him," he asks with sincerity.

I look down and peer up at him, never normally questioning his authority but curiosity gets the better of me, especially lately.

"Demetrius, I don't deliberately seek him out, it's as though he's following me…but, may I ask why I should avoid him?" Demetrius' eyes rumple together in disappointment from my lack of respect to not have full confidence in him.

"I know…but his father is…" he looks around seeming to be somewhat nervous, an expression I've never seen him portray and continues, "not to be trusted…nor his son." His dire need to explain is covered by an underlining sense of fear which I cannot explain. So, I nod as he adds, "The apple never falls far from the tree…" as though there is a long story behind a filter of events involving Leon.

After we finish climbing numerous amounts of steps and what seems like hours upon my now exhausted legs, still carrying the heavy bag filled with my precious medicine, we finally reach our destination: 'Orbis Bellum,' written above large doors that appear to be rotting, small amounts of moss, fauna and tiny flowers grow from its soft exterior. It appears to be quite moist at a closer glance as though a leak may be the cause. The Cancers stand first in line to the entrance.

"There appears to be no handle?" one questions from their group and I realize she's right.

Their overseer steps forward and says, "Well, why don't you take a look for yourself?" Their male overseer steps to the side and the new-blooded female Cancer steps forward, from behind she has short black hair and a tiny frame.

Standing in front of the strange entrance, she cautiously extends her bone spear from beneath her forearm, each serrated edge looking sharper than a newly made sword from the blacksmith. She nudges the soft wooden wall and bits cut easily from her sharp bone blade, falling to the floor in front of her. Now with confidence, she withdraws her spear back into her forearm and determinedly lifts bits of grass and overgrown weeds in search of some kind of knob or handle. The now suspicious Cancer girl looks at her SNC overseer for guidance and he looks back encouragingly to continue. She places both hands on the decaying door, pressing her head against it, now trying to listen. And in that moment, the fauna comes alive, wrapping weeds and roots around her wrists and ankles then her waist, gently withdrawing her into itself. She immediately panics and vigilantly extends both bone spears from her forearms and attempts to cut herself free, but the position she is being held in stops her, the spears flattened against the surface.

Everyone is shocked with what they're witnessing. Her Cancer companions lunge forward towards the door, extending their spears and attempt to cut the fauna away from her, but their overseer abruptly says, "Leave her!"

With clear hesitation and dismay, they step back and do as their overseer commands. The girl sinking into the door looks terrified, even distinguished within her pitch black eyes. I become apprehensive watching as roots grow and twist hard around her mouth. More greenery continues to engulf her until she is gone, now embodied within the decaying wall, quickly returning back to its original state. All the Cancers now lean up against the group of zodiacs, some with their hands covering their mouths in astonishment and one with tears in her eyes; she steps forward.

"What just happened?! Where is Naida!? Where is my sister... Is she okay? Tell me she is okay?" she says between broken sobs.

The Cancer overseer steps forward with reassurance. "It's okay, Naida is fine. She is now confined within the safety of Orbis Bellum. The entrance you see before you is known as the Bainbridge Plant. It only accepts zodiacs who are allowing. It protects the arena from bad creatures or entities such as the Infernum which it can confuse with fearful energy. Once Naida put her guard down, the Bainbridge Plant took that as an offering. But when she struggled it became agitated, fighting against her. Once absorbing you inside the arena, you cannot die or be harmed, technically. Because you still feel the pain of a harmful blow, but it's only simulated by your mind from what it's observing. The purpose is so you can practice your skills and abilities in safety."

Everyone looks at him in disbelief from what they just witnessed. So he puts both hands up in forfeit and says, "I'll demonstrate. I'll attack it first, allowing it to presume I'm a threat and then I'll put my guard down, disregarding all negative energy."

Both his bone swords extend fiercely from his forearms, making a shimmering noise, echoing within our proximity. His back is facing us but he glances behind and says, "Step back." A pulsating aura begins to make a pronounced circle around him as dust and dirt circulates and pulsates away. Then a large oval blue shield is produced around his hard, lean, athletic frame.

A few of the fellow zodiacs gasp, one commenting, "Cool!" in awe. The overseer Cancer now begins slashing and stabbing the wall. Leaves, wood, bark, flowers, and moss fly everywhere until we can no longer see where he stands. Then it all comes to a standstill and we can hear him breathing slightly heavier as the dust settles, the moist, fragile wall appears to have been untouched with not a leaf fallen. His shield instantaneously disappears and he withdraws his spears back within his arms. Turning around he says, "Now watch as I allow myself to be taken without resistance."

He gracefully jumps back into the wall and he is held ever so gently by the fauna as it pulls him in without hard restraints unlike Naida. Now all the Cancerians, one by one, allow themselves to be taken by the wall and as each one is consumed, every one after becomes more relaxed and confident. We're up next; Europa bounds forward for sheer thrill and eagerly allows herself to be taken with a big smile planted across her face as she yells, "Woohoo!!! This is cra—" and she is gone.

I'm next, stepping forward I can now see more detail on the wall and I notice it breathes, exhaling a wheezing, whistling noise. Trickling water falls within its cracks and collects in little pockets. Taking my right hand, I press it firm but gently against the wall, the soft rotten wood feels cold beneath my palm. Then stems of flowers begin curling around my wrist, sprouting as it twirls around my forearm. I nearly panic until I remember Naida's petrified face wrapped within the wrath of weeds pulling hard against her mouth. I take a big breath telling myself to stay calm. I shut my eyes as I feel it consume me gently, pulling me into the bounds of its diversity.

Chapter 6

Orbis Bellum

Beware ignorance, it lays unconsciously beside one's ego.

I slide out and down into a puddle of slime; I peel my arms from my sides and flick a clump on to the saturated ground, wiping the remnants from my face, I peer at it within my hands. It doesn't seem to smell but the texture is clammy, clear, and thick. I turn around to see a large plant that appears to be in decay. It climbs the walls, sprawling out from a dense area from where I slid out. The dense part moves up and down as though it were a heart, pumping blood to the crawling stems that grow sporadically and cling to the wall, a depiction of a poorly built spider's web.

I see Europa standing beside Naida, the Cancer who is now at ease. I stand up, wiping off as much slime as possible and see the place we now stand on is on top of a large platform with two small sets of stairs laying either side with a drop just behind us. Naida and Europa converse peacefully until Europa notices me and waves me to come over. I go to move but my feet are securely stuck within the heavy slime.

"You have to pull hard!" Naida calls. But as I do, I fall flat on my face, making a pathetic splat sound. Europa runs over and helps me up.

"You alright?" she asks.

I nod and she rips me out and slides me on to a more secure, none-sticky spot, where I can now walk. I follow her over to Naida and she introduces us.

"Naida Odette, this is my best friend Taura Andreas."

Naida, now with a friendlier demeanor, nods her head in acknowledgement.

"Nice to meet you," she says in a kind conservative voice.

Her short black hair is now pulled back from the remnants of the slime. She has beautiful porcelain skin; her mouth is small as though she purses the whole time, with a tiny nose that surely isn't functional for breathing and has an almost pixie appearance. But it is her large black eyes that capture me. They go on forever, you could become lost within the darkness.

I notice Europa and Naida are both dry to the bone apart from their hair. Looking down at myself, slime still drips off me in clumps. I look at Europa.

"How did you…" I begin to ask as she points to the ground. A large slug-like creature lays at the back of my heel trying to attach itself to me. I jump out of the way.

"What is that thing?" I yelp. It has a long and slimy body with big lips, large eyes that attach to long muscular tubes, growing endlessly from its body, its eyes searching over me.

"It's okay! It just sucks the slime off you," Naida explains. The strange creature begins sliding over towards me, its eyes analyzing me from head to toe with a delicious expression. It lifts its large lips and latches on, beginning to suck the slime from my skin, and it quickly evaporates. The creature burps and slowly heads back towards the large pool of slime from where I fell in.

"What is that?" I ask.

Europa shrugs. "Who cares, I'm just glad it did its job," looking at herself to make sure there is no residue.

Naida chuckles, becoming more comfortable with us.

"It's just a Potator, they're harmless; they live off all different kinds of slime, mold, and bacteria. They are very important for the echo system. They must use them to clean the slime from that Bainbridge Plant. They love that kind of stuff!" she explains enthusiastically as we watch Isa clumsily slide down the slime trail.

I ask, "How do you know that?"

Naida explains, "We have a few colonies that live around the outskirts and within Vadosus, our large village inside our huge rock pool. They're essentially our little cleaners, keeping our inhabitants clean of any nasty and unwanted diseases – handy little guys."

Everyone watches others in amusement when they see the Potator for the first time. Isa kicks one, which flings straight into the wall and goes completely flat but appears to be unharmed. Its soft body, with the appearance of no bone, must allow it to squeeze into small places and change shape easily. It comes out completely unscathed from a hard kick to the body, unlike myself. For a moment, I daydream, how handy it would be to have that ability.

Then Naida's soft conservative voice captures my ear, "I don't mean to sound rude, but aren't you a Taurus? Shouldn't you harbor sheer strength?"

I look up at her in question and she adds, "I just don't understand why you couldn't pull yourself effortlessly from that slime, like the others of your kind?"

I go stiff as I had forgotten how noticeably weak I am. Before the situation becomes awkward, Europa steps in, "She was born with a condition that prevents her from harnessing her inner strength. It makes her unfortunately weak."

Europa says no more and I am grateful for her simple explanation. Naida's face becomes inquisitive and I wish her curiosity would be satisfied. "Oh, I'm terribly sorry, that must be incredibly hard. But I'm just interested, how did the Elders – well, you know…"

We both look at her, hoping she won't ask the question, but she continues hesitantly, "How come they let you…live? We were taught your village in Herba killed those born with any kind of weakness, which I always thought was very sad as I believe each child has some kind of great purpose. But I respect your way of living as you wouldn't be the great warriors we know of today if it wasn't for certain sacrifices."

As those last words fall out of her mouth, she instantly purses her lips in forgiveness. My mouth feels as though it has sewn shut and I feel myself becoming furiously angry. I had never been asked that question before, as everyone within the Herba community was already aware of me and my condition. And they hate me for it. I've never had to explain it before, it was just accepted and resented at the same time, and I could deal with that as I never had to justify it to myself or anyone. But now knowing I'll have to explain my existence time and time again within this place, makes me wish I could just go live with my father and never return.

Then Naida's voice is heard again, "Oh my, I do apologize, I didn't mean to make you upset."

Was my facial expression that obvious? Thinking my thoughts were purely internal.

She adds, "I was just curious as I thought you must have some unbeknown power or something."

The world around me becomes still for a split second as the words from the strange hairy creature that entered my room just one night ago leaks into my mind: *"You have an unbeknown secret power you do not know of yet."*

Then Naida's words slowly bring me back into reality, "It was just a thought. But I shouldn't have presumed. Your situation must be very hard for you already, without me or others prodding into your business."

The anger subsides and I slightly smile at Naida in acknowledgment.

"Thank you," I say sincerely.

Then Europa cuts in, "Naida, I'm not sure if you'll have any information but do you know of the purpose number…10?"

I become slightly irritated that Europa is now involving another. But Naida seems to be trustworthy and I know Cancerians are very faithful friends and very intuitive. It makes sense how she had read my body language so well. But Europa must be in the same thoughts as myself when Naida mentioned an unbeknown power.

Before Naida answers, she thinks on it for a moment. "I'm sorry, I thought there were only 9 purpose numbers and the master numbers. But I have never heard of such a number. But I know who you could ask."

We look at her eagerly as she says, "The Gemini, Bibliotheca, she's the Librarian of the Doh. I am yet to meet her but I know everyone calls her Bib. She has read every book in this place over one hundred times! So I'd imagine she's your best bet. My mother always says: once you're settled in the Doh and you begin your lessons, if you need any assistance with your studies, ask the Gemini Bibliotheca, you'll find her in the library."

My mouth slightly drops open, thinking, *Why didn't I think of that when she was standing in front of us?*

Europa cuts in again, "I've heard she's up to reading through the books for the five hundred and twenty-six thousandth time."

Europa winks at me and I shake my head as though that wasn't necessary.

Naida adds, "Well, I doubt that, you'd have to be a ghost in limbo to be able to have that kind of time… Anyway, I should be getting back to my sister, since I nearly gave her a heart attack before. I know it's not much but I hope that helps!" She smiles and moves over to where her sister stands.

Europa and I look at one another.

"Maybe Bib was over-exaggerating when she said that. Because that would take an awful lot of time!" Europa exclaims.

"Never mind that. We should try to get back there as soon as possible and ask her," I say. Europa nods in an affirmative agreement.

By now everyone has fallen through the slimy Bainbridge Plant and the platform is getting overly crowded. I feel a large hand grab my shoulder as does Europa's. "Come on, you two. Stay close to the group." It's Demetrius and he stays close by our side as all the other zodiacs slowly start to split down either side of the narrow staircases.

Europa leans into my ear and whispers, "What's with all the bloody stairs in this place? This is madness," she says nudging me. I smirk with amusement and nod, until I hear an aggressive grunt in earshot. A Sagittarius looks at us with a judgmental expression and I'm uneasy as to what he is about to say as Sagittarius don't shy away from the brutal truth.

"That's because your Constellation is only interested in your gluttony for food instead of fuelling your brain, blinded by an over-indulgent cholesterol inherent diet, constipating you from appreciating the beautiful diversity of this magical building," he says without remorse, probably not even realizing how insulting that was. Europa and I look at one another with astounded expressions and without knowing what to say, we say nothing.

Then a deep familiar voice is heard amongst the crowd, "I wouldn't call stairs beautifully diverse, when the only diversity they contain is the change in direction," Kendall says plainly, slowly coming back into existence after this morning's collision with Isa. The Sagittarius holds Kendall's stare without conviction, as though showing some kind of respect for the intelligence he obviously doubted within our race, stated within his comment, probably thinking we're imprudent brutes. The Sagittarius nods in deference and Kendall responds with validation and with a flick of his tail, he clops on. Kendall has always been the more serious and wise beyond his years, always very humble towards those around him, which makes sense as his purpose number is nine: worldly, giving, altruistic, self-aware, old-school, intuitive, and wise. Demetrius's body language becomes stiff beside me as he watches the Leos who are slightly in front of us; he slows us down to see which staircase they'll take. They move down the right and he immediately signals us to go down the left. I linger at the beautiful Leo girls, who are mesmerizing with their long golden hair, golden eyes, athletic bodies, tanned skin with a promiscuous aura, probably drawn from their Lion ancestor which adds to their exquisiteness. But the bad side is that they know it, making their arrogance even more distinguished in addition to their own admiration for themselves. But I remind myself they are ruled by the Sun – indicator and interpreter of everything revolved around self and energy.

I'm jolted back to the present when Europa pulls me to her side as we walk down the stairs. I become instantly mesmerized as I step down each step; holding the handrail, I'm now able to see the magnitude of the Orbis Bellum Arena. I now hear the astonishing crowd that cheers below as thousands of seats are cultivated proportionally around the over-encumbered arena. Two small figures stand below either side, appearing to be waiting to start. One paces back and forth while the other waits patiently as though a statue. Then I notice a message is being brought up from below the stairs from where we stand. A whispering message is quickly moved through the long crowd up the narrow stairs. Demetrius is now being informed by a Pisces SNC overseer and for the first time I see Demetrius express some kind of excitement, displaying the first of any exaggerated emotion that I have ever witnessed. He gestures for us to listen and instantly changes back to his stiff and rigid demeanor. But I know he is holding back some sort of excitement, trying to keep the usual authority in place.

"We've just walked into a battle involving the renowned and legendary Sagittarius, Ahearn Orion, who has served the longest time in the SNC army within his Constellation. As you probably know, part of a Sagittarius SNC criteria is to go off the grid to search within the Infernum habitat to uncover any new geographical areas; during these journeys, they may discover new monsters and creatures. Ahearn has discovered some of the largest unknown lands, fought some of the toughest unknown creatures within the uncharted forest and still continues to come back alive. His bravery and courage is something admired within our lands. His opponent is an up-and-coming Scorpio, Imelda Kore. Both her parents died when she was very young, no one knows how or why but it made her the relentless warrior she is today, the first SNC Scorpio woman to ever show up and humiliate the men within her Constellation. Her determination and focus outdo those who have thought to have natural talent. Imelda never had natural talent; she worked hard to prove to those who never thought she'd ever amount to anything other than a NC. Possibly breeding potential offspring but nothing more. She is one of the fiercest women and a true Scorpio at heart, although she is much younger and less experienced than Ahearn and still only new to being an SNC. So the odds are in his favor. He hasn't taken up a battle in centuries as he hasn't needed to prove himself, but the rumors of his old age must have gotten to him. There has been a lot of controversy about these two. So, all who witness today are watching history in the making. I'm surprised I wasn't informed earlier. Now we must move, they won't start until everyone is seated."

Now I could tell the one pacing back and forth was Ahearn the Sagittarian and the other stiff dark figure was Imelda the Scorpio, obviously impatient to start and we're the cause. The seats we take are wooden, hard, and far from the front, barely in eye view of either figure, and so small, you can hardly tell what's going on.

Demetrius claps to get our attention and points down beside his chair. "There are Oculi under your armchair. They look like two round crystal balls plastered together. Place them on your eyes and they'll latch on, enabling you to see the arena up close as though you are sitting at the front." He sits back down and places these unusual looking crystals on his face, which instantly stick to his face and he glances at us to demonstrate but quickly looks away rubbing the side of his head. It looks as though he has large bug eyes and on Demetrius, who is such a serious zodiac, it is comical. Europa giggles once he's looking away.

"I'm actually impressed he is able to maintain his usual stern stature with those things," she says chuckling in between the words.

"He's got to maintain appearances, Europa," I reply with a smile and we both laugh taking our Oculies out from under the armchairs and they latch on effortlessly. Instantly I can see the Orbis Bellum Arena in front of me as though we have front row seats. I hear Europa's voice beside me.

"Wow, these things are handy! Who needs front row seats when you have these?!"

I unexpectedly hear Henrietta a few seats down, "Oh wow! Ouch! Owe ou! Where am I!"

I hear a slap as Isa replies, "Look at the arena, you idiot, you're going to give yourself even more brain damage by doing that." Europa chuckles and I turn to look at the commotion, and I'm instantly met with immense amount of pain in my eyes and head as everything enlarges immensely, obviously too much for my eyes to handle.

"OU!" I yelp, quickly looking back at the Orbis Bellum Arena as everything goes back to normal size.

"Oh not you too," Europa laughs.

"I'm guessing that's what Henrietta did?" I reply, now understanding why Demetrius only glanced our way. These things are deadly up close. Europa rubs my arm in sympathy.

"Don't worry, your secret's safe with me," she says sarcastically.

I look over at Ahearn who steps hard and deliberate back and forth, not once taking his eyes off Imelda. He is large bodied and strong with incredibly lean muscles, long, brown, wavy hair that falls behind his back with half of it tied up with striking prominent features. As I look closely, you can tell the man has been through a lot of rough collisions with large and small scars covering his whole body. His deep dark eyes that watch intently with a slight leer planted across his face. His horse body ripples with muscles as he clops along. His tail that has been cropped short, probably to keep it from getting tangled or used against him within these types of scenarios. A bow hangs by his side in his right hand with arrows tightly secured to his back. The bow held at a ready and a small sword sits securely by his left hip within a worn brown leather case. I scan across to take a closer look at Imelda, realizing the arena is a desert environment as sand blows around, even though there is no wind from where we are seated. The stillness is completely contrasting.

I capture Imelda standing motionless as though nothing is apparent other than this crucial moment, her focus is clear and profound. She is a powerful looking woman with long black hair, braided along her scalp and into a high prompt long ponytail, and strong features highlighting her pronounced cheekbones and defined jawline. The independence of a woman like Imelda makes her incredibly unattainable and exceedingly attractive. She wears nothing but a small black leather crop, matching a barely noticeable skirt as they both blend into her hardened black exterior. She stands with two daggers in separate hands with the blades facing towards her elbows and her tail stands high above her head at a ready. Ahearn needs to be wary of that stinger. Suddenly, the sound of a loud old horn is ejected into the atmosphere and I notice a large old shell sitting above Imelda as a deep echoing sound vibrates through the arena.

It must be the sound to begin as Ahearn now gallops hard against the sand, clearly working harder than normal as it pulls his hooves in with every gallop. Imelda elegantly leans down towards the ground as though crouching into a scorpion-like imitation as her tail extends high into the air. She waits patiently as he approaches fastidiously; her arms are sprawled out either side, the daggers at a ready. Ahearn begins circling around her, drawing back his bow, carefully picking his target and shooting. But the shots seem to be off target, some landing into the ground beside her. Imelda slashes against the arrows with her stinger, the end of her tail obviously impenetrable. The arrows are invisible to our naked eye, only apparent when sparks fly from hitting the end of the stinger, making a sharp crisp sound penetrating to the regular ear. He shoots another and another circling continuously around her, never getting close enough to be in range of her long stinger, which reacts every time he shoots an arrow.

Imelda never allows her back to be turned towards him. The distance he keeps allows her to move in position to his circumference, giving her the upper hand as her defense appears to be impenetrable. But he doesn't allow her the range she needs in order to attack. Both stay within their comfort zones, trying to figure one another out from a safe distance. Ahearn comes to a standstill as his arrows are becoming scarce. His muscles swell as blood pumps hard through his veins, easy to see from the low body fat percentage. Imelda is not letting her guard down.

"I guess you shouldn't have been so tactless to think your own self-image couldn't be beaten within any environment now, Ahearn," Imelda says patronizingly. Ahearn begins pacing back and forth, pulling out and cleaning the sword against his coarse horse-haired body.

"Contradictive words from one so self-assured as herself. The battle hasn't even begun," he says intently, glancing up and smirking. I realize the Orbis Bellum must be able to simulate any given environment, Ahearn obviously wanting the battle to take place within a similar environment to the Scorpio's Solitudiem Desert where they reside within their Constellation, most likely to prove his capabilities undoubtedly after being compared to one much younger and inexperienced to himself. Those around rumored to be doubting him. But maybe his own heroic image has gotten the better of him, believing in his own legend. I've heard it happening before as Imelda appears to be impenetrable and fearless at this point. It could be seen as he underestimates her. Imelda smiles and says no more, crouching down slightly lower, preparing herself for the next attack. The crowd begins to go wild for the stir talk as it adds drama and excitement to the battle, making everyone cheer harder for their preferred fighter.

Ahearn gradually places the sword back in its case, clipping back effortlessly as if trying to create everlasting suspense. With five remaining arrows left, he pulls three out at once, placing them against his bow steadily and aimed towards the ground. The silence in the stadium could be broken by a pin drop. Imelda does not move an inch, carefully watching Ahearn's every movement. He begins to gallop gracefully this time as though the sand no longer cripples his disposition. Imelda follows, this time he steadily comes into range of her stinger; she smirks as though she's got him. But as the large intimidating stinger lurches at him, he fires all three of his arrows and the highly reactive stinger now responds to the fast movement of the arrows, first lurching at the first primary arrow then at the following two. The stinger destroys the arrows that aim for the ground behind her, appearing to be deliberately off target as he now rides hard in the opposite direction, circling around her and shoots his last two, which penetrate the base behind the stringer which are vulnerable under armored plates and now securing it to the ground. Imelda's face is astounded by shock and before she has any time to react, Ahearn has already leaped into the air with his sword in a downward position, aiming for her spine. She pulls at her tail then as a last-minute decision, she attempts to run, but it's already too late, not that it would have mattered any way. The sword has now pierced deep through her body and sturdily into the ground beneath her, only the handle visibly from above as Ahearn holds it securely, deep within her, his body crushing hers. No scream or sound escapes through her mouth, only a gasp followed by a curdling sound of blood as it furiously falls from between her lips like a bursting water pipe, her eyes still wide open in shock as she never saw it coming. They cloud over into a clammy gray color as though she were now blind. Then she relaxes as though her life had mysteriously escaped her.

No one says a word and I grasp the side of my seat in question. I thought you couldn't die within the Orbis Bellum? I take off the Oculi from my face, dropping it clumsily on to my lap as I cover my mouth with my hands, staring stunned into the distance. I have only been told stories of murder but never have I witnessed it, forever knowing this is what we've been preparing for but never ready for the actual reality of death. Then I hear Demetrius's voice as others around me are heard to be making a commotion.

"Calm down! The slime you were covered with from the Bainbridge Plant protects you. The slugs only remove the unnecessary bulk, so you can function. She is not dead, put your Oculies back on and watch!" he retorts with impudence and lack of empathy. I place my Oculi back on and focus on Ahearn who has already stepped off Imelda and is now cleaning his sword with an already dirty cloth kept within another leather pouch on his side hip. I look over at Imelda who still appears to look very dead. Then the same slime from the entrance begins to pour out from the wound in her back, flowing out until her body is completely immersed within it. It pulls her into a tight ball and turns white like a pearl until we cannot see one part of her anymore. Ahearn then walks over to the now white ball and pokes it with his sword and it bursts as though it were as delicate as a bubble and slime gushes everywhere. Imelda slides out on to all fours, gasping for air, dropping her head as though she had been reborn. Ahearn walks over and offers her a hand; she glances at it and turns away. Kneeling on to her knees, she steps up on to one leg, using her hands to push herself up on to her feet, obviously tired.

"Still so defiant, Imelda. Why can't you just admit defeat? It wouldn't make you any less of the great warrior you clearly are."

She squeezes out her slime-covered braids and flicks them behind her. "Not until you or anyone else officially…kills me. There is no point admitting to something that is yet to be true."

Ahearn smiles humbly; even though she may have taken the defeat badly, depending on how you look at it, her ambiguous belief in herself could be seen as admirable in the face of defeat.

I remove the Oculi from my eyes and place it back under the armchair and rub my eyes as they readjust to their usual vision. I look over to see Europa at the end of her chair, raveled with excitement. "Wasn't she amazing? I hope I'm as strong and fierce as Imelda by the time I finish the Olympus Trials. She kicks butt."

I glance back at the arena and watch both Ahearn and Imelda disperse either end and look back at Europa and say, "She definitely is something else."

Europa grabs my shoulders and rattles me. "To even take on a zodiac of that caliber says so much in itself. She was defiant even in the face of defeat…she was the definition of the underdog."

I smile and nod in admiration. And then Imelda's name begins to be chanted amongst the crowd and the feeling of profound respect grows with every encouraged chant.

Demetrius calls out, "Alright, we'll be heading to your classroom where you'll meet your first mentor and have a small introductory session. Now follow me and don't get lost amongst the crowd."

We stay close together, pushing past other zodiacs. Some grunt, judge, analyze, stare, and others apologize. The dynamic of each region is so animatedly vast.

Once we step down to ground level, walking behind the walls of the arena, we come upon a large, deep dark hallway. It looks old, decayed, and easily lost within its unseen passage. Vents are installed on either side and on the roof. The ground angles down either side and the flat path in the center is made up of a drain with a metal crate, like material sitting on top for us to walk upon. Rust seems to have riddled all the vents, leaving an orange decomposed tinged color leaking down towards the drain. Demetrius turns to us as the other overseers do the same, announcing, "We're all going to walk through this together as a group. And this tunnel is going to rid you of the residue slime you still contain within your skin." Everyone looks at the eerie tunnel with unkind thoughts.

Unexpectedly, Dalton speaks, "But I like knowing I'm invincible. Wouldn't something like this help us fight the Infernum? Besides, that tunnel does not look inviting," he retorts overconfident, trying to cover his prudency.

Demetrius says, "Do you understand the term rejuvenation?" Dalton nods unconvincingly as his expression says otherwise. Demetrius adds, "Well, that's what the slime does, rejuvenates you, in other words, restore. So when you die, a chemical reaction occurs. When cells start to die due to death, the slime encapsulates you and revives every dying cell. It may look like you're dead but you're not. It's okay to have it on for a few days maybe even a couple of weeks before you start noticing certain side-effects. Imagine if you had such a substance on at all times. As the natural process of cells die, the substance will continue to rejuvenate them, making your skin unable to shed, your hair unable to fall out and so many more natural process of life and death subside within your body. Your skin will become thick as it will be too overcome with skin cells, making you bleed and crack, only producing more skin cells. You'll begin to grow an immense amount of hair all over your body as you are unable to shed through the daily process. There are so many other problematic side-effects. But yes, you will never die. But the pain that accompanies it is immense. You wish only for death to find you."

Dalton's mouth drops open, "Well, what are we waiting for! I ain't turning into some behemoth! No siree."

He begins striving determinedly for the creepy dark hallway and we unquestioningly follow behind, along with the other zodiacs, who too take the queue.

The tunnel is cold and damp. The humidity increases dramatically and you instantly feel as though you could suffocate within its density. Darkness completely consumes us and we are basically walking blind. The overseers are constantly repeating themselves, "Continue walking straight and do not walk up the angled concrete, stay on the flat crated platform."

Europa places my hands on the back of her shoulders.

"Hold on to me and don't let go," she says, whispering as she does the same from the feel of her shoulders. Soon the humidity begins to increase again and I hang my head down between my heavy arms that Europa carries upon her back. Sweat starts to heavily drench my whole body, dripping down every segment of skin. I hear everyone around me beginning to pant hard and I too begin to breathe deep and heavy, feeling as though every breath is harder than the last. Now no murmurs are heard amongst the crowd as that task would take further energy. The oxygen continues to deplete, the temperature continues to rise and it's as though we have walked into an oven. Anxiety now takes over, my eyes dilate, my breaths become short and fast. My heart beats hard into the surface of my chest, and I know I'm about to go into a full-blown panic attack. But just as I feel I'm going to pass out, the air pressure changes. Hard, cold wind pushes against us. And my hair stands high on end from the severe atmosphere change. I now shiver, squinting through my eyes. I see a light beaming in front of us. Everyone's footsteps pick up pace, turning into a fast-paced walk and nearly into a jog as we all spurt out of the dark tunnel, panting. Some lean down on to their knees, others leaning against Doh's twisting wall, trying to catch their breath. The overseers stroll out as though they had just gone for a gentle stroll, their breathing appears to be unchanged and their stature is calm and somewhat relaxed.

We all look at them contorted. The Pisces overseer steps forward with an amused but compassionate smile; he speaks with a soft but confident undertone which is easily understood. "Don't worry, new bloods, you'll soon become used to it after a while. It's necessary to place the body under threatening circumstances. It's the fastest and most efficient way to rid the body of toxins such as the slime. The body tries to survive under severe conditions due to the massive temperature alteration, killing any foreign bacteria. For some reason, the slime cannot survive these types of conditions within our genetic makeup. No other technique has been found to completely destroy it – believe me, we've tried – unless you want to turn into a Bwbachod."

We all glance at each other in question to see if any one appears to know of Bwbachod.

Then a Pisces girl asks her overseer, "Apologies, Meredith…but what's a Bwbachod?" Everyone nods in agreement, whispering to one another, wanting to hear about this unheard creature. The fins on the side of Meredith's face sprawl out in anticipation to tell the story. Pisces love telling stories, it compliments their imaginative minds to elaborate on things they know. He gestures towards the rest of the other overseers and they nod in agreement.

"Well, before I tell you the story, I advise you not to judge your ancestors harshly because this is an unfortunate bit of history known within the Nirvana land which everyone learns of eventually. Plus, it'll stop you from ever avoiding the tunnel."

He rubs his hands together in preparation and uses them animatedly as he tells the story, "In the beginning when Apophis started possessing zodiacs and the Infernum began taking over our forest and the twelve Constellations were just beginning to work together, we had to figure out a way to replicate a battle field scenario, where zodiacs naturally fought against one another in practice. But egos and differences got in the way and we ended up injuring each other more in preparation than in battle. After a while, many zodiacs were unable to fight due to bad injuries or on rare occasions, death. Because of the vast conflicting diversity between Constellations, we found it hard to get along in the beginning, especially Constellations that had a reputation for clashing. Then, a now well-known Pisces alchemist known as Bainbridge Blaine, who had been studying the Potator for many years, came across an amazing discovery. The slugs could not be injured nor could they die. This life or death dictation was only enabled by their environment, as they did not fornicate with one another either to reproduce as a normal species would. After studying their food substances, like particular bad slimes and bacteria, Bainbridge found the more the bad slimes and bacteria accumulated – hurting the surrounding natural environment – the more the slugs appeared rejuvenated within the trail of slime left behind by another Potator. He found that this was brought on by the number of bad bacteria in the environment. If a high concentrated amount was found within the Potator's residue slime, it caused a natural chemical reaction to reproduce more slugs. Once the concentration went down, the slugs died off – fizzled out. Then by studying these slimes and bacteria, he created his own slime. Then he had to find a plant that could inhabit the slime. Then alter its genetic makeup in order to keep reproducing the slime on its own. This resulted in a soft rotten moldy-looking plant, the one you now know of as the Bainbridge plant. To keep reproducing this so-called slime, it must absorb a zodiac, withdrawing particular minerals from your skin which it utilizes for its survival but leaves the by-product of this rejuvenation slime, which is also referred to as Bainbridge slime. After this Bainbridge creation, little was known about the long-term effects," Meredith shrugs and sighs in an uneasy manner of regret, very theatrical in his whole description of the story.

"The strongest and most powerful zodiacs, now known as the SNC, were tested time and time again. They began getting stronger. Everyone thought this was great and a major breakthrough to destroy the Infernum and take down Apophis. But not long after, they started turning into…monsters, unable to listen, short-tempered, and irritated most of the time due to the body's inability to shed everyday cells. It made them go…insane. Most died but some who had a complimentary makeup to the bacteria, flourished and were unaffected mentally from the disturbing physical side-effects, although they suffered from a low IQ, unable to follow orders which made them chaotic at times and unreliable. But over time as they started to breed, they kept enhancing, the cells genetically heightened over generations. They were never tested against the Infernum until they knew everything about them as they were unaware if they were susceptible to the enchanting lullaby and didn't want Apophis to have control over such a creature. They developed an ability to morph into anyone just by consuming a small portion of their blood. They'd transform into a perfect physical replication, able to use the zodiacs' special abilities and power. This was thought to be incredibly dangerous, so they were soon eradicated. One still remains but he is enslaved to Theophilus and is controlled heavily upon his hand, no one knows why he was spared. It is told that he's kept as a safety resort because if anything were to happen within Orbis Bellum and the genetically enhanced slime adapted, becoming unaffected by the tunnel, his blood could hold the answer… Anyway, that's the end of today's history lesson. We better get you to class." Everyone is now recovered from the tunnel's effect and we now follow our overseers.

Chapter 7

Nature Elements and Quality Signs

It's those of our enemies that unbind us.

We've now split off from the other new-blooded Constellations and no one has spoken for a while as the journey has been long through the new unexplored area of the Doh. I now use the handrail to pull myself up each step as Europa leads in front of me and I slowly fall behind, carrying my heavy backpack which adds to my struggle. I stop for a moment to peer over the edge. Down the center, there is only darkness, and I'd hate to think how far you'd have to drop until you come face to face with the surface. I'm sure your body would be unrecognizable, a pile of moosh. Then I hear Henrietta yell over the ledge, "Echo!" and I glance up at her. Dalton is standing beside her as their expressions are curious and enthralling to hear the sound of their own voice. I look over the ledge again to hear her one convicted word travel down the deep chamber, repeatedly echoing back as it dilutes into the distance.

Dalton then joins in, "Taurus Rule!" and the words continuously travel down the large passage, vibrating into one another and it's a terrible melody to listen too. Europa places both her hands over her ears in irritation, stepping up each step with deliberation to express her annoyance, probably wondering why Demetrius hasn't put a stop to it. I wonder the same thing as I squint at the repeated word that follows each other. Then unexpectedly I hear the sound of rustling coming from below where we climb the twisted staircase, as though paper flails in the wind at high speeds. Everyone stops to look over the edge, except Adonis. We peer down the Doh's deep, infinite center; the rustling squeaking noises become stronger as though a stampede of something travels up from within the dark eluded center. Unexpectedly, before I even see anything, I'm clipped in the face by a white feathery thing and I stumble back to the wall and watch hundreds of white furry creatures fly up the Doh's center. But I can't get a good look at one as they travel incredibly fast.

"Everyone, gather 'round!" Demetrius announces from above the high twirling stairs. Europa looks at me and gestures to follow, running up around to where Demetrius stands, as the strange white-feathered animals continue to fly up the Doh's center by the dozens, not appearing to slow down. I see Demetrius holding one in his hand; we gather around.

"This is a Nuntius. They are as fast as a hare and as swift as a falcon. They deliver messages from the zodiacs who live within the Doh's premises to loved ones within their Constellations or to other zodiacs in different parts of the Doh. But you won't get one of these until you have proven yourself worthy."

The strange white-feathered creature that he holds around the top of the neck, has a similar body to a large mouse with a long, thin tail that curls around and grows a bunch of feathers at the end, where it holds a letter securely. It has big black eyes and tips of black at the ends of its hands, feet, and wings. It twitches around, attempting to escape at an unearthly rate. But it has no chance against Demetrius's grip. Europa approaches the Nuntius, gazing at it affectionately.

"Aw, it's so cute. Can I pat it?" she asks, already reaching out before Demetrius has given his approval, and just before she touches its soft head, it nips her on the end of the finger.

"OUCH!" she cries.

Isa snuffs. "That'll teach you," she spits.

Europa now flicks her hand back and forth, rolls her eyes at Isa as Demetrius says, "I would have warned you not to get between a Nuntius and its letter as it'll defend it with its life."

I curiously ask, "Why haven't we seen any within our own Constellation if they deliver messages to and from on a regular basis?"

Demetrius lets the Nuntius go and it immediately joins the last few Nuntius that trail at the end of the large group. Everyone moves over to the edge and peers up, watching them disappear into the distance. Demetrius answers whilst standing behind us, "You've probably had one brush past you but most likely mistook it for a gust of wind or a mouse. But you're just unable to see them with your naked eye. Their speed makes them pretty much invisible… But we best keep moving otherwise you won't get to your orientation session."

We eventually come to a small corridor with the Taurus emblem engraved into the concrete structure. It glows green and white as we approach. Demetrius holds the tall, thin creaky wooden door open as we all pass through, and I wonder why it's so old and conventional compared to the rest of the Doh's premises. The classroom is bland, with small glazed windows, singular wooden tables and chairs stand lifelessly in the center of the room. Large stone bricks make up the area and there is nothing stimulating about the atmosphere, only dust that riddles the air and clogs my lungs, probably produced from the large black board at the front of the room that is covered in chalk residue. Once we have all entered, Demetrius announces, "Well, I'll be leaving you now. I'll be back later to escort you to your dorms, before dinner." He shuts the door and leaves us to our devices. Waiting for our mentor, I notice our individual names are carved into a small plank of wood placed at the end of each small working table. Mine is centered at the front with Europa on my right, bringing a smile to my face until I see Isa's name to my left.

I sit down and Europa places my heavy bag between my legs and I smile in gratitude. "Thanks, Euro."

She slumps down in her chair next to me. "That's okay…but what the hell is in that thing!? Didn't you bring enough the first time? Never thought you were high maintenance."

I smirk amusingly. "Yeah, neither did I," I answer convincingly, without giving much away in front of the others and try to cover my medicines as my father insisted so heavily upon.

Once we are all seated, Isa blurts out ignorantly, "What a dump," scraping dust from her table and blowing it of her finger. "My granny would keep her grave in better condition," she adds.

Dalton abruptly replies in confusion from the table behind, "But Isa…your granny's dead?"

Isa rolls her eyes not even bothering to turn around to insult him about his idiocy, which is standard. Then Henrietta punches Dalton in the arm. "Exactly…stupid." Dalton doesn't retaliate to the punch as he is too conflicted about the joke he did not comprehend.

"Don't hurt yourself," Kendall says uncaringly. Dalton glares at him with fury. But Kendall just draws in the dust on his desk, not taking any notice of Dalton. As our attention is preoccupied, we're given a shock by the sound of a pronounced clearing throat, followed by a cough. We turn around to see a Capricorn standing in front of us on the platform that sits higher than the rest of the room. And I recognize him from the dining room. It's the Capricorn elder, Aldous Darcy, as his features are memorable. Big elongated horns bend slightly back to the shape of his head, following his hairline downward but not curled. His goat tail sits upright from behind, dark long brown hair tied back neatly with two thick bits, draping down either side of his pointy ears. He appears contained but has a wise and noble demeanor. His orange-tinged skin glimmers under the tiny bits of light that pierce through the dust-covered windows and his large eyes blink slowly in contempt.

"Good afternoon. You may call me Mr. Darcy," he says politely and we all follow suit, "Good afternoon, Mr. Darcy." He smiles.

"I'll be your general mentor for this year. I'll be teaching you about all things to do within our world and life itself. Us Capricorns are the general mentors and teachers within the Doh. But anything that is specific, like alchemy, is taught by any classified PNC alchemist Pisces. Healing spells and procedures would be taught by Aquarius PNC healers and so on. You'll never master any of those skills but it's good to have basic knowledge and ability within all areas. Plus, it lets you have a broader understanding of all your brother and sister zodiacs. I don't normally take on first years but I felt I needed to challenge myself this year as young zodiacs are quite unpredictable and genuinely more challenging. You seem to react on raw emotion which directly relates to your instilled traits from your Constellation. But that is what you are here for, to grow, condition, and broaden your horizon of our world."

Aldous turns around to the blackboard and sighs at the mess that has been left. As he proceeds in cleaning it competently, he says, "I'm not used to the first years' classrooms, there's always such a mess and disorder. I'm sure you've noticed."

He turns back, glancing at Isa, who glances away from his intent stare. "Unfortunately, there is a reason for it. Being that you're so easily stimulated, we believed you needed an environment that was literally bland and boring so you could concentrate more easily on your present studies. Don't worry, this won't be forever, only for the time being. Everyone has to start somewhere."

After he finishes cleaning the board, he writes with white chalk: 'Questions?'; turning around, he adds, "Now before I dive into what I was planning on talking about today, I want you to think about anything within the Doh you do not understand and I'll try my best to explain in layman's terms, so you feel more comfortable and confident within your environment."

He stands patiently as Henrietta yells out, "Yeah, why are there so many blood…I mean stairs, why are there so many stairs? How are you supposed to get to places within this maze of a place if you are in a hurry? I mean what if there's an emergency?" Henrietta asks in a manner of disapproval.

Aldous smiles, "Good question. Don't worry, you will only ever need to travel to every area once within the Doh. Remember how you teleported back home? That was because you had already been there and you could teleport back to the Doh as you could visualize exactly what it looked like. Now that you've been to this classroom, you'll be able to teleport here every time you have class from your dorm. Although you can only teleport once you have your purpose numbers, so unfortunately everyone must venture through the uncharted forest as you know."

He waits for the next question, but then Dalton adds abruptly, "But why stairs? And why is everything so far away from, well, everything else!"

Aldous smirks in amusement and adds, "Well, anything that is good is never easy, is it? Imagine if we had everything close you'd take everything for granted. The layout teaches you discipline and respect for everything you obtain within the Doh. Besides, you haven't even seen an eighth of this place. The zodiacs who live within its wall, such as most PNC, haven't even seen a quarter. It has more to do with the fact that most don't want to travel the distance in order to see everything. The more you see, the further you must travel. It would probably take a zodiac a lifetime and make it their dedicated purpose to uncover all its secrets. Next question."

Kendall raises his hand respectfully and you can tell Aldous is impressed with his mannerisms. "Yes, Kendall, what is your question," he says, reading the nametag from his desk.

Kendall gently places his hand in his lap and asks, "From the times we teleported, we chanted Unum. I was wondering, why that is? Considering the obvious?"

Dalton utters under his breath, "What's obvious?"

Aldous smiles again.

"What a great question."

He glances at Dalton who is ignorant of the dim-witted facial expression he has written upon his face. Aldous takes a breath, maybe feeling as though it was a mistake to take on first years. He goes on to explain, "The obvious being because he no longer speaks or converses with us in present times. You feel as though he abandoned us? So why would we acknowledge his name in a chant for teleportation?"

Kendall nods. Aldous draws a big circle on the black board and turns around.

"First off, he does still speak to us. The only problem is, no one is yet to speak or understand his language. Except through death will the Wisdom Tree guide our essence back to Unum. And unfortunately, Apophis never taught anyone Unum's language. But without Unum, we would cease to exist. He connects us to everything and everyone. He completes us like this circle here. We call his name as he is the one who gives us the power of teleportation and every other power we withhold within this world. He is our connection to all things. Our purpose numbers give us direct connection to him. Every time we teleport, it's reassurance that he still exists within Nirvana. Because if he were dead or ceased to be, we would not be able to teleport. In fact, we wouldn't be able to do anything, we'd most likely turn into the instinctual animals of our ancestors without a conscious mind. Our whole world, as we know it, would collapse into an oblivion." He crosses a line through the circle he drew on the blackboard aggressively and continues, "That is why we chant his name and that is why we still acknowledge and praise his existence till this very day. We may not know the reason why he chose Apophis to comprehend his dialect, but I'm sure it was for good reason; we cannot judge something we do not understand nor know the reason to. We can presume and make assumptions, but that is all it is. A presumption is not truth. You should remember that when you hear of any murmured rumor within these walls about any one." Aldous explains with conviction and passion as though personally affected by the very repercussions of rumors spoken about his fellow Unum, who he still feels to have a deep connection with.

He cleans the board, noticeably not wanting to answer any more questions as he begins writing 'Nature Element.'

"Now, I'm presuming you know your own nature element, unless you didn't pay any attention within your Halls of Ivy classes." He glances at Dalton. We all nod murmuring the word 'Earth.' He nods in enthusiasm and goes on, "Good, and I presume you know the other earth zodiacs." He writes Capricorn, Taurus, and

Virgo. We all nod once again. "Now, I'm going to explain to you what defines us as Earth signs along with Fire, Air, and Water zodiacs." He places the chalk down and stands in front of the class diligently. "Now, take out your writing books which are within your desks as you'll need to know the definitions of each element." He becomes animated with his hands as he speaks about the elements, clearly completely competent and confident within this area. Opening our desks, we find books and pencils to write with.

"Earth signs are practical, grounded, and dependable. We generally don't like to take big risks and we much prefer a sure thing. In contrast, we believe in what we can see, hear, touch, taste, and smell. We know we can't live on just inspiration alone and have to put in the grounded footwork in order to obtain what we want. We are down-to-earth signs and like to take care of the finer details of living. Taureans, you are impossible to stop once you have your mind set on something. Virgos like to stay busy, paying very close attention to the smallest of the details. Their work is always seen as flawless within the eyes of others except themselves, forever seeing the finer details of improvement. Us Capricorns can organize many diverse details into a whole easy-to-follow structured project, planning and knowing how to get to the top of our field." It reflects his clear understanding within this field, not having to look at any textbook as he explains this all in detail. He turns back around writing Fire element. "Now who can tell me the Fire zodiac signs?"

Europa puts up her hand and Aldous gestures towards her. "Uh is it Aries, Leo, and um…Sagittarius?" she answers hesitantly, unsure of her answer.

Aldous gives an assertive nod. "Absolutely correct. Aries, Leo, and Sagittarius are your three fire signs." He writes on the board.

"Those graced by Fire are enthusiastic and genuinely larger than life. Being incredibly fiery, if left unattended, can burn out of control like any fire within a forest. So, they must be aware to mind those embers." Aldous winks at us acknowledging the witty joke. No one laughs or even cracks a smile but since he is in his element of mentoring, he doesn't appear to be bothered, caught up in his own world. He continues, "Although they are magnetic, like any fire, they have the reputation for being hotheaded and very much into themselves at times. They find it incredibly hard seeing things from others' point of views but are actually one of the softest signs deep down. They have giant hearts and want only the best for those they care for around them. Fire signs like to tackle obstacles head on, so you must be wary and have patience with them. They are the most adventurous signs of the zodiacs and have a strong sense of self. Aries tend to initiate things immediately and directly. Leos are creative and enjoy putting their heart into their craft. Sagittarius are investigative, free, and able to use their mind very well intellectually." He waits patiently as we quickly try to keep up with his enthusiastic fast-paced lecture.

Turning around and writing Air, he says, "Now, who can tell me the Air zodiacs?"

Kendall puts his hand up and softly speaks with confidence, "Gemini, Libra, and Aquarius."

Aldous flicks the chalk in his hand with an affirmative nod. "Absolutely, Kendall," murmuring the words Gemini, Libra, and Aquarius as he writes them next to Air.

He slaps his hands together after placing the chalk down followed by the explanation, "Now, the Air elements are the maker of the intellectual, smart thinkers and handle abstract reasoning very well. They love to analyze and can work out most dilemmas. That's why they enjoy indulging in relationships, communication, sociability, and intellect. Although humans are only known as a legend within our lands, the Air elements have been described as having the most human-like traits out of any zodiac. Even though they may find it more difficult to understand emotion at times, they always need to discuss things to have higher insight towards a greater understanding in all forms of life. Gemini relies on communication and a constant flow of information as they are easily bored. Libras gravitate towards partnerships, justice, and more beautiful forms of communication, which is why many have been known to be quite the flirts. Aquariuses love to exceed the boundaries in any area. They thrive on seeing themselves as vastly different from everyone else and gravitate towards close friendships."

Aldous looks at the time and goes straight on to the next element, writing 'Water' followed by the zodiacs, calling out their names as he writes. "Now, our last element, Water, which I'm sure you can all tell me is Cancer, Scorpio, and Pisces." He turns around clasping his hands together and continuing, "Water signs are intuitive and sensitive; they feel their emotions more intensely than any other zodiac. They are emotional and nurturing, like a river they run deep. Water elements are guided by their emotions in whatever they decide to pursue. They have strong emotional bonds and much empathy towards others, falling into the 'artistic' realm of the zodiac as they have intense and vast imaginations. They are incredibly selfless towards those they care deeply for, as they'll happily sacrifice their own happiness in order to see the fulfilment in others. Though, their emotions can get them into a lot of trouble as they have a tendency of taking advantage of others, like water manipulating the earth's surface. The water elements are great craftsmen when manipulating any situations in their favor, without many realizing. When dealing with high levels of stress, don't be surprised if they disappear for a while as they like to seclude themselves when dealing with hardships. Cancer often wants what they can't have and holds on to anything that has value. Their passion drives them to succeed in any area that fulfils them with great purpose. Scorpios are natural-born detectives, great at understanding the logic behind others' way of thinking and reasoning. They come with intense emotion but contain it within a strong barrier. Pisces have more compassion than any other sign and are incredibly intuitive, reading clear emotion within any given situation, where most may remain ignorant. This makes them susceptible to taking on others emotions, making them drained." Aldous dot points important parts about every sign and turns around. "That's why they like to keep things cool and neutral. Now that's all the nature elements, time to move on to our quality signs."

Aldous gives everyone a moment to write the information down then cleans the board. I begin to wonder if I should have asked about my purpose number at the beginning of class. Aldous seems incredibly knowledgeable. But I don't want to bring more unwanted attention to myself. Especially from Isa, whose fire continues to be fuelled without my support; her anger grows with every passing year towards me. And I don't want others making accusations either. I have too many unanswered assumptions as it is. I guess I'll just see Bib first and see if she can explain anything.

Aldous appears to be looking for more chalk, gesturing to give him a second. I glance over at Isa who angrily carves something into her desk with her pencil, ruining its ability to write.

I reminisce about the time when we were briefly friends. The time when children have no judgment of one another and aren't aware of the world's dynamics and social differences. It would have been around the time I started at the Halls of Ivy when my father deemed me well enough and I could leave the house without his shadow. I remember how we used to play in the grass fields just in eye view of our houses, laying in the grass where the poppy flowers bloom as they have the perfect amount of shade and sun. They used to make me sneeze but I still enjoyed the tranquility; we could sit in silence with one another for hours talking about nothing and everything. She used to have a kind smile and loving nature. She even brought extra food from home for me, telling me I was too skinny and needed to build some much-needed muscle. Then one day, she stopped coming outside. Days, then weeks went by, and I eventually got the courage up to knock on her front door which was answered by her mother. Petra Edlyn, a stocky, unattractive woman whose skin had broken capillaries riddled all over her large nose and cheeks as though she drank too much. Her horns had decayed and the hair at the end of her tail had mostly fallen off except for a few strands, and it dragged solemnly on the ground behind her. She had a lot of residing anger within her that she still carries visibly on her face to this day. It has aged her far beyond her years, portrayed as a curse. She may have been an attractive woman once, but that time had long passed. She leered at me with a glare of impatience and imprudence. She angrily told me with spit spraying from her mouth that Isa couldn't come out of the house to play with me anymore as it was unhealthy to play with a sick child such as myself, that had no resemblance of a Taurus; it could teach her bad habits. And from now on, I should leave her be.

Her mother was an angry woman, giving the same resentful feelings Isa shares towards me to this very day. As though the curse had been passed down to the generations within the Edlyn family. I remember Petra spitefully saying as I walked away, "Your father is a wretched being. And there's a proof in the offspring."

I never went back after that and I stopped playing outside. Instead, I read every book I could get my hands on within the small Herba library. And there were not many, considering our race is defined by brawn not brains. But brain was the only ally I had. There were only the necessary books for schooling, which I memorized over time. Those hateful words grew deep resentment inside me and my father Adonis said to me one day as he noticed my angry and isolated behavior worsening over time, *"My dear, be careful whose words you decide to harness as you might be drinking their very own poison."* I soon realized the same curse had entered my heart and was consuming me. And those words had been a blessing, because I now harness power within knowledge, something no one could take away from me. I began reading books within the rays of the suns fields, amongst the poppy flowers I enjoyed the company of. Months later, reading in the fields, I heard a door shut from a distance, poking my head up from beneath the grass. I saw Isa walking up the dirt footpath from her house with a small backpack. Without the constant shadow of her mother, I ran up to her with excitement. She saw me running and her expression turned into the same hateful look her mother had given me on that same day.

"What do you want!?" she retorted. I stared at her blankly, astonished that I was looking at the same Taurus. She was covered in horrible bruises but she had buffed up an immense amount, cropped her hair and one eye was severely bloodshot. "Well!?" she spat.

"Isa, I was just excited to see you. I missed you, I thought since your mother wasn't around, you might like to hang out?" I asked. She snorted at me and continued walking, I grabbed her backpack from behind and tugged on it, "What's wrong, Isa?" She did not answer and I continued tugging. "What have I done? What lies did she feed you!?" Then I felt a sudden large pain in my chest. Isa had punched me right in the rib cage and I flew about five feet back. Skidding on the hard gravel, tumbling and ripping my already ragged pants, bleeding from all sort of places. And my sternum was broken; I could not stand nor barely breathe. With short distorted breaths, I looked up at her with remorse and tears in my eyes. The friend I once knew was no longer standing in front of me. This was somebody else, someone I did not know.

No remorse had stricken her, all she said was, "It's all your fault, all of this is your fault, Taura. You'll clearly never understand the pain I've been through. You just pretend it never happened. You're not my friend... We can never be friends and we obviously never were. It was you who fed me a lie."

She pulled the singular strapped backpack over her right shoulder, glanced at her home in the distance and continued walking up the path. I reached my hand out not for help but in remorse. Because although I did not understand, I could see she was in pain. I whispered between gasped breaths, "I'm sorry. Please don't leave." My book had split in two from taking the majority of the impact as I had been holding the book over my chest where Isa had hit, which probably saved my life. Glancing at her home, I started sobbing. I saw her mother in the small crooked window smirking as she pulled the curtain across.

I dragged myself into the side of the road where the tall grass grew. Where no one would see my tears and hear my sobs. Fearful of my father being punished for such displayed weakness as I painfully brought my knees up to my chest, curled my arms around them and sobbed hard and muffled until I fell asleep from pain and exhaustion. I soon woke up within the arms of my father and saw the stars in the blackish blue sky and the fields had been lit up by the planet Venus herself. Nightfall had taken place and as I watched a shooting star sprint effortlessly through the night's stars, I shut my eyes and did not wake for a long time. It was a long time until I allowed anyone to enter my life again. Keeping everyone at a far distance. So, if any one left it did not break my heart again. It was safe, it was protection against my now scared heart. So much time went by developing this strong dynamic I did not know how to let the wall down until I met Europa, she forced her way in.

Europa has a way of doing that to others; she gives you no choice; she is the one who decides who will be friends and who won't. That is why I love and adore her. But to this day, I still don't understand the words Isa said to me on that particular day; she broke my first bone. Now, there are many to match the caged vertebrae that still protect my beating scared heart. But for some reason, I carry around some essence of guilt, which I cannot explain. What had been my fault? What had she been told to believe that I had done so wrong by her? But maybe I'm not meant to understand the pain carried around by another.

I'm taken off guard as I catch Isa looking at me as I have not taken my eyes off her since I started daydreaming about our past life.

"What are you looking at?" she questions sternly, leaning towards me and pushing the carved bits of wood on to the floor. Then Aldous brings everyone's attention back to him as he raises his hand up with a box of new chalk.

"Perfect! Thought I'd never find one. I should really reorganize this chaos. Okay then, quality sign. Who can tell me your sign along with the residing zodiacs? I'll give you a clue. Us Caps aren't related to you in this one. And I want to hear from someone who is yet to speak."

Europa and Kendall both slowly place their hands down and I feel everyone's eyes on me and Isa. I stare intently at the ground, then Aldous says, "Alright then if neither of you are going to decide, I'll decide for you. Isa, can you tell me your quality sign along with the residing zodiacs who you are related to you within this region?"

My head is pointed towards the front of the room but I glance to the side to see Isa's fist bunched up in frustration. Refusing to make contact with Aldous, she says nothing. Aldous turns towards me with impatience, knowing no Capricorn likes a dilly-dallier. "I'll take that as a no then. Taura, can you inform us of your quality sign?"

Still looking at the floor, I feel the blood rushing to my face. I nod and say with soft words, *"Fixed.* Taurus, Leo, Scorpio, and Aquarius."

Aldous claps his hands together, "Very good, Taura! Now, I'm going to test you even further. Can you give me a small definition of a fixed sign? I'm aware you probably haven't learnt of this yet. But maybe you can give me an idea of what you think, just to expand your minds. Make you think for yourselves."

I feel Isa's fuming glare burning into the side of my skull as though she is telling me 'don't you dare' as it'll make her look incompetent. But I say it any way, "Purpose of a *fixed* sign is to maintain, uphold, and defend possessions, responsibilities, goals, or desires in everyday life. They are not easily distracted when a goal is in place, although this can get them stuck in a rut." I recite it exactly out of the textbook which I have read numerous times.

Aldous mouth drops open. "My girl! How did you know that!? I'm very impressed, you're the first new blood to ever recite the exact definition written within the text! You must be quite the bookworm. I'll be keeping my eye on you. I like the unassuming ones." He turns around and begins writing dot points on the board, and I hear the pencil break between Isa's hands, making my reflexes abruptly turn in her direction. We make eye contact, and she mouths the words with a slight whisper, "You're dead."

Then Aldous turns around and continues, completely oblivious to Isa's concentrated death glare. Or maybe it isn't his place to interfere as we are not from his Constellation. But I diligently make a point of turning around and forcing myself to listen, taking my mind of Isa's unbroken intense stare. Aldous continues, "Now, I'm going to add on to that if you don't mind, Taura." I look down at my desk and shake my head. "Great, because what you also need to know is there are twelve houses making up each of these qualities. Each one is made up of four of the twelve. *Fixed* is made up of 2nd house Possession, which includes emotions, self, ability, needs, and wants. Fifth house: *Pleasure*, which includes creative acts, self-satisfaction, procreation, and children. Eighth house: *Sex*, which includes relationships, and 11th house: *Friends*, which includes clubs, organizations, and groups. Now I'll explain the last two qualities along with their four houses. Make sure to write all this down. The next quality sign is *Cardinal*. Aries, Cancer, Libra, and Capricorn, these signs are restless, active, self-motivated, ambitious, and they are often leaders in their community although they can be overly domineering. The four houses making up *Cardinal* are:

1st house, *Self*, which includes life and body;

4th house: *Home*;

7th house: *Partnership*, which is away from self to another;

10th house: *Social Statues*, the role they take within the community. And the last Quality sign is *Mutual*. Gemini, Virgo, Sagittarius, and Pisces, they are highly adaptable, flexible, and communicative, coming up with solutions faster than they can bat an eye, but they can get lost in detail. Their four houses are:

3rd house: *Communication*;

6th house: *Health*;

9th house: *Philosophy*;

12th house: *Unconsciousness*, trying to make sense of one's self."

He waits as we all write the information down, although I'm already aware of all this, but I don't dare make it known, still writing the information down as is. Isa doesn't write down a single word, only fixated upon my existence at this very moment. Now I'm thankful for not asking about my unknown purpose number ten.

Then Aldous looks at the time; bringing his hands together, he announces, "And that just about sums up our time together. I hope you enjoyed it as much as I did. Make sure to study those notes as you'll be tested on them. Now, if you exit from where you came, I'm sure you'll find Demetrius waiting for you outside to take you back to your dorms."

We all stand, picking up our books, and I make sure not to forget my backpack, carefully placing it on my back so the vials don't clink together as they could have moved amongst the hay. Isa gives me a patronizing smirk, suggesting she has me now.

Then I hear Aldous's voice, "Taura, may I speak to you for just a moment?" A big wave of relief falls over my body and I nod attentively, heading up in his direction; even if it's just for a moment, it allows me to think. He waits for everyone to leave then looks at me directly with his large eyes and says with kindness, "Thought you might appreciate a savior." So he has noticed Isa's angry behavior towards me.

"You noticed?" I question.

"Let's be honest, it's not hard to miss. But I'm sure within your Herba community, a blind eye is given or even encouraged by most."

He looks me up and down and I nod.

"I'm used to it, I just try to stay out of her way," I say.

He grimaces, "Unfortunately, that approach won't work in such close proximity of each other and within an everyday environment, especially since no one is around to protect you twenty-four seven. If, or should I say when, she snaps, your death won't be seen as any loss in your Constellation. I'm sure no one thought you'd last this long."

The blunt words chill me to the bone and I feel the blood drain from my face. I'd never taken that into account.

He continues, "I apologize for being so harsh but someone needs to inform you before it's too late. The hatred in that girl's eyes isn't of any small quarrel. It's a deep darkness and it's eating her alive. It grows with pure hatred and you appear to be the catalyst. Do you know why?" I shake my head. "That's a shame, if we knew, we might be able to find a solution. If it were within another Constellation, it'd be different. Unless you were Scorpio, although I've seen them on many accounts to have sympathy towards one so helpless as yourself. Their austerity appears to be related to actioned failure, not an uncontrolled one. I've always believed their water element helps compliment their harshness. But regrettably when your Constellation sees red, there is no stopping them, ignorant of anyone's feelings. And unfortunately, you were born within this harsh Constellation's upbringing; it wasn't always like that. One such as yourself gives them the appearance of weakness, lack of determination to make the perfect warriors, which has, unfortunately, made them blind by their relentless tunnel vision to accomplish the obvious goal. And that's why babies such as yourself are killed at birth. So, Isa would get a slap on the wrist, if that. Because every zodiac's murder is dealt between their own elders and I know Iden Terran is a religious believer in the Taurus law. Even if Constance Terran disagreed, he would have the last word."

I nod, his words must be to prepare me for what's inevitably to come, my fate, ending by Isa Edlyn's hands. Then he uses his index finger to lift my chin, peering at me with slight annoyance.

"Are you just going to lay down that easy?"

Confused by the gesture, I shrug with an unsure assumption, and he continues, "I have said these words to warn you, to be aware of what may appear inevitable. But to also prepare you. And not to lay down like a dismissive dog."

His words have spirit and angry passion behind them.

"I've always barracked for the underdog, and I believe you can stop this if you grow a pair. You clearly have been beaten down so many times you no longer hold belief in yourself. Because any one can do anything, so much as you want it with all your heart. So, Taura Andreas, do you want your life and to live it, with all your heart?"

I become conflicted by his words as I've been told my whole life to take it easy, as my life depends on it keeping me alive. I look up at him and explain my illness I've had since I was born and he replies, "Puppy squash," and I'm instantly taken back, "You're going to let some supposed illness which no one can explain, define you? When there is no actual proof of it killing you? I'm surprised your father didn't encourage you to become strong in order to help your immune system considering your Constellation and their regard for beating the undefinable."

I stare at him and say, "I'd never thought of it that way," thinking of the medicine in my backpack and maybe some training would have been complimentary for my condition.

Aldous throws his hands up in the air as though it were obvious. "Well, of course you haven't! Your reality and world are made up within the walls of your Constellation. Like every other new-blooded zodiac who comes through here each and every year. Thinking they know everything! Naive to the outside world, presuming their Constellation has taught them everything they need to know, no regard for question. Maybe now you can see how our world fell into turmoil when Apophis created 'The Infernum' and we were unable to reunite. No one could see past their own noses. Now, do you see why we must all learn each other's way of living to get a broader understanding?"

My eyes grow with acuteness as Aldous's direct and assertive passion about our world exceeds to a whole other level. He is a true Capricorn, but I do think he needed to let off some steam.

"I'm sorry for being so abrupt, my ambition for a restored world gets the better of me. And so many answers seem so obvious to me, too," he says this whilst leisurely walking over to the small dusty window, fixated on something through its obscurity. Then he unexpectedly pulls open a tiny draw in the small wooden desk that lays before him. Taking something out, he lingers at it for a moment and curls it up in his hand. Staring at that engrossed point on the window again, he turns around and the light makes his orange-tinged skin gleam, identifying his true beauty.

"Here, take this." He opens my hand and places a circular cold object on my palm. It's a small, old, rusty ring. I look up at him in misunderstanding.

"I know it may not look like much, but that ring will give you unimaginable strength. Once you put it on, you'll be able to defend yourself, but you must also believe in yourself and the capabilities it will enable upon you." The ring is so tiny, it only fits on my pinkie. For the first time, my small frame pays off. I twist my hand back and forth, looking at the ring at all angles to see if it has some sort of magical gleam, but it looks completely ordinary. But maybe that's the whole point to keep its power hidden.

"How does it work?" I question.

"That is the part you must figure out on your own as it's harnessed differently within every zodiac. And don't be eluded by its exterior; misjudgment is probably its most powerful enchantment… Alright then, you better get a move on, I'm sure Demetrius won't appreciate being held up." He smiles encouragingly. I pull my backpack up securely on to my shoulders and head out the door. As I pull the door open, I'm stopped again by Aldous, "Oh, and just remember, Taura, you hold the strength within you. Use it when the time is right."

I nod confidently with assertiveness. "Thank you, Aldous," and I head out the door.

Demetrius is waiting and stands with the others upon engraved markings on an extended part of this floor. The same markings with all the Constellations fitting into a circular alignment. The same markings Demetrius had drawn terribly with chalk on our classroom floor, used for teleportation.

"Taura, I was just explaining to the others that these engraved markings are specifically made all around the Doh. So you or anyone else can teleport at any time. They're genuinely found outside specific destinations, such as classrooms, chambers, library, and so on. No one should have to look far. Now come stand with us so we can teleport back to the dorms. Now remember, when standing on the platform, you must shut your eyes, visualize your destination, and chant Unum's name."

Chapter 8

The Dream

Reality and time do not define, they entwine.

After teleporting back to our dormitory, Demetrius leaves us to our devices and informs us he'll teach us to teleport on our own in the morning. The door clicks shut, and I look over at Isa instantly readying myself. But she is already in bed along with Henrietta and Dalton. This puts me on edge as it's unlike her to let something of this nature go so easily. Kendall sits up and reads, and Europa is putting up photos of her family around her bed. I look up and watch the little yellow totem orbs fluttering around the large upside-down tree that constantly drops leaves. It keeps the room smelling of grass fields, trees, and fresh air that remind me of our Constellation. One leaf swiftly falls down, delicately swaying from side to side as it's quickly salvaged by one of the yellow orbs. Floating back up to the tree, it uses the leaf to secure a nest.

I feel my bed tip to one side, Europa sits on the edge with her head hanging down. She is staring at a photo she holds in her hand. She extends her hand out towards me and gestures me to take a look. I grab the photo and I notice it's been badly worn as though she has held it on many occasions. It's of me and her on the first day we met. Her arm is thrown affectionately around my shoulders and she has a big smile sprawled over her face as the sun shines illuminatingly over her long blonde hair. Her small horns are shiny as though she had just oiled them that very day and her Taurus tail sticks up behind her. Perfect skin, beautiful features, and magnetic aura still consume her, and she hasn't changed since that day. I realize I had been gazing at her for so long, I didn't notice my thumb covering my tinier child frame within the photo. A shadow falls over me, making my mousy brown hair look darker than normal. My head slightly hangs in embarrassment. Only slightly seeing my green eyes as I cautiously glance up towards her, probably admiring her beauty as I do now. I always hated photos; I guess that's why Adonis has no recent ones around the home as I always refused to be in any. Apart from when I was a baby, as I had no choice. But Europa always seems to encourage me into doing things I wouldn't normally do. My hair covers the majority of my face and I clutch a large book desperately against my chest as though it were some sort of comfort. My porcelain skin looks translucent. I feel Europa watching me from where she sits on the other side of the bed as I analyze the photo and she begins shifting towards me.

"When I first saw you, I was captured by your beauty. Did I ever tell you that?"

I look up at her as though she was delusional. She smiles at me in amusement and chuckles.

"It's true! You were unlike anything I'd ever seen! Kind of reminded me of the ancient creatures Bibere Sanguinem."

I raise an eyebrow. "The blood drinkers?"

Europa laughs. "Without the blood drinking, of course. Just their beauty."

I shake my head. "You should really go see an Aquarian for treatment."

She tilts her head trying to work out if I'm being sarcastic.

"What for?" she asks curiously. I press my thumb below her eye and index finger against her eyebrow.

Opening her eye and peering in, I say, "Because I think your vision is impaired." She smacks my hand away and rolls her eyes, defensive like every Taurus.

"Do you remember that day?" she asks.

I shake my head. "Not really. Only that you forced me to be your friend."

She smiles, looking at the picture.

"You don't remember how it came about?"

I look at her contorted. "Should I?" as I try to recall details that no longer inhabit my memory. She glances at the green and white bed linen and begins playing with a loose tassel. She looks at the others who appear to be in their own world then lowers her voice to a tiny whisper and leans in, "Ever since you told me about that strange creature and this unbeknown secret power you presumably have, it triggered memories I thought I'd forgotten as it was so long ago. And I'm surprised I'd forgotten. Because it was so bizarre at the time and still is. It was on this particular day when I first met you, I'd seen it."

I grab her hand.

"My power?" I say with anticipation.

She nods slowly, staring at me as though it's too bizarre to say out loud and I wonder how she had forgotten and how I don't remember.

"At least I think so, there is no other explanation. You know how Adonis always kept you locked up inside and you rarely came out to play with anyone when you were very young? Only until later when you were allowed to attend school?"

I nod my head and murmur, "Because of my illness?"

She nods. "Well, there was a day I found you playing alone near your house and he wasn't with you for the first time. I had always been curious about you, because you were so different to everyone else. But I'd never dare go near you. Your father was and still is so feared within the Herba community. And he made it damn clear to everyone that you were a very sick child and no one was to go near you. I understood why he was so over-protective as you were the only precious being left within his life. But the fear fell away when I saw you talking to a large tree beside your home."

My expression becomes indifferent. "That's not anything special, all children talk to animals and wildlife."

Europa begins playing with the tassel again nervously. "I know, Taura, it wasn't that. I know this sounds crazy but the…the tree, it was responding to you. As though it were a conscious being. It wrapped its branches around you as though it were hugging you; it responded when you spoke to it with nods and shakes. It drew in the dirt and you drew beside it as though you were both communicating. And being the child I was, I didn't realize how odd it was at the time. You know children are ignorant to the conventional reality of the world. And a Taurus talking to a tree, that's not normal. Only the Sagittarius are presumably able to do that and that's only after going through a tremendous journey through the woods when they're very young for many years learning its language. And so many don't come back. But you were a small child, a Taurus child. And no tree comes alive for a Sag, they're only able to read it and understand its indiscrete signs. Don't you remember, Taur?" she questions.

I shake my head. It's as though my brain has blocked out important details of my life, only remembering events but no detailed elements of the memories. Probably because that part of the day doesn't exist in my mind. I recall meeting Europa but that might only be evoked as she told me, creating memories from the words others bestow upon me. I look up at her and she continues trying to trigger my memory.

"Once I saw this, I had to speak to you. I wanted to know how you were talking to the tree and I wanted you to teach me. I wandered up to you from within the fields where I was playing with my brothers and sisters, taking prints of insects with the Memoriae device. No one took any notice of me leaving. But as soon as I got near, the tree froze as though I'd been imagining the whole thing. Then you noticed me, intensely stared at me with stiffness and fear. You abruptly looked around for Adonis but I told you it was okay. That I was a friend and you glanced at the Memoriae in my hand and asked, 'What's that?' in your tiny voice, and I had explained it was a device that captured special moments in time. And I gestured for you to stand next to me so I could show you. You hesitated then insisted on picking up that ginormous book that laid next to you. I thought maybe you were going to use it to defend yourself." She laughs. "And this print is from that special moment." She points to the worn picture within my hand and I can see the branches of the tree falling beside me as the light hits her from the outskirts, but I still don't recall the memory. "Afterwards, I asked you how you were speaking to that tree and you looked at me with confusion and softly said, 'Can't everyone do that?' That was when your father Adonis came roaring out of nowhere and asked what I was doing, and to leave right at that moment, taking you within his arms. I ran as fast as I could back home; I was terrified of your father. I kept this photo, pulling down all the random pictures I had from our Constellation and placed us right in the middle of my wall. Lingering at it, I knew we'd be best friends." She squeezes my hand. We lean back against the headboard of my bed and we look at one another.

"The annoying thing is, Euro, I still can't remember. And it just makes more unanswered questions. How could talking to trees be seen as an unbeknown evil power?" Europa ponders on it for a moment and says, "I know it doesn't make much sense. Maybe we need to sleep on it. And will go ask Biblio…Bibo…whatever her name is, tomorrow."

I smile looking at the picture. "Maybe you should stick to calling her Bib when we see her, she might take offence to saying whatever your name is."

Europa chuckles. "Yeah you're probably right, I'll make sure to do that." She kisses me on the forehead, smiles and hops into her bed. I pull the warm doona over my shoulder and lay my head on the soft pillow. The lights automatically go out and the room is illuminated by the small yellow totem orbs that leisurely hover above us. They sway in and out of the tree, which slowly put me to sleep.

I find myself staring into the big blue eyes of the woman who holds me tight within her grasp. And I watch the same singular tear fall from her eye and I wish every time that I could save her. "*Te amo*," she says softly. I stare intently at her face but it's impossible to get a full profile as she's distorted within the shadows of the forest. "Who are you?" I ask within my penetrating stare as she lovingly holds me. And for a moment, I hope time might stand still. But once again I find myself falling and I feel the air stolen from my lungs from the impact of the ground.

I am woken by some sort of felt smothering my face. I begin to panic, not knowing what's going on as I can't see anything. I become claustrophobic from lack of oxygen as my breath becomes short from adrenalin and anxiety. Several hands and arms are restraining me on my bed. And I try to scream, which is immediately muffled by a large sturdy hand. Harsh words are whispered close to my ear and I recognize it instantly.

"If you make another sound, I'll slit your throat from ear to ear. You got it," Isa's voice is angry and filled with immense rage. I nod slowly and she carefully takes her hand away and her breath leaves a horrid smell as I'm given little relief to breathe within the thick cloth. I am easily lifted up, placed on a shoulder and taken out of the room. I feel for the ring that Aldous had given me not too long before and I can feel its rustic texture still secured around my pinkie, which gives me some hope as I know Isa Edlyn is going to kill me.

I soon lose track of where we are, my body bouncing to the rhythm of the steps taken. Then I hear a squeaky sound of a door opening. The one who is holding me punches another.

"Careful, stupid. Open it slowly." I recognize Henrietta's voice and I know Dalton would be opening the door. I am placed on a hard chair that feels old because it becomes unstable as soon as my body weight is placed upon it. The cloth is ripped from my head. Isa, Henrietta, and Dalton all stand before me. I choose to say nothing and wait, before adding fuel to the fire.

Isa begins, "So, you think it's wise to humiliate me in class, do you? What makes you so special that you think your life is held above all others?" she spits, presses a hard fist against my face, knowing she is about to boil over.

I look down at the ground, thinking carefully before I speak. "Isa, I never asked for any of this. I understand the way you and others feel about me and it's completely justified. Why should I live when others who are stronger than me are still deemed unworthy, I get it. But it isn't my fault."

I know deep down words aren't going to be my savior today but I try to prolong the beating, in hope I can figure out this ring in order to save my life. Her fists squeeze hard into her palms and suddenly a hard-stricken pain burdens me to my right cheek. I feel the rupture of bones breaking beneath my skin. Drool begins falling from my mouth, saturating my pants. She laughs hysterically, turning around abruptly and says, "That's right, it isn't your fault, is it? Because you're just a victim, never taking responsibility of your own life and repercussions it has caused. It's all Daddy's fault, isn't it…well, sure your dad has played a massive part but you should have done us all a favor, Taura Andreas. You should have taken your own life if you feel so forsaken about the other lives taken. But once again, someone else has to take out your dirty laundry and I guess today that person is me."

She looks at me exasperatedly, but the pulsating pain in my cheek has stricken me into shock. "Now your father, feared Adonis, can feel the same pain he has relentlessly bestowed upon others, thinking he has any right to override the rules of our Constellation. They should have taken more than just your mother. They should have taken you too! But now we must be reminded every day of your existence and what horrors it has brought upon our land!" Her words instantly pain my heart. I couldn't bear to burden my father with any more agony than he's already endured. Then anger begins to riddle my veins. I won't allow her to hurt him. I twist the ring round and round my finger, praying for the ring to work. But the throbbing pain of my upper cheek seems to prove otherwise.

Isa becomes angrier about my non-responsive behavior and begins beating me harder than she ever has before. The psychedelic expression on her face has turned her into a rage-stricken monster, fuelled by red and blinded by her own self-conceited tunnel vision. Foam falls from her mouth as blood sprays on to her face

123

with every blow. I feel and hear every breaking sound of bones, one after another, face and body. The color of blood fills my vision and becomes impaired from the intense swelling. Then unexpectedly she stops. And any sort of anger I had, has now subsided. My head drops, my body goes limp, and I now realize my back is broken, losing complete feeling and function of my body. All I can see is the blood drain profusely from my face and mouth as my head hangs lifelessly. I strain my eyes to glance up through the bare vision I still retain to see the repulsed expressions of Henrietta and Dalton who hold either side of Isa's arms. Isa rips away from their grasps, panting, and says, "What are you two doing! You knew the plan was to kill her." They say nothing.

Both glance at one another expressionless and Henrietta says, "Because you just continue to beat a dead battered body. She was dead after the first few blows. Her neck's clearly broken."

Isa snuffs, "She's lucky it wasn't prolonged. Hell, it's more than she deserves. Her and her wretched father."

Isa wipes the bloodstained hands on her clothes. Dalton pointlessly adding his two cents, "Well, she definitely looks dead." I feel the blood draining coherently from every inch of my body, watching the pool of blood expand from the outer perimeter of the chair at a rapid rate. But instead of feeling the life drain before me, I feel it slowly becoming profusely stronger. I want to live with all my heart, I internalize. I don't want to be known as the girl who got beaten to death by the bully. The one that should have died at birth.

"Alright, let's get rid of the body," says Isa.

"Wait, I think I saw her move," says Dalton.

Isa whacks him in the side of the head. "Don't be stupid, have you seen the bloody broken mess in front of you. She's unrecognizable… In fact, I think she looks better that way," she snuffs. Dalton shrugs, walks over, and throws me over his shoulder as I continue to bleed.

We make a small journey to the twirling stairs in the center of the Doh.

"Alright, get rid of it," Isa says.

Dalton peers of the edge and I can't even see the bottom, we must be far up.

"You want me throw her off the stairwell?" Isa gives him a dumbfounded look and gestures to throw me off with her hands and Henrietta asks, "But they'll find the body?"

Isa smacks her forehead with her palm.

"That's the point, idiots. Make it look like a suicide. No one will care about her life any way, she was worthless to our Constellation. Even if they did notice the battered bits, they won't think to question it. They'll think it's for the best. Everyone knows her life was insignificant."

With my neck being obviously broken, my body is a complete rag doll. I'm only able to watch my life end before my eyes. And with a pulverized jaw and swollen tongue, I can't even muster a scream as she's also crushed my voice box. Dalton takes one more look over the edge and with ironic care, he gently slides me off his shoulder.

I fall face first. My hands sprawl out uncontrollably. My body rotates upwards and I'm now staring at their three unremorseful faces. Is this really my fate? I feel the wind press hard against my back, knowing any minute I'm going to impale the ground and my whole body will be an unrecognizable broken mess.

"I'm sorry," I say inside my head, thinking of Adonis. I squeeze my eyes shut and as I do I see the image of the lady's big blue eyes from my dream. If only I knew who you truly were, other than the loving woman in my dream.

"*Te amo*," she says again.

"I'm sorry," I say repeatedly inside myself. Tears fall delicately away from my body and I can watch them float right in front of my eyes, following me down to the end of my journey. The feeling is too overwhelming and I can't stop crying. "I don't want to die!" I scream with curdled words from the broken trachea as blood leaks down my throat and spits out of my mouth as I cry and speak at the same time. "Please! I don't want to die!" Then I feel the number ten on the back of my neck begins to burn like it does when I teleport. My neck jerks and hangs as my whole body comes to a halt in mid-air. I slowly glance either side of me and I can see the beginning of twirling stairs either side and notice the floor just beneath me. I've stopped just before I've hit the ground. Unexpectedly, I begin to become aware of my body again as though my broken neck has healed itself, but that's impossible. Then immense amount of pain begins to take over my body; my broken bones begin to snap, crack, and pop uncontrollably into place. My skin begins to burn and my body jerks sporadically with uncontainable movement. I continue to scream incoherently as my vocal chords realign. I hope someone will hear my call. But no other life form comes to my aid and I don't have the energy to go on. The pain is so overwhelming, why didn't I just impale into the ground. The agony continues to increase and as it becomes too unbearable to withstand. I black out.

I awake with a slight headache. My cheek and body lay hard against the stone-cold ground and my left arm has gone numb as though I'd been laying on it for a long time. How long had I been out?

I sit up, suddenly realizing my body is fine. Maybe even better than before. I look over my hands, arms, and the rest of my extremities, lastly feeling my neck and face which are both completely intact. "How could this be?" I murmur aloud. I take note of the ring, lingering at it. I guess Aldous had come through with the goods after all. I begin to become aware of my surroundings and realize I am no longer in the foyer of the Doh. I am concealed within a tiny corridor. How did I get here? There is a larger corridor a few feet in front of me. I peer around each corner, startled by voices in the distance. I abruptly move back into the shadows and listen to a couple of earthly voices approach. I glance around and see one male and one female PNC Aquarian healers carrying a large coffin-like case, one at either end.

"She isn't exactly big, I don't know why we have to carry her around in this overly sized tomb. Plus, it mustn't be very comfortable in there, I feel sorry for her," says the woman. "I know, but unfortunately Theophilus doesn't want to chance any one seeing her. You know it would cause an uproar. She's meant to be a mythical legend. We're nearly there any way then she can stretch her legs, have something to eat and we can go get a bite before we begin testing. I'm starving!" The woman laughs in a warming way.

"You are always hungry, where does it go anyway?" he glances over his shoulder with a sarcastic expression.

"My arse!" they both crack up laughing and place the case down as they come to a large steel door, pulling out some sort of device that scans the back of their necks. Their purpose numbers light up and the door clicks open. They pick the tomb-like casket up and continue through the door. Then something hits me on my shoulder, giving me a shocking fright, and I see it's a handle from a broomstick. Glancing back and seeing the door slowly closing, I spontaneously grab the broomstick and run over to the door with the handle extended out in front of me, stopping the door before it closes. I look down each end of the large corridor, with its red velvet carpet and high ceiling walls, some sections of the roof built out of slabs of extended glass with clouds moving idly by against the bright blue sky. The only life that exists within these halls is the large old paintings of legendary zodiacs caught in a moment of a war-stricken time. Fighting the Infernum, which looks contradictory as zodiacs fight other zodiacs. They hang on either side of the tall walls. Their ancient eyes watch on, stuck within the chamber of limbo. Decorative gold is incredibly suggestive as it illuminates with great detail on an already over-exaggerated wall. Vases stand tall with the remnants of the once beautiful flowers lay lifeless below, ornamented by wilted beauty.

I step inside, taking the broom with me so no one suspects a prowler. Another dark, short narrow hallway leads to another secure door with a tiny dusty window that beams with a bright light. I carefully walk up to the door and stand on my tippy toes, wiping away some of the residue. I peer through the base of the window to see an immensely clean white room with infirmary equipment everywhere. Small and large tubes of strange mutated creatures lay with water-encased capsules, looking to be small babies of some sort, but I can't place the species. They look to be dead and deformed. Some with two merged heads, bulging eyes, insides hang out of their body and some don't have a single limb with a barely formed head. As I scan the room, I come across the encapsulated tomb which has been opened and is now empty. The two Aquarians stand over something on a table, injecting some sort of shots. The male opens a small compartment and pulls out a tray with some kind of sustenance and places it next to the specimen. The Aquarian woman reassures it with her humanitarian customs and gestures to the male to get a move on. They pack up some things and the male rubs his belly with enthusiasm. She gathers her things and they leave through a back door, gesturing to the creature that they won't be long.

A soft, creamy pink creature lays on a table with no physical protection but the bare skin that looks delicate to the touch. Long mousy brown hair grows on the top of its head and falls delicately off the table as its back is turned towards me as it lays on its side. It has no scales, horns, tail, claws, or hard shielded exterior. It's the first species I've seen that looks weaker than me within this world. Unexpectedly, it sits up, its back still facing me. It lingers at the contents of food on the tray the male Aquarian had left, rummaging through the bits and pieces but decides against eating. Its ribs stick out profusely through its back next to its bony spine. And I become troubled by its fragile exterior; it clearly needs to eat something because it appears to be starving to death. Struggling to step down from the counter, it places one foot down after the other and holds its weak frame up with the support of the steel table. *What is it?* I ponder. It begins to turn towards me and my eyes widen with curiosity. My mouth drops wide open, it cannot be. But it is, the woman from my dream.

Those same big blue eyes linger at the tubes of deformed babies, their color has faded to a translucent surface of decay. Although she looks different, her cheeks are sunken in and she has a kind of sad gray pigmentation upon her skin, but I know it's her from the eyes. Shutting her eyes, she places one hand against a tall tube and presses her head against it. The same single tear falls from the same eye from my dream. *Are they her babies,* I wonder. Why are they deformed and dead in a tube; they should be laid to rest next to the Wisdom Tree. I place my hand on the glass and tears begin flooding uncontrollably from my eyes. I want to know if she's okay; why isn't she eating and why are they preforming tests on her. I begin banging on the glass lightly at first with one fist but the glass proves to be immensely thick. So, I start using both fists hitting it as hard as I can to get her attention. She suddenly glances my way, not noticing where the noise is coming from at first. Then we make eye contact and I instantly know the dream was not a dream but a memory.

At first, she turns whiter than before as though she had seen a ghost. And I continue to bang on the window as she stands in shock to what she is witnessing, clearly unconvinced about her own sanity. She runs over with tears now, flowing from both her eyes, staring at me with bewilderment. We stand looking at one another, and I notice we look incredibly similar, apart from the color of our eyes, plus my horns, tail, and slightly more athletic frame. She places her hand against the glass and I place mine against hers.

"You're alive," she manages to muster with a soft delicate voice, which I can barely hear through the thick glass. I nod, although I don't understand why she'd presume otherwise. Maybe she thought I was abandoned in the forest on that particular night, the only memory of her that still clings to my subconscious, reminding me every night of her existence.

"Who are you?" I ask. She looks at me confused as though I should know the answer. Her big blue eyes stare lovingly deep into mine, piercing my heart just like that very night. And I feel the answer already lays within me, but it couldn't be.

"Your mother," she says with tears still falling down her dry, sunken face.

My world begins to spin. My mother? But my mother is dead? And this lady looks nothing like my supposed mother. Thinking of the picture that lays beside my bed, I don't even know what species she is. So many unanswered questions begin to consume my already muddled mind.

"Penelope?" I ask. She shakes her head in confusion,

"Penelope? What lies have they been feeding you!" she spits lividly. "You know who I am. I'm…" The two Aquarians come barging in. Both gasp, staring right at me. The frail creature turns into uncontrollable rage. "You told me she was dead! You told me they left her in the forest! I thought the world was doomed! What did you do with what's inside of her!?" The male runs over, cautiously approaching her with his arms sprawled out as though trying to calm a wild beast.

"Please, you must come with me. I don't want to have to give you the injection," he says with sincerity. She picks up a small sharp object on a nearby steel table and starts flailing it about.

"If you lay one finger on her, I swear, I'll kill every last one of you!"

I'm instantly taken back by her hostility; she reacts so instinctively on emotion unlike any other specimen I've ever seen. The Aquarian soon restrains her and she turns towards me with struggle. "Run!"

I stare at her big blues eyes. The eyes I thought I'd never come to know. I don't want to leave her here. Then I notice the other Aquarian female charging toward me. I instinctually run to the door from where I came, but it's locked, realizing I don't acquire the two Aquarians purpose numbers. I press against the corner of the wall and she comes through, approaching me calmly. She kneels down to my height and holds her large single hand out to gently seize me. "It's okay, I won't hurt you. Come on, you'll have to come with me. This is no place for someone like you."

Chapter 9

The Bwbachod

Ugliness is the most misunderstood of beauties.

Now being led down hallway after hallway, I have no idea where I am or where I'm being taken. All the surroundings appear to look the same as the previous one. I wander across to get to that infirmary. I'm being escorted by the Aquarian female who caught me within the chamber of my supposed real mother, which would explain my lack of Taurus appearances and ability. But now I question the story I have been told all these years. Who am I really? And what am I if my mother is that strange, weak, and fragile creature?

I manage to get the courage up to ask, "May I ask where we are going?" The Aquarian glances behind her.

"You don't have to linger so far behind, I won't bite. I promise." She smiles kindly. I manage to produce some sort of comforting expression, recalling what I've read about the Aquarians, admiring their friendly, kind, and magnetic mannerisms. I can see why they make friends so easily and why animals love them. Their aura is powerful yet neutral and inviting. Even though she found me in an area that is completely off-limits to someone of my stature, she still manages to keep a warm but detached demeanor as she probably takes me somewhere that is not all that kind but makes me feel comfortable. I walk slightly faster, trying to keep up with her large steps and as soon as I'm hurriedly walking beside her, she says, "May I ask how you managed to not only get into that restricted infirmary but find it in the first place?"

I instantly become hesitant as I don't really know myself. I peer at the ground and say, "It's a long story."

She smiles. "I bet. Well, you get to explain your long story shortly."

We eventually come across two large wooden doors, made out of a warm dark timber with beautiful artwork crafted upon it – a large snake, I presume to be Apophis, stands upright; the giant Wisdom Tree with all its animals and creatures surrounding its trunk, basking in all its glory, encapsulated within the twelve zodiac emblems, circulated around the perimeter. My eyes slowly gaze over every element, all the tiny animals and the immense detail that's gone into them. As my eyes crawl across a small rabbit, I notice the two humans standing above it. I didn't notice them at first amongst the busy portrait but I recognize them as they are always mentioned in our historic studies, drawn in the exact same way: the legendary Adam and Eve. I look closely at Adam's face who I recognize from all the books and then I turn to Eve who at first I only recognize from the books until I peer closely at those same big eyes. The woman from the infirmary, that was.

I turn to the Aquarian woman. "That creature in the infirmary, that…that was Eve!?" I don't even ask for confirmation as I already know it was Eve, the female human. The Aquarian doesn't look at me; in fact, she keeps the same composure but does not disagree with my theory either. Then I realize I had been so taken by the artwork, I wasn't aware we had been standing here for quite some time. She could have hurried me in before I had noticed, but she didn't. Did she want me to know? Am I half human? And what did Eve mean by what did they do with what's inside of me? Is she implying my supposed unbeknown evil power?

The doors begin to creak open to an even larger room with even taller ceilings and ostentatious artwork, unlike any I have seen before. A giant marble open fireplace burns diligently, creating the warmth that gently presses upon my face as the doors had opened. A giant glass window makes up majority of the room and stares over the whole Nirvana valley as though this place were separate from the Doh as it sits in the center of Nirvana. Because we now peer at the world from a place where only the gods should bear witness.

A long seamless table stands isolated at the end of the room in perfect center of the glass wall with a stuffed trophy animal sitting beside it on the right-hand side. It looks to weigh around four to five hundred kilos with high front shoulders and a sloping back, over six feet tall, positioned snarling with its mouth open and lips curled, showing off its large sharp teeth. It's ferocious and a powerfully built carnivore who I'd hope to never bump into and I wonder what Constellation it's from. We approach the table and before I take another step, the Aquarian places a hand affirmatively in front of me as though there were some kind of danger. Then a deep fierce growl starts to penetrate the air, coming from the animal whose life I'd thought had been robbed long ago. My heart begins to pound so hard, it's all that bounces between the walls of my ear, *thump, thump, thump.* Now profusely sweating, my body prepares itself going into fight or flight mode, but before my reflexes find the courage they need to react, the Aquarian gently holds my arm and says, "Don't make any sudden movements. It's not a dangerous animal, unless you provoke it. It may come across as cold and detached but that's only because it's an independent creature. Slow to show emotion unless they deem you trustworthy. It just doesn't trust you as yet. It's actually very humble and loyal soul. It's only doing what it's told as it's an incredibly faithful and protective friend." I don't take in much of what she says as I am fixated on those sharp teeth, dripping with saliva, clearly hungry for its next meal.

Unable to calm myself, I try to hide, shifting my rigid body behind the Aquarian as she still maintains her calm and comforting aura. Amazed by this, the animal doesn't take its eyes away from me. In fact, it hasn't even taken notice of the Aquarian. How could it define me as the threat in comparison to a large Aquarian who could be mistaken for a close relative of a giant. Then a familiar voice enters the room.

"If you don't calm yourself, he'll be able to follow that wretched scent anywhere you go, no matter how far or quick you can run. He won't harm you unless I say otherwise. His name is Kerit, he is my most dearest and trusted friend." A large live bird is thrown from behind Kerit, screeching as it falls. He catches it effortlessly in his mouth without even having to glance where it had been thrown. It squabbles loudly until a loud crushing sound of bones deform between his teeth, making it apparent how easily he'd devour me within those large jaws. I wince, listening to the bones pulverize, blood dripping from his jowls. I try to breathe deeply to calm myself as I can see he thrives from my fear, saturating my scent. Single white feathers are scattered in different parts of the room, leading toward small piles laying around Kerit. Then two large white wings appear, feathers fall leaving a trail behind as they drag on the ground, followed by a prominent scraping noise. And now I place the voice to the overgrown wings – Theophilus. He turns towards us and for the first time I'm able to identify his facial features as I've only seen him from afar. His piercing green eyes peer through squinted eyes, slanted downward with thin lips and high cheekbones. He is cleanly shaven with short white hair, sleekly pulled back with not one hair out of place and wears the same elongated robe from the common room, with the Virgo colors of green, white, and yellow. For an ancient zodiac, he doesn't look a day past twenty-five but his demeanor and prodigious wings say otherwise. His presence in this close proximity makes me feel as insignificant as a mouse. His large wings face me as he lingers out the large window. "He needs to eat whilst his food is still alive so he obtains the most efficient nutrients. Once a creature is dead, most of what is good dies with them," he says blandly as though lives were nothing but to be objectified, to be used at will.

"So, I hear you have been prying around restricted areas?" His once welcoming tone of voice has disappeared from when we first entered the Doh. A complete contrast to a now stern and direct manner.

He glances my way, waiting for a response, and I stand completely stiff not knowing what to say but the truth. "Uh…yes. It is true, Patriarch," I say in a quiet tone. I don't see the point in justifying it as I myself don't understand how I came about it.

"So, tell me how you knew about it, as it's incredibly far away from any area you've travelled too? It would have taken you weeks on foot, unless you had already been there before. So teleportation could have been an option." I twist the ring around my pinkie, hesitantly thinking of Aldous and wanting to explain without involving him as this might be a ring that's forbidden against some one of my caliber. I look up as he still stands turned away from me.

"To be completely honest, Patriarch, I'm not entirely sure how I found that particular infirmary." I explain the story on how I was kidnapped during the night, beaten so brutally my spine was broken, paralyzing me from the neck down. Then thrown off the center from Doh's twirling stairs. I informed him of the recurring dream and that woman's eyes had been one of the last images I had seen until I had stopped above the ground. The brutal pain that followed, inflicting me from what I believed was my bones rejuvenating and how I had passed out then woken right next to the infirmary. I added about the supposed ring I had come across in the library and noticed it had some sort of power on other recurring days I'd had it, trying to divert the story away from Aldous. I take the ring off and go to place it on the table but Kerit insists on growling heavily.

"It's okay, Kerit, leave her be." He obediently stops, but his ears are pressed hard against his head and his expression is angry and untrustworthy. Turning around without meeting my gaze, he picks up the ring and looks at it carefully. He holds it up high and brings it back down. Turning towards the table, he holds his hand out flat with the ring sitting delicately in the center of his palm.

"So, you presume this rusted, worthless junk teleported you there?" I nod cautiously. He crushes the ring effortlessly within his fist then allows the crumbled pieces to fall from his fist to the table as though it were powder. My mouth drops open and my eyes widen as he stares emotionlessly at me with a serious countenance. "Wherever you found it or…should I say, whoever gave you that ring had told you a lie. It's just an old, rusty, worthless piece of trash. And I want you to remember there are eyes everywhere within this place. So be careful the lies you decide to feed me next."

The blood drains from my face and I nod, pressing my chin against my chest. Kerit's heckles are now standing high on end as he doesn't take his eyes off me.

Theophilus turns back around and asks, "Now that we have that established, do you know what the creature in the infirmary was?" My eyes glance at Theophilus whose wings now face me again and I quickly shift my eyes back to the floor.

"The female human…Eve?" I hesitantly answer. His head turns towards me, only seeing the side profile of his face.

"Indeed, you are correct. And I presume she told you, you were her daughter?"

I nod again, with a bewildered expression. I wonder how he knows all this information.

"Before I explain why that is a preposterous concept, let me explain the story behind Adam and Eve. They were created to be a part of our world as another creation of Unum, but to be honest, I never understood their purpose or why Unum had created them in the first place, as they are weak and unable to defend themselves as you have seen. Plus, they're too chaotic when it comes to their emotions and as you also saw, unpredictable. Many of us could see they would slowly kill one another due to their own greed, gluttony, laziness, wrath, lust, pride, and envy. And we knew due to these over-encumbered emotions, they would destroy anything that got in their way. So when Unum left, Adam disappeared and Eve went crazy as she had lost her first daughter and developed many complexes about Adam's abandonment. Now you may presume that it could be you. But that would be impossible as that happened centuries before your time. You may look alike but that's only because you represent certain traits to that of her long-lost daughter, considering your physical qualities. She has done this before, reached out. We believe she has a strong telepathic power and you probably do to, that is probably how she connected to you. And that is why we keep her hidden and only known as a legendary tale. Because unpredictability is not something that can be controlled, only contained."

Suddenly, the door creeks open and slams shut behind us. I turn around and to my disbelief, I recognize the creature that stands in front of me as he had been standing in my bedroom only one night ago. We make eye contact and his expression becomes instantly tense, probably not noticed by others who aren't aware of our first encounter. His eyes quickly dart away, pretending not to recognize me, and hurriedly walks past me with a pan and brush.

Kerit uncontrollably starts to foam from the mouth, trailed by small broken rumbles followed by a big roar, making the creature jump in fear and clean even faster. Theophilus waits, being amused by the torment Kerit induces upon the poor creature, verbalized within his facial expression. Then Theophilus slowly holds up his hand and says, "Calm yourself, Kerit, there is no need to do that every time the Bwbachod enters the room. I understand his presence is irritating but we have to allow him to do his meaningless jobs. Besides, everyone must have a purpose." He smiles patronizingly and doesn't even acknowledge him as he sweeps up the tiny bits of crumbled residue from the ring. He's the Bwbachod? I hadn't known what they looked like. So, it didn't occur to me when the Pisces SNC overseer was informing us that Theophilus had the last one enslaved. The Bwbachod quickly cleans up the impetuous mess and leaves as quickly as he entered, deliberately avoiding my intent curious stare.

"Now as I was saying, before I was rudely interrupted… Taura Andreas, you appear to have some sort of gift you were unaware of until now. And it also appears you don't want to recognize it by yourself, as you seek other superficial objects, such as that pathetic ring, to give it justification. You must learn to harness this gift, but don't make it aware to anyone. Many don't like someone different within this place.

"We genuinely like to know what's certain, otherwise you might end up like the Bwbachod race. And you might find yourself in that same recurring position again from last night. And I don't know if this strange power of yours will save you every time, as you yourself don't know how to control it. So instead, I encourage you to try to understand it. Bring forth its true identity in your own time. I understand you don't have much time between your studies for such things. So, I'm going to allocate someone to help you, who will also report your progress. But this, too, must remain a secret.

"And last of all, you must not inform anyone about Eve, otherwise I will have you eliminated. I'm willing to help you but I'm not willing to help one who causes unnecessary rumors which could be detrimental to the Constellations' unity. Something of this nature could cause those to lose faith in the system and I am willing to eradicate anyone who disrupts the balance and peace that has taken years to build. Do you understand?"

I nod repeatedly with assertiveness. "Yes, Patriarch, and thank you. I promise not to tell anyone." He turns towards me and forces himself to look at me; it's as though he tries to hide some kind of disgust.

"Good. Now go on with your day as if nothing had happened and I shall call for you again."

The Aquarian woman escorts me to a room that resembles hundreds of others from the outside. But as we enter, I see it's a planetary site for teleportation. And I ask as we enter, "May I ask what that Kerit creature was?" She glances down, closing the door carefully behind her not making eye contact with me.

"He was once a bear. But now…" she shuts her eyes for a moment, searching for the right words, "now he is more like a distant relative." She lays her hand out, introducing me to the room, not wanting to add anything more. There is another planetary orbit of golden planets representing our ruling gods that spin around in their usual trajectory. It looks identical to the one in our dorm, just more exorbitant, like everything else within this sector of the Doh. The golden planets slow their trajectory as we approach so I can step on the platform. The Aquarian woman grabs my hand delicately and unexpectedly. She glances around as though there could be someone listening and realizes a small frustrated sigh. Looking at me with purpose, she says, "Be careful."

Not understanding the intent of the comment, I nod.

"What is your name?" I ask, she lets go of my hand and steps away from the orbiting golden planets and says, "Cordelia Dion."

I slightly smile as the planets now begin to pick up pace.

"Thank you, Cordelia," I acknowledge as she had been kind to me even though I'd placed her in a difficult situation. Shutting my eyes, I begin to chant the name Unum, visualizing our dorm.

Chapter 10

Inhabitants of Living

Belief lies within the stories of our upbringing.

Now standing back in familiar ground, the planets spin at a protracted speed, coming to a slow halt, so I can step out. Pausing momentarily to catch my thoughts, Eve's big blue eyes and fragile body enter my mind from the infirmary. Do they have other incredible powers such as the telepathic abilities Theophilus spoke of; their fragile state must be a ploy to be underestimated, being overly protected in that infirmary. And who's going to teach me to connect and control my supposed power? Walking towards our dorm, I glance up at our Constellation's poem. Before entering, I murmur the last two lines:

> *Beware color red,*
> *fixed arrow makes his bed.*

Isa comes to mind. Theophilus didn't give me advice on how to deal with her. Now she'll be well aware something is just not right as she saw me fall to my death. I wonder what she'll do in response; the thought brings me chills. And I'm given a fright by a startling voice, "Well, hurry up and recite the rest of the poem. I haven't got all day."

I frantically glance around the dorm, but it appears to be empty.

"Up here, genius."

I look up and notice the impatient and irritated expression of the Taurus doorknocker peering down at me, beneath his large golden eyebrows.

"Oh sorry, I haven't entered on my own before."

He rolls his eyes. "Memory of a gold fish you have."

I quickly read the rest of the poem in a hurry and he sighs. "Don't breed them like they used to," he remarks disappointed. The emblem above the door glows bright and the door begins to open.

To my relief, no one is there; class must have already started. The little yellow totems dance around me as I enter; softly pushing them out of the way, I grab my books and as I turn to leave, the other backpack catches my eye. I had nearly forgotten to take my medicine. Thinking of my father, I grab a vial and shove it in my pocket as I'm running late. Walking back through the door, I turn around and say to the doorknocker, "Maybe you shouldn't be so quick to judge… I mean, you're the one who knocks on doors for a living." He rolls his eyes as though he's been alive for too long and has lost all patience. He now looks at me as though seeing me for the first time; he stares for so long, it becomes almost uncomfortable.

"You know…I've seen those eyes before." His eyes drift away and his expression becomes hard as though trying to recollect a lost memory. "You can read a lot from someone's eyes. I see the same ignorant eyes coming through this door each and every year. But those eyes, they were different from the rest," he pauses, thinking on it for a moment and I curiously answer, "Was her name Penelope…May?" I suggest my mother's maiden name as she would not have been married to my father when starting the Olympus Trials. His large eyebrows raise in recollection.

"Penelope May. Yes, that could have been it," he says with reminiscence. "She represented the old Taurus ways of life… Not like now, all brawn, no brains. You should be grateful to have such eyes. They have a history that tells no lies."

I go to ask about my mother, but he shuts his eyes and transforms back into the lifeless doorknocker he deceivingly portrays to be.

I catch myself in a reflection of a glass mosque, peering at the abstract image that stares back at me. I wonder who I am if not my mother's daughter, represented within the universal depth of my eye. I take a big breath and head over to the planetary teleportation device; hopefully I'm not too late for class.

Standing hesitantly before the door, I feel for the vial in my pocket. I take it out, popping the lid and shoot it down, wishing I had some water with me to wash the horrid taste out of my mouth. I wait in procrastination before I enter, taking a big breath. I glance at our Taurus emblem above the door and enter the classroom. As I push the door open, I hear Aldous's voice. He's has only just started, "Alright, today's lesson is all about the Constellations' inhabitants and living." He stops as I enter. "Well, look here. Taura! I thought you had gone astray," saying the last word with slight spite as he glances at Isa. "No one knew where you were. I hope you're okay?" he gestures sensitively. I nod, feeling the discomfort of everyone's eyes staring at me.

Everyone waits for my explanation and I manage to croak out, "I wasn't feeling well. So, I went to the Aquarian healers in the early hours of this morning."

He smiles warmly, signaling to my seat.

"Well, we're all glad you're feeling better. Please take a seat." Europa is beaming at me with excitement, clearly relieved of some previous concerns. I notice Isa's expression through my peripheral vision, but I don't dare acknowledge her. She stares at me as though she too has seen a ghost, which seems to be a recurring expression of late. Dalton and Henrietta stare blatantly too. Aldous glances at all three of them.

"Did you three want to take a picture? Or did you have something to share with the class?" he says with an impertinent expression.

Isa quickly readjusts herself.

"No, Mr. Darcy," she says, searching for her voice. But continues to glance at me periodically as though I might disappear.

"Okay then… Now as I was saying, constellations and inhabitants of living. Unfortunately, this lesson won't be a very interactive one. You'll need to read this important content and take notes as you can't take the books with you. I've placed spare copies of the particular book you will be needing inside your desks. And be careful, they're very old."

I open my desk and take out the neatly placed book. It's old and tattered, with a dark green tinged color and a fading golden boarder. Written in bold writing is *The Deeper Understanding of the Twelve Constellations*. Aldous begins writing on the board with his new chalk he found from last class and I suddenly notice he has tidied up the whole classroom. No more cobwebs hang from the corners of the room, there is not a speck of dust in sight, and the air is no longer dusty as I see the windows have all been cleaned and remain open to air out the room. Even his desk is neatly organized.

'Page number 55' is written on the board and underlined. He continues to write more underneath as he speaks, "Alright, turn to page 55 and get started. You will need to know the names of where each Constellation inhabits, certain rituals, how they go about everyday life, why they do things the way they do and how it has shaped them into the particular zodiacs we have come to know today. And the allocation of each NC, PNC, and SNC. I'll be doing some marking at my desk, so if you have any questions, please put your hand up and no talking. This is learning time."

I see Europa beaming at me and I smile with reassurance. Aldous clears his throat in attention and I turn my book to page number 55.

"Constellation Inhabitants and Living"

The Scorpio Constellation

Scorpios live within a desert called Solitudiem, inhabiting houses made from bark, rock, or clutter; they love the warm sand and hot sun. Scorpios are possessive of what's dear to them, keeping their families well protected, not interacting with each other all that often, unless they have profound respect for one another, they do not waste time on those who they do not deem worthy; even their children must interact and marry those who are respected amongst the community. Although they may seem hard, Scorpios feel an immense amount on the inside being a water sign. These zodiacs are taught to fight from the moment they are born due to their harsh living conditions. To be the highest sought-after male and female within their Constellation, they must defeat every Scorpio of their sex at the age of 20 in a combat field known as Mortem Arena. This displays an example of ambition and bravery, striving to be the best. And depending on what young Scorpios exemplify will depend on how sought-after they are within Solitudiem. The bravest of the brave marry one another, to breed stronger, fiercer offspring, obtaining the highest respect within their community which Scorpios hold most pertinent. After Mortem combat, the weakest Scorpios commit a ritual called Secundum, by which they stab themselves in their intestines and pull the blade up towards their sternum, if they accomplish this ritual, they will keep their dignity and respect within their family. But if unable to perform this Secundum ritual, they will be banished from the community, as they are believed to breed weakness within the tribe. And living on the outskirts of Solitudiem is incredibly dangerous as terrifying monsters live within the desert, and without the protection of the community means these Scorpios generally die not long after they've been banished.

NC Scorpio

Stay within Solitudiem, working within the community and every month the mediocre Scorpios are taken to have their serums drained, as it's needed throughout the Nirvana land for both medical and felonious reasons (used to put those who have done wrong by Nirvana to death). As their serums replenish plentifully after a month and are left with plenty to spare, the stronger ones are left to protect their tribe from the monsters that challenge their existence.

PNC Scorpio

They are mostly seen as guards within the Doh alongside a few other zodiacs like Cancer and Sagittarius enforcing the law.

SNC Scorpio

They are great fighters, as their bravery and focus has no bounds along with their skill to fight as it's bred within them from the day they are born.

The Sagittarius Constellation

They live within a forest called Maga. From the time a Sagittarian can walk, they are sent out in the wilderness, with only a bow and arrow on their back. This ritual is known as Deambulo where they must learn how to become one with the forest Maga. Hunting and gathering all that mother nature has to offer but no more than one needs. This is how they develop the skill to talk to the forest and obtain an incredible skill in archery, rarely missing a target. Being in solitude for so long, they become finely tuned on how the forest speaks and once they become one with the forest, they are able to find their way back to the Sagittarius village called Philoponus to reunite with their family which is followed by a month of celebration. The ones who do not find their way back, disappear, never to be seen *again. It is believed they become a part of the forest and are thought to be the ones who whisper to the Sagittarians who have the ear to listen to Maga as they speak through her. The Sagittarians who are now one with Maga are worshipped as it is thought that without their silent whispers through Maga, the Sagittarians and Philoponus would cease to exist, never able to find their way back home.*

NC Sagittarius

Stay within their constellation, hunting and gathering for all who live within their village Philoponus.

Breeding and mentoring the new generations to come.

PNC Sagittarius

Hunt and gather for the Doh's food supply. They're able to go deep into the forest, places that are hard to track even with a well-developed map, gathering and hunting for rare delicacies.

SNC Sagittarius

They venture to places far off the grid, certified and deemed capable to search for Infernum inhabitants and other geographical information which is given to the PNC Geminis, adding to Nirvana maps. But even they can go missing or be obtained by the Infernum within this territory, that is why this is a highly skilled stature; very select few Sagittarius make an SNC statues. They are also used within the Nirvana army, taking advantage of their great skill in archery, but only the ones with the greatest potential. Never missing a shot, no matter what the condition.

The Capricorn Constellation

Live on a large Crater Lake, their main village is called Aquaterra, residing between the large mountain known as Deus and the water surrounding the land inhabitants known as Motus, as they need constant access to both. When a Capricorn is born, they are either physically gifted with a fish tail or goat's tail. This representation determines where the child will reside for the next 11 years, before coming back to Aquaterra. If one is born with that of a fish tail, they will live in and beside the water Motus, learning all it has to offer about life's erratic, unpredictable, passionate, and exhilarating emotion, represented in the metaphysical form of water. It is believed this creates their deep philosophical wisdom of understanding the ways of life, being as unpredictable as water. One born with a goat's tail will reside within Deus. Learning all about life's sturdiness, durability, resilience, and strength which they also believe is the representation of the harsh, dry living conditions residing around Motus. There is no nonsense played out there as it's kill or be killed. It is believed this creates their highly ambitious trait. Once the 11 years come to an end, they come together within Aquaterra, mentoring each other for what they now lack. Those who were taught by Deus lack empathy, kindness, and emotion. Whereas those who come from Motus lack strength, sturdiness, and resilience. By the time they turn 21, they have become momentous mentors, combining each other with the strength of Deus and the emotion of Motus. Due to this severe combination, Capricorns are perceived as hard and cold, showing no empathy. But this cold exterior is due to Deus's teachings, covering the deep emotion they feel intensely inside taught by Motus. Never allowing any one to read or see their true state of mind emotionally, until one has earned respect and trust. This mysteriousness gives them an eluding beauty.

NC Capricorn

They spend their time with the children within Aquaterra, teaching them about philosophy and wisdom. Some residing in either Motus or Deus, attending to those who spend those short precious 11 years to understand the unpredictability of water or the harsh merciless mountain.

PNC Capricorn

They are the mentors and teachers within the Doh as they have a higher understanding of life which is vastly sought after. SNCs still look up to their Capricorn mentor, as a PNC Capricorn is carefully selected amongst the few greatest mentors.

SNC Capricorn

They are a small selection who have an incredibly strong connection to their telekinetic powers. If shown to have great potential, they are put through grueling training to perfect this ability.

The Aquarius Constellation

They live hidden behind a giant waterfall within a giant cave that leads to a secret village called Coelum. Only the animals of the forest know of its location along with the already residing Aquarians, but they rarely venture from Coelum. They only come out to speak to the animals who come by the waterfall when they're injured or in need of assistance; they must make a home calling noise to make it known. When an Aquarius is born, they're taken out of Coelum and placed beside the waterfall, where a family of animals will be waiting to take the Aquarius baby to make it a part of their own community. This is how they learn to talk to the animals and once this ability is obtained, the family of animals will guide them back to Coelum to reunite with their Constellation. But if an Aquarius does not come back, it is believed they turn into the animal itself and this is thought to be *the reality of every animal within the forest. They too were once Aquarians themselves and this is how they're able to communicate with all the animals as they stare into the eyes of their ancestral bloodlines.*

NC Aquarians

They heal the animals of the forest who fall sick or become injured. Although they'll never interfere with the balance, for example, those who eat flesh must survive. If an animal is being hunted and comes to the water that lays before Coelum, an Aquarius will not appear. It is only within an unpremeditated action without an effect on a reaction will they assist.

PNC Aquarians

They are the Healers within the Doh, healing those who are sick or become injured in battles. The general Aquarius has a couple of strong languages for particular animals, especially the ones who brought them up.

SNC Aquarius

They have a vast range in mystical animals and creature tongues. They are the few selected who show great potential for communicating with other animals and creatures beyond the ones who brought them up. They are constantly learning new dialects for creatures and animals who are believed to come in great assistance, especially in battle. But the rarer the animal or mystical creature, the more complicated the tongue, this skill takes years to master as there are many dialects within the Nirvana land. Over time it has also been documented that a powerful Aquarian such as an SNC are able to persuade and control the minds of animals, becoming one with them.

The Pisces Constellation

They live in a beautiful giant lake that travels for many miles, called Mollia. Surrounded with many different types of plants and agriculture. Pisces can walk amongst the land zodiacs but they need constant access to water or moisture, otherwise they'll die from dehydration. They'll carry around Scindet, which is water castrated into the shape of a tear, expanding into a large sticky sheet of illusive water. It covers their whole body, keeping them hydrated for up to 24 hours. Once a year for a 12-hour period, there will be a blood moon. This is the time when the Pisces will reproduce as it turns all of Mollia Lake red, allowing them to see a violet-lit pathway to a secret protected location, where they go to mate and lay their eggs, because their offspring will not survive the treacherous environment within Mollia Lake. Once born the Pisces start out as a fish, now having to use their intuition to find their way back to Mollia as it grows a particular fungi called Colstridium – their only food supply. If their intuition is weak, they will die from starvation, becoming a part of the lake, which happens to most Pisces born into this realm. But the ones who have strong intuition survive, growing into the Pisces we know of today. Since they are incredibly intuitive, they make great alchemists and or sorcerers.

NC Pisces

They stay within Mollia, living within their small community, helping one another out with everyday living and marine life. They use their water control, helping to improve the environment to thrive abundantly as they can control the water's temperature too. Being selfless beings, they enjoy nurturing externally from themselves. They also study the herbs and agriculture within their environment.

PNC Pisces

They work within the Doh, making large scales of powerful potions. These Pisces are carefully selected as they have a high level of intelligence regarding science. They are able to make potions that are incredibly complicated and dangerous. There are also the sorcerers: Pisces who are born with a strong psyche are capable of reading bones and casting spells.

SNC Pisces

They are born with a great connection to the water, as they are able to control it in a remarkable way. Creating tornados, tsunamis and manipulate into other external objects. But this type of Pisces is incredibly rare. On record, only one shows this kind of potential every decade.

The Aries Constellation

They live on the largest mountain in Nirvana called Hircum Mountain. The main village is called Cornibus Village, inhabiting the majority of the Aries population which lays at the peak. Some live in small huts scattered around Hircum. Being half goat, they love to be up high. Aries are renowned for their constant confrontational arguments. Being ruled by the planet Mars, the god of war, it is no wonder they'll never back down from a fight, which is a great endeavor on a battlefield. Winning many battles with enemies as they never give up until the last breath. But this trait kept causing too much destruction within Cornibus Village as fights kept breaking out, causing a lot reconstruction of homes and communal areas. These constant battles also took Aries away from their daily duties. So, the Aries Elders, Ardon and Athena ordered a fighting stadium to be created to satiate their urge to fight. They called it Compono Stadium. Now when two Aries clash verbally, they have to settle it within Compono, which entails smashing into one another until one is defeated or the other gives up (a rare occurrence). Keeping count on who has the most wins and loses within Compono, the one with the most wins is vastly sort after as many try to challenge him/her.

But with such a magnetic charisma, they definitely know how to celebrate a victory. Never holding a grudge against one another, they genuinely just enjoy a good battle which is how respect is earned within their region. But this can be taken as arrogance from other Constellations as many don't enjoy a confrontation like an Aries.

NC Aries

They stay within Cornibus village, finding a mate and breeding many children. As they are the child of the zodiac, Aries are great with kids. They tell the ancestral stories of their courageous ancestors to not only their children but all offspring of the Constellation. Teaching them the ways of the dynamic, fiery, adventurous Aries. They also clear mining tunnels within Hircum Mountain, mining for gold and other prized stones and minerals.

PNC Aries

They clear areas for construction within the Doh, uncharted forest (create new pathways) or other Constellations to erect new edifices. On occasion when a Sagittarians is searching a deep part of the dangers of the uncharted forest, they sometimes come across a blockage, which inhibits them from venturing into a particular area. An Aries will then be sent in to clear the blockage for the Sagittarius.

SNC Aries

An Aries is a rare individual, they are gifted with an immense amount of strength. Like most Aries, they can destroy anything by charging through it (allocated area). But these Aries are able to destroy a considerable amount of area in one hit. Their impact creates a domino effect. Once they hit one object, if that object hits another, it creates a ripple effect, causing great destruction, which comes in great use when fighting a large army as it can kill a vast number of individuals at once.

The Taurus Constellation

Live within a village called Herba on a large, green, flat paddock. Although Taureans are known to be natural great warriors, this talent comes with the upbringing of toughness and rigid routines. Once a Taurus is born, they are inspected by the Elders, to determine if the baby is strong and suited to represent the land. If determined weak or feeble, the baby will be carried to the woods and laid to die to become a part of the land. If determined strong, the baby will be brought up learning how to fight from the day they can walk. This protocol is established for both male and female. If a Taurus wants to make it to adulthood, they must be fastidious in their approach otherwise they'll perish as the Elders are incredibly regimented, constantly testing them, placing them in situations where they must fight for their lives, whether it's proving themselves physically or mentally. Their psychologically challenged too, enduring camps which leave them without the comfort of little clothes, feeling all elements and they must hunt for their own food and water. But it's these challenges that make the Tauruses who they are today: grounded, independent, patient, stubborn, possessive and incredibly determined zodiacs, which causes their tunnel vision affect. Also, it's these teachings that also keep them humble as they appreciate the good in life, seeing the beauty in all things. They are the type of zodiac who won't go down unless you put them down. Their greatest pride is to die within the battlefield. However, due to their harsh, brutal lifestyle, this Constellation must be monitored as it's the sector with the lowest population.

NC Taurus

They have simple but important lives within Herba as they love the routine for daily life. They also keep the foundations for the Taurus generations to come by implementing the ancient grueling teachings of great past warriors. But also own their own small shops within the small community village and they love to farm and grow their own food.

PNC Taurus

They are personal bodyguards for zodiacs who need protection when going into different Constellations or venturing into the uncharted forest along with the guidance of a Sagittarius. They also help soldiers within the Doh to learn a vast variety of skilled weaponry.

SNC Taurus

SNC Tauruses aren't rare but aren't common either. As their upbringing is so harsh, they're taught to strive for the best, this is where their tunnel vision for a particular goal comes into play and their patience genuinely gets them to where they desire. An SNC Taurus is an incredibly skilled fighter, strong and hard to kill. It is warned not to make one angry because once they see red there is no stopping them.

The Gemini Constellation

They live within a habitat that constantly alters, called the Labyrinth. It's a diverse and complicated habitat, where not many choose to venture. Walls and passages constantly change. And at times colliding with creatures which must be defeated in order to move forward or riddles given by fays, you must solve or perish. The main village in the middle of this puzzling Labyrinth is called Simul Village. This is where all Geminis reside. It's a beautiful, dynamic place where there are constant and forever changing tasks and activities as Geminis get bored easily. A Gemini can get around the Labyrinth effortlessly, without colliding with monsters or having to solve riddles but that's if you know the right way, although if unfortunate enough to take the wrong turn a Gemini has no dilemma in solving riddles or defeating the Labyrinth's strange creatures. Because when they're children, one of their daily tasks is solving the Labyrinth; they believe this is a great way to stimulate their active minds. Some do perish or become lost forever, believing to become the monsters within the walls themselves. That's how the Labyrinth constantly changes, never being the same at any point in time. The Geminis just become accustomed to reading its walls. They're able to guide other zodiacs through to Simul, if permitted. But if another zodiac ventures in alone, they normally die or go insane. This environment represents the Gemini's dynamic and forever changing and growing personalities. Teaching them to be dynamic, never to miss a thing, enthusiastic and versatile. It's what gives them their charismatic personalities. But since it lacks consistency, this too reflects within them along with boredom as they're accustomed to constant stimulation.

NC Gemini

NC Gemini stay within Simul, helping to build towards their vivacious community, this expresses their serious ambitious side to strive for constant growth and stronger community. This makes Simul a place where many would love to reside, as it's beautiful and animated. They constantly hold festivals and competitions/tournaments where Geminis are continuously having a good time and challenged to grow – forever stimulated.

PNC Gemini

They put together geographical maps of areas discovered by Sagittarians or design beautiful pieces of architecture (example; The Doh). These Geminis are carefully selected amongst the few who are able to channel their highly strung energy into large in-depth projects, never missing any small detail.

SNC Gemini

A Gemini is one of the rarest SNC zodiacs born within Nirvana. Being so ardently dynamic and mastering their ability to control their individual yin and yang, once split (an incredibly hard ability to master), Gemini can actually fight like a bird, dancing in flight as they hit with perfect precision, knowing where each other will be at the exact moment. This makes them highly sought-after but incredibly rare.

The Cancer Constellation

They live in a large shallow rock pool within a village called Vadosus. Smaller rock pools are constructed on the outskirts of Vadosus as some Cancers like solitude with their family, only having to come to Vadosus when in need of supplies or a village communion. They enjoy the water from their crab descendants but don't depend on it for their survival like the Pisces. Since Cancers are incredibly family orientated, they genuinely have large kinship. With an average couple having up to six Cancerian children, creating a community of their own which makes them unbelievably protective. Within each family, grandparents play a huge part, passing down their wisdom and are shown great respect. They learn to become agile and quick from their rocky environment, having to pounce from rock to rock in order to get to any place of importance. From falling on the rocks from a young age, their skin becomes tough and hard. Creating such secure family structure, a Cancer develops deep feelings and passion as they are brought up surrounded by unconditional love, this gives them this uncanny ability in believing in themselves, without unreasonable doubt just like those of their loved ones. This belief and passion can come off as unrealistic, but not to a Cancerian. Be warned when their Planetary Moon is full in the sky, as their strength triples and their emotions become psychedelic with irrational behavior, it's highly stressed for all other zodiacs to avoid Cancers at all costs during this time, until the full moon has passed. This transition is called 'the Lupus period.'

NC Cancer

They are set on having a large family of their own within Vadosus. Bringing up their own children and teaching them the ways of the crab and traits of their own family. All they want is to love and nurture. To create an environment which they can call home and watch their children grow up.

PNC Cancer

Have a passion for protecting, helping, and serving their world to become a better place. So, they can be seen as soldiers within the Doh alongside the Scorpios, or are used in secret assignments within the Doh as they are light on their feet and can genuinely go in and out of places unseen.

SNC Cancer

They are highly sort after as they make great assassins; light on their feet, they move at unfathomable speed and are incredibly quick to react. These particular Cancerians are also able to produce a shield so powerful, it goes beyond their own body to cover a small army.

The Leo Constellation

Live on a large rock called Superbia, which stands above a vast valley that contains many animals in which they hunt. Although Leos have their own distinct bloodlines, they will never separate from their pride. They sleep together, eat together, train together, and hunt together. Learning all about team work, they take it in turns on leading the pride into a hunt. The main leader holds all the control within the Constellation and is known as the Silverback. The Silverback has a special ability which is mental persuasion over the pride. If a Leo somehow manages to resist this and becomes rebellious, they're declared exiles and they have to live on the outskirts of valley where food supply and shelter is nearly non-existent. But to disobey a Silverback comes with great difficulty as the whole pride is strongly connected to the Silverback. Once exiled, they'll most likely die soon after as a Leo can't live in isolation; they depend on others to give them purpose. Although a Silverback is not an Elder, the pride will always follow his instruction unless Elder commands otherwise. The pride will not like it, but they will obey, unless the Silverback objects then they will stand by him until death. Nevertheless, an Elder can challenge him to an Imperium: a battle to death to take leadership of the pride. In fact any Leo can request an Imperium, even those who are declared outcasts as a last resort or because they believe their leader has become incompetent or too old to lead but they must prove themselves to the pride in order to take over control. An Elder cannot have both roles, on the contrary, this has happened in the past so the Elder can pick a more suitable Silverback. It must be a Leo who the pride respects, otherwise they will not follow his leadership, which will lead to a breakdown of the pride and the whole Constellation which would disrupt the zodiac balance. Since Leos are able to transform into a more animalistic version of themselves, they make incredibly hunters. There isn't much about their makeup that suggests weakness; they are natural born killers.

NC Leo

A Leo who just wants to be a part of the pride and nothing more. Maybe wanting to achieve a Silverback statues one day, but they genuinely enjoy everyday Constellation life.

PNC Leo

They are generally the commanders within the Doh soldier community. Rarely seen amongst Doh soldiers, they keep order behind the scenes, organizing and scheduling a rock solid system. Their great leadership skills make others gravitate towards them. Rarely having a problem with others challenging their authority.

SNC Leo

The commanders or leaders within other regions of the Nirvana Army. They are never seen watching from a far, as they love to get in amongst the thick of battle. Showing off their animalistic killing ability and basking in all its glory.

The Virgo Constellation

They live on a floating island called Insula Island. It constantly moves around the sky within their Constellation, although this one area is incredibly large. To find Insula on the surface is like trying to find a needle in a haystack. But there is one distinct landmark: a small patch of rain where it continuously pours and above is where you'll find Insula Island. The reasoning for this strange occurrence is due to the large river called Iudicium. A dormant Volcano captures water from the sky and within the volcano water collects and creates a river called the Iudicium River which integrates into Insula's landscape, Insula, eventually finding its way to one of the many cliff points, falling down to the surface, so flooding doesn't occur, creating the strange patch of rain that never stops falling. The river also supplies water to the Virgo population and is also known as 'the judgment river.' The day a baby Virgo start walking, they are placed into the river until they make the journey off the cliff. This is how they learn to fly. If a baby Virgo does not fly, they will perish upon the hard surface. When other zodiacs come by their small bodies, they are renowned as fallen angels. It is believed if they do not fly, the baby is simply too weak, determining a birth defect. Virgos only want perfection within their Constellation. On the island lays an ancient village made out of pristine stone called the Lapis village where all Virgos reside. They are constantly seen coming and going from Insula. No other zodiac is allowed to step foot on the island. As the Virgos believe they'll simply disturb the perfect serenity they've created over many generations. If one wants to talk to a specific Virgo, they must meet them on the surface where the rain falls ceaselessly.

NC Virgo

They stay within Insula, keeping the perfect order of their routine way of living. Genuinely spending a lot of time within their organic farming estate as Virgos will not eat anything they have not grown or fed themselves. Their diet is a plain one, perfect nutrition to keep their bodies in optimal health and this diet is a main priority within the village as they want to achieve the perfect mind, body, and soul.

Regularly seen meditating and training rigorously with great discipline, the Virgos never complain nor boast about achievements as the Virgos are humble zodiacs.

PNC Virgo

They are generally in politics within the Doh, trying to find order and perfection throughout the land. Coming up with new ways to make sure everyone has a purpose within each Constellation and the land. These ideas and concepts are then passed on to the Patriarch and Matriarch.

SNC Virgo

Although most Virgos can control elements of the wind, an SNC Virgo isn't a common one. As they can control the weather, they create havoc, like hurricanes and tornados or the perfect day filled with sunshine and blue skies. Once they have mastered this ability, they are given long golden swords to shine bright in the sky. A signal to those on land that they are being watched upon by safe eyes. Flying above scouting out particular areas, especially if the Nirvana army goes into battle.

The Libra Constellation

They live within a village that is concealed within the tallest trees of their Constellation called Arbor Domus. It displays beautiful huts, constructed out of wood, ferns, flowers, plants, bridges and rope made from roots of particular trees, creating an illuminating and beautifully gorgeous residence. Libras live amongst the flora and wild as nature gives them balance and harmony. When a Libra becomes unbalanced, clearly portrayed in their eye color, they are sent to the forest floor, known as Pacem, until they find peace within themselves again. An unbalanced Libra is careless, erratic, over emotional and irrational, saying or doing particular things that are extremely out of character. Once placed on the forest floor, they'll frantically look for Arbor Domus again. But the village will only appear when they stop looking and find harmony within themselves again. And it will appear as if it had been there the whole time. This is the same for any zodiac who steps foot in the Libra Constellation. As they'll firstly be stepping into Pacem. Anyone is welcome, unless a zodiac has turmoil within their soul, then they'll never find the village. Every zodiac is warned, because if your soul is corrupted, the forest will never allow you to leave either. Not unless you find peace, if not you'll become a creature of the shadows until the end of time. Some believe the turmoil causes one to transform into a Wendigo creature, similar to a cannibal. The same goes for the fallen Libras who do not find themselves again.

NC Libra

They take care of the forest, helping it flourish and grow. Some spend more time with the animals, making sure not one baby is unattended or unfed. Some work on the trees and flowers, every Libra has a place. But once the sun goes down, they'll return back to their haven Arbor Domus as the Wendigo's live within the shadows and that is when they hunt.

PNC Libra

They deal with quarrels within different Constellations, settling matters by offering solutions as they are natural born diplomats and have great influence over others. If this doesn't work long term, they'll use their power of telepathy to influence the zodiacs to help maintain peace, if this technique fails, the zodiacs involved must sit a trial.

SNC Libra

Although all Libras have influence over others and telepathic abilities, an SNC Libra has incredible telepathic power. Hearing the minds of all who are near and if channeled, this power can search out particular zodiacs who have disappeared, if still alive. They can also control others physically and speak to them through their minds. This type of Libra is not only rare, but in fact the rarest amongst the SNC zodiacs; this kind of power takes decades to master along with a disciplined and gifted mind.

Please Note:

All SNCs within each constellation are incredibly hard to come by, some more than others. There is great potential if more were obtained to conquer Apophis and the Infernum. But, unfortunately, there are only a few number of SNCs. It wouldn't be difficult for the Infernum to take over our land as they mask the same abilities as we do, only more powerful as they are not in control. Apophis is the only one who has the ability to encourage the true authentic power of any individual. This is why testing is so grueling as we must find the trigger for each zodiac to release their true power as it is the mind that dictates our level of power we relinquish. We must conquer the mind to unlock one's true and endless potential. Sending zodiacs in to fight against a force like the Infernum controlled by a powerful and ancient spawn, such as Apophis without proper preparation, would be suicide and the end of life as we know it.

I jot down small dot points since I've already read this book and feeling grateful for Constance who used to secretly bring me books like these from the Doh when I was young as I was always unable to participate in most activities. I only make notes of elements I had forgotten in detail, wanting to get out of class as quickly as possible, but the time drags. I begin to feel the lack of sleep from the night before as my adrenalin has worn off. Aldous walks around the room checking our work. He stops beside my desk and picks my book up, glancing at me with a suggestive smirk, knowing I must have read this book too. Aldous places my notebook down, delicately moving to the front of the class. "Alright, that'll do for today. Make sure to go over those notes and memorize them," he says sternly, pausing and adds, "You'll have class with your Aquarian Elder, Cassidy Dion, tomorrow, learning about your totem animals. Demetrius will guide you there and I'll see you later in the week." As we get up, Europa becomes ecstatic, quickly collecting her books and now abruptly stands beside me in anticipation. But before she opens her mouth, Aldous speaks again, "And Taura. Mind if we have a word? Won't take a moment."

Europa's expression becomes annoyed, rolling her eyes subtly.

"I'll wait for you outside," she whispers. I nod. Turning around, I catch Isa staring at me as she walks out of class, being her usual focal point of attention.

He waits as everyone leaves the room and I stand facing him, feeling for the ring that was once sitting around my pinkie.

"So, I see the ring gave you the strength and courage you needed?" he says, looking down at my hand, his expression now becomes curious. "Although I'll admit I didn't expect it to work so fast," gesturing towards my naked pinkie.

I shrug, "Mr. Darcy...what was the ring actually designed to do?"

He gives me an entertained expression as if to know something I don't.

"What do you think it was designed to do?"

I shrug. "I'm not entirely sure...to give me courage and strength?" I say unsurely.

He smiles. "Precisely, and it's done exactly that, hasn't it?"

I feel as though we are on two separate pages. So, I ask without trying to give too much away, but insinuate, keeping Theophilus words in mind, "Well...by courage do you mean finding places unknown to you? And by strength do you mean...the strength to heal one's self?" For the first time, Aldous appears to be without words, thinking on it for a moment.

"Well, not entirely, unless those sorts of things were already hidden within you." I look at him with frustration.

"What are you trying to say?" I say blatantly.

He stares into my eyes with earnest. "The ring was nothing but an ordinary ring, it held no power. But by telling someone otherwise beholds and gives great power to an ordinary object. It gives them the inner strength and courage they wouldn't have thought otherwise. Essentially, it makes you believe in yourself. Now would you have believed in yourself if I had just told you too?"

I shake my head.

"Exactly, some may see it as deception but really that's an ignorant way of thinking. It's a gift of encouragement to lift a blind fold, that otherwise would have been lost within darkness. Sometimes, we have to find belief in something as ordinary as we see ourselves in order to see the magic we chose to ignore."

Aldous's wise words of wisdom cease to astound me, now I understand. I nod with enthusiasm, not knowing what else to say as he adds, "Well, I'm glad you found your feet. And whatever did happen last night, it appears Isa won't be bothering you anymore. Just don't let your head get the better of you, keep an eye on those inner thoughts. Now you better get a move on. I'll see you soon."

He turns around and returns back to what he was doing during class.

"Thank you," I say quietly as I walk out of the classroom, knowing he refers to my negative mind that cripples my reality. I now walk out of the classroom to the twirling stairwell. Europa stands in front of the entrance, twirling around, surprised by my arrival and quickly insinuates for me to look at something. I peer from behind her to see Leon, my mouth drops open as he shoves a piece of paper into Demetrius large chest and suddenly my hearing comes back to the present moment.

"You have no jurisdiction here, I've been asked by Theophilus himself," Leon says domineeringly. Demetrius rips the paper from Leon and begins reading it fastidiously then throws the paper on the ground, stepping on it with disregard.

"Well, it doesn't make sense for a zodiac of your caliber to teach her how to fight, especially from another Constellation, she should be learning from someone of her own region."

Leon shrugs. "Well, isn't it obvious? Clearly, no one in her Constellation took the time to teach her. Seeing as you all saw her as worthless. They must think highly of me if someone of my caliber has been assigned to help her harness her natural-born skills. Something in which she should have been taught in the first place."

Leon's pent-up anger towards Demetrius begins to show as his muscles begin to ripple and his rage begins to take over, but he contains the transformation by closing his eyes momentarily, taking a big breath and it subsides.

Demetrius smirks at him. "Clearly…because you have so much control over yours… Didn't realize how much influence Daddy had."

Europa pushes me back against the wall as Leon's bone structure begins to change, bones break and expand as his muscles ripple with growth and blood supply. Then he transforms into the more animalistic version of himself: the natural born killer I've read so much about. He relinquishes a giant lion roar, echoing through the whole serenity and covers Demetrius's face with saliva. He stands completely still and without fear, he wipes the drool from his face and with a patronizing expression, he spits on the ground beside Leon as though he has just proven his point. Turning around he sees me and says, "You've seen what he's capable of, Taura. He's reckless, not to be trusted. I'll be keeping a close eye out, don't worry."

And he disappears down the twirling stairs.

Chapter 11

The Care Taker

Careful the thoughts you nourish – unknowingly you'll grow a forest.

Leon Sol is hereby the caretaker of Taura Andreas, holding complete responsibility in teaching Taura on how to reach her full potential within her region. He is given full access to Taura, after class hours to teach her how to harness her inner powers. Anyone who interferes with this process will have to answer to Theophilus Malis.

Signed
Theophilus Malis

I fold the crimpled piece of paper back in the envelope Leon had given me as I follow him up the numerous number of stairs. He gently takes the piece of paper and places it back in his pocket, holding on to my hand a little longer than comfortable.

"Thanks," he smiles charmingly, "and I just want to apologize about before. That genuinely isn't like me, but your overseer definitely knows how to get under my skin. He's a very serious kind of fella, wouldn't you say?"

I'm taken aback by his charismatic way of talking as I found him rather arrogant when I first met him. It's kind of appealing, I'm not used to one expressing so much, but he makes me feel comfortable. Taureans don't talk all that much, they just learn to get on with it.

"Yeah, he's always been like that," I say.

"I guess I'll have to get used to it," he chuckles. "So, are you okay with this?" he asks kindly, staring at me but I look away from his penetrating golden eyes.

"Why wouldn't I? Theophilus did assign you to me."

He laughs again. "You Tauruses, it's all yes sir, no sir. You never think twice about anything, do you?"

I shrug. "I'm aware you're going to help me find my inner power and I'm going to do the best I can. What else is there to think about?"

He smiles. "This is true. My purpose number probably doesn't help me overlooking every detail."

I glance at the back of his neck, noticing the number four, the same as Isa which makes me cringe momentarily, but I quickly remind myself it's their purpose, not personality.

"Maybe," I say as we come to an average-looking door and Leon pulls out a small crooked key.

"Here we are. Here, you'll have to do it so it works properly." He hands me the small ugly key and I look at him with slight misunderstanding. But he gestures for me to open it and without question I insert the key and turn it. A glimmer of green and white light shimmers across the door as I open it. Walking in, I'm taken back by the ordinary room that's not much bigger than my old room within my cottage. Old wooden floorboards with old wooden panels make up the walls and ceiling, with two tiny cracked windows either side, only showing darkness on the outside and not a star in the sky. The temperature drops significantly and the energy makes me feel lonely and sad. Leon becomes incredibly amused by my facial expression, as he circles in beside me, kneeling on his hands and knees, remarking, "Wow, you don't even need to talk. Anyone could read your face like an open book. So that's how you guys express yourselves, can't hide your face, can you?...relax, this is only a reflection of how you perceive yourself currently, which helps me out a lot since you're not a talker." I become angered by his insensitivity.

I sternly look away with a rigid expression on my face and he instantly knows he's hurt me. "I'm glad you find this all so amusing."

I proclaim between my teeth. He puts up his hands in submission and says, "I apologize, I can see why you might think I'm mocking you. I promise that is the last thing I desire. Let me explain: I know this isn't a true reflection of you, it's only an illusion. A story you have heard or told yourself so many times you now believe it to be so, but I know that isn't the true story. And that's why I'm here to tell you the new story, the one you have piled beneath years of negative thought."

I become stiff, my eyes begin to well up. I look down, piercing the ground with my eyes. I've felt invisible for so long, I don't know what existing really feels like. A single tear begins to fall from my face and I curse it as it escapes. I don't even know this zodiac and he has broken me down in a single sentence. Am I that predictable? The room begins to shrink and he gently grabs my hand.

"It's okay, this room isn't a make-up of who you are. There is so much more to discover, don't you worry. Come on, look over here." He walks to the middle of the room and points up. I find my hand becoming clammy within his, so I pull it away holding on to my elbow. Looking up to where he points, I notice a tiny little white ball that moves in and out on itself with tiny bolts of lightning.

"A cloud?" He nods. "The cloud is a perception of your inner power, what you currently harness. And this room demonstrates how you feel about yourself which can tell you a lot about what a zodiac feels and the power they withhold at any current moment in time. But not the details and make-up of an individual. I don't think anything could replicate the unique imperfections of one's soul."

I stare at the tiny cloud that stays secure in the center of the room and ask, "What is this place called?"

He glances at me then at my tiny cloud.

"Well, it's a little too obvious really. It's called the 'Reflection Room.'"

I nod in agreement and ask without facing him, "What does your reflection room look like?"

He smirks, "I'm flattered by your curiosity, but right now I don't think that's a good idea as you'll only compare. How about when you achieve everything you came here to overcome, I'll show you. But until then, we have a lot of work to do." He gestures to the room. "By the way, Theophilus explained that your power isn't the usual strength endowed ability from the Taurus region. What does he mean by that?"

I shrug. "No one really knows. But I have a feeling it has something to do with my purpose number."

I turn around lifting my hair and he gently touches my neck which makes my hair stand on end. I pull away and turn around.

"Have you seen it before?"

He shakes his head. "Never. What have you experienced, power wise?"

I become hesitant to tell him as to say it out loud sounds preposterous. But I remind myself that's the purpose of these lessons.

"I've self-healed?"

He shrugs unimpressed, "Pisces and Aquarians can self-heal with their knowledge."

His comment angers me. "I've healed a severed spine from paralysis from the neck down. And I've teleported to places that I've never seen before," I say with a stern tone.

He grins. "Now, that's impressive. You're going to have to use more words when you're around me." He winks.

His ego begins to irritate me again.

"Why is a new blood like yourself teaching me how to harness my power anyway?" I ask.

His facial expression drops to a more sincere composure. "I thought you guys didn't second-guess authorized decisions?"

I cross my arms, angered by his stereotype way of thinking.

"Well, I'm asking. I thought you said everyone is uniquely imperfect, which means I'm not that predictable! I'm not like everyone else! And I don't know why!" my voice deepens to a powerful dark tone and as my rage boils, my vocals become unrecognizable.

Droplets of rain begin to fall and his expression is now a serious one, "You need to calm yourself, Taura."

He points to my cloud. Tears begin to flood from my eyes and rain now falls hard to the ground. The room quickly begins to flood as the walls crack and shake. Leon presses up against the wall.

"Taura, you need to breathe. Everything is okay, you're safe. This is a safe place. Breathe!" I look up to see my cloud has turned into a dark storm, engulfing the whole ceiling with lightning sporadically shooting from unpredictable directions.

"What is happening to me?" I whisper, collapsing into the flooded water that is now as high as my shins. Drawing my knees up to my chest, I rock back and forth. Squeezing my eyes shut, I'm suddenly overcome by a lost memory.

Penelope's face appears, my mother? She holds me up high within her grip and spins me around; the spinning makes me laugh as I become more and more dizzy. Then she drops me down into her grasp and holds me tight. She looks so beautiful as I stare into the eyes that are now mine. She begins walking, looking at an object in front of her and I just stare at her exquisiteness. Turning me around, she faces me to the tree that Europa spoke about on the day she had met me, the one that hangs over my cottage. But it's currently riddled with some kind of dark disease, spreading from its roots all the way up into its branches. She stands beside it and places my tiny hand against its rotting bark and I can feel its pain. It's in so much pain, it brings tears to my eyes. She gestures for me to do something. I shut my eyes and I feel a deepened warm sensation build up inside of me. Opening my eyes, I notice my whole body is glowing a vibrant blue. I gently place my tiny hand on the tree. At first, nothing happens, but suddenly the disease begins to subside. Drawing away from its extremities into the palm of my hand, leaves sprout and flowers blossom instantaneously, and the disease quickly dissipates, merging into a dark black stone that I now hold in the fist of my hand. Unexpectedly, I'm shaken by someone who grabs Penelope from behind, it's my father Adonis and he is yelling at Penelope. But I cannot hear their conversation as though all sound has gone silent. He throws his hands up in the air, gesturing to the field beside us; Penelope yells something back bringing me to her chest as she storms inside the cottage and Adonis follows with a dark expression saturating his face in despair.

"Taura, Taura!" I'm shaken awake, "Taura!"

I see Leon's face worriedly staring at me.

"Thank Unum, you're okay. You passed out."

I press my palms against the ground, looking for the water that had filled the room. But the room and the cloud are as they were before I lost all control.

"What happened?" I ask.

He looks at me in disbelief.

"Well, your power grew at an immense rate and then you passed out. I've never seen anything like it. This room takes down any mental walls, spells, or potions that hold control over you. It's so you can harness and connect to your powers without fault. Although I didn't expect that to happen so fast, but anger is your current trigger and anger is unpredictable and can't be controlled. So, it can be incredibly dangerous as you just experienced."

I touch the cold wooden floor. "How do you know so much about this room?"

He brings his legs into a crossed position and sits upright. Looking away with a slight glimmer of shame, he quickly turns it around, making intense eye contact with me, enthralled to share his story.

"Well, partially what Demetrius had said was correct, I guess that's why I lost it. My father Cedric Sol."

I glance down at his forearm, remembering the memorial tattoo of that name displayed in bold writing, clearly expressing the pride for his father.

"He's the Head Commander of the SNC army. So he has a lot of influence within this place and was able to take me to the Doh from a young age. He introduced me to the 'Reflection Room' and taught me how to harness my deepest inner powers earlier than any other Leo. On record, I'm the strongest animalistic Leo hunter for my age. I've even gotten the upper hand on a few SNC Leos before. But I still have a lot to learn and have to go through protocol like everyone else. I guess that's why so many don't really like me as they have this perception about my identity, until they get to know me of course."

He winks again and I roll my eyes. He grabs my hand and shakes it.

"I'm just kidding, just don't do what you did before. I promise I'll behave." I instantly smile without meaning to.

"See, I knew I'd make you smile."

I punch him, hurting my hand and I hold it with discomfort. He puts his hands up in retreat. "Alright, I think that's enough for today, you're probably going to feel really tired after releasing such power like that."

I nod in agreement and shake my hand to release the pain, and he can't hide his amusement.

As we go to leave, the sound of glass hitting the wooden floor echoes. I turn around to see my tiny green vial, innocently rolling around in a circle. Adonis's voice instantly penetrates my mind, *"You must never, and I mean never, inform any other of this medicine."*

Leon's voice gives me a sudden fright as I feel for the missing vial in my pocket as it stares blatantly at me from the floor. He walks over and picks it up, analyzing it as he stands.

"This yours?"

I'm good at keeping a secret but outwardly lying is another story. But what would be the harm in telling him either, it's only medicine, and he is helping me, like the medicine. Using it to sabotage me wouldn't make sense.

"Taura!?" he questions again as I've gone deep into thought. "Words, remember, I need words. I can only read so much from your face. And right now you look like a constipated bull, can't do much with that."

My eyes glance up at him.

"Right, sorry, I was just deep in thought. It's nothing really." I go to take it from him but he pulls it away.

"Well, if it's nothing, why can't you tell me?"

I look away. He's right, why can't I tell him? It would only make sense. But there is a part of me that's holding back for the loyalty of my father's word.

"It's, just uh, my medicine. You know, to keep me healthy." He looks at me inquisitively.

"No, why would you need medicine?"

I just realized I hadn't told him about my condition. So, I tell him the usual story from when I was born and that's why I look the way I do. "It's just for my immune system is all."

He hands it back to me.

"I see, I thought you were just the runt."

I scowl at him, and he raises his hands again.

"I mean it in a positive way. Don't take this the wrong way but I've never found the Taurus women to be exactly, well...attractive."

I raise an eyebrow.

"Can you blame me?! They are masculine, hard, and tough. As tough as some blokes, that's not genuinely something you look for in a woman. Men like to feel needed from their woman, otherwise what purpose do we have?" he says sarcastically.

I smile.

"So what are you trying to say? That I make you feel needed?"

He smiles.

"Not exactly."

I tilt my head to the side and he throws his hands up in the air.

"You're attractive alright! Small, petite, and well...beautiful. That's the way most men like them, I guess that's why Libra women are seen as the beauties within Nirvana. Until they lose the plot, good thing they got that give-away eye color alteration," he says humorously.

"I'm glad you find humor in objectifying women of any race." He looks at me with confusion.

"Well, I wouldn't want to make you angry, that's for sure."

I feel myself losing control so I storm out of the room instead,

"Oh, come on, I was just kidding!" he yells out after me.

I lock the door with the crooked key and I turn towards Leon.

"You know what I like about you, Taura," Leon says as I hand him the key.

"That I'm not intimidating like every other Taurus woman." He laughs.

"Not quite…you're different."

I look at him in question.

"Now you're the one who needs to elaborate."

He smiles. "Well, I call you beautiful and you tell me off for objectifying women."

I glance away. "Oh, yeah. I guess I don't take compliments all that well."

He laughs. "I'll keep that in mind. Insults only?"

I smile and nod. "Yeah, I can work with insults." He draws up the same teleportation circle as Demetrius does.

"How did you memorize that symbol, it's so complicated," I say. He looks up at me and stands clapping the chalk from his hands.

"I told you, I've been coming here since I was a young lad. Now stand in the circle." He's drawn the circle smaller than normal, which makes me have to press up against him, "Go back to your dorm and I'll be seeing you soon." I glance up at him and nod.

"Where are you going?" I ask.

He smiles. "To objectify some women," he says sarcastically and I shake my head in amusement. Visualizing the dorm, I chant the name Unum and open my eyes to the usual fast spinning planets that come to a slow.

Other zodiacs come and go as they please through their dorms, stopping to watch me for a moment and then continuing on with whatever tasks they were doing. I step out and I'm unexpectedly confronted by Demetrius who I did not see amongst the crowd.

"What did he make you do?" he asks interrogatingly.

I instantly recollect Theophilus's words, *I'll allocate someone to help you, who will report your progress. But this too must remain a secret.*

I glance around the room knowing he sees all and I don't want to reap the repercussion as warned.

"Taura!" Demetrius says impatiently.

I instantly stiffen and look directly at Demetrius.

"Nothing, he didn't make me do anything." I go to walk past him towards my dorm and he aggressively grabs my arm.

"Don't ever walk away from me like that again!" he says with an undertone so no one overhears. He intensely stares, penetrating my eyes with his sheer anger. I feel the pressure of his grip harden.

"Demetrius, you're hurting me, let go!" I begin to make a scene, pulling at his reinforced arm, securely attached to mine. Not moving an inch as I plummet my body back and forth to release his grip. He suddenly lets go and I fall back on to my arse, my books scatter and everyone has stopped to watch the commotion. But I am now riddled with antagonism.

"What is your problem?! He is just trying to help me! Something you never took the time to do!"

Demetrius's expression softens to a remorseful composure, but before he answers, I abruptly pick up my books and storm off to my dorm, slamming the door behind me.

I lean against the door and slide down, allowing my books to slide out before me and I bring my hands up to my face. Unexpectedly, I feel little warm sensations browsing against my skin and I notice the yellow orbs nudging me and settling down against my shoulders in comfort.

"Taur! Finally!" Europa comes rushing out of the toilet. "I heard the door slam. I see they've warmed up to you too. Cool, aren't they?"

I nod holding one within the palm of my hand and she effortlessly starts playing with another yellow orb within hers. Then looks at me with intrigue.

"So…what the hell has happened to you this past two days!? I knew something was up when Isa and her duo kept making sarcastic jokes about your disappearance. And now they're looking at you as though you're a ghost and then you're taken away by Leon!? What the hell is going on?"

I take a moment and linger at the yellow totem orb that nuzzles into my palm, wondering where to start and what to say, still wanting to keep my promise but wanting to tell my best friend everything at the same time.

"I'll tell you but you must understand I can't tell you everything…right now."

She nods with a concerned expression from the tone of my voice. "Isa, Dalton, and Henrietta kidnapped me last night. And Isa beat me so bad she severed my spin, paralyzing me from the neck down."

Europa's mouth drops open in disbelief as she looks me up and down.

"They threw me of the Doh's center stairs…but before I hit the ground, I stopped just before, levitating. My bones began to rejuvenate, breaking back into place and healing themselves but the pain was so excruciating, I passed out. And that is all I can tell you right now. And we must go to see Bibliotheca as soon as possible to find out if she knows about this number."

Europa's eyes nearly drop out of her head. "Wait, she did what!? And you did what!? That good for nothing…piece of…" She mumbles curse words under her breath in spite then pauses momentarily, "Well, at least it makes sense why they were all staring at you, the way they were. Definitely thought they'd seen a ghost."

I nod. "And that's why I must try to avoid that scenario again as I don't know how to control it, kinda happened spontaneously. I'm not sure if I could do it a second time."

Europa's mouth still hangs wide open.

"Wow, I'll never complain about a bad day again. Well, I don't think you have anything to worry about. When Isa saw you, she became petrified and Isa doesn't easily scare as you know." She instantly stops and realizes something. "Wait, why can't I ask about Leon? Where did he take you? And what was that piece of paper, jurisdiction thing? Helping you out with your power? But he is only a new blood himself?"

I smile at her eagerness to know what's going on.

"Like I told you, I can't tell you everything right now. Let's just say he's helping me."

She rolls her eyes.

"Oh alright, but you'll have to tell me eventually. Because I swear that lion has a thing for you and I don't trust him."

I laugh.

"Don't be ridiculous, have you seen the female Leos; they're absolutely stunning: small, lean, athletic, long golden hair with tanned skin but not overwhelmingly masculine." I realize I repeat the same words which Leon had said not too long ago as I too now objectify my own sex. Europa shrugs, unintrigued.

"I could kick their arse, that's all that matters,"

She appears to be slightly jealous by the comment and tensely staring at the ground.

I nudge her. "And I don't doubt you, you'll be just like Imelda Kore."

I smile and she peers up at me, containing her enthusiasm, nodding assertively. "Alright, let's go find Bibo, biblilo, bibly…whatever her name is."

I laugh and nod. Putting my books away, I notice *Language of the Purpose Numbers* corner edge sticking out of my other backpack, knowing I need to return it. I take the backpack with me, with it concealed inside. As we leave, Europa lets out a sudden thought, "Oh bonkers, it's 3:30. We have to be back in our dorms by five and be ready for supper in the common room by six. We were told that when you had your secret flirting lesson with Leon." I roll my eyes.

"Oh, shut up. Okay, we will have to be quick about it."

Chapter 12

The Photograph

Memories harness the power of invincibility.

We stand idly in front of the library's immensely huge wooden doors. "How are we going to get these open? I mean Demetrius struggled on the day he messed up the teleportation and got us into that mess with the Aries new bloods. Maybe we should wait until someone comes out?" I suggest.

Europa smacks my shoulder. "Argh, we don't have time for that. C'mon." She walks up to the doors and lingers at the golden open-paged handles that appear to be pristine and never touched. As she touches one side of the golden book handle, the book begins to flip through its thin glimmering golden pages at an unearthly rate and the doors begin to open as the pages turn, loudly creaking as they swing wide. The smell of old books is drawn into my nostrils, one of my favorite smells but with a library this big the scent is all the more enticing.

Europa looks at me with an eyebrow raised in suspicion.

"So, our humble SNC overseer was just showing off his big muscles after all." I chuckle.

"Maybe it's different when you have to open it from the inside."

Europa snuffs, "Yeah right, you just think his dingleberries don't stink," and she walks into the library.

"His what?" I retort.

Books fly past us, glancing behind them as zodiacs inconspicuously try to follow them without starting a full-blown chase and other zodiacs nearly bump into us as they read whilst walking to their study area. I begin to admire a beautiful Libra woman, reminiscing about Leon's spoken thoughts as I had not taken notice of their profound beauty before, although I was aware logically but I'd never had admiration. Or am I only admiring now that it's been brought to my attention or because he said it to be so. Unexpectedly, I bump into a Pisces and his books are knocked out of his hand and his thick glasses become contorted against his face; he stares off into the distance as though he hadn't realized what had hit him, becoming stunned in the process.

"Oh, I'm so sorry! Let me get those for you," I insist. He suddenly looks down, only noticing me after I had spoken, readjusting his glasses that are already broken, taped with thick tape in the middle, and I become aware that those particular glasses look incredibly familiar. Now his already large eyes become even larger through the lenses.

"That's quite alright, you just caught me in a train of thought is all." He now becomes transfixed on me. "Mind me asking what creature you might be? You appear to be that of a Taurus but you seem to be a cross breed. Too petite to be compared to the brute of a bull," he remarks as I pick up his heavy book. I strugglingly pass it back to him.

"You could say I'm the runt of the bunch," I say with minimum sarcasm, noticing I use another one of Leon's quotations. What's wrong with me, I don't even sound like me.

The Pisces laughs.

"I like it, you could say I'm the blind of the bunch. These glasses aren't exactly flattering, but they belonged to someone who I dearly cared for. Besides, they have character and I do believe they bring out my deep blues." He pushes his face into mine, blinking frantically, trying to act flatteringly beautiful in an amusing way. I chuckle at his awkward quirkiness but I love his confidence in his imperfect sense of humor. The idea someone can be completely comfortable in who they are is intoxicatingly magnetic. Now standing up straight, he pushes his webbed hand out towards me.

"My name's Manfred Harwood. What might yours be, mighty runt?" I grab his cold hand that's wet and damp, remembering they must always stay hydrated.

"The mighty runt's name is Taura Andreas," I say, trying to keep my deceptive confidence that somewhat resembles the Leo I have unreasonable attachment to. He profusely shakes my hand frantically, making my whole body move along with it. "It's a pleasure to meet your acquaintance." I nod and smile in agreement. Thinking it's nice to be in a place where no one really knows who you are.

"Taura! Taura! Taur!" I hear Europa calling. Manfred turns around, fiddling with his glasses as he peers at the charging bull now heading our way, her blonde hair floating behind her as she walks with intent towards us. "There you are! What are you doing? You know we don't have much time? And I can't find whatever her name is anywhere!" She now stands in front of me but before I can answer, Manfred has already stuck his hand out into her personal space.

"Hello, I'm Manfred Harwood. I ran into your friend just now, my mistake. And she insisted on picking up my book when I clumsily knocked into her." He winks at me as if trying to save my arse, knowing too well it was I who knocked into him.

"It's okay, Manfred, she's my best friend, Europa Castellanos," I say reassuringly. Manfred's expression becomes confused as if to wonder why your best friend would be yelling at you in such a domineering insolence; clearly he hasn't spent too much time around Tauruses.

"Oh, well, in that case. It's a pleasure to meet Europa Castellanos, the best friend of mighty runt." He forcefully makes Europa shakes his hand and she rips it away in anger.

"What did you just call her? Mighty runt?"

Manfred becomes flushed and confused at the same time.

"I do apologize, I thought it was an inside joke?" he questions.

Europa spits back, "You think calling someone a mighty runt is a joke? What's wrong with you! Clearly no Pisces I've read about," she says with ignorance towards his feelings and it's instantly obvious she's hurt them.

"No, no Europa, you've got it all wrong. I told him I was a mighty runt." She stares at me.

"Why would you call yourself that?" she questions as if wondering who I am, as I too was questioning that not too long ago.

"I was kidding. Look, it doesn't matter, he was actually being very friendly and nice."

Europa takes a big breath to calm herself down.

"Sorry…Manfro," she says bluntly, fixated on the ground as it's hard for bulls to admit when they're wrong, that's why our most common known trait is our stubbornness. Manfred smiles, probably knowing our traits as Pisces love their broad knowledge,

"It's Manfred, but that's quite alright, easy mistake. It's nice to see a deep love for a friend," he suggestively says to Europa as if to see her in a way no one else does. She suddenly goes bright red and I'm now confused to what he might have suggested. Although I know Pisces are incredibly intuitive, but they're never to the point which makes their motives hard to interpret, that's why they make great subtle manipulators.

"Now, who is this 'whatever' her name is? You are looking for?" he asks curiously. Europa, who has gone as stiff as a plank, says nothing. So I answer, "Bibliotheca the Librarian. Europa struggles to say her name is all."

He nods his head, knowing whom we speak of and his expression forms into an admiration. "Oh yes Bib, well, you may find it a little harder than you presumably thought. I'm sure others have spoken about her but I'm sure they too are unaware of a certain inconvenience to her existence, most are."

Europa now loosens back to her normal and pushy demeanor.

"What do you mean?"

Manfred gives an awkward expression, "Well…she's dead…but not gone."

Our jaws drop open in disbelief. "She can't be dead unless it's been recent, we only just met her a few days ago!" Europa adds.

Manfred takes a moment, letting the information sink in. "She's been dead for decades. You would have met her ghost; she has never left this place since her passing. Many don't think she ever will. So, unfortunately, to find her is more difficult than originally thought. Most zodiacs like yourselves stumble across her. But when wanting to find her again, can't seem to do so. Some say it's when you're not looking for her will she appear."

We both look at one another, knowing we're in dire need of finding her.

"Who's the living librarian?" I ask. Thinking Bib's wisdom and knowledge must have been passed down to another. Manfred's expression once again doesn't look too promising.

"That's the other mishap, there isn't one. Bib is the current and still remaining librarian. She still does all the same duties as she did before her death. Just no one sees her doing them, so the Elders thought instead of upsetting her unresting ghost, they'd let her continue doing the job she always loved and maybe that might help her pass over, thinking maybe there was something she'd left unfinished. But decades have gone by and she still remains. What is it that you needed from her?"

Europa looks at me, knowing she doesn't want to answer such a question for me.

"Oh, it was to do with the purpose numbers."

I pull out the *Language of the Purpose Numbers* residing tightly within my backpack. But as I lift it out, its eyes open, becoming alive again within the library's walls. It sporadically wiggles hard, back and forth to win its freedom.

"Hold on to it tight! Must be an older tucker!" Manfred says, helping me hold on to it and Europa now jumps in too. And I struggle to say the words as I try to keep a grip on the book.

"It has…a page inside, that's ripped out…the theory behind…number ten," I manage to say with sheer struggle.

"Man, this thing is strong!" Europa adds.

Manfred tensely says, "I need you both to keep a hold of it. I'm going to let go, ready! 3, 2, 1. Hold on!" As he releases the book, it begins to get the better of me and Europa but Manfred quickly acts, gently gliding his middle and index finger down the spine of the book and it begins to calm, appearing to fall asleep as its eyes shut. We both relax and he quickly takes it from us. "We must be fast, it'll wake soon." As he flips through the book, looking up the index and gliding through to the page I spoke about, he runs his finger down where the pages had been torn. "Hmmm," he says as the book now sprouts awake, slamming shut and fastidiously flies away through the other thousands of books that soar through the library's high-ceiling walls.

"What the hell is that book's problem?" asks Europa.

Manfred answers as he still watches the book from above, "The oldest books within the library have the strength to fight against you and will only allow you to read them if they deem you worthy. The new bloods like yourselves are seen chasing them around the library as they hold the most ancient information from the beginning of time. Very useful in end-of-year exams, but they never catch them. They're usually the ones who are looking for a quick fix as they didn't take the time to study all year." He smiles as though amused by an off-distant memory. Adding, "And that book is the most ancient book I have ever held," staring appreciatively at his hands, "It must have wanted you to see something. Probably to do with those torn pages which is an act so traitorous, if caught would be sentenced to death by the Scorpio's death serum. Old books like that are very precious to our history." He still lingers at the flying books.

"How do you know so much about the library?" I ask.

He smiles gently, reminiscing. "Bib told me. When I was a new blood, she used to visit me all the time as I lived in the library, bit of a loner I was…well, still am actually, which I know is a strange trait for a Pisces but I still love a good chat, maybe I chew too many ears." He laughs. "And I too was unaware she was a ghost until much later on. But she no longer visits me as I now yearn for her and her company. But back then I was too preoccupied with my studies and found her more of a nuisance when studying. She would just appear when no one was around and share random factual information with me about the library and other things. I miss her dearly, she was my first and closest friend," he says as his eyes well up, recalling the time he spent with her. His glasses begin to fog up and he wipes the tears from his large eyes. Taking off his glasses and cleaning them, carefully avoiding upsetting the messy tape that keeps them from breaking in two.

Then I realize. "Those glasses…they're Bib's, aren't they?" He places them back on the bridge of his nose as they too do not fit his frame, constantly falling down his face.

"Indeed they are. She left me the original ones from her time in this realm on the last day I saw her. Now I can't bear to part with them," he says, readjusting the frames so they sit comfortably.

"How did she die?" I ask.

He blinks a couple of times now, getting the position right.

"To be honest, that was one story she had not shared with me, unfortunately."

"I wonder if anyone else has read all the books in the library," Europa says, hoping someone else withholds the valuable information we seek and changing to topic as we are short of time. Manfred shakes his head and the glasses slide down, pushing them back up on to bridge of his face.

"Unfortunately not, it would take several lifetimes," pausing and thinking on that remark. "Actually probably more, for someone to read all the books within the library and not only that, all the ancient books would need to deem you worthy, so life experience is a necessity. Only Bib would have such profound respect from those books as she takes the utmost care for them," he pauses for a moment, looking at me inquiringly. "Why would it want to show you the theory behind number ten, I wonder?" asking in a way, knowing I already know and with curiosity gives me the benefit of the doubt. I turn around and lift my mousy brown hair from the back of my neck, displaying the unbeknown number ten. He holds the side of his glasses so they don't fall down as he bends over to get a closer look. He squints, peering at the strange number. "I see, that makes an awful lot of sense now," he says as I turn around. "Do you know of such a purpose number?" He shakes his head, "Unfortunately not, but I understand why the book came to you. Obviously wanted you to know something, but someone else clearly didn't. And they've gone unbelievably out of their way to make sure you wouldn't…because to risk such a crime is, is insane."

Then, unexpectedly, Manfred becomes stiff and rigid in his appearance, his eyes now glaze with a contrast of moving white and gray, as though he is seeing something we cannot. Grabbing my shoulder, he presses against me, glancing around as though someone could be listening and whispers in a strange voice that is not his own. Europa leans in.

"Taura Andreas, you must heed this warning… There is something greater here than you could ever imagine. There are powers at will, greater than I've ever felt before… Taura, I have a feeling you are in great danger and I believe you must find out the truth in order to save yourself. But there is much conflict and turmoil within such a journey. Things aren't as they appear."

He stands back and stands up straight again, readjusting himself, and his eyes slowly return to normal. I feel the hair on the back of my neck stand on end and Europa becomes overwhelmingly emotional. "What do you mean save herself? What's going to happen? How do you know?"

His eyes blink hard as though trying to readapt them to the present moment, readjusting his glasses again.

"Blimey, darn it… I apologize for that. I've been studying within the Olympus Trials for many a year now to become an SNC sorcerer as I've proven my strong capabilities within my psyche. But my intuition can be quite strong at times and comes on quite spontaneously without my prediction. I'm still learning to control it, but it seems to be taking longer than most, and they won't deem me worthy until I have full control of my powers. I came to the belief Bib could help me as she is so knowledgeable and it was on that very day I sought her out; she disappeared from my reality and I still subconsciously search for her, that's why I can no longer see her. But what I felt after you showed me that number was the strongest message I've ever received, you must not ignore it," he says with urgency.

I stare at him sternly. "Okay, but none of it makes any sense. How am I supposed to discover the truth and be careful of such powers when I don't know the purpose of the power?"

He tries to look at me reassuringly. But his emotions are clearly visible on his face. "Unfortunately, I can't answer that for you, only you can discover that truth. All I can tell you is when you search for something that is of great importance to your essence, Unum has a funny way of helping us. I believe it has something to do with seeking out clarity within purpose, but that is only a feeling I withhold. But I must get back to my studies…and please, Taura…" he places his webbed cold hand on my shoulder, squeezing it tight, "be careful, I know nothing makes sense right now. But soon all will be revealed in due time. And remember to keep your mind open and clear." Not knowing what to say, I say nothing, only nod in acknowledgement. He smiles kindly at Europa and says, "Take care of her, I know you will. And both of you. Be careful." And just as abruptly as he came, he disappears into the crowd.

"Well, that only adds more questions. I wish someone would tell us what the hell is going on," Europa says impatiently with an edge of acidity.

I then realize that the only other creature that seems to know any more than we do is the last remaining Bwbachod. But I don't know how we will find him.

Europa looks at the big clock displayed high above the big entrance doors.

"Oh dingleberries, it's almost five. We have to get back to our dorm! Will have to figure that our later, C'mon." We move passive aggressively through the crowd, towards the doors.

As we approach, I notice a tall, slender Virgo staring directly at me with piercing bright green eyes, appearing to know me by his expression. I look behind me, thinking he must be looking at someone else, but his stare does not alter. He has light brown hair that's parted in the middle and like every other Virgo, there's not a hair out of place. As the large doors creak open, another zodiac enters, Europa yells, "Hurry! Before it closes!"

She grabs my hand and begins to pick up pace as I'm dragged behind her. And as we pass the Virgo, who still continues to hold my gaze, he deliberately bashes into me, making me lose Europa's grip, and I fall to the ground with his book dropped beside me. I look up to see him slowly disappear into the crowd, he glances back and continues on.

"Wait!" I yell, picking up his book, standing frantically to my feet. "You dropped your…" But he's already gone as if he were only a ghost, which does make me question as nothing is out of the ordinary within this place.

"What are you doing?" Europa is now in my face and grabbing my hand again. She swiftly pulls me through the big doors that nearly squash our tails within its heavy clutches as it closes behind us. Holding the book the Virgo dropped under my arm. Europa and I teleport back to the dorm.

As we return, all the SNC overseers are standing out front of their residing regions. The Constellations' stones glow above the doors which means the zodiacs can come and go without reciting the poem every time they enter. Demetrius stands outside of ours. I quickly hide the book within my bag before anyone notices and as we approach. Demetrius locks eyes with me, still looking regretful for the commotion that went down between us not too long ago.

"Are you two okay? Where have you been?" he asks genuinely without his usual assertive approach.

Europa smiles.

"Just to the library, had to catch up on some study," she says charmingly and I say nothing, continuing to follow Europa into our dorm. Demetrius grabs my arm to stop me then quickly releases it, trying to control his strength.

"Taura..." he glances around as the other SNC overseers watch and for the first time I see Demetrius's demeanor become somewhat edgy.

"Yes?" I question as Europa also intently stares too.

Appearing to be tongue-tied and not knowing what to say, he answers, "Never mind. Make sure everyone is organized before six for supper," now regretful of the words that instinctively fell out of his mouth. I stare at him for a moment, giving him a second chance but he does not budge. He holds the door open, I enter and he shuts it behind us.

"What was that all about?" Europa asks.

"Don't worry, just something trivial," I remark.

"Oh good, because I'm not sure if I can live up to your level of drama at the moment," she sarcastically chirps.

"Yeah, me neither," and we both laugh, finding humor in a mysterious situation.

Isa lies on her bed staring at the yellow totem orbs that hover leisurely around the room. Dalton and Henrietta quarrel over some contraption and Kendall lies on his bed reading. Isa glances over as we walk in laughing, becoming instantly irritated by our presence but also inquisitive as she watches me from the corner of her eye. Dalton and Henrietta stop quarrelling and begin to whisper, sitting on the bottom bunk side by side. Ignoring their stares, I sit beside my bed, facing away from them and Europa stares at Isa challengingly until she slowly looks away, sitting beside her bed on the opposite side facing me.

She leans over and whispers, "We will have to talk about our next step when these vultures aren't around."

I nod in agreement.

Pulling out the book from my bag and to my surprise it's a common book found in any Constellation library. It reads: *Zodiacs Appearance, Abilities & Power*, the exact same book I keep beside my bed and the one I read just before I ventured through the uncharted forest for the first time.

Europa asks, "Why'd you take that from the library?"

I look at the book from front to back.

"I didn't mean too. A Virgo dropped it beside me when I fell before we left the library."

Europa becomes disinterested and I begin flipping through the pages and as soon as I do, a photograph falls out, landing face down.

"What's that?" she curiously questions. Picking it up, I notice in small writing, 'Vaughn and Benedict.' Turning it around, I see the same Virgo I saw in the library standing next to what appears to be his twin, very similar at first glance but both uniquely different the longer you stare. The one from the library is happier and attractive in stature with a big smile spread across his face making his eyes squinted whilst the other stands rigid with a solemn expression, with a slight smirk but obviously not wanting to be in the photo. Both have their arms wrapped around one another and you can feel the unconditional love between them. Their wings pushed up against each other as feathers are captured falling down within the photo.

I hand it over to Europa and she observes both sides.

"Who are they?"

I shrug as she hands it back.

"I don't know. I recognize the Virgo called Vaughn to the left, he was the one who bumped into me in the library. He's the one who dropped this book. And I think it was deliberate. He was staring right at me before he bashed into me, dropping the book next to me."

Europa stares at the photo. "But why?" she says rolling her eyes up to the ceiling and frustratingly sprawls her legs out in front of her as if she's had enough of unanswered questions. Then there is a knock on the door.

"Dinner's up, time to go," Demetrius says as he pokes his head through. I slide the book under my bed and put the photo in my pocket.

Entering the dining room, all the elders are already seated and all the new-blooded zodiacs enter together. But the room is on a much larger scale than we had originally been exposed and monumental in its presence. It's as though they had reconstructed the whole premises within a day. We're seated at our usual tables that are much longer than I recall. Already seated are the other zodiacs who live within the Doh studying the Olympus Trials, but clearly years ahead of us. Egos that were once written are eradicated. Being the new bloods, we instantly know our place.

Once everyone is seated, Theophilus stands, elegantly pushing his already sleeked hair back with both hands, tiny white hairs curl perfectly around his ears, poking out from underneath. Clasping both hands together, he begins to speak. "As you all can see, a few things have changed within our dining room. The new bloods will now be dining with the reputable zodiacs who have been within the Doh's premises for many a time now. Depending on their potential, it will determine where their journey leads and how much time they'll need to spend within the Olympus Trials to obtain their classification. Some of you may only need to spend a year here, whilst others may need to spend five, ten or more. At first, we like new bloods to feel comfortable, so we don't introduce you to your fellow betters, until later. And for you, that time would be now. I'd suggest picking their brains if they allow, you may find they have valuable information you'll be needing later on in your studies. Now, let's all enjoy the company over a well-earned meal. Please begin."

He sits back down upright in his grand chair and the food slowly begins to appear as if it had already been waiting, invisible to the naked eye. Steam lingers off the food and I didn't realize how hungry I was until the scent hits my nose.

I pick at my food, admiring the reputable Tauruses that sit beside us. They too still enjoy their food just as much as we do and do not talk in the meantime. Europa leans back in her chair with a full belly.

"Ahh, that was good. I needed that," she says rubbing her now prominent food baby. Isa is still gorging herself senseless as she stares at me beneath her thick eyebrows. Henrietta and Dalton both play with their food, flinging it at one another, and Kendall eats deliberately and assertively with a relaxed presence.

I place my hand in my pocket, feeling the photograph I just attained not too long ago and a flash of Vaughn's face projects in my mind from the intent stare he pressed upon me. And I have a feeling he wanted me to have this photo; why else would he deliberately bash into me, dropping the book? I continue picking at my food, glancing at Europa, who now lies in a food coma, knowing she won't be much help. I attempt to look over at the Virgos, but it becomes apparent that it's too hard to see past Gemini, Cancer, and Leo's Constellation tables. Accidently I catch a glimpse of Leon, my heart begins to skip a beat as I notice another female persistently flirting with him, obvious by her body language, and she too is incredibly beautiful, more so than I. I unexpectedly become hot and angry, realizing my blood now pumps with jealousy, and I find myself no longer hungry. My possessive streak begins to take over, as I realize I have feelings for another zodiac I barely know. My father would be furious.

Unable to help myself, I glance over again and see them both flirting. I become infuriated, taking a few deep breaths; I close my eyes but feel the pressure of tears behind them. How could I be so stupid. He's just doing his job. The tears wallow up uncontrollably; I squeeze my eyes tight. But I know I won't be able to hold them back for long. I feel a hand grab my shoulder.

"Taur, you okay?" Europa asks. I shake my head, stand abruptly as the tears bellow down and I run for the door.

Europa grabs my hand to stop me and I turn around to face her as tears flow profusely down my face.

"Taur, what's wrong? You can't leave; it's forbidden to leave the dining room when eating has commenced. C'mon it's okay." But I'm engraved to the place I now stand as firm as a tree and unable to move. No other table has noticed me yet but I know they soon will. Unexpectedly, another reputable Taurus male stands with a compassionate and calming aura.

He walks over to me with an unreadable expression and says, "The food's spicy, ain't it? Gotta be careful of that grass curry, hits you right in the you-know-what. Don't worry, I've been seen running out of here crying from it too. Retched stuff, don't know why they still serve it." He smiles at me and hands me a napkin and guides me back to my seat and he casually goes back to his. I blow my nose and everyone continues eating as if his excuse was sufficient and reasonable explanation.

Europa leans in and whispers, "It wasn't really the curry, was it?"

I smile, thinking how stupid I could have made myself out to be and become immensely grateful for that Taurus, I should thank him. I shake my head.

"I knew it, are you okay?"

I nod, and she looks at me understandingly and knows I've been through a lot recently, so she decides not to press the question, and I'm happy to allow her to assume it's related to recent occurrence of events.

The chattering in the room begins to rise and others leave their table to converse with other zodiacs, firstly initiated by the reputable zodiacs, but most of the new bloods stick to their Constellation's tables, clutching to familiarity.

"We should casually walk past the Virgo table. I want to see if I can find that Virgo I ran into, he might be connected to all this," I suggest to Europa.

"Do we have to? I really couldn't be bothered carrying this food baby around." I look at her, unimpressed with the laziness she conveys. But this trait is renowned within our zodiac; when we work, we work hard and fast like a charging bull, but when we're lazy, it's as though you're trying to move a five hundred ton sleeping bull, especially after a well-induced meal.

"Are you serious?" I ask, trying to guilt trip her.

She sighs. "Alright, alright, let's go," standing up at a slow pace.

We walk past the charismatic Gemini who banter continuously as I watch a few who attempt to split and miserably fail whilst others tease them, but none of them are offended by the mockery as they throw it back and forth. They move at such high speed, your eyes are unable to keep up with their fastidious changeability as though in a constant fast-forwarded state. Now, we are approaching the Cancerians and I hear our names being called.

"Europa, Taura! Over here!" I turn to see a familiar face, Naida the Cancer, we met at our first introduction to Orbis Bellum.

Europa grabs my hand and insists on going over.

"We won't be long," she says. I find I'm becoming reserved as all the Cancers watch us carefully with their mysterious and robust black eyes; they don't trust strangers. But Naida continues to smile as we approach. I stand just behind Europa.

"Where are you guys headed? Far from your own territory for new bloods," she comments, squinting with a perky smile. And I find this Naida different from the last encounter, probably feeling more comfortable within her own community. Europa unexpectedly pulls the photograph from my pocket.

"Actually, we're looking for one of these Virgos."

She points to Vaughn, determinedly wanting to get this over with. Europa continues, "He accidently bumped into Taur in the library, dropping his book with this inside. We thought he might like it back," trying to make it sound more subtle. I surprisingly look at Europa, and she shrugs at me to suggest we haven't gotten anywhere so far on our own and I know she's right. Naida looks at the picture for quite some time then shrugs.

"I'm sorry, I don't recognize either of them, but I'm only a new blood myself."

As she goes to pass it back, the Cancer sitting next to her grabs her arm, taking the picture from her hand and says, "Yeah I know one of them, not the one who you ran into though," says the Cancer inexplicably and Naida jumps up with inquisition.

"How do you know, Artemis? You're only a new blood too!"

Artemis smiles. "You know I don't tell you everything."

"Don't be stupid, of course you do," Naida smacks her playfully and turns to us, "Europa, Taura, this is my know-it-all sister, Artemis Odette," she says stirringly. Artemis has long black hair that's braided all the way down her back but it's obvious she's the more contained sister with prominent features and harder facial features than perky Naida who's more delicate to the eye. But you can see the similarities once it becomes apparent that they are sisters.

"Nice to meet you," Europa says with warmth, and I nod with a welcoming but less eager demeanor.

"Might I ask how you know the other Virgo, Benedict?" I ask, getting straight back to the point.

"You don't mess around, do you?" Naida says light-heartedly.

I smile and shrug, and look straight back at Artemis who still stares at the photo, handing it back to me and says, "It's no secret. He's Theophilus's boy."

Europa and I look at one another in surprise and Artemis looks uninterested, as the information is useless to her.

Naida turns around to her sister and asks, "If it's a not big secret, how come you didn't tell me?"

Artemis glances at her sister with obvious annoyance, like siblings who spend too much time together.

"Because if you didn't spend your whole time talking, you might actually hear something other than your own voice." Naida pokes her tongue out at her sister and smirks.

Turning to face us, "It's true, I do love a good chat," she says, not being obviously offended by her sister's harsh words. But I guess having such large families, you become exceedingly comfortable in who you are, as they'll always pull you up, not afraid of offending you.

Artemis adds, "It's no big deal, he was pointed out to me by our older brother, Derk, who's a reputable zodiac," she says with pride towards her brother who she clearly looks up too.

Europa then asks in astonishment, "How many siblings do you guys have?"

Naida laughs.

"To be honest, I've lost count! But I wouldn't recommend it. I mean look at what I have to put up with!"

Artemis chuckles but with a crude expression, "It's you who everyone else has to put up with," and they both laugh looking at each other affectionately.

I tug at Europa's arm and she nods. "Alright, best be getting this picture back, great seeing you again Naida, and nice meeting you, Artemis."

We both continue walking down the aisle between Cancer and Gemini, and Naida yells, "Don't be strangers!"

We wave, turning the corner of their short width table, rapidly approaching the Leos. Their gold, orange, and yellow become profound compared to the sea green and silver Constellation colors of Cancer's table, standing side by side. Not establishing where Leon is, I keep my eyes fixed to the Virgo's green, white, and yellow.

Europa then says, "Your boyfriend's spotted you."

I become tense. "You know that's not true," I say with a tad of disappointment and Europa's expression becomes irritated, unable to look as I might explode into an emotional storm again, unable to hold back the tsunami of tears. But to my dismay, I find my eyes unable to look away and he is staring right at me from quite far down the table, which gives me hope that he won't call out to me, making it known to everyone in his vocal path. The same Leo female sits near him, lingering at him which draws jealousy into my blood stream. Then curiously she follows his gaze. My hairs stand on end and my sweat becomes cold and nervous. She spots me and I quickly look away but just as quickly I find myself staring back. Leon's eyes have not yet broken away from mine. And just like their close relationship with fire, the Leo female eyes light up with flamed fury, hitting a golden cup over beside her, followed by an enraged confrontation with Leon, but I am too far away to hear. She storms off down the other end of the table, glancing back to see if he follows, but he does not and seems unbothered by her tantrum. She suddenly shoots me a livid glare and I'm quickly taken by Leon as he smiles subtly gesturing a small wave of acknowledgment my way, and I realize he too would have been told to keep our affair a secret. I awkwardly smile and quickly turn away as I become flushed but relieved at the same time as my heart flutters.

The magnetic, warm table of vibrant Leos is soon transitioned to the Virgos' upright and practical composures. No one's ego is seen over-encumbered by another and they all socialize appropriately with superb mannerisms. Still eating modestly as some still slowly consume their meal, probably wanting to make sure to chew their food properly. A few who sit at the end of the table look up at us as we try to look on inconspicuously, but nothing goes past the Virgos, knowing their great attention to detail does not go unnoticed. Some even separate the colors of food on their plate into a pie-like assembly.

"May we help you?" one asks, and I even feel Europa become intimidated by their penetrating green eyes that pierce straight through you. They are all incredibly different but similar at the same time as their movements are all dictated in the same way, portrayed within their upheld moral value of no one being no better than another.

"Uh, we were just looking for someone within your region known as Benedict?" I ask apprehensively. Without acknowledging our inquiry, he calmly places his knife and fork down gently and ever so slightly leans over, looking down the long table, holding his robes against his chest, making a point of not getting them dirty. His eyes swiftly shift back to us and I can't help but stare, his eyes are so intensely beautiful.

"He's down the other end of the table," he says, not seeming interested as to why we ask for him. Picking up his knife and fork once again, he continues eating, thoroughly chewing his food slowly.

"Oh, uh…thank you," I say, expecting him to question us, but he does not.

"You're welcome," he replies plainly. Europa seems surprised too as she prolongs her stature, waiting for him to enquire as every other zodiac we have met seems curious in who we are. I guess being so preoccupied in the detail of your own life, the idea about asking about another would make things too complicated and not asking would seem logical to a Virgo as it would drive attention away from their own inner complex thoughts or he's just being modest and keeping to himself, either seems likely.

I gesture to walk down the aisle beside where the Libras lie, their blue and jade green colors calming to the eye. And as we pace down towards the other end of either table to find Benedict, I find myself lingering at the contrast between the Constellations of Libra and Virgo. The Libras touch each other affectionately with ease as the expression of love and romance comes naturally. Their pleasing manner is warming as some gesture a welcoming hello as we pass by and you can't help but be captured by their flirtatious self-expression. Some gesture for us to sit with them and we politely decline.

Europa whispers in my ear, "The women are incredibly beautiful."

I nod in agreement and add, "Yeah, the men too, they are as pretty as the females." You'd almost think they'd stolen the beauty from the elves themselves but the Libras are more enticing to the eye. Elves are more subdued to the forest, representing nature in a physical depiction, but their eerie beauty is profound.

Approaching the end of the table, I carefully look at each individual Virgo, pulling out the picture in my pocket and comparing it to make sure I don't mistake him for someone else, not wanting to offend anyone. And just as I'm scanning through, I see him at the very end of the table, playing around with his food. He appears to be uninterested, deep in thought. I nudge Europa and gesture over to him and she sighs with relief and we hastily wander over. He has separated all his food into the appropriate colors like most, but unexpectedly proceeds in crushing them into an unrecognizable mess. The Virgo sitting across from him notices us and stops eating, but we eagerly stare at Benedict who doesn't seem to notice our presence or just ignores us.

"Uh, excuse me, are you Benedict Malis?" Europa asks. He stops playing with his food momentarily, glancing up at us but does not look at us and continues playing with his food.

The Virgo sitting across from him intervenes, "Yes, that is Benedict Malis. Excuse his mannerisms…he's not like the rest of us," he says without emotion but conviction, disappointed by his representation of how he portrays himself within his colony. We nod with acknowledgment, looking back at Benedict who now stares at the other Virgo with empty eyes, unaffected by the isolating words. Once again, mashing his food more deliberately than before, gathering other bits of vibrant colors that lay on the table and mixing them into the mess he's created but never placing anything in his mouth and is obviously malnourished. His cheekbones stick out from his face, his hair is untidy, even his wings welter, clearly thinner than the rest of the Virgos. He has a slight dimple in his chin and long eyelashes with prominent eyebrows. And it becomes obvious that he'd be an attractive male if he'd just put some meat on his bones. The other Virgo intervenes again, "It'd be best if you just ask him what you are here for as he's in a particularly bad mood today. He's not going to acknowledge you, he barely acknowledges us."

We nod again in gratitude and he continues thoroughly eating his nourishing meal, appearing to be uninterested as to why we are here but gives us some handy advice. I look at the picture then glance at Europa and she nods, clearly feeling uncomfortable as I am.

I place the picture down in front of Benedict and say, "Your brother Vaughn, he uh…bumped into me in the library and dropped this picture of you two. I thought you'd like it back. Seems to be a priceless one to lose." Benedict instantly stops, becoming stiff as he sees the picture, lingering at it momentarily and for a moment I thought I saw a tear build up in his eye. But he quickly composes himself again.

"That's impossible," he says with an uninterested monotone that's stern to the ear. Europa and I look at one another, waiting for him to explain, but he doesn't.

So, Europa determined to get some answers, asks, "Why is that impossible? We went out of our way to find its rightful owner and this is the thanks you give us."

I nudge Europa for her to stop and she does but relentlessly scrunching her face up. But he doesn't react to her probing, now focusing delicately on a green leaf, placing it carefully next to bluish mushroom that blends together perfectly. But once again he squishes them together with slow intent then Europa gestures for us to leave and as we turn, he says, "He's dead."

We both become stiff, glancing back to see he now holds the picture in his hand and as we turn back to ask another, Theophilus's powerful voice echoes through the now extensive dining room.

"Alright, it's time for everyone to go back to their seats. You must get an early night as I'm sure you all have a big day of study tomorrow. I hope you enjoyed your meal and I shall see you all tomorrow for breakfast. And always remember, allow strength to lay beside you."

Everyone quickly begins moving back to their table and we know we won't be given leniency over the reputable zodiacs who immediately obey Theophilus's commands. But as we attempt to hurry back to our table, I'm unexpectedly grabbed and I turn around to see Benedict's skinny hand grasping on to my arm with large veins that pulse from his thin skin, my skin protruding between his large knuckled fingers as he asks without looking at me, staring at the ground.

"Where did you see him?" he asks plainly but with clear motivation behind it.

"The library," I quickly answer and he instantly lets go without acknowledgment of my response, which makes me question if he even heard me. I wait a moment but he sits deep in thought again and I know that is all I am going to get from him. Sitting back at our own table, all the zodiac Constellations begin moving out of the dining area; first the reputable zodiacs, starting with the Capricorns and we follow after the Aries whose red and scarlet colors beam bright, representing the differentiated colors of blood reminding me of the near-death experience I had, feeling the unknown danger that continuously follows blindly behind me.

Walking out of the dining hall, Europa turns to me.

"Well, that was a waste of time… Are you sure it was Vaughn who ran into you in the library?"

I nod affirmatively, remembering those exact eyes that penetrated me.

"I'm sure…the only other explanation is he could have been a ghost like Bib?"

Europa nods in agreement.

"Yes, that would make sense. But then why did he leave you that picture? And more importantly, why you?"

I shrug. "I don't know, nothing makes sense at the moment. Could be connected to Manfred's message he received."

Europa sighs. "Maybe. Still doesn't help. The more information we find, the more confused we seem to become."

As we wait for teleportation up to our dorm, I notice Benedict walking down a tiny corridor with an estranged Leo who is large and more muscular than any other Leo I have ever laid eyes upon and covered in thick armored plates with giant peridots that decorate his already extravagant attire. His Constellation colors, gold, orange, and yellow stain the armor with the symbolic emblem of Leo engraved prominently on either side of his shoulder plates. I nudge Europa and gesture to them both as they sneak into a smaller room. Quickly looking around, she says, "Quick, while no one is looking."

We follow agilely down the corridor. As we come to the door where they entered, we can hear voices growing louder as we approach. Europa turns to me, placing her index finger over her sealed lips and we hear a voice.

"I can assure you that is not true," says a deep powerful voice that is more robust than Theophilus's stern and assertive tone, this one more intimidating to the ear as roughness coats the undertone.

Then Benedict's voice is heard. "Dad told me he was dead! How is it possible then? No one knows he even existed, do you think they know it was..." he says without finishing his sentence as though he can't bear to say the words.

The deeper voice replies, "Your brother? No, definitely not. How would they? You know he is dead, you saw what happened with your own two eyes, no one could survive that. She must have been making it all up and a ghost would be very unlikely."

Then a loud bang is heard. Me and Europa both jump, ready to make a run for it but it's soon followed with Benedict's now upset voice, "Why would she make it up!? And if he is a ghost, why haven't I been able to see him!? He was my brother!"

There is a brief silence followed by sobs.

"Vaughn did not die during the fracture of time, so a ghost is impossible. Only those whose passing got caught within the broken transition of that war-torn day stayed within limbo. You know that, that's why the librarian will never leave that library; she is forever caught within a loop and you should be grateful your brother isn't. Because that is what I'd call hell," the deep robust voice says sternly.

Europa and I look at one another in shock then lean in closer.

"And you know if it were known that one of the Malis boys was nearly taken by the Infernum, it would portray weakness within your bloodline and Theophilus's Patriarch stature will be re-evaluated by the rest of the Elders. And if that were to happen, everything he has been working towards will fail, years wasted."

Benedict suddenly stops sobbing and says patronizingly, "Yeah...because killing him seemed like the more logical decision to save his own arse."

Suddenly, an exasperating curdle is heard, and Europa and I lean around the corner to see the huge Leo holding Benedict up with one hand, his fist curled effortless around his scrawny neck in comparison, lifting him up without effort. Benedict's wings sporadically expand and contract in distress, and more of his weltering feathers fall. Then the Leo throws him into some shelves, making them collapse on themselves.

"Your father has given you everything! You spoiled little brat! You know it killed him to make that decision. To see your own blood nearly taken by the Infernum, any one would prefer death than to see their own son turned into one of those mind-controlled creatures. He would have done the same for you, if he hadn't taken your place... Or is that what you wanted for your brother? Just how you selfishly wished he were in limbo so you could see his ghost. Vaughn was ten times the Virgo you ever were and he should have taken the throne. It should have been you that day but he decided to give his life to save yours and that was the stupidest decision he ever made. And how do you repay him? By continuously humiliating not only your loyal father but your Constellation. Now get yourself together. You can see yourself out."

Benedict immediately replies solemnly, "I wish it had been me too..."

The Leo snuffs in disgust, murmuring, "Pathetic," and begins to leave as Europa and I quickly make a quiet run for it, regaining our position back in our Constellation just before they're next in line to teleport back to the dorm.

Chapter 13

Garden of Eden

Murder stands consciousness at the cross road.

Europa and I now lie restless on our beds as we wait for everyone in our dorm to fall asleep. After a few hours, we cautiously hop out of bed, both looking at each other in bewilderment.

"What did he mean he didn't die on that war-torn day? So he couldn't be a ghost and if that's the case, who did you see?"

Europa looks down sighing in frustration, adding, "And Bib's in limbo, what does that mean? That doesn't sound pleasant."

I shake my head, unable to justify it. "I have no idea, but it was definitely that Virgo in the photo. I can't believe Theophilus presumably killed his own son. No wonder Benedict is the way he is."

Europa nods, saying, "Yeah, depressed beyond reach, they must have been incredibly close. I wonder how long ago that happened."

I shrug, answering, "I'm not sure, but they were both quite young in the photo, at least 12."

Someone begins snoring which is followed by a toss and turn, and I gesture to go to the bathroom just in case we wake someone without realizing, as we could be crucified for discussing such information.

Quietly shutting the door, Europa lets out a big sigh of relief.

"This is so frustrating! It's as if we only find tinier bits from a much larger puzzle. None of it makes sense!" Europa says in defeat. I nod in agreement and I think of Eve, whom I'm forbidden to talk about. But I can no longer keep it to myself, telling Europa seems like the logical thing to do at the moment and might help us solve this baffling puzzle. So, I tell Europa the whole story of what happened after Isa had nearly beaten me to death. Europa's eyes nearly fall out of her head, not blinking once during the whole saga. "Adam and Eve are real, not mythical? I can't believe it! And she's kept within these walls told as a legend! And Adam's in the uncharted forest? Surely he's dead now or enchanted by Apophis's Infernum army. Why didn't you tell me this sooner!?"

I shake my head.

"I couldn't. Theophilus has literally threatened to execute me if I spoke about such secrets. So you can't let this go any further than this room."

Europa nods asking, "Of course not. But tell me, what was Eve like?"

"We didn't speak much; she just told me she was my mother, which at first thought, made sense, since we both have very similar feeble physiques and she's the lady who's been reoccurring in that same dream most nights.

"But Theophilus informed me that it was impossible, considering the time frame when I was born… Basically told me she's insane, due to her being a human and all. It's common in their species as they are quite chaotic when it comes to their emotions and I'll admit she did reflect that."

Europa hangs on to every word, thinking on it for a moment. "It does seem strange though. I mean you've been dreaming about her your whole life. I wonder if you're connected in some other way because let's be honest…you're not exactly good with handling your own emotions at times."

She smirks jokingly, trying to cautiously handle each remaining word. At first I become hot and angered by her comment, but thinking on my irrational emotions around Leon, I do see her point, especially after my display in the dining room this evening. "Yeah, I guess I see your point," I say direly, speaking through my teeth. Being a Taurus and admitting that you're something you perceive as weak can be a hard dynamic to face.

Europa adds, "Don't take that the wrong way. Obviously there is something special about you, otherwise you wouldn't have that purpose number everyone keeps warning you about. But the emotions could have something to do with it… Look, let's find that Bwbachod, he is the only one who appears to know anything. And he was the first one to warn you of this secret power before you were even aware of it. Because I doubt we'd be able to find Eve again. Let's think smarter, not harder."

Suddenly, I realize something.

"Wait, if the Bwbachod already knew of my power, do you think Theophilus knew? Do you think that's why he warned me? He is enslaved to him?" I question.

Europa shrugs, saying, "Who knows, before we make any more accusations, we first need to find out the truth. Just like Manfro told us…then we can save you. Whatever that's supposed to mean."

I smirk, "You mean Manfred?"

Europa rolls her eyes.

"Does that really matter right now? Anyway, we better get to bed before someone notices us missing. Will decide on a course of action tomorrow."

We are woken early to be taken to the new destination to meet with Cassidy Dion to learn about our totems, which means there is going to be another long journey throughout the Doh. I make sure to take my medicine before we leave. I find a large dirty fingerprint on the vial, which brings comfort of my father's presence whose picture sits next to my bedside table. Memories of when I was young, leaving my clothes tarnished on numerous occasions from picking me up effortlessly after a long day of hunting in the uncharted forest, gathering our food for the following week. Winter was always a hard time as animals went into hibernation and nutritious vegetables and fruits would wither in the colder months. I was always curious what he'd seen but he'd never discuss those ventures with me, told me visions of those dark places should not tarnish that of a small child. Although not much time has passed, I miss his shadowing presence. I look at a stain on my tethered clothes that still remains from when we used to play in the meadows just by our front yard, near the large tree which I presumably cured, and I wish I could ask him the many questions that now continuously linger in my mind, and I begin to regret not telling him about the Bwbachod that had entered my room that night.

We walk up more stairs than we ever have before, entering through several doors and down several long corridors, all decorated differently to the one before. Demetrius approaches me as I'm now walking on my own, as I've grown tired and Europa walks a few feet in front of me.

"How are you travelling?" he asks.

"Can't complain," I say as he looks ahead with clearly something on his mind.

"How are your lessons going with…the…Leo?" he questions.

"His name is Leon," I say and he nods, conflicted.

"Yes, I'm sorry…Leon. How is it all going?"

I look up at him curiously as I can see he's really trying. I look around to see if anyone is listening.

"I was told I'm not allowed to discuss my sessions with anyone."

He glances at me with slight irritation but takes a big breath instead coming to his senses. "Well…he did show me the jurisdiction letter. So technically, I am already aware he is attempting to teach you to harness your inner power."

I think on it for a moment, knowing it would be nice to discuss with someone who is a classed, reputable zodiac. Although I do trust Leon, but I've known Demetrius my whole life.

"Yeah, it's going okay. I've only had one session but I was able to conjure up some power. But I don't know how to control it. It's only when I'm angry does it uncontrollably come about."

He nods, carefully listening and I wait for him to ask me about the power, but he doesn't.

"I'm presuming you're training within the Reflection Room?"

I nod. "But I presume you haven't been able to conjure up the same power by your own free will outside of that room?"

I contemplate on it for a moment, thinking about the time I healed myself but I hadn't done it by my own will. So, I shake my head, knowing telling another would make things more complicated than they already are. He nods affirmatively with confirmation.

"Do you know something I don't?" I question.

His expression becomes transfixed, ignoring the question and asks with deliberation, "Have you told Leon about the medicine you take?" I become puzzled and anxious, feeling guilty about going against my father's word and now I feel as though something may be very wrong.

I answer with insinuation, "What if I had?"

Demetrius expression becomes rigid and cold with concern, "Did you give him the medicine or not?"

He now looks at me with urgency and I become completely confused.

"No, why would I do that? Why would he want the medicine?" He thinks on it for a moment, once again ignoring my questioning.

"Taura, you must listen to me. You must promise me not to give him a sample. It's very important, as I'm sure he will ask you for a vial. Probably say along the lines of being able to improve it somehow…as he thinks its impairing you from your true potential. He'll probably also ask if you've been able to use your powers outside of the reflection room and that's how he'll go about obtaining it. But you must refuse, no matter how charming he may seem; it's very important. Do you understand me?"

I bewilderingly stare at him, annoyed that he is hiding something from me.

"Why? Tell me why? What are you hiding from me?"

He sighs with frustration, looking away in despair.

"I'd tell you, Taur, if I could. But I can't, it'll only place you and others in great danger and then I won't have time to save anyone. You just need to trust me on this." He stares at me with sincerity, and I nod in agreement.

"Okay, I promise. But you must promise to tell me what on earth you're talking about, eventually."

He nods with assertiveness. "In due time. But right now, it's too dangerous."

He looks ahead and I follow his gaze to see a dead-end down the path we take. Then unexpectedly Demetrius places one of his large hands on my shoulder and says, "Thank you, Taur," and paces ahead to get in front of our whole group as Isa now stands in front of the blank, high-ceilinged wall and stares up.

"Dead end!" she says annoyed, rolling her eyes and turning around, presuming Demetrius has led us down the wrong path. Ignoring her ignorance, he walks up to the wall, placing his right hand gently on its surface and says, "For the power beseeched in me, I promise to do no harm. Or I am only the primitive animal known as the bull."

Suddenly, several tiny green lights appear and at an incredibly speed begin to work together to draw up a giant door with decorative plants and animals grown and lay beside it. As it finishes its perfect picturesque image, the animals and faun begin to move and the picture takes a life of its own. Then the door begins to open.

A large beautiful garden with the smell of fresh air brushes against us with the fragrance of blossoming flowers. Large trees sway, animals and strange creatures I've read about wander within. I stare at a particular tree that moves in a peculiar way as its green leaves move independently until they all fly off, realizing they were never leaves but strange birds that camouflage themselves as leaves. They leave the tree leafless and I notice it's not a tree either but a strange creature that looks like a dead tree and gets around by using its roots as legs; its face droops down and its eyes are disguised into its bark-like skin and it slowly begins moving along, now revealing a small footpath. Demetrius turns to us, "If you took notice of the words I spoke before summoning this door, you'll be aware if you harm anything within this realm, you'll be turned into your ancestral bull and forever live out your days as an animal. So, if you want to get back out of here in one piece: Don't. Touch. Anything."

Europa and I look at one another in wonder and turn back to admire the flawless beauty within this weird place as we all follow closely behind Demetrius, trying not to step on anything as he explains, "This place is known as Eden, some refer it to as The Garden of Eden. It's where all the animals and fauna from all regions live together as one. It is believed that if something disastrous happens – say a disease or illness drives a species into extinction or if the balance of nature goes out of whack, like if we interfere too much – we can use the species within Eden to restore their existence, although this is a rare occurrence and it's not confirmed if this is the purpose for this place."

As we follow Demetrius – now in a single file as the pathway has now become quite narrow through the growing thickness of the garden – we come across a large lake, pitch black in shade.

Dalton proceeds to ask, "What's with the black lake? Is it poisoned or something?"

Before Demetrius answers, Kendall stands beside the lake and gives Dalton an idiotic expression as he gently touches its surface and a rainbow-like glow follows his touch as he draws a picture of a book within the water.

"Do you read?" says Kendall, patronizing Dalton. Dalton now becoming angered, snuffs through his nostrils. Kendall adds whilst playing amongst the water, "It's called a Fingunt Lake, it's found within the Sagittarius forest, Maga. It's black because the fish and insects that live within it are albino in appearance and are incredibly sensitive to light. When their eggs inhabit any kind of water, this beautiful occurrence happens, as their feces destroy the translucent effect in the water, causing it to go black but leaving a by-product fungi causing this rainbow effect when touched. But it is incredibly nutritious to particular animals that inhabit the area, killing off bad bacteria that might cause certain diseases, although only some will drink it as it is poisonous to others but it keeps a sort of balance in the area."

Then unexpectedly, Demetrius begins clapping hard and deliberate, "Yes, that is correct, Kendall, feel free to enlighten everyone else when idiotic questions are asked." He glances at Dalton, who is now looking conceited. Kendall's expression stays neutral as he continues drawing with the rainbow fungi.

Demetrius continues as everyone but Dalton now pokes at the lake, creating the strange but remarkable rainbow effect. "Adding on to that, in reference to the balance, there is one specific animal called the Albous Aqua which thrives off eating the albino creatures within a Fingunt inhabitant lake. They keep them from spreading to every other bit of water in the area, which would throw out the balance and kill off other specific animals who don't thrive from their existence." He stares at the lake then gesture to follow, "Anyway, best be moving on, Cassidy will be waiting our arrival."

Not long after, we come to an opening with a large tree that grows directly in the middle, its old large roots twist up high into the sky as multi-colored leaves grow and fall delicately to the ground. Lush green grass thrives, moving on its own accord as no wind blows. Much smaller, droopy trees sit around the outskirts with white light bulbs that grow at the end of their branches, lighting up at different times to make a brilliant show as though they were welcoming our arrival. Smaller creatures scatter back into the thickness of the garden and the same multi-colored totem orbs hover amongst the colorful leaves of the large twisted tree that grows in the middle. Then, unexpectedly, the tree groans, revealing a large mouth that yawns. Dark yellow eyes appear, molded from the twisted trunk that grows from the earth. It does not say anything, only observes us. Then Cassidy Dion, the Aquarius Elder, appears from behind the tree and it watches him as he walks out in front. His long blue dread-locked hair drapes down in front of him with different fauna immersed within it with freshly bloomed flowers. He wears a comfortable white robe, his large belly hangs over the belt he wears around his waist. His eyes are kind and eyebrows bushy with slight pinkish cheeks and a long itchy beard. And with him is a fat little otter that sits on his shoulder cleaning itself.

Demetrius bows and looks at us in an aggressive and suggestive manner to show respect, and we mimic as he does.

"Good morning, everyone! I hope the beautiful scenery made up for the long journey." Cassidy smiles warmly and we all nod affirmatively.

Then Demetrius steps forward.

"I do apologize for the inconvenience and short notice, Cassidy, but I must attend to some…important business that cannot be left unattended. Do you mind if I collect them after class has ended?"

Cassidy nods without a bother. "Of course, I'm sure they won't cause me much trouble." He winks at us, but our faces stay expressionless.

Cassidy chuckles, "I forgot how serious and rigid you Taureans can be. That's okay, this lesson will loosen you up; we just need to wait for the others to arrive, which I'm sure will be in any moment. I shall see you after, Demetrius, carry on your…important duties." Demetrius bows to express thanks, looks intensely into my eyes as he is leaving and disappears back into the thickness of the garden from where we came.

Europa whispers to me, "Others?" and at that exact moment, all the other new blooded zodiacs appear from other parts of the outskirts where the light bulb trees hang.

Then Cassidy says with a bellowing loud voice, so everyone can hear, "Come! Come! Everyone, take a seat around here and we shall begin. All the zodiacs look around as we did when we first entered and even more little creatures that had stayed within the grass now scatter to the outskirts of the garden. Cassidy continues to gesture towards the other zodiacs who are guided by their overseers.

"Come sit around the luscious green grass where the Taurus lie; you'll notice it's incredibly soft to the touch, like a newly knitted blanket. Babies could fall asleep in this stuff." As everyone gets comfortable, sounds of gasping comfort are heard as some sit down into the grass. Europa plays with a few strands, gently scraping it along her skin. Once everyone is seated, the overseers stand in the back behind everyone and Cassidy delicately places his little fat otter friend on the ground next to him and gives him a tiny dried-out fish from a little pouch on his side pocket and says, "Alright, let us begin! Now your totems have been mentioned as you know. They live within your dorms, but I'm sure you still don't really know what they are. But the little colored orbs that hover around your premises while you sleep." Everyone nods in agreement, some distracted by the environment. Cassidy's expression now becomes excited. "Yes. Well! I bet you didn't notice that for every one of you there is one of them in your dorm." Now I immediately remember there being six little yellow orbs in our dorm. He now points to his fat friend who rolls around on his large tummy kicking the dried fish with his back feet and I hear from behind me a few awwing noises as they adore the small animal, especially from the Libras that sit close by. The little otter soon tires himself out and falls asleep, and the fish falls to his side. "This is my totem, Obog the otter, and he is a complete reflection of me. As you can see, I love my food and sleep. I don't believe I tire myself that easily but he seems to prove otherwise! Maybe it's something I need to work on and maybe a little more exercise." Cassidy laughs in amusement of himself, holding up his big belly within his large sturdy hands, jiggling it.

He continues, "They are your guides; they teach us many things about ourselves and show us what we are turning into metaphysically. Each Constellation has their own animal representation, but each distinct animal is a complete representation of you. Obviously, otters are the Aquarians' totem as you can see from my friend." He raises one hand high and a silver-gray orb comes floating down into the palm of his large hand. "For instance, the Aquarius would

186

see this little silver-gray colored orbs in their dorms, where a river flows upside down on their ceiling, leaking down the walls. This is where the first stage of a totem otter's life begins, just the same for all zodiac totems." He gently pushes the orb back up into the large multi-colored tree where the others inhabit and the tree watches it with its big yellow eyes. Cassidy lingers at it momentarily then clasps his hand together with enthusiasm. "Over time you'll become more connected to your totems, but at the moment they are just getting to know you and still in the fetus stage of development. Once you obtained your purpose numbers, your totem was born into the tree you see behind me and they awaited your arrival within the other tree you first saw in the dining hall. You'll soon learn which specific one is yours as it will continue to approach you. They all look the same at the moment. But you'll start to notice distinguishable differences from yours to others, especially over time, as it will transform into its physical form; one can't say when that will happen, it'll be determined by the individual and how quickly they grow within themselves over time."

A Scorpio puts his hand up in question and Cassidy gestures to him, he asks, "Why don't we see our superiors or anyone else with their totems around the Doh? Or in our Constellations?"

Cassidy raises his eyebrows. "Great question! You probably have seen others with totems, but didn't realize they were their totems. Your overseers don't like to keep their totems around when they're on duty as you can't control your totem, because in a way they have their own entity and feed from your emotion. So it becomes impossible to cover up how you are truly feeling. Right now, I'm a bit tired as I had one of those sleepless nights, so Obog here…demonstrates my fatigue… In regards to your Constellations, totems aren't allowed to be kept within Constellations as they react on how you feel and can be too unpredictable as they can't really be controlled by any normal NC zodiac. And without a Libra diplomat around at all times, it would cause too much chaos between residing zodiacs. So, NC zodiacs totems lie dormant within their orb forms and live within this beautiful Garden of Eden."

The little otter now snores with large amounts of drool seeping from its mouth and Cassidy shakes his head in an amused but disproven expression, "As you can see, it can be quite embarrassing to have them around when you're not feeling your best," he chuckles and I now notice the dark bags under his eyes from lack of sleep, which I wouldn't have noticed if it wasn't pointed out by Obog.

Now an Aries puts his hand up and Cassidy gestures to him. He asks, "What do you mean they represent us metaphysically?"

Cassidy raises his eyebrows again and smiles warmly.

"What I mean by that is, physically you may have the same animal as your other Aries friends and family, but they'll never look the same as each other. For example, if you contain a kind essence, your totem will be incredibly innocent looking and welcoming to everyone who comes into its presence as they feed from your essence. But if someone, say…holds a deep dark resentment in their heart, their totem will appear to be monstrous or scary or both, and sometimes they can be very dangerous, some have been known to kill others. But those totems are locked away and the zodiac will have to be treated to clear any darkness within them. But even if two individuals had the same natures, neither totem would look the same, as everyone expresses themselves differently, they are a complete representation of who you are at that current moment in time. Now before we have any more questions, I'm going to go through each zodiac's totem and explain their traits as every animal chosen is in fact an actual animal representation of each zodiac. So, everyone should keep your ears open as you may learn something you didn't know about your neighboring zodiac."

Cassidy clears his throat, places his hand out again and this time a blue orb glide's down into the palm of his hand, and he gently brings it out in front of him. Whispering a few soft words which no one can hear, the blue orb turns into a giant black bird. "Libras, I'm sure you recognize the color of the orb. This is your totem animal, the raven. Friendly, social, and greatly enjoy being part of a group. Despite their talkativeness, Libras and ravens are very discrete and are therefore great at keeping secrets. The ability to keep an objective mindset allows them to see all sides of an issue, making them great mediators and diplomats. It is this ability, however, that can cause hesitancy in decision making as they strive to be fair at all times. While genuinely cheerful and upbeat sorts, an atmosphere of distortion and confusion may send them spiraling into moodiness or become unbalanced, which is soon known by the contrast in eye color. So as long as you are clear in expressing your point, you will find them an exciting friend or partner." Then the raven flies off and turns back into the blue orb and returns to the multi-colored tree.

Cassidy does the same gesture again but this time a violet orb floats down. He looks towards the Scorpios this time and the orb turns into a slithering snake.

"Scorpio! Your totem is the snake! Scorpios and this reptile embody intensity and transformation. With a love of secrets and a penchant for uncovering the mystery of the universe, those of this totem are able to entrance those around them. Even those who are daunted by their intense nature will feel drawn to his or her mysterious psyche. Just as a snake periodically sheds its skin, Scorpios of the snake totem will undergo occasional life transformations, sometimes leaving others in the wake. While the feeling of new situations and experiences enthralls snakes, it is important they do not completely alienate their old companions in the process, or they will find themselves unable to sustain life-long relationships." The snake now begins to grow longer and thicker, curling itself around Cassidy and he calmly smiles, opening up his hands and allows it to then slither back up the tree. Soon after returning to its violet orb.

The next orb is gold, transforming into a large bird with large eyes and appears to turn its head nearly three hundred and sixty degrees which astonishes everyone. "Sagittarians, your totem is the owl! The guardians of the underworld. Sagittarius and owl are good at embracing their personal darkness, spotting deception, and keeping secrets. Intuitive and perceptive, owls love the acquisition of knowledge and bringing the mysterious out of the dark. They place a high value on integrity and ingenuity. While genuinely easy-going and friendly, they can also be bold and reckless. It is important for them to remember the art of tact while dealing with others, as they can be accused of lacking compassion. Characterized by a constant need for freedom, whether real or perceived, they have trouble with the sensation of feeling tied down. They are very adaptable and thrive on change, and while this is advantageous in many ways, it can lend itself to trouble where solid commitments are required." The owl expands its humongous wings and flies up into the tree turning back into the golden orb.

The next orb is pristine white and it turns into a large fat bird with a black neck and head with a white body. It honks loudly and Cassidy follows up with, "Capricorns, your totem animal is the goose! Capricorns and goose are powerfully insightful, focused, and determined. Resourceful and imaginative, they're more likely to reach his or her big lofty goals than most. While their perfectionism allows them to perform tasks with the highest integrity and care, it is important for them to not be overly critical of themselves. Though much of their energy is focused on their life's many goals, they make extremely dependable partners and friends. As practical sorts, they tend to dislike insincerity and tend to be more tolerant of it in others and able to spot it better than anyone else. While never insincere, it is common for them to adopt a masked persona, hiding their feelings from others. While sometimes a hard nut to crack, those with the goose totem are wonderful zodiacs to get to know and well worth the effort." The goose walks up to Obog who's still fast asleep and honks loudly in his ear making him jump out of his skin and running up behind Cassidy, making everyone laugh and the goose turns back into a white orb.

Obog climbs up Cassidy's shoulder and he scratches him on the head as he proceeds to get comfortable. "Well, Aquarians, it's time for our own totem. As you know it's the otter. And what we have in common with these tiny animals are friendliness, adaptability, sociability, inventiveness, and creativity. These original thinkers often times use their creativity to produce unconventional ideas which may seem wild at first but brilliant upon second glance. Born during 'cleansing time,' we enjoy reformation efforts and helping others succeed. True humanitarians, we possess the amiability and intellect necessary to succeed ourselves. We can be more spontaneous than others are comfortable with. And our dislike for conventional ways can cause friction with others who we work closely with. We should learn to hone our creative ability to produce unique ideas, while respecting others' needs for rules."

The next orb is bluish green in color and turns into a large dog which immediately releases a penetrating howl. "Pisces, your totem is the wolf! Pisces and the wolf are highly intuitive and empathetic sorts. This intuition allows them to see what others may not, allowing them to act instinctively. Sensitive, romantic, and protective. Both make loyal companions. They need love, which at times come in conflict with their need for independence. Though their intuitions are usually correct, sometimes they may neglect 'thinking' or 'feeling.' Their deep capacity for empathetic feeling may cause them to absorb others' negative emotions. It is important for them to spend some time alone so they may return to their normal compassionate state." The wolf prowls around, sniffing after the scent of the otter who teases the wolf from the safety of Cassidy's tall and broad shoulders. And just as it prepares to jump up to where the otter sits, it turns back into the bluish green orb and the otter sighs with relief.

The next orb is yellowish green in color which turns into a medium-sized bird with a yellow beak.

"Aries, your totem is the falcon! Aries and falcon are energetic to the core, leading exciting lives, full of whirlwind activity. They are thrilling to be around due to their exuberant and self-assured nature, even despite the touch of arrogance many exhibit. A natural leader, others are often infected by its enthusiastic and enterprising spirit. Although they should reframe from making hasty decisions as their impulsiveness and exuberance can cloud reason. It is also important for them to learn to follow through even when a project or relationship loses its zest of novelty. While they love being on the go, they benefit from taking a step back and relaxing." The falcon takes off, soaring around the tree and turns back into its orb once it zooms up through its tall branches.

The following orb is yellow and I immediately recognize the color from our dorm. Cassidy places it on the ground and it turns into a fat hairy creature with large front teeth, and I soon see why he didn't proceed in holding it. "Taurus, your totem animal is the beaver! Those represented by the beaver are hardworking, dependable, and industrious. If you want a job done right, ask these guys. Their attention to detail, mental acuity, and persistent effort makes them excellent workers. They work best when the seas are smooth and work hard to transform their home into a secure, comfortable retreat. Interior décor is often times important to them due to their fondness of beautiful items. Their love of stability makes them excellent long-term friends and partners; however, their tendency towards continual improvement in themselves and others may come off as controlling if left unchecked. If they learn to be more flexible, they can become a modelled worker and a loyal friend." The beaver now begins gnawing on the tree, which immediately moves its roots out of the way and flings the fat animal off and it goes flying, turning back into its yellow orb and returning to the tree.

The next orb is orange and turns into a large animal that stands on all fours and has large antlers.

"Gemini, your totem is the deer! The Gemini and deer are engaging conversationalists, tending to be broad and knowledgeable on a large range of topics, exhibiting a charming enthusiasm for life. Popular and well liked, their finer qualities often times make up for their tendency towards moodiness and narcissism. They can just about make any one laugh, and entrance listeners with their animated stories. These zodiacs thrive on life's challenges and love variety; however, this adaptability often times leads towards flight behavior. They should learn to slow down once and a while and to temper their moods when needed." The deer proceeds at nibbling the grass then turns back into its orb.

The next orb is rose in color and turns into a tiny little blue bird with a thin beak. "Cancer, your totem animal is the woodpecker! You are both warm, emotional, and deeply sensitive, empathetic and great listeners. They are the ones who we come to at times of need. These great nurturers make great parents and invest considerable amounts of efforts into their homes, desiring a beautiful haven that is both comfortable and beautiful. They are considerate friends and loyal workers. They're generally ruled by their heart instead of their head. But it's important for them to remember to not always sacrifice their own needs for the sake of others." The woodpecker now begins violently drilling into the tree at an unimaginable rate. He turns into a blur as he moves back and forth. The tree pulls him off with a small root, curling around his tiny body and he quickly turns back into the rose-colored orb and the tree trunk quickly heals over.

The next orb is red in color and turns into a pink fish that stands on its back fins on the other side of Cassidy's shoulder. "Leos, your totem is the salmon! Leo and salmon are warm, exhibiting enthusiasm and protrude energy that is contagious. Just as the salmon do, Leos like to swim against the current. Confident that their way is the correct way. In most cases, it is. It's this determination that makes them great leaders, easily getting others to hop on their bandwagon. They are emotional beings, choosing to invest a lot into their relationships. Because they give so much, they also expect a lot back. They are easily hurt if not shown adequate approval and affection. While appearing confident or even arrogant on the outside, they require the positive attention of those around them to thrive." Obog tries to catch the fish by sneakily trying to jump over to Cassidy's other shoulder where the salmon stands but the fish glides out of the way, now using its bottom fins as wings and Obog falls straight down to the ground but Cassidy quickly catches him within his large hands, laughing at the attempt.

The next and last orb is brown in color and turns into a large, thick hairy beast that positions itself on its hind legs and stands at about seven foot tall. "Virgo, your totem is the bear! Virgos and bear are independent, work best in routines, and are often times resistant to change. Practical with an eye for detail, those born under this animal make great workers, though they are humble almost to a fault. Their hard work and good ideas may go unnoticed if they do not learn to praise themselves occasionally. Virgos born under the bear are fond of familiarity which makes them great partners and friends, though they may come across as cold and aloof to some. This is because their independence makes them slow to show their emotions, not because of a lack of feelings. A true diamond in the rough, once you get past their humble exterior and reserved nature, you will uncover invaluable work ethic and lifelong friends." The bear relinquishes a powerful roar and I instantly recognize it. Fear trembles through me, remembering what the Aquarius Cordelia Dion had told me when I asked what Theophilus's creature Kerit was: *"He was once a bear. But now…now, he is more like a distant relative."*

Cassidy now asks as the bear turns back into its original brown orb. "Now, are there any more questions?"

I look around but no one appears to have any. So, I hesitantly put my hand up and Cassidy eagerly points to me and says, "Ah yes, the small Taurus girl."

Europa looks at me curiously as I've never had the courage to speak in front of more than a couple of zodiacs. I swallow hard and pray I don't trip over my words. "What if your totem…was incredibly dangerous and scary…but, uh, did as you commanded? I mean…in regards to you saying they act on our emotion…what if it did express it but didn't act on it? It did as you see fit?"

Cassidy looks at me strangely and I feel the eyes of every zodiac penetrating me as it's a very specific question. "Do you mean hypothetically, because I've never heard of such power over a totem? I mean you can have influence which relates to you controlling your own emotion, but do you refer to complete dictated control?"

I nod, then begin to wonder if anyone has seen Theophilus's totem; referring to Cassidy's information, they are most likely to keep them hidden, especially when they have something to hide and I now begin to doubt it.

"Well, hypothetically to have such a power over an emotionally controlled entity, I'd say the zodiac would have to be incredibly powerful because they'd need to have great willpower over their strong dark emotions that would clearly be embodied within their totem, but to control it would take power beyond one lifetime, I'd imagine. And to increase a zodiac's lifespan, well, I don't want to even speak of such evil that would entail."

I become increasingly curious by the last statement. "A zodiac can increase their lifespan?"

Cassidy's expression becomes hesitant, probably wondering why I would want to know such information. But instead, he smiles warmly. "My gosh, you are a curious one, aren't you. Well, yes, but to speak of such treachery is forbidden as it's punishable by death, inseminated by the Scorpio's death serum…but we are going off topic now. Are there any other questions regarding your totems?"

I take that as my queue to sit down and as I do, Europa looks at me in question.

"What was that all about?" she whispers and I don't dare want to speak of Theophilus amongst such close proximity to others.

"I'll tell you later."

A few more questions are answered but I become too deep in thought to pay attention. After they've been addressed, I notice Demetrius is now back. Everyone disperses back from where they came and Demetrius guides us back through the Garden of Eden.

Chapter 14

Sample

Truth seekers are courageous but they walk alongside loneliness.

Walking up to our dorm after teleportation, I see Leon leaning against the wall beside our door, with one leg bent against the wall and the other stiffly planted to hold him up. He has his arms crossed leisurely; he turns towards me and smiles flirtatiously.

Europa whispers, "He doesn't leave much to the imagination, does he?"

I smile.

"No, he does not."

Then Demetrius is determinedly by my side and I look at him, his expression impatient but forcefully contained, "Remember what we spoke about. You promised."

I glance at Leon and sternly look at Demetrius, whispering so no one can hear, "I promise, just so long as you tell me what is going on."

He nods firmly.

"I will. A day has already been set."

I stare at him in question.

"What day?" But we can no longer continue as the group comes to a halt.

They recite the poem and walk into our dorm as the doorknocker sighs with irritation on hearing that same old poem, each word spoken, appearing to be torturous to the ear. Each Taurus sternly stares at Leon as they enter with untrusting eyes, especially Isa, keeping me in her peripheral vision. She gives me a strange expression of doubt and caution. She stops momentarily and snorts with judgment as she follows the others.

Europa stays by my side as I stay to speak with Leon. Demetrius too stands firmly beside me, and Leon looks up at him, two prides just as proud as the other.

"You take care of her, you hear," says Demetrius.

"Of course, I'm already doing a better job," says Leon challengingly.

Demetrius snuffs at him, "Yeah, we'll see about that." He abruptly turns his back and storms off, saying out loud, "Enjoy it while it lasts. The blindfold will soon be lifted...Leon Sol." Leon watches him as he disappears into the crowd of new bloods who now come and go within their dorms.

"He sure hates you," says Europa with conviction. Leon looks at her, clearly holding back the fire that now burns within him.

"That he does." He stands up from the wall and gestures to me. "Shall we get going then, Taur?" he says with warmth.

Europa's energy becomes possessive.

"Since when did you start calling her Taur?"

He glances back at her vigilantly as she adds fuel to his already raging fire.

"Since now."

Her eyebrows draw together and she looks like she is going to explode; she turns away and says between her teeth, "Your ego stands up to its reputation!"

She looks at me with caution and storms into the dorm, slamming the door behind her.

"Oh, that'd be bloody right, no consideration for the guy who lives on the door!" the door knocker yells. Everyone in the premises stops to look at us momentarily.

Leon glances at the door and remarks, "I guess she hates me too?"

I shrug. "She just doesn't trust you is all."

He smiles. "Well, that's something knew…let's get going, shall we?"

We teleport to the Reflection Room, and as we enter, I notice it hasn't grown in size but it's more confident in appearance. The small windows on either side no longer have sporadic cracks and the wooden interior is now more welcoming as opposed to feeling cold and lifeless.

"Well, I can see you're becoming more confident within yourself," says Leon, walking up to the tiny cloud with small bits of sparking electricity that sporadically lights up.

"Hmmm, although your power still remains the same, which I find surprising."

I walk over and linger at the cloud.

"Why's that?" He looks at me.

"Well, since becoming aware about your unbeknown power, it's curious to me to see your cloud remain the same. Generally, when awareness occurs, it gives it general growth, just in knowing about it even if you haven't used it."

He walks closer to me and I become rigid.

"It's kinda like negative attention; it's still attention. But ignoring something altogether makes anything wither. Ignorance made your power weaken without you even knowing it."

I watch him carefully, wondering if he is going to bring up my medicine, just as Demetrius foretold. But before the conversation heads down that path, I ask, "Who was that girl in the dining room? She seemed awfully mad at you."

Leon smiles with intoxicating warmth. "That's a random question and quite off topic? Why? Were you jealous?"

I become angered by the arrogant comment, wanting to dismiss him. "Why would I be jealous? There is nothing to be jealous about," I say with spite.

He smiles again, appearing to be amused by me. "Well, she was jealous of you…" I feel the blood drain rapidly from my face, this conversation is much worse. He watches me carefully and I know I can't hide the now obvious, no matter how hard I stare at the ground.

"She's just a Leo who has been wanting to court me since I was a young lad but I've never been interested in her." I feel myself becoming calm again.

"Why?" I ask curiously.

"Because she isn't interesting… Although I probably lead her on every now and then in boredom, which I should probably stop doing. But I'm not going to lie: it's flattering to the ego."

I roll my eyes. "Yeah, you should probably stop."

He chuckles, "Probably. Now you tell me. Why did you ask that strange question to Cassidy Dion in the totems' class? It seemed awfully specific."

I forgot he would have been in that class for new bloods. And I realize he might know some information about the Bwbachod, considering his father is Theophilus's right-hand man and he's ordered by Theophilus to conduct these sessions.

"If I tell you, do you promise not to report it back to Theophilus?"

He stares at me carefully but out of curiosity he nods. "I promise."

I linger back and forth from the ground to his gazing stare and explain when I first met Theophilus I had also met his totem called Kerit. Explaining he was able to control it even though it looked monstrously deformed in reflection of his inner image and was able to command it even though it clearly wanted to rip apart his enslaved Bwbachod and myself.

Leon listens carefully, thinking on it for a moment, reminding me of my father's expression when he selectively chooses the right words. "Yeah, I've met Kerit, not many have. I'm actually surprised he allowed you to see him as those who do generally take him the wrong way, especially knowing the information we were taught in that class."

"What do you mean?" I ask.

He explains, "It is believed that Kerit was manifested that way from all the turmoil Theophilus has been through, and still holds to fight the Infernum, to keep us alive. The stress of creating a systematic structure for us all to work together has deemed more difficult than originally thought and that task landed in his lap. And being a humble Virgo enables him to control his emotions so rigidly that he is able to control Kerit and since our totems change due to our growth, I also think going into such a powerful position has also enabled him to grow these particular elements. But many wouldn't realize this so, he tries to keep Kerit hidden as those presume he has turned evil, but maybe he thought indifferent of you, that's why you were allowed to see him." I become guilt-ridden, feeling I had judged Theophilus too harshly. "And I bet you feel bad now as many have before you. It's okay, it's completely understandable that you would presume that, knowing what you knew. But knowing what you now know makes you realize you shouldn't jump to conclusions. There's always more to the story than appears."

I nod guiltily.

"Can I ask you another question?"

He stares back at my cloud. "Sure, but we should be getting on with the lesson soon."

I begin perspiring. "Do you know why…he kept that singular Bwbachod alive and enslaved?"

Leon's eyes raise and his face relaxes, thinking on it for a moment then his expression comes to some sort of epiphany.

"If I tell you…you must promise not to repeat it. Spreading such information could be traitorous. Do you promise me?" His big golden eyes stare deep into me and I nod assertively, my eyes widening. He turns away and starts pacing as he tells the story. "Good, I'm also telling you this as I believe I can trust you… That Bwbachod…was once the son they never knew." I look at him in confusion and he continues, "You know how Bwbachods over generations obtained the ability to become any one in personality, ability, and power? They would shed their skin and turn into whoever they wished, just so long as they drank some of their opponent's blood as it has in their genetic DNA make-up." I nod again in understanding. "Well, that Bwbachod who is the remaining was swapped at birth by its mother Bwbachod for the twin Vaughn Malis. She made him drink some of his blood and he turned into the baby Vaughn who she stole and disappeared, never to be seen again. It's not really known information but baby Bwbachods are more powerful when they are young so they can make it to adulthood, increases their chance of primitive survival. But anyway, as time went on, the baby continued to grow, only knowing himself as Vaughn Malis, ignorant to his mother's actions. And once he turned thirteen, puberty set in and the reality he had only known started to become distorted as he started unwillingly transforming into the Bwbachod he really was, probably confused and scared half to death but not wanting to be found out, he continually transformed back but it became harder with each transformation. It's believed puberty had changed his hormonal imbalance in regard to the Bwbachod gene or he just ran out of juice, but no one really knows. Anyway, Theophilus soon found out and banished him to the uncharted forest. Benedict originally was going to be told another story to protect the memory of his brother Vaughn. But unfortunately, life doesn't always go as planned and Benedict somehow saw his brother walking into those woods that day as the brother he had only known. He ran after him and was never able to remember what happened after he heard that magnetic lullaby which we all pray to have a deaf ear. The Bwbachod disguised as Vaughn protected the only brother he knew by saving him and taking him away from the forest as quickly as possible and hoped he could save him before he became completely cursed. Fortunately for Benedict, he snapped out of it and came to, which is the only case I have ever heard of. But unfortunately, Benedict awoke to see his brother walking back into the uncharted forest, thinking he had been enchanted by the lullaby. And it was then he saw his own father Theophilus stab Vaughn in the heart from behind with his Virgo golden sword. And has forever been told that his brother had saved him from the Infernum by giving his own life. And his father, Theophilus, couldn't bear to see his son taken by that kind of evil and wanted to kill him by his own hand. But as everyone knows, Bwbachods can't die, another reason why they're so dangerous. So, what Benedict saw wasn't his brother dying but it was actually the Bwbachod going into shock from the penetration from the sword as a diversion as Theophilus never wants Benedict to know the monster he really was, a genetic mutation of a zodiac. He wanted him to remember him as the Virgo he only knew, not wanting his memory to be tarnished. Once he had been taken away, the Bwbachod rejuvenated into his original form, never able to transform back into Vaughn again. The Bwbachods had already been eradicated at this point in time and Theophilus kept the Bwbachod, pretending he had kept him hidden this whole time before Vaughn's disappearance. Explaining if anything were to ever go wrong in Orbis Bellum, his genetics could be used to help, so in logic it would be appropriate. Others believe he kept him for other purposes. But I believe it's because he is the only thing that links him to his real son. So, as much as he loved him, he resents him for taking away the son he never knew and feeling like a failure as a father, unable to recognize his real son from fake, which has caused deep conflicting turmoil. Probably another factor as to why his totem looks the way it does. Not many know of Vaughn's existence, which I think makes Benedict increasingly resentful towards his father, having to pretend his own brother never lived who he loved dearly. But he is too naive and blinded by emotion to see the bigger picture of the responsibility his father must uphold within Nirvana."

My expression becomes solemn. And I feel deep sadness for the Bwbachod, reminiscing on the day I was in Theophilus's domain. How could you treat someone so badly when you used to love them as your very own son? Why did the Bwbachod risk so much to warn me?

Leon brings me back to reality. "Love and hate. The most contradicting yet closely bonded emotions. Either one can be used unconditionally…and either one can be used against you," he says, lingering at the tiny window in my room that now begins to break again slowly as a reflection of the sadness I now feel.

I ask, "And the Bwbachod has never confronted Benedict…to tell him the truth?"

Leon shakes his head.

"I used to play with the twin brothers when I was young before any of this was known as our fathers have worked closely together for many decades. And from knowing the Bwbachod as Vaughn and conditioned to a Virgo way of life, I'd presume the Bwbachod doesn't want to tarnish the memories he has of him either. He doesn't want him to be conflicted in the way his father is. He'd rather remember him for what he was, not what he is. I guess that's why he stays so immensely loyal to the Malis family."

I think on that for a moment and question it from the first night I met the Bwbachod as Leon adds, "May I ask why you wanted to know about the Bwbachod?"

I become flustered by the last question. Shrugging, "I was just curious really, I was told they were eradicated. And the remaining Bwbachod was enslaved to Theophilus... I guess I just wanted to understand why."

He looks at me questionably, then drops the suspicion and nods his head in understanding. Then I ask, "Why didn't you tell me the story Theophilus has told everyone else? That it was for the purpose of the Orbis Bellum?"

Leon shrugs just as I did.

"I guess it's nice to share the truth for once as opposed to constantly keeping secrets, to keep the ignorance guarded within faith. Sometimes, the more you know, the bigger the burden. So it's nice to share the load sometimes."

I nod in relation to the burden of my own unbeknown secrecy. "Yeah, I can understand that."

We both stand in silence for a short time then Leon says, "Alright, let's lighten up the energy. Let's try to harness some of those powers of yours without conjuring it up randomly with sporadic aggressive emotion. You told me you could self-heal?"

"Yes?" I answer as Leon randomly starts jumping up and down on the spot, breathing deeply with strange grunting noises as if warming up to something. "What are you doing?" I ask.

"Well, genuinely if you can self-heal, you should technically be able to heal others too. So you're going to try it out on me."

I look at him puzzled. "But you're not hurt?" I question.

"Precisely."

He continues jumping up and down on the spot, breathing in deeply and unexpectedly smashes himself into the wooden wall like a rag doll, over and over again. The room begins to tremor, until I hear a snap, crack, and pop, followed by an exasperated groan.

"You're going to seriously hurt yourself! Stop that! A small cut or something less extreme will suffice!"

I run over to him as he holds his shoulder and I notice it's dislocated and possibly broken.

"Are you crazy?" He smiles with clear pain written over his face.

"Only a little…now I need you to kneel down and I'm going to sit next to you. You'll take a big breath and imagine my arm back in its original condition. But you must believe you can heal me, that is the most important part," he says with clear struggle.

We sit down and I place my hands over his muscular, lean shoulder, and I can feel his now physical warmth beneath my skin and instead of fixing his arm, I think this is the closest I've been to any male other than my father, who would not be pleased by this image.

"Concentrate," he says sternly. "Now breathe in deep and slow. Imagine my arm in perfect condition. Feel yourself healing my arm," he says with a tone that's harmonizing to the ear. I breathe in deep and I imagine the bone going back into its original stature, I feel warmth going from my hands to his body. There is silence for a moment, until he groans again in immense pain, followed by sounds of rapture and deep inner popping. I open my eyes briefly to see the same blue aura I remember from when I presumably healed that tree and the same one from my dream when I reached out to Eve after she'd fallen to the ground. Then the aura begins to fade and Leon opens his eyes in panic.

"Don't stop now!"

I shut my eyes once again and continue imagining it in perfect condition. Leon now groans even louder in pain as the breaking sounds of bone and muscle are clear as they go back into their original place, my whole body begins to heat up and I can see the light blue aura beneath my eyes.

Leon unexpectedly pulls away, collapsing on to the floor, looking exhausted, and he looks up at me in astonishment, his mouth slightly opened in awe. And I notice my whole body is now saturated in the blue aura, my hair even stands on end. and I feel the number ten on the back of my neck pulsating. He looks toward the cloud as do I, but it no longer represents the contorted cloud with sporadic electricity, instead it appears calm and powerful, bounded within the same blue aura. Now it begins to leak the blue orb on to the floor as though turning into water. Splashing into the floors' surface, it absorbs into the cracks of the decaying wood, splintering through. Lighting up like tiny veins and shooting up the walls, it glows and infests my surroundings. I feel the number ten continue to pierce with burning heat and the pain becomes more intense. I become agitated, panicking, I fall to the floor, squeezing my eyes shut. I curl into a ball holding my knees to my chest, wanting it to stop but it's as though this force has a life of its own, living dormant inside of me and I cannot control it. The room goes dark and I feel a hand placed gently on my back.

"Taur, don't be afraid, that was amazing!" I still lie their scared at the power I withheld and Leon continues, "You did it. My arm's all better, in fact, I have something else to show you."

I open my eyes and come to a stand, noticing the room has returned to normal and so has my cloud, except the little sporadic electricity, that's a little fierier than normal. Leon pulls up his shirt up to reveal his incredibly physique and not an ounce of fat on him, rippled with lean muscle but hasn't taken into account what happened after I'd healed him. "I used to have a giant scar at least 10 inches long from a battle I had with my father when I was quite young... Taur, it's completely gone!" He twists and turns, showing his incredibly torso, not realizing I don't take notice of the scar I never saw. "It had faded over the years but my skin appears to be brand new. Not even one of the hundreds of little nicks are left on my arms." He laughs with excitement. "I'm going to be underestimated now as our Constellation finds someone with many scars to be a great warrior and threat, clearly demonstrating the physical pain that they've embarked upon." He continues looking at himself and the shoulder he broke, moving it up and down. I grasp my hand over the other arm, feeling insecure and conflicted about what I'd been able to do and seen.

"Did you not see what happened to my cloud?" I question.

He continues to admire himself and takes a moment before realizing I've spoken. "Huh? Your cloud? Yeah, it's a little more powerful now. We're definitely on the right track!" But I instantly get a bad feeling. The memory of Penelope encouraging me to heal that tree but my father seemed angry about it. Is the Bwbachod's warning true? Is this some sort of evil? Has my father just been trying to protect me?

Leon is now looking at me. "Taur, have you been able to do anything like this outside of this Reflection Room?"

Demetrius's words now find their way back into our premises. I now know what he is leading too and my body becomes rigid and untrustworthy.

"Well, yes, when I was thrown from the stairs?"

I can tell he is now reading my body language so he approaches me carefully. "Yes, but that was out of extreme circumstances, your body probably acted on instinct for pure survival. What I mean is, have you ever been able to do this just as you did then, thought something and it happened?"

I nod again. "When I was very young I think, but I'm not sure if it's a memory or a dream. I healed a tree."

He nods calmly. "Yes, but it hasn't happened since you started taking that medicine, is that right?"

I become angry at him as I feel he is about to break the bond we have created with mistrust, why else would Demetrius warn me against him and predict this. But I still nod, curious to what he will ask next in hope it is all a misjudgment. He smiles warmly.

"I think you should give me a vial; we may be able to change it somehow as I think it's affecting your ability outside of this room. I could give it to one of our top Pisces alchemists or sorcerers, see if they can improve upon it?"

I become livid with anger, my face fills with fury and his expression becomes worried, glancing over at my cloud.

"Taur…what's wrong…calm yourself, remember what happens when you get angry in this room."

He worryingly looks at my cloud as it continues to grow. Bolts of electricity now spray off my body and I know I'm about to lose control as I feel my heat rising and the number ten pulsating harder than ever and there is no sign of it ceasing. I squeeze my eyes shut, feeling the power that wants to take control and before all is lost, I run out of the Reflection Room and I don't stop.

Leon does not chase me and I eventually come to a stop as my legs become tired and I can no longer pursue the temporary flight. And without knowing I've come to the library, the giant doors open as a group of Scorpios exit. They talk amongst one another until they notice me, covered in sweat and frizzy hair. They become silent and curiously analyze me with unreadable expressions. But without a care, I walk into the library and find a quiet and reclusive spot to sit to gather my thoughts. Sitting silently, watching the lively books fly above me, I catch site of Emun, the book purifier leaping from book to book as they fly about. He agilely cleans them as they go, sometimes falling but his tiny wings find the strength to carry his awkward, skinny, long body for a short time until he lands on another nearby book and vigilantly continuing his duties.

"Isn't it fascinating? The sight of purpose, it can overcome any obstacle." I nearly jump out of my seat to find Bibliotheca standing beside me and I stare at her as the blood drains from my face; she kindly looks at me, adjusting her large glasses that remind me of Manfred, and I now notice the slight translucent tinge in her skin that I did not recognize before, reflecting the ghost-like image that stands before me.

"Bib…" I say, barely able to muster up the vocal chords in my throat.

"Yes? Are you okay, my dear? It looks as though you have seen a ghost."

Frozen in my current position, staring at her broken memorable glasses, I remember what Manfred had told me, *"It's when you're not looking for her will she appear."*

I slowly begin to relax but not wanting to take my eyes off her, just in case she disappears. She begins fluffing around the bookshelves.

"So, did you find what you were looking for with that ancient book you…borrowed?" she says, glancing behind her, looking at me as her glasses slightly fall down her nose and she uses her index finger to press them back up hard against the bridge of her nose, clearly the glasses were never made to fit a

Gemini or Pisces' face and I wonder who they might have originated from. I become speechless.

"How...how did...you know?" I question.

She turns back around fluffing over the books again.

"When you've lived for as long as I have, you pick up a few things...especially in this realm." I get the distilled feeling she is aware that she is a ghost.

"Well, not exactly..."

I stand up and walk closely behind her just in case anyone is listening. "The information I was searching for was torn from that exact book."

She glances down toward me as I am at least a foot shorter than her, her glasses annoyingly fall down her face again.

"*The Language of the Purpose Numbers*? Was that the book?"

I nod. "The secret behind number ten section had been ripped out. That's the information I have been looking for quite some time... Do you know what had been written within those torn-out pages?"

She lingers at me, pushing her glasses back up to her face again and continues to tend to the books. "*Tu es via, veritas et vita. Nemo venit ad Patrem, nisi per te.*"

My whole world comes to a standstill and I feel sick as though I have spun around too fast. The exact words spoken within my dream from Eve, who presumably believes I am her daughter.

"That was our first language ever spoken. Although it has been lost amongst this time, the Patriarch doesn't see it necessary to learn within the new-blooded generations. So, soon it shall die amongst many other sacred things of our time... ludicrous, I think."

I grab Bib by the arm, ignoring what she had just said. "What does it mean? Those words?"

Bib blinks at me as though she thought I knew.

"You are the way, the truth and the life. No man cometh to the father except through you." I look at her expecting more, but she does not continue.

"Is that it? There was nothing else written in that section? What does that mean?"

She pats my head. "My dear, it cannot be explained by another, only you can find its meaning. And although you may not remember, this is what you wanted, so only you can embark upon this chosen journey. By walking the path you elected, it will show you everything you need to know in due time. After all, you are the number ten, you should tell me."

She smiles gently and my eyebrows crease together in frustration.

"I should tell you? How would I know? None of this makes sense to me!" My frustration escalates. She looks at me kindly, patting my head patronizingly again and she disintegrates into the sandy color of dust. Sighing, I quickly find a pen nearby and write the meaning down on a scrap of paper before I forget. Shoving it in my pocket, I notice on the large clock in the library above the entrance doors that it's nearly hit five o'clock. Redoing my hair, I gather myself together and quickly venture back to the dorms.

No one is walking around the dorm and all the overseer SNCs stand by the doors of their new-blooded Constellations as per normal, awaiting to take us to supper. And I catch Demetrius standing by our door as I approach.

"Where have you been?" he says with urgency.

"Just the library, I needed some time alone."

His eyebrows crease together and he looks around and the other SNC overseers, who seem to be angered by my incompetence, suddenly grabs my arm, appearing to be furious and I become frightened as he whispers, "Relax, this is just a ploy for them to think I'm angry at you because you didn't stick to curfew. Just to cover both our arses."

I relax for a moment then go back to being rigid, pretending I'm intimidated as he jerks me around and asks, "Did you give Leon a vial?" I shake my head and he sighs.

"Why? What's wrong?" I ask as I don't think he believes me.

He looks at me intensely. "Are you sure?"

"Yes, I'm sure, that's why I ran away to the library…because you were right. When are you going to explain all this?"

He glances away momentarily then intensely looks back at me again with acted anger.

"Thank you for trusting me. Obviously I can't explain here. I just need you to go inside and make sure all your vials of medicine are still there."

I nod. "Okay, I'll be right back." He releases his grip and I quickly go inside. Europa is quick to stand from her bed as she had been playing with her yellow totem, which now floats by her shoulder.

"That was a long lesson? How did you go?"

I unintentionally ignore her, quickly going to my bedside. I search for my bag, but I cannot find it. I look under my bed and around my draw set but find only my necessities backpack is visible. I become infuriated, storming over to Isa who lies leisurely on her top bunk also playing with her yellow totem.

"Where is it, Isa?" I sternly ask.

She looks at me with growing anger. "What did you say to me!?" she says defensively.

"You heard me, give it back." A stern line becomes visible between her thick eyebrows; she ignores me and continues playing with her totem.

Europa now stands next to me and whispers, "Is everything okay, Taur?"

Ignoring Europa once again, I walk over to Isa and ruthlessly push her off her top bunk, which she did not expect as she falls clumsily on to the ground with a giant thud. Everyone is now staring at me in confusion. Dalton and Henrietta now stand side by side but don't interfere as fear still lingers by my living ghost. Kendall sits up on his bed, placing the book he was reading beside him. Isa pushes herself up and flicks her frizzy hair back that had fallen on to her face, abruptly standing she walks up to me and stands over me with rage.

"I'm not afraid of you, you're still just the same old pathetic runt. You're just harder to kill than I had originally thought. I guess you tricked everyone though, huh… I can see why your father went to great lengths to keep you a secret. Even killing those who suspected him."

I push up against her. "Just give me my backpack back, Isa. And don't you dare say another thing about my father, you don't know anything!"

She shoves me and I stumble back.

"I don't have your stupid backpack, why would I want to touch anything of yours?"

I walk back up against her. "Because you have been out to ruin my life since we were kids. All I ever wanted was to be your friend!"

Isa suddenly laughs with an over-exaggerated act as though she were some kind of wicked creature.

"Don't play coy with me. How could you think we'd continue being friends after what your father did; my mother blamed me you know!"

I suddenly become confused; I step back.

"Oh, I guess you still don't remember, that's convenient… Even after my father died, I consoled you. But you forgot, just like now… What kind of friend does that! I needed you!" I look around at everyone and I get the feeling everyone knows something I don't.

"What do you think my father did?" I question.

Isa rolls her eyes, throwing her hands up in the air in frustration, then Europa steps in and says, "Taur, don't you know why everyone is so terrified of your father?"

I shake my head. "I thought it was because he was a fierce warrior and because he was allowed to keep me when no one else is allowed to have a weak Taurus baby. To be honest I…I never really thought too much about it."

Europa grabs my shoulders and looks at me in the eye.

"Taur, you know Tauruses respect and celebrate warriors, they wouldn't be frightened by one. Our whole Constellation revolves around being a great warrior and they wouldn't be afraid of someone who was allowed to keep someone such as yourself. Sure they think it's unfair but that's not the reason they're frightened…"

I can see Europa struggling to tell me, and I look at her with eager sincerity. She looks down and glances back at me.

"Taur…Adonis killed Darius Edlyn… That's why they're frightened of him, because he killed one of his own kind. Everyone knows that."

I shake my head.

"No, he couldn't have…why? Why would he do that? He has no reason to. I don't remember this?"

Isa smirks.

"Do you know how many times I told you when we were kids? I've actually lost count. It was as though you had been brainwashed, every day forgetting another memory as the days went by. And you would pretend as though we were still best friends. That's why I hit you that day… I'd had enough. I just wanted my friend to be there for me but you only seemed to remember when I was mean to you. So, I became your tormenter because at least you'd remember that. My mother beat me relentlessly you know, she blames me for his death because I was friends with you. Thinks I got too close."

I shake my head again and again.

"Why would he kill Darius? Tell me why!?" Isa looks at me intensely and I look at Europa.

"I'm not sure if any one really knows why, no one speaks of it since it happened," says Europa.

Isa snuffs, "I can tell you why."

She pulls out a necklace that is hidden under her garments, a round black stone is attached to a thin old rope. The black stone is encapsulated within melted glass.

"Recognize it?" she asks and my mind begins to have flashback of the memory being held in Penelope's arms. That black stone had fallen into the palm of my hand after I'd cured the tree from a terrible illness. I walk up to Isa and she allows me to hold it. "From that expression I guess you've remembered a few things. Your father used this pebble to kill my father Darius. He pushed it down his throat and he became immensely ill, dying soon after."

I pass it back to her. "But why? Why would he do that?"

She puts it over her head again and says, "Because since the very first day my father saw Penelope, he unconditionally loved her, even though it ruined his relationship with my own mother, Petra, who hates you as you resemble the woman who took my father away from her in every way. My father knew Adonis was only using Penelope as he never showed an interest in her. But he could never put his finger on what he was using her for. He never trusted him and always kept a close eye on him, especially when you came soon after. Knowing Penelope had struggle conceiving, no one even knew she was pregnant. But one day, he did find out the truth and your father killed him for it, so he was never able to tell anyone the truth. As soon as he forced him to swallow this, he was bed-ridden and died by drowning on the black infectious tar that filled his lungs. This was the stone that came out of his mouth once he had passed."

Europa now stands in front of me.

"And how are we supposed to believe you, since you say he died before he was able to tell the truth. How do you know all of this?"

Isa snorts at Europa.

"Because he did!"

Tears begin to well up in Isa's eyes and she furiously says as spit flies from her mouth. "On his death bed, he was able to splatter all this out in tremendous pain and before he was able to tell me the truth…he died. In front of my very eyes! I was only ten years old! Because of him! He took my father away from me! I tried to tell you! But you never remembered! And you played the victim! Where were you when I needed you?"

I become stiff and guilt-ridden, as I now understand the cause for Isa's tremendous pain and hatred towards me; how could I not remember. I look up at her, tears stream continuously down her face but her expression stays stiff and stern as though the tears aren't falling.

"Isa…I'm—"

The door suddenly opens and Demetrius's face peers in.

"Taura, you're going to have to come with me immediately." He looks at everyone who is now standing in a tense circle; glancing at Isa, his demeanor becomes firm.

"Is everything okay?"

Isa wipes the tears aggressively from her face.

"Everything is fine," she says bluntly. She looks at me and gestures me to go. Turning around, she hops back on her bed and rolls over. Demetrius, clearly not wanting to get involved, accepts Isa's word and signals for me to come. I stare at Isa's back and I genuinely want to stay and talk to her and tell her how sorry I am for not being there for her as I start to question my father's actions. What was he trying to hide and why can't I remember anything? Without saying any more, I follow Demetrius out the door as he says to the others, "The Gemini SNC overseer will accompany you to the dining hall with his Gemini new bloods. As I have some important business to attend." He shuts the door and guides me out of the dorm.

"Demetrius, what is going on?" I ask. He glances down at me looking to be on edge.

"Did you find your medicine?" he asks. I shake my head.

"No, I thought Isa had taken it. But I don't think that's true either." Demetrius sighs.

"No, it isn't. It's just as I thought. We've been found out."

I look at him urgently. "What do you mean you've been found out? Who's we? Demetrius, what's going on?" I say in frustration.

Demetrius looks around and stops me in a quiet secluded area. He kneels down to my height and places one of his large hands on my shoulder. "It's too dangerous to tell you within the Doh's walls, there are many ears. But just know, everything your father has done has been to protect you. Some of the things you may hear from here on out may be conflicting, but know deep down, Adonis truly wanted to protect you. You're very special, Taura, more special than you could ever imagine. And some way, somehow, we will resolve this."

He looks around again apprehensively, "Listen carefully, you must not release your true power. You hear me? It's very important. As soon as you do, we are all doomed." He looks around again. "Luckily, I was able to inform them of my suspicions before this happened. But know that they'll come for you and don't be frightened when they do; just know, you must go with them. That's all I can tell you."

He looks around again and sees another zodiac SNC approaching and he quickly stands whispering to me, "Now, you must not speak about anything we've discussed even though none of it makes sense right now. But it will, I promise. You must trust me on this, Taura. No more suspicious questions." He looks at me intensely and I nod, still unsure of anything and now I'm also frightened.

Then I see an SNC Cancerian approach. "Demetrius! What's taking so long? Theophilus is waiting." Demetrius nods and takes me to a teleportation area accompanied by the Cancer. I'm asked to envision Theophilus's premises. Now I know where they're taking me and I know this can't be good. I chant the name Unum as we teleport to the Patriarch, knowing the last time we'd spoken he'd threatened to kill me.

Chapter 15

Father

Loins of truth; conditioned, created identity.

As we approach the same ornate doors that will bring me face to face to Theophilus, I linger at the same detailed artwork placed on display, the ancient ones from the beginning of time; Adam and Eve, Apophis the snake who has declared war against our world; the Wisdom tree in all its unspoken glory, now kept hidden for reasons unknown. All the remarkable creations of Unum drawn into this ostentatious piece of artwork stand proudly upon these doors, creating an intimidating atmosphere before entering.

I stare at Eve's portrait and think of her from the woman in my dream and hope she is okay. The doors creak open and the power they withhold is tremendous as we step through. If only they could speak and tell the unspoken truth. The old pine moves as though it were alive, breathing as it opens. And I see Kerit, who lies leisurely by the large marble fireplace, sprawled out on an old rug camouflaging him as a dead stuffed animal as he sleeps peacefully; his body raises and falls as he inhales and exhales, seeing the true resemblance of him as an unconscious entity not blocked by anger or hate by a conscious state.

I look around the room that's made up mostly by glass, displaying our land from a bird's eye view, and I watch the gray clouds slowly go by the window as rain saturates the glass. Peaceful atmosphere amongst the giant fire which burns calmingly in my ears. I linger at a large portrait of Theophilus that must have recently been hung. It only shows a half profile of his face, his clean white-sleeked black hair visible and his large wings curl around in front of him, taking up most of the picture, his green eyes penetrating as they glance over the top of his wing as though he hides something behind them.

"Good evening," says Theophilus in a stern and unemotional voice. I turn to see those famous wings turned towards us as he stares out into the cloud-covered sky, watching the rainfall. Demetrius stands closely beside me and I feel his tension. It's the first time I've seen him this way, attempting to disguise the obvious fear in his eyes. I unexpectedly feel a large presence walk up behind us and I soon smell the terrible breath of Kerit as his pungent breath presses against the top of my head, pushing my hair down with each exhale. "I'm very disappointed to find out that treachery is amongst us," says Theophilus. The blood drains from my face as my eyes widen. *How could he possibly know?* I only told Europa and she wouldn't have told a soul. Unless someone heard us? My heart begins to race and as I go to admit my treason, Kerit grabs Demetrius by the shoulder and he relinquishes a sudden and subtle shriek of pain and I know it hurt more than what he is portraying. Tears begin welling up in my eyes.

"What are you doing? Let go of him!" Without thought, I grab on to the Kerit's large jaws and begin pulling on him. But he does not move a muscle, they're completely locked and I look pathetic in the attempt, but I do not care. His large eye, that's nearly as big as my head, shifts over to me and he snarls.

"Taura, we discussed this in our last conversation. You know what happens to those who try to implement treachery in what we've worked so hard to achieve as a unity, they must be eliminated. It disrupts the peace and causes chaos to a system that's taken many decades to create…it's a shame too. Demetrius had great potential and SNCs are few and far in between these days."

I ignore his statement and continue pulling on Kerit's jaws and Demetrius has now fallen to his knees. Blood now profusely pours down his chest and on to the floor, growing from a small puddle to a large one.

Demetrius grabs me with his free arm and looks up at me with a reassuring expression, "Taura, it is okay. Please stop before you hurt yourself."

I fall to my knees by his side and begin sobbing.

"But he didn't do anything. Let him go! Can't you see you're killing him!" I shriek.

Theophilus now turns to his usual side profile but doesn't look directly at me. "Now, Taura, we both know that is not true… I know he told you not to give a sample vial to Leon when he was only trying to help you. I'd call that sabotage. No one was allowed to interfere with your sessions. So now I've had to intervene and take the whole lot, which has interrupted an already busy day. This could have all been avoided if Demetrius just worked with us."

Theophilus signals Kerit and he picks Demetrius up as if he were some kind of toy. He groans as he now hangs by his shoulder, pulled down by his heavy body. More blood pours down, leaving a large trail of blood as he takes him out of the room. I scream, followed by, "Where are you taking him? He's losing too much blood! Can't you see he'll die?!"

I collapse on the ground and continue to sob in my hands.

"I know you were fond of him. But sometimes we have to do things for the sake of a larger purpose. Besides, I didn't bring you here to witness that, you're here for a more important reason. That just had to be dealt with in the meantime."

My tears stop and I slowly look up at him, my eyes red raw and anger begins to burn and spread through my veins, growing like an unremorseful cancer pulsating through me with every heartbeat and the number on the back of my neck begins to throb with fury as a small crack on the large window behind Theophilus

210

starts to splinter. His head glances towards the crack, watching it grow as he continues.

"The Infernum, we haven't had an attack in years but unfortunately today Apophis has decided to strike…within the Taurus Constellation." My anger subsides momentarily and time begins to slow as I feel a deep hole in my heart begin to concave. "And it comes with great regret to inform you of this unfortunate news at an already hard time. But your father Adonis…has died in the process of protecting the village Herba." The words slip into the air idly, lining up to penetrate my chest as the now growing hole begins suffocating my heart and I feel as though I can't breathe. I collapse to the ground unable to move. I press my hands into my aching heart, feeling the pit of my stomach fall beneath me and I stare into the abyss; the world around me becomes distant and all I want is to hold my father one last time. My heart keeps beating and I wish it would stop just so I can be with him in the moment of death.

"Love preys on those with an ignorant eye, hiding behind a beautiful mask, waiting to reveal the identity of one's worst nightmare.

"And that face is a representation of the hate that was blinded behind the ignorance of love. Realizing hate is unpreventable if you allow love to exist within the chambers of your heart. Love is dangerous, as it is forever fleeting in one moment until one day it is taken…unforgiving in its essence. Turning into the monster that rips us apart from the inside out." Tears fall painfully down my face and I wonder why I haven't stopped breathing. Theophilus continues, "Two such conflicting emotions yet one can't exist without the other…" he pauses for a brief moment, staring into the clouded stormy bliss through the cracked window. "I know this is an inconvenient time, Taura, but you're going to have to be isolated from everyone else for a while as your unbeknown power has proven to be too unpredictable and we just can't have that around others, it's too dangerous, especially when it has been reported that it's currently controlled primarily by your emotional state. So, when you're going through a time like this, I believe you are too hazardous to have around others." The crack on the window starts to splinter into a large web as I stare intently at him from the floor, thinking what an inconsiderable monster he is. And I become blinded by my anger as though I've fallen into the black hole where my heart once laid. A thick singular crack prominently falls straight down the center of where Theophilus stands and for the first time I can see the full profile of his face up close. His expression emotionless, his eyes piercing as he stares penetratingly into mine. "Remember it was you who wanted this. Now you too will feel the emptiness," he says.

The words ignite a large pulsating rush of energy that throbs from my chest to my head and a purple aura begins to raise from my skin, another power takes over and the splinter in the glass sporadically crawls in random directions from the main crack that falls down the center behind him, creating a theatrical affect as lightning now dissipates from the stormy clouds. And just before the glass shatters, I feel a sharp pain hit me in the back of the neck and my body goes limp. As I fall to the ground, I see the Bwbachod's face standing above me.

"Vaughn," I mutter under my breath and I feel I too am falling into my own black hole and I pray it consumes me.

Unfortunately, I feel consciousness begin to awake me. Opening my eyes, I find my vision is quite distilled and blurred. I slowly sit up from what feels like a cold steel table. I have a splitting headache and for a brief moment from the unconscious to the conscious, I forget the pain I am in, a brief moment of ignorant bliss until the aching pain of my heart begins to pump through my veins and the tears find the cracked, dried-up river down my cheeks as my eyes provide an everlasting supply of pouring heartache. For what feels like a long time, I sit motionless at the end of the cold table, growing a small puddle beneath me in hope it'll grow large enough to drown myself in.

My father Adonis, he may not have been perfect but he was and always will be my father. I can still smell the bark and woodland smell from his itchy beard, which scraped against me as he'd kiss me goodnight from since I can remember. I still feel the callus from his hands, representing the hardworking Taurus he'd always been. He always smelled of dirt even when he bathed, but that smell always brought comfort to me as it reminded me of home. I still remember when he picked me up when I fell, brushing me off and pushing me on. He'd listen to me speak of nothing and everything without a single interruption and looked at me as though I was the apple of his eye. I'd follow him everywhere, sometimes in complete silence just because I wanted to be in his presence as he made me feel safe. He was my hero and now he is gone, and all I can think about is that solemn expression he had lingering at me as I left the cottage that day; what was he hiding and why couldn't he tell me.

Unexpectedly, I hear the sound of a compressed door opening. I look up to see that I'm confined within a pristine white room, so white, in fact, you can't tell the floor from the wall as though each corner of the room goes on forever. A rectangular door shifts open and all I can see is darkness behind it. The Bwbachod steps in and I become angered by his presence.

"What are you doing here?" I question bluntly. He glances up at me but says nothing, only coming over with some food and pills in a small cup. He glances around as though someone could be watching.

"I know it was you in the library. Why did you want me to know about Benedict and you? What is the purpose of all this secrecy! What is this stupid power?"

He presses his index finger to my mouth. "Shh," and looks around as I smack his hand and the tray falls abruptly to the ground.

I glare at him, impatiently waiting. "Tell me!" I yell.

He anxiously blurts out, "Remember the day you teleported to the library by accident with Demetrius and the other new-blooded Tauruses."

I now become confused as he hurriedly continues, "That was you. You did that. You must have been thinking about something important that was related to finding out particular information within that library." My memory flashes back to that day when *The Language of the Purpose Numbers* found me, and we met Bib, and I had been questioning my purpose number beforehand. He nods, realizing my expression recalls that day. "And you know how you randomly teleported to the infirmary and met Eve. You must have been thinking something in relation to that. Anything you feel closely connected to, you can teleport to. You don't need the teleportation device or markings like everyone else. You hold it within you. You are the one, Taura."

I intensely linger at him, noticing his anxiety heightens as he becomes increasingly fidgety.

"What do you mean I'm the one? The one of what? That only adds another question, nothing is being answered! Tell me what is going on!" I yell again.

The Bwbachod takes a big breath and quickly whispers, "There isn't enough time to tell you the truth! I came here to help you! I warned you this would happen if you made your power known. I wanted nothing more than to keep you and others safe. I thought your father was in on it, but he wasn't. And now I feel terrible as I could have possibly saved him but there may still be time…to save him, but only you have the power."

My eyes widen. "What do you mean he was in on it? You're not making sense! Theophilus already told me he was—"

He grabs my hand in comfort. "He may still be alive, there is still time. Your powers are significantly disabled within this room…but if we create a diversion, you can escape and do as you did those last couple of times when you teleported unknowingly…Taura, you must teleport back to your Constellation and find your father before he is murdered. But you must not delay as they'll be on your tail."

I look at him sincerely. "Why are you doing this? Why are you helping me?"

He sighs, "Because I know how it feels to lose everyone you love." The hole in my heart is triggered by those words and the story Leon had told me reminisces in my mind. I look at him not as the race of the mutated zodiacs but for the beautiful being he truly is. "I saw you in the library as Vaughn, I thought you couldn't transform into him anymore?"

He now looks at me curiously. "I don't know who you saw, but it was not me. It is true I no longer hold the power to resemble the image of the son they once loved. I now and always will remain the mutated zodiac who took their son…but you will not carry the load of a heavy burden as I do, otherwise this place will never be restored to its prior glory. You are the one, Taura."

He looks at me determinedly and as I go to comment on the last statement, he yells, "HELP! HELP! SHE'S ESCAPING!" He proceeds in throwing himself into the wall incredibly hard as he leaves a splattered blood mark. He draws out a small button pressing it then crushes it within a clenched fist. "Go!" he whispers urgently as the door opens. I jump off the table and run as hard as I can through the door and don't stop.

My lungs begin to burn and I have no idea where I am, every corridor I turn down looks exactly the same as the one before and I'm completely disorientated. I pass room after room which looks identical to the last and I can hear the tremor of footsteps gaining ground. I stop and remember what the Bwbachod had said, *"You don't need a teleportation device…you hold it within you."*

I breathe deep and hard, bending down on to my knees, trying to catch my breath. But every breath feels it's needed more than the last. The tremor of footsteps becomes louder.

"Quick, she's over here!"

I hear from a not so far distance and déjà vu hits me as I'm reminded of the dream with Eve when she is trying to escape with me in her clutches. I try to concentrate on what I had done before when I had teleported unconsciously but I don't know how and I'm rushing due to panic. I continuously think of home as I squeeze my eyes shut, time and time again thinking of my small cottage, the smells, the feelings but I continue to open my eyes to the same place and I know they'll be here any minute. I can't let the Bwbachod down, he's risking his life and this will be the only chance I have to save my father. Tears begin streaming down my face as I feel the over-encumbered sensation of defeat.

PNC soldiers have now turned down the hallway, spotting me, and I squeeze my eyes shut one more time thinking of home, opening my eyes I see them coming towards me, only meters away now and it ceases to work. I sigh and let go in the face of defeat and murmur, "I'm sorry, Dad." I think of his large hand scraping against my soft skin, caressing my face. And he would always tell me, *"It's okay, my dear."*

I burst into tears, falling to my knees. And one of the soldiers grabs me, tears flowing down my face. I wait to be obtained, but the next words spoken surprise me, "Thank the planetary gods, we got to you in time." And as I turn to look up at them, the sensation of their hand is gone and suddenly I feel a cold impression of wind caress against my wet cheek and the gentle tickling of grass against my hand. I open my eyes to see the familiar field of my Constellation, right outside my house.

I slowly stand, looking around, thinking I must be dreaming or they tranquilized me. I check myself over and everything seems to be in place, but I'm still not entirely sure how I did it or if I did it. I suddenly recall what Theophilus had said about an attack by the Infernum as I now stand cautious with alert, carefully looking around the premises but as I scan across Herba, nothing appears to be untarnished. It looks exactly the same as how I left it. Unexpectedly, I hear a crashing noise coming from behind my cottage, and without thinking, I dash through the field and head for home. As I approach, I slow down, hesitant of what will be revealed from behind my cottage as I look intently in the direction from where the noise came. Then a gust blows fiercely and the large tree that hangs over my small cottage home rustles violently within the wind. It continues shedding leaves on to the rotten roof which helps build up resistance against the rain, keeping us dry. All feels eerily still and I wonder if everything I now remember and have been told is true about that old tree because now you would not believe it to be so, too normal in its stature. I reminisce about the memory of Penelope encouraging me to heal the tree as a baby and think of that tiny black stone that fell from within and presumably went on to murder Darius Edlyn, Isa's father, dictated by my father's actions. But it makes me wonder about the balance of life taking its natural course as we cannot do as we please without repercussions of our actions…like saving a tree that was meant to pass. Induce a karma effect by taking another, maybe Darius' death is really blood on my hands. Who am I to dictate who lives and dies?

Suddenly, another undisturbed crashing noise brings my attention back as I anxiously and gently scrape my hand along the side of the cottage, not pressing too hard, a lesson learnt from the many splinters I had as a child. I breathe in the smell of old damp pine, keeping my body close to the old raggedly aged wood. I hear a familiar voice that I cannot put my finger on, but it's not my father's.

"I always knew you were a traitor. I just never had any proof until now and Theophilus was blinded by who he thought you were."

I hear another crash followed by my father's voice, which brings me conflicted comfort as his life is still in danger. He snuffs, followed by, "You're all blind if you think what you're doing is for a great purpose. Don't you see the repercussions?! Things weren't supposed to be this way. You're going against the natural process of life."

I take a big breath, slowly peering behind the corner of the cottage and I see the same Leo that was with Benedict and wonder who he is.

"You're just stuck in the old ways, Adonis. It's your typical Taurus trait, familiarity. Things aren't what they were, you need to embrace change. It's for the greater good. Your mind has just been poisoned by them… I cannot believe you used that potion to prevent her from developing the one true power. How stupid do you think we are?! Of course we'd eventually find out." He smashes a small wooden bucket over in anger, which effortlessly breaks into several pieces. Adonis walks over to the Leo whose back is now turned and I suddenly notice something uncanny about my father. It appears he's aged several decades; he looks like an ancient old man, even his voice is husky and worn out.

"Cedric, I would have done anything to keep her safe from what she's meant to be used for and I'd do it all again if I had to… Besides, Unum is our creator, Theophilus has become tarnished by jealousy and hatred. How can't you see that what he is doing and ultimately wanting to do is the most traitorous out of any crime within Nirvana. It'll destroy any chance of returning things to the way they were and who knows what will become of him and our world." Cedric abruptly swings around and backhands Adonis right in the jaw, making him stumble back. I nearly scream but quickly restrain myself. Cedric Sol? Leon's dad? Theophilus's right-hand man?

"Unum abandoned us, Adonis, along with that traitorous snake! He wanted to use us for the benefit of those under-developed creatures. Nobody wants things to return to the way they were! Can't you see Theophilus wants to embrace us as opposed to being used as a pawn within another world."

I can see my father becoming angry now and the supposed old age doesn't seem to inhibit his ability to take a hit. But he controls himself by taking a big breath and shutting his eyes, glancing away briefly.

"We would have lived our usual lives; it was only in death would that existence become our reality; he wasn't going to take anything away from us, it was just going to be part of the natural process. If you had been ignorant of that fact, you wouldn't have known any better." Cedric smirks. "Well, it was his own mistake in telling us then, wasn't it? Why do you think Theophilus keeps so much hidden from the Constellations…to protect them! Otherwise everything would fall apart just like it had on that day and the Infernum would have consumed the whole of Nirvana by now."

They both stare at each other with conviction of personal opinion and I can feel the tension building.

"You know the Infernum is a natural manifestation from what we've broken. And how would any of you know what Nirvana wants, our world is currently made up of deceit and lies. What is Theophilus offering you to make you think this is for the greater good…immortality? Without the killing and murder of essence. Tell me, Cedric, how is Theophilus going to share such a power with you when there is no evidence it'll even work?"

Cedric's frame starts to ripple as anger poisons him from the inside; if he becomes any angrier, he'll turn into the animalistic version of himself and by looking at him, I don't think my father can take him on in his current state.

"That's ironic, coming from the SNC who never questioned Theophilus's authority, you took the essence without question. And now look at you, growing a conscience, you've become weak and pathetic," says Cedric fiercely.

Adonis looks down upon the ground in regret then faces Cedric with a confident and stern persona. "Yes, it is true, I was a part of the original murders to take control and prolong ever-lasting life. At least in death I can be happy knowing

I was no longer like you as I tried to save our world not destroy it due to my own selfish greed."

Those last words now send Cedric into an uncontrollable fiery rage and my heart begins to race as his armor now slowly begins to break off piece by piece and his body begins to expand into a muscular lean killing machine. Adonis grabs the same old axe he has used for decades to chop wood; he is defiant even in the face of death but a glimmer of hope still sits within me. My father's demeanor still remains calm and collected, breathing in a controlled pattern. The top of Cedric's armor has now broken off, fallen by the waist side, showing an incredibly muscular upper body with large veins pulsating hard, clearly prominent from an onlooker, his facial features have become more animalistic in appearance much like that of his lion ancestor. He breathes deep, which gives a rippling echo within his throat, his ears are pressed back hard against his head, and his eyes look intoxicated with that of blood, and he has my father in his projectile. I stand stiff and rigid, looking on from afar, still unnoticed.

Adonis stands at a ready and says, "So…this is how the story ends."

A tear drops delicately from my eye and I feel it land on to the top of my dirty foot. Cedric's feet shift deep into the ground, his large claws piercing the soft dirt as though he is about to pounce and my father stands at a ready, and before I have a chance to blink, Cedric pushes hard off the ground, sprinting after my father who swings but Cedric dodges one after another, darting from side to side, but Adonis never turns his back on him, switching the axe from hand to hand in diversion to not leave an opening. But Cedric closes in, pressing to the ground, preparing for a giant leap and as he does just like a cat pouncing on its prey, I relinquish a frightening scream.

And in that very moment, time comes to a slow as Adonis turns around and sees me. Tears stream down my face and his guard instantly drops in fear of my watchful eyes. He drops the axe and it bounces on the ground from side to side, and I immediately realize I have locked in my father's fate. Anticipation surges through me. Cedric comes down upon him, claws sprawled and giant teeth ready to penetrate. I instinctively run as hard as I can and as I blink, I stand between my father and Cedric, who sees me unexpectedly and tries to quickly withdraw his claws and ginormous fangs. And as I accept my fate, coming to peace with saving the one person who I truly love, something grabs me from around the waist and I'm pulled away and held up high. Watching from above, I glance back to see the branch of that same tree who I doubted to be so now holds me within its grasp. I scream so penetratingly, I hear glass shatter from around the area and I watch on as Cedric now collides with my father, pinning him to the ground as he engages his large jaws around Father's neck. Blood begins to drain from his body and during this whole saga, he has not ceased to look anywhere but at me, apologetic in his expression as though he had failed me, his aging eyes more sincere and true as though I'm looking at him for the first time. His expression lingers at me adoringly as he slowly begins to fade into the darkness. The tree places me down gently beside him, staring into his gray old eyes, crying as blood drains from his neck. He smiles at me, lifting his now heavy hand and lays it as gently as he can upon my face.

"Taura...how did you?" he says curdling.

"Shh, shh, don't speak, Dad. I can heal you. I promise. Just hold on a second..." I say, broken by congealing cries as I try to stop the bleeding. I close my eyes, holding the wound and I try to imagine him as he was. I attempt to harness my healing powers, but all I feel is blood seeping through my hands and it fails to work.

He coughs blood everywhere and determinedly says before he passes over, "Taura, you are...the one. The only one...who can save the zodiacs..." He coughs several more times and the deep red of his blood now warms my quivering body, saturating my clothes. "I told you. You...were special. I love you...so...so... mu—" His hand slides off my face leaving a prominent bloody hand print as his last breath escapes him and I continue to place his hand on my face, trying to feel those same calluses and hardworking hands that had always warmed my tiny face. But now the warmth and smell begins to fade and his body begins to shrivel up as though he had been dead for many decades and has become an unrecognizable empty rotten shell of the man I once knew. Unexpectedly, hundreds of blue orbs begin to escape from his body and I watch as they disappear over the large walls into the uncharted forest.

Still clutching my dad's decaying old hand within my grasp, I scream, "Daddy! Daddy! Wake up. No, no, you can't be dead! I'm sorry, why won't it work! Stupid, good-for-nothing power, why won't you work when I need you...Daddy!" I scream.

I relentlessly shake him and push down hard upon his now unrecognizable wound, crushing the trachea into dust. I gather the bits and pieces together trying to make it heal, but I know his life is long gone. I now stare at an empty, broken vessel of my father. I sob in uncontrollable cries, still in disbelief as reality hits and another overwhelming sensation of pain consumes me. I cry harder than I ever have before, throwing my body over his, never wanting to let go.

THE END

The Language of the Purpose Numbers
Table of Contents

Meaning of a Purpose Number

A purpose number is the sum of the day you were born. They are the traits you'll carry through life and foundations you'll be drawn towards. Our purpose number gives us great insight to our desires that give us satisfaction and purpose within this journey we call life. It gives us an element of understanding of why we came into this world and what we are here for.

Find Your Purpose Number

To establish your purpose number, you must add your whole birth date together. For example: $15/05/1990 = 1+5+5+1+9+9 = 30$.

You always round it up to a single digit $30 = 3$ purpose number. If you had say, 31, as a total you'd add $3+1=4$ purpose number.

Master Numbers Are the Rule to the Exception

The only numbers you don't round up to a single digit is the master numbers, so if your date of birth equals to either,11, 22, or 33, you do not add these two-digit numbers to a single as they would be your purpose number.

Purpose Numbers

Purpose Number One

Leader
Hard-working
Determined
Self-Motivated
Ambitious
Independent
Innovative

Strengths
Great at beginning new projects
Fantastic multi-tasker
Focused and driven
Making decisions doesn't scare them
Embrace every opportunity
Huge goals and dreams

Weaknesses
Lack sensitivity and patience
Have a tendency to be selfish at times
Pride can get the better of them
Inclination to be a 'know it all'
Too concerned about vanity
Can come off as too aggressive at times

Ideal Career Paths
Self-employed or entrepreneur
Politics or Corporate leader
Anything that allows them to embrace their independency, as they don't like to take orders.

Life Challenges
Acknowledging that they're wrong and that's okay.
Understanding that the journey is as good as the destination.
Accepting and dealing with authority figures.
Feeling unrecognized for their talents and hard work Implementing the big dreams and plans in their head.

Life Friends
Two and seven
Two for their sensitivity
Seven for their spiritual and introspective demeanor

Purpose Number Two

People person
Intuitive
Sensitive
Team player
Peacemaker
Caring
Spiritual

Strengths
Great team player
Considerate and thoughtful
Handles pressure incredibly well
Sincere and Honest
Tends to see the best in others

Weaknesses
Putting others needs before their own
Oversensitive
Evades confrontation
Reluctant to initiate
Can be quite shy

Ideal Career Paths
Teaching in any form (not just school system)
Humanitarian fields
Creative pursuits that allow them to express themselves
Being in service to others (medicine, nursing, counselling etc...) Career in spirituality and personal growth

Life Challenges
Placing your needs before others
Voicing personal opinion
Not taking things so personally
Being indecisive and knowing what you want
Learning to be happy on your own

Life Friends
Two and four
Two for their ease and friendly nature
Four for their honesty and hard work

Purpose Number Three

Creative
Generous
Charismatic
Playful
Joyful
Optimistic
Witty

Strengths
Their incredibly creative and innovative
Communication comes easy to them
Others are drawn to their charming and magnetic personality
Their energy uplifts and your happiness radiates to those around you

Weaknesses
Tend to hold grudges when hurt by those they trust
Tough time with money and managing finances
Lack of focus and procrastination
Need for praise and affirmation by peers

Ideal Career Paths
Career in entertainment (acting, writing, directing etc…)
Career that allows them to use their creativity and express themselves (artist, musician, performer)
Ventures that allow them to work with others and use their communication skills (marketing, public relations, project management)

Life Challenges
Have a tendency for escapism when things become hard
Frivolous and superficial
Tendency to be moody for no apparent reason

Life Friends
Two
Their intuitive and understanding nature helps ground you while feeding your need for self-expression.

Purpose Number Four

Strong
Honest
Determined
Practical
Hardworking
Down-to-earth
Organized

Strengths
Their perseverance and organizational skills help them achieve large projects and huge goals.
Because their honest and have high integrity, others know they can trust them.
They are comfortable with growing a small project or business into a larger vision.

Weaknesses
Have an inclination to be bossy and a bit of a know-it-all
They can be rigid at times and quick to judge their co-workers or peers.
Overly cautious and careful nature, which can lead to missed opportunities

Ideal Career Paths
Anything that incorporates a methodical and disciplined approach, such as construction, law, engineering, finance, or science.
Teaching to pass on skills and talents is something they highly value
Careers that value their organizational skills and ability to see through large projects, such as project management, marketing or producing.

Life Challenges
Since others easily trust and depend on them, they will often find themselves shouldering the burdens of others; they need to learn to say no.

Have a tendency to become biased, judgmental, and stubborn when under stress, which can create unnecessary conflict. They must learn to see things from others points of view.

Life Friends
Seven
Their spiritual and genuine nature complements and inspires them.

Purpose Number Five

Magnetic
Fun loving
Adventurous
Curious
Flexible
Restless free spirit

Strengths
Ability to adapt to any new situation
Unafraid of the unknown or uncertainty
Great at meeting new people
Captivating personality
Persuasive and have a way with words

Weaknesses
Have a dislike for routine and repetition
Easily distracted by adventure and change
Tend to lack focus and direction
Self-indulgent

Ideal Career Paths
Sales, marketing, and public relations
Careers that allow them to travel and explore
High-risk careers, like firefighting, stock broker, or stunt man
Project base careers so they don't get bored

Life Challenges
Balancing their need for freedom while staying focused on their dreams and goals
They have many talents but need to embrace discipline and perseverance
Learning to manage their self-indulgent side and avoiding extremes
Allowing and understanding others desire for security and stability

Life Friends
Seven
To keep them balanced and grounded

Purpose Number Six

Loving
Warm
Compassionate
Reliable
Understanding
Responsible
Sensitive

Strengths
Natural sensitivity on relating how others feel
Deep desire for responsibility and leadership
They understand on how to make others happy

Weaknesses
Their caring desire can turn into meddling
Jealousy
Perfectionistic tendencies

Ideal Career Paths
Careers that reward their responsibility, such as managerial or leadership roles
Humanitarian career paths
Teaching, philosophy or justice

Life Challenges
Learning to balance work, emotions, and responsibility
Accepting that their desire to be in control by finding a career that rewards that tendency Allowing themselves to release control when their on holiday or vacation.

Life Friends
One
For their drive and ambition, which you can relate too.

Purpose Number Seven

Mystical
Intuition
Sensitive
Dreamer
Playful
Introspective
Perfectionist

Strengths

A natural connection to the spiritual world
Intellectual and analytical – able to turn date into knowledge Independent and comfortable being alone
Incredibly intuitive nature that usually proves to be right

Weaknesses

They can have trouble connecting with others as they've be found to be aloof and mysterious
Perfectionistic tendencies which can inhibit them from starting anything at all
Can be found to alienate and isolate themselves

Ideal Career Paths

Anything that incorporates seeking truth and wisdom, such as a priest, teacher, or researcher.
Analytical, scientific or technical careers.

Life challenges

Learning to rely and trust others
Moving outside of their own reality and being social with others. Letting go of the belief that everything must be 'perfect.'

Life Friends

Four
Their hardworking and determined ways keep them grounded

Purpose Number Eight

Ambitious
Visionary
Organized
Authoritative

Efficient
Tough
Materialistic

Strengths
Can take on big projects and complete them.
Natural manager and leader.
Unafraid of hard work.
Their ambition and organizational talent will get them far in life.

Weaknesses
Materialistic gains masked by greed can cloud their perspective Self-recognition and statues may cause self-harm and pain
Can have a tendency to be self-righteous or dictatorial
Workaholic

Ideal Career Paths
Law
Business
Politics
Management of large organizations
Positions of influence and leadership

Life Challenges
Balancing material world with the spiritual world
Knowing their limits so they don't burn out
Knowing the importance of what they can't buy (friends, family, love, compassion)
Tendency to be detached

Life Friends
Four
They're grounded and practical just like them, but while they see the big picture, they see every detail.

Purpose Number Nine

Worldly
Giving
Altruistic
Self-aware
Old school

Intuitive
Wise

Strengths
Since they are highly intuitive and wise beyond their years, others often come to them for help and advice.

Their inner strength and perseverance carry them through obstacles and challenges most cannot bear.

An intense and incredibly vivid imagination that allows them to create with ease and joy.

Weaknesses
Disappointment is often met when they work towards goals that have the intention of acquiring wealth and materialism. Tendency to allow emotions to flare up and carry them away, which can lead to unnecessary conflict.

Their humanitarian side can get the best of them if they don't set boundaries and learn to say no.

Ideal Career Paths
Career that allows them to help others

Their strong creativity that allows them to express themselves (arts, literature, drama, travel or luxury services)

Natural born leaders as they are great at resolving conflict (project manager, teacher, judge, healer)

Can also be great in positions dealing with money and business but can be a bit more of a challenge.

Life Challenges
Leading towards a life that allows them to work towards a higher purpose, benefiting humanity and the world.

Finding an outlet that allows them to express their deep emotion and intense creativity.

Learning how to manage finances and overcoming negative emotion towards wealth and money.

Life Friends
Three.
Creativity and imagination that matches theirs.

Master Numbers

Master Number 11

Intuitive
Visionary
Charismatic
Inventive
Dreamer
Deep
Thinker
Spiritual

Strengths

Great ability at picking up on others' emotions and intentions.

Because of their great energy and clear vision, others are inspired by them and drawn to their charm.

Their incredible intuition allows them to act as a bridge between higher and lower realms of thought – consciousness and subconsciousness, subtle and blatant.

Weaknesses

Perfectionistic tendencies that may inhibit them from finishing a project.

Because of their highly intuitive senses and intelligence, most things come easily to them, which may express impatience and frustration within others.

They are delightful when everything is going their way but once they have one or several setbacks it can place them into self-blame, depression and pessimism.

Ideal Career Paths

Anything to do with spirituality, mysticism, and personal growth.

Art, Literature, music or anything that allows them to express their creativity.

Academia teaching, science – careers filled with discovery, research, and revelation.

Life Friends
Seven
For their insight and spiritual nature.

Master Number 22

Balanced
Determined
Materialistic
Powerful
Strong
Practical
Influential

Strengths
Have the ability to manifest their dreams and goals more easily than others (But only when disciplined and organized).
Have great influence and charisma, making them excellent leaders.

Weaknesses
Generally want total control and micromanage everything.
At times have a tendency to be materialistic, caring about status and personal achievements only.
Can become overbearing or dictatorial when their patience runs out.

Ideal Career Paths
Careers that have ascendance through promotion, job title or income as they'll genuinely rise to the top wherever they reside.
Careers that allow them to show the world how things should be run: politics, policy-making, leadership roles, teaching, or writing.

Life Friends
Seven
For thought-provoking conversations and their spiritual nature.

Master Number 33

Intelligent
Philosophical
Wise
Inspiring
Loving

Nurturer
Compassionate

Strengths
They are master teachers
Many will come to them for guidance as they have great wise advice that resonates with many.
Born to lead as their compassionate and nurturing natures captivate those around them.
Their energy is incredibly uplifting and many will just want to be in the company of a 33.

Weaknesses
Compulsive lying in order to save others' feelings from being hurt.
Can manipulate the truth to project an image of themselves of being more superior or special than average.
Can have a tendency of dependency which can inhibit them and destroy self-confidence.

Ideal Career Paths
Careers that involves being in the service of others (helping those who are less fortunate).
Make great spiritual leaders, healers, humanitarians, and teachers.

Life Friends
Six
As they are an extension of the purpose number 6 they can relate to them on many levels.

Next Addition

The Ring of Fire

Coming Soon